CAPTIVE'S RANSOM

BY BETINA M. KRAHN

ZEBRA BOOKS
KENSINGTON PUBLISHING CORP.

ZEBRA BOOKS

are published by

KENSINGTON PUBLISHING CORP.
475 Park Avenue South
New York, N.Y. 10016

First printing: November, 1983

Printed in the United States of America

*For the big Viking
who takes my breath away*

One

The South of England, 1787

The cool, crisp air of the morning was alive with expectation. The long winter of waiting was past and ahead lay the promise of spring—warm sun and rich green abundance. Brien Weston pulled her mount to a halt at the top of a knoll overlooking her home. She had ridden hard this morning and farther than usual, enjoying the sense of freedom in ranging where she would. Now her face was flushed with excitement and the exertion of containing the spirited mare. She sat a moment, feeling the thudding of her heart and surveying the peaceful scene below, then allowed the horse to set her own pace at an easy trot down the grassy slope leading toward the stable.

The lady turned her thoughts to the satisfying picture that spread itself before her. A great gray-stone manor house dominated the little valley, several smaller buildings of stone and half-timber huddled near. Low stone walls and a tree-lined lane threaded in and among the structures, then wound up and over the gentle slopes leading to the outside world. The noble old trees that lined the lane and crowded around the lake were dark and silent except for their murmuring response to the playful breeze. Just behind the great house was an expanse of pure lawn, dearly bought with labor and care, perfectly groomed even now in its yellow-brown dress. Nearer the terraces of the house were borders of hedges and flower beds that would soon be ready for a bounty of bright blossoms.

It was so fair a place, the young woman mused. Her Weston Place, her home. Smiling now and filled with early morning joy, she urged her animal on toward the stableyard. The mare, sensing the promise of a good rub and cool sweet water, pranced with anticipation.

As the groom helped her down, she smiled genuinely into his youthful face and straightened the dark hunter green wool of her jacket about her waist. "Thank you, Frederick. She's done well this morn." Brien placed one gloved hand lovingly on the mare's neck as the young man took the reins. "See she gets a good rub for me—and a carrot or two."

Before the young man could reply, a confusion of angry shouts and wails assaulted them from the open half-door of the stable. Brien's eyes flew wide, then narrowed and darkened as the sense of the noise burst upon her understanding. Her lovely jaw set with determination and sudden anger as she turned, speaking only a word to the groom over her shoulder, "Go!"

Inside the darkened building, a shirtless young boy cringed back upon a mound of straw in an empty stall, writhing under punishing blows from a broken bridle made murderous by bits of metal still clinging to the joints. The boy sobbed and jerked spasmodically in his misery and shielded his head with his thin arms as best

8

he could while the torrent of blows continued.

Halted in the opening of the stall by the grisly sight, Brien was unable to speak or to move for a moment. Her eyes were drawn inexorably to the red oozing from the boy's side and arm and her heart pounded wildly in her chest and her ears. Suddenly the blood on the boy's body was all she could see.

"Stop!" she shouted with such force that it tore at her throat. The large figure meting out the punishment paused a moment at the strangeness of the voice and the anger in the command. But the big man brushed aside any caution produced in him and again raised his muscular arm to strike.

Brien was instantly beside him and grabbing his arm with every bit of strength she possessed. She barely succeeded in holding back the blow's finishing stroke. "Cease!" she snarled. "For every blow you deal that boy, I vow you'll feel ten!" Her anger poured unaccustomed strength into her limbs as they strained against his.

The man's watery gray eyes turned on her, slitted and simmering at this unexpected impedence to the venting of his wrath. His blunted nose and fat lips gave his face a cruel cast, now magnified by the evil of this deed.

"Out of my way, Lady . . ." He sought to shake free of her grasp and jerked his shoulder violently, but to no avail. In the angerlust that gripped him, he failed to remember that she was the lord's daughter, and the lady of the manor. Still she hindered him and he growled, "Let me go! The wretch needs a taste of the lash to teach him to heel to his master."

"You set lash to the lad again and you're fired! Put that piece of cruelty down, or I'll see it used on you next!" She growled the last part and something in her voice caused him to turn his face to her. The smol-

9

dering determination there arrested him long enough for his wits to reassemble and he began to realize the gravity of his mistake. For a moment their eyes were locked in a test of wills. Only the easing of his muscles hinted as to the victor.

Brien drew her hands from his arm as if the contact repulsed her and the feeling manifested itself on her face. "Mr. Seaton," she spat, "your cruelty knows no limits—but it has found my own! Your abuse of this boy has been your last act on Weston land." She pulled her shoulders back squarely. "You shall pack your belongings and be gone by sunset this eve. Mrs. Herriot will draw your wages. Never—never set foot on Weston land again." Her voice was an ominous whisper at the last.

The dull anger in his face turned to shock and quickly back to anger. "I'll see first what the lord has to say," he ground out between gritted teeth, his fists clenching violently at his sides.

Brien's fury went cold at his challenge. "You shall not," she uttered with deadly calm. "My father will not return until tomorrow. If you are found on this land after sunset this eve, any who find you will have my permission to properly chastise you. Your manner has so endeared you to those who live and toil on these lands, you would do well to see the dawn again. There are many who would delight in meting out to you your own measure."

A long, hot moment passed as the stablemaster searched the lady, finding only that same determination he knew instinctively would carry the day. Yielding with a vile, blasphemous oath, he hurled the blood-flecked bridle against the bare wooden planking of the stall and stomped out past two grooms who stood gaping in the alley.

The young Lady of Weston closed her eyes and

sighed jerkily with relief. She knelt beside the boy who moaned and sobbed into the straw before her. Unmindful of her own garments, she gathered the thin form against her, careful of the oozing stripes on his back and side. She held his head against her breast and made soothing, shushing sounds as he cried against her.

Some moments later she turned to the grooms who stood respectfully at the opening of the stall and ordered, "Carry him into the house—the kitchen. Cook can tend his back and he can stay in the empty maid's room until he mends." Wide-eyed, they looked wonderingly at each other, then bent to the lady's bidding. She gave his hair one last reassuring stroke as they took him gently from her.

The lad's large, brown eyes, filled with tears of pain and gratitude, nearly pulled her heart from her as he looked back. "Thank 'e, milady." Sitting in the straw alone, she closed her eyes against the blood on her sleeves and skirt and let the tears come.

Lord Lawrence Weston was later than usual returning from his solicitor's home in the nearby town of Eddington the next day. Just at dusk he reined up in front of the great house and handed his mount over to the waiting groom. He had barely settled himself into a chair by the blazing hearth of his study when Mrs. Herriot, the housekeeper, appeared to give him the news.

Now, at dinner, the usual quiet of the meal in the great dining room became strained silence. The brash clang of an etched crystal goblet against a china plate caused Brien to jump slightly and her heart to beat faster. She fastened her gaze on the elegant tableware before her, refusing to raise her eyes down the long polished table to where her father sat. But for an occa-

11

sional scrape or tinkle of silver against china, there was no sound to mitigate the growing anxiousness she felt.

Lawrence Weston, the wealthy sixth earl of Southwold scrutinized his daughter carefully over a tall goblet of rich claret and his anger threatened to bloom anew. The girl was a puzzlement to him always and now she had affronted his authority mightily. She must be chastised properly, he knew, but he dreaded it all the same. It had been a long time since he had felt such emotion; it was quite disturbing and another reason for his stern countenance.

He pulled deeply from the goblet, draining it. A slight, authoritative movement of his hand brought a liveried servant to his elbow with a decanter to replenish his glass. His manner was efficient and abrupt; he was a man who was used to being obeyed. Over the goblet he paused, his eyes never leaving the silent figure of his daughter.

"Brien," his tone was a command for attention and the girl's head snapped up in surprise, her wide, blue-gray eyes dominating her rounded face. It struck Weston just then that her features seemed different somehow than he remembered and the thought lodged uncomfortably in his mind. But his voice was controlled, demanding.

"Yesterday morn you fired Seaton. I will have an accounting for that headstrong bit of behavior now, miss."

Brien's fork dropped to her plate with a clang and she swallowed hard. Taking a deep breath and clasping her hands tightly beneath the table, she launched forth. "I was returning from a morning ride when I came across him beating the new stableboy mercilessly. I ordered him to stop and he refused. I fired him." Her chin lifted slowly under his scrutiny.

Weston scraped his chair back angrily and rose,

12

pounding his fist down on the table top. "It is not your place here to hire and fire stablemasters!" he roared. "Decent stablemasters are hard to come by. Your meddling has cost us dearly."

Brien was trembling now, but rose to meet him as he aprproached her end of the long table. "How can you say the man decent? He took a cat's equivalent to a boy of nine years. And he was no better with horses. He used cruel bits and whipped some of the carriage horses until they trust no man now; they are ruined!" Her blue eyes flashed and her cheeks flushed crimson. She would stand her ground in this matter, whatever her father intended.

Weston was taken aback at her outburst and her defiant mien. He had not known exactly what to expect, but more toward tears would have been to his liking. Instead, here she prated at him as though it were his fault.

"That is not at issue!" he bellowed, surprising even himself with his vehemence. "You had no right to—"

"No right!" she interrupted, incredulous at his concern over a lost stablemaster while the blood of an innocent boy he made a trivial thing. "I had every right!" She took a step toward him, but stopped herself. "I am lady here in your frequent absence, and I see well to that duty. It has been my lot numerous times to guard the well-being of both great and small with equal care. Seaton was a brute, hateful and mean. Frederick, as young as he is, knows more about horses than that cur."

"Enough!" Weston's face was red and puffed with ire. "The man was in charge and was held accountable." His balled fist smacked the polished table top with great force. "And it was not your place to meddle in the affairs given into his charge."

"No!" She felt the bile rise in the back of her throat.

"The lad was my charge! He was trusted into my care from the orphanage at St. Anne's. He needed a place to live and grow, not an overseer with a lash! It was my right as it was no other's!" She had thrown caution to the wind and could no more hold back this next than she could fly. "Will you say me wrong and call him back?"

Weston turned to the side, more furious with her speech and manner than her deed. She edged a bit closer to deliver the final thrust.

"Will you, my father, hand him the bloodied straps to finish the job?"

The contempt in her face and voice goaded him beyond all limits, and he shoved his face downward into hers. The muscles of his square jaw worked furiously under his skin, and his gray-blue eyes now blackened with rage.

"You will never," his voice was low and deadly, "never presume to such again. You will keep your place and do whatever women do—and never again interfere with the running of this estate. Is that clear, girl?"

Trembling now, Brien only stared evenly into his heated face, unblinking. Fleetingly she wondered if he would strike her. As if in answer, Weston pivoted away, stomping and muttering to himself and grinding his teeth in frustration.

The silence was charged between them. Brien stood tall, shoulders square and hands clasped tightly in front of her. She drew a deep shuddering breath, feeling—hoping—that the worst was past.

Weston snatched up his goblet and went to stand by the ornate marble fireplace, anger blatant in his every move. Then he turned to stare at his daughter, taking in her erect posture and noble bearing. That seemed to be what bothered him most, he realized now—her uncommon pride and assumption. Why did she not yield and weep like any other woman? What was wrong with her? He tore his gaze away from her own level return of it and lashed out once more at the woman-child who waited almost patiently for her chastisement.

"If you cannot learn to be a real woman, at least learn to bow to the God-given authority of men like a real woman does." He stared into the glowing coals on the hearth before him and missed her reaction completely.

His words assaulted her physically; she reeled and steadied herself against the table. She felt a pricking at the backs of her eyes that warned of tears to come. She closed her eyes briefly and put one hand to her waist, as if to hold herself together. Whirling, the next thing she saw was her own hand upon the door handle.

Weston heard the swish of her skirts and the door latch and looked up just as she closed the door behind her. His last taunt rumbled about inside his own head. What had he said? It was a mean and little-minded thing to throw in the face of his own daughter, Lord knew. To make it right with himself he assured himself that he only did it to teach her a lesson, but a deeper part of him scoffed at the thin logic.

He snatched up the decanter of claret, and with his goblet in the other hand, he made straight for the comfort and quiet of his study. There at least a man could have some peace.

Slamming into a chair before the fire, Weston drank with determination and brooded over the confrontation with his headstrong daughter. Dear God, she had made him angry—more angry than he had been in years. Why?

He reddened to admit, it but knew she had been right about Seaton. He had seen evidence of the man's cruelty himself, but had brushed it off with one excuse or another. He was too busy to be bothered with such

15

stuff. And his conscience prickled anew. If he were too busy, why did it bother him that she saw to the staff and set the matter to rights? He scowled deeper and pulled again from the goblet.

It bothered him because she was his daughter, not his son. It wasn't right for a woman to mix in such things. He thought of her standing there, meeting his anger without the slightest quailing. She had courage, he would admit that—but who wants a woman with courage? She should be soft and tender and . . . womanly.

Brien . . . he thought of her as she reasoned hotly against him and then as she regally suffered his abuse. What was it about her that was so different? Her appearance was more womanly than he remembered, ripened, though a bit more rounded than was fashionable. Her hair was an odd combination of streaked blond colors, and her fine features were sculptured and well defined. Her eyes were striking as he remembered them flashing at him. A pleasant enough combination to the eye . . . What was it about her?

Glumly he picked up an andiron and poked at the dying embers before him. She was uncommonly quick of mind for a girl of sixteen? Eighteen? Nineteen? How old was she anyway? The question skewered his last untouched piece of conscience and his stomach lurched. He didn't even know his own daughter's age!

Once the door was opened, a horrid flood of doubts and worries assailed him, staggering and engulfing him on all sides. Was his daughter of marriageable age? Did she have friends? Did she ever go out? When had she been to a party or a dance?

Lawrence Weston, Earl of Southwold, put his graying head in his hands. What had he done?

Two

The firing of the stablemaster had been all but forgotten in the four months since the unsavory incident. The wealthy Earl of Southwold had stayed at Weston Place long enough to see another freeman hired for the job and then had left for Paris, blaming urgent business as the reason for his haste. Now the lord had returned and with him came an air of urgency and a need for action. It was felt everywhere in the manor: in the stables, the granaries, the barns, and most of all in the great house itself.

Brien was called to her father's study on the third day after his return. Recalling vividly their last encounter, Brien approached the massive mahogany doors to his private haven with an understandable dread. She had dressed carefully at the summons, choosing her best blue silk with the voile inset at the throat and the large white cuffs at the wrists. Her maid had taken pains with her hair, but its style was simple at best. She knew her father felt her lacking in feminine graces and thought to make the best impression possible. There was no good raising his ire needlessly against her.

Her palms were wet and she swallowed hard. He was her father, true, but just now she felt the urge to run—to be anywhere in the world but here. Drawing a deep breath, she smoothed the soft folds of her skirt, squared her shoulders, and opened the door.

Lawrence Weston sat behind an ornate teak desk, immersed in a document in his hand. Brien thought of the many times she had entered this room as a child, sure of the arms of an indulgent father. The slight rustle of her skirts was the only sound as she crossed the thick carpet to stand in front of him.

"You wanted to see me, Father?"

"Yes. We have a matter of some importance to discuss, Brien." He smiled briefly, his large hand ordering her to a nearby chair.

"What matter, Father?" Her heart began an agonizing crescendo. It was not his wont to consult her in the running of the estate . . . he had made that clear enough. For the last three years few words had passed between them. Sheltered by the same great house, they led entirely separate lives. What could be so important between them now?

"I've received a letter from France." He lifted the document in his hand before placing it on the desk and rising. "We shall have visitors this fall for the hunting season. Among them will be two members of the Trechaud family of Paris." He paused; he had started badly. He clasped his hands behind his back and began to pace.

Brien knew with dreaded certainty that whatever matter her father put before her, there would be no deliberation. This was an audience to announce a decision; it pleased her a small bit that he seemed to be wrestling with how to best put it. She felt a welcome knot of resistance forming in the small of her back as he

18

began.

"You will be twenty years next May, Brien." His strong features and rich brown velvet garments made him a formidable figure as he loomed over her. Under his appraising stare, Brien's face grew warm and pink. "I have of late realized how remiss I have been in planning for your future."

He paced again, avoiding her eyes. "But I have taken steps to remedy the situation. While in Paris, I made the acquaintance of the Marquis de Saunier, a man well respected in French financial circles. He has four sons, the younger two as yet unmarried. He and I agreed that a marriage between our children would be most desirable."

Brien felt her stomach surge.

"Having you well married in such a prosperous family will set my mind at rest." He smiled a bit too coolly. "We will reopen Dunstan for the fall hunting and entertain there. Raoul Trechaud, your intended husband, will join us. Arrangements for the nuptials will be made at that time." He returned to his massive desk, his sharp features and steel gray eyes making him appear a stranger to her.

Her mind raced to sort out all he was saying to her. But it all pressed itself into a lump in her throat and her voice sounded pitifully small even in her own ears. "I am to be married to this man? As simply as that?"

The impact of her own words broke through the shock that enveloped her. "I supposed that I should have to marry someday . . . but not like this. You have promised me in marriage to a man I have never seen . . . with no regard for my feelings or wishes!" Her fists were clenched in her lap and her heart seemed to beat in her throat. Was this her punishment, long delayed, for the crime of presuming upon the lord's position?

"Of course your feelings are to be considered." Weston's voice was at once solicitous. "I have made this match with your interests at heart. There are few families about with sons whose fortunes make them a suitable match for you."

Brien's eyes burned with unspoken anger. Suitable matches—she knew what he meant and the words stung. Rich though she was, he thought she could not afford to be so choosy in her suitors. She felt some of her resolve weakened.

"I had hoped to have some choice in the matter of a marriage. . . ."

Weston frowned. "You were unlikely to find suitable candidates in this modest local society. I have saved you the trouble of a season in London—and arranged a better match than you might have hoped for there. The marquis is a wealthy man." He watched her struggle to master her emotions. "You've been too long with your books and tutors and charities. Too much learning impedes a young woman's sense of balance—importance. It's time you took your place in society and set about giving me some grandchildren."

Her cheeks burned with the shame of his meaning. "But what if the man is not . . ."

"Agreeable?" he offered.

"Acceptable!" With his prodding she found the word she searched for. "What if the man is not acceptable?" she repeated angrily.

"Brien!" But then his voice became solicitous once more. "How could you think I would marry my only daughter to a man she found distasteful? He will be acceptable in every way."

Was that his opinion or a command? A hot wave of fresh anger flooded through her and she bit her bottom lip to keep from lashing out at him. A verbal battle here would do no good, only confirm his conviction that she had been allowed to run her own life too long already.

Taking her silence for surrender, he smiled thinly. "We should see Dunstan before the first of September. That will give you time to . . . prepare."

Brien stood to go, trembling violently, but his voice called her back.

"This was sudden for you, I know." His voice seemed to mellow, or was that a clever diversion meant to persuade her of his sincerity? "In time you will see this is best."

Choked with fury, she moved to the door, her feelings warring for expression inside her. A quick glance back told her he was again satisfied that his decision had been accepted. As the door closed behind her, she gathered up her skirts and ran through the great hall and up the staircase.

Only in the safety of her own chambers did Brien's anger boil over into hot, scalding tears. She fell on her bed, drained of strength by this unaccustomed torrent of emotions. She felt betrayed, and yet chagrined that she had been unable to foresee so inevitable an outcome. She turned over onto her back and stared at the canopy and hangings above her, the tears trickling back toward her hair. Dolt! She smacked her forehead with the palm of her hand. How could she have been so foolish! She should have reasoned there would be retribution for Seaton . . . but she could never have dreamed the form it would take.

Feeling caged, trapped, she rose from the bed to pace the room. How could he force her to marry like this . . . promise her to a man she had never seen—a Frenchman at that! Seizing the bolsters from the bed she flung them with all her might across the room, smashing a small vase on her dressing table and sending a bright laquered box crashing to the floor. She stood fighting for control, her fists clenched at her sides as a young woman in servants' gray appeared in the doorway. The maid stopped short when she saw Brien, a frown creasing her forehead.

"What's happened, milady?" she whispered, aware that she had intruded.

"He means to have me married off to some mindless French fop!" she spat as if the words themselves defiled her mouth. "He just called me in to announce it. 'You'll see this is best,' " she mocked him, " 'It's time you took your rightful place in society,' he says. What does he know of my place—he's barely spoken to me for three years!" Her words were an angry wail and she staunched them for a moment, trying to control the raging forces within her.

"Why must my life by sacrificed to see him provided with heirs?" It was more a complaint than a question. She knew it was the way of things for women of her station; it was her destiny.

In the silence that followed, Brien sank into the cushions of the window seat and leaned her head against the windowpane. The gardens below were alive with color, living out their perfect symmetry as ordained by human eye and desire. "Everything so neatly arranged. Everything in its place . . . and me in mine." Her voice broke.

Ella crossed to her mistress' side. With familiarity beyond her servant status she put her hand on her lady's shoulder in a consoling gesture. She had been with Brien for several years as maid, companion, and friend. She had helped to cushion the blows of the deaths of Brien's mother and beloved sister, and of late had helped to ameliorate the loneliness of the great house and the coldness of the nobleman whose word was law here. She knew well this was the thing Brien dreaded most and now must face alone.

"There will be parties and dinners—and the Hunt

Ball. Dear Heaven, how shall I get through it all?''
Tears again coursed her cheeks as painful memories
washed over her. ''I cannot abide the thought of people
staring and making polite comments, all the while
smirking about how the Earl of Southwold has finally
bought a husband for his poor daughter.''

Since the death of her sister, Denise, three years ago,
the Westons had retreated further and further from the
world. They accepted no invitations and offered none.
Brien had been no farther than the Abbey for Sunday
mass. Weston Place had become a veil of mourning
that cloaked her from the world and the expectations of
wealthy society. For three long years the gulf between
father and daughter widened and Brien's spirit seemed
to wither within her. A welcome numbness had enveloped her and the entire household, all but Lawrence
Weston. The Lord of Southwold, already titled and
wealthy, threw himself into his business ventures and
found himself possessed of the Midas touch. And as in
the fable, father and daughter found riches of little
comfort, a poor substitute for love.

It had been different before the tragedies, only three
years apart. Brien had been a bright inquisitive girl,
preferring always to listen to her father's discussions
with his sailing captains rather than other girls' chatter
over tea. Weston had indulged her in this and taken her
everywhere, dubbing her his ''little shadow.'' He had
hired a tutor for the girls when Brien was yet only nine
years old, claiming he would not have his daughters as
witless and uninteresting as contented most men.
Denise, then twelve, had little interest in such learning
and soon ended her education, but Brien continued to
study under the kindly and learned M. Duvall. The
Lord of Southwold noted with pride that his younger
daughter progressed well in her studies, learning lan-
guages, history, geography, and even natural philoso-

phy.

Then, only three years after the death of her beautiful mother, her beloved sister died in a fall from a horse shortly after her engagement. Weston decided to close Dunstan Hall, which had been their home for most of Brien's girlhood, and to move farther out from London to their smaller house, Weston Place. To Brien it was as if the closing of Dunstan had sealed them off from the world. And now it seemed as though she were thrust again through that portal toward an unknown life.

Her tears had stopped in the gloomy silence. "I shall go from obeying my father to obeying a husband and never have known the world as myself. I'm no person to him—but a commodity, labeled 'daughter,' to be dispatched to its proper place."

Ella impetuously hugged the sorrowing young woman and retreated discreetly to allow her some privacy. She would have little enough time to herself in days to come.

The next days were a blur of activity for the entire Weston household. A French dressmaker, now living in London, had been summoned and arrived three days later with a massive entourage. After laborious fittings and measurings, the slight, genteel M. Lamont agreed to finish six new ball gowns, four riding habits, several day dresses, and assorted accessories within the month. The elegant little man seemed to like Brien from the start, advising her on the selection of colors, the cut of the gowns, and the effects of the various rich fabrics and laces he had brought with him. He declared he would create for her his finest.

Heretofore, Brien had been content with the creations of the dressmaker from the village nearby and preferred to delay as long as possible the dreaded fittings that were required in the purchase of new apparel. Her conscience pricked at the thought of the cost of her new wardrobe, though her father had given express orders that no cost was to be spared in seeing her suitably attired. She could not help but think of the numbers of pairs of shoes the parish might buy for the orphans and poor of St. Anne's with so great a donation. She had become accustomed to thinking of the needs of others as above her own and did so even now as she stood poised at the brink of a new life.

On the day of the last fitting, Brien withdrew from the noisy entourage, seeking the solitude of her rooms. She tried to sleep but found it impossible and instead paced her rooms, warm and growing peevish in the strong afternoon heat that invaded her chambers. She felt completely out of control. Everything was happening to her so fast; there were so many changes all about her—and even within her. And none of it was her doing . . . it was to please the vaunted pride of her father. She felt a queer heat building in the bottom of her stomach at the turn of her thoughts. Her father thought little of her womanhood, he made that plain. . . .

She seized the door to the ornate, carved wardrobe in her sleeping chamber and threw it open. In the large gilded mirror inside the door, she studied her reflection.

The young woman who stared back at her was a bit taller than average, though not uncommonly so, and was dressed in a rumpled blue-gray silk dress, made with wide collar and cuffs. But for the rich texture of the silk and the hint of snowflake Belgian lace at her throat, she might have been a village vicar's daughter instead of the daughter of a wealthy lord. Her hair was a tawny blond with streaks of lighter colors and was pulled back severely from her face into a neat braid that made a figure eight at the back of her head. Her large, dark-fringed eyes were the same striking gray blue ones that had stared across the desk at her just days before, declaring and sealing her fate. They were larger in her face than she remembered and they wandered over the image as if seeing it for the first time.

Defiantly, she pulled at the fastening of her skirt and it soon sank about her knees, followed shortly by her petticoats. She was not accustomed to seeing herself in a looking glass and scowled with indecision, unable to assess the image before her adequately. She struggled with her bodice buttons, soon disposed of it in like manner, and stood in corset, thin chemise, and stockings. Above the whalebone of the corset she saw full breasts and smooth white shoulders. Her waist was a bit thick, she judged, but her hips were curved in the manner of the regal sculptures she had studied in her art books. Her legs were long, well curved about the calves, and trim about the ankles.

There was more that she could not have known how to appraise: fair, cream-smooth skin; fine even features in a heartlike oval of a face; a straight nose above full, delicately hued lips that revealed straight white teeth.

She felt a telltale burning in the corners of her eyes and a tightening in her throat. She had not Denise's dark, delicate beauty, it was true, but was she so horrible that her father could not wait to have her off his hands . . . to be rid of the liability of her? Was she so lacking in feminine graces and qualities that he would sell her to a foreigner and give it not a thought?

She threw herself on the big canopied bed and buried her face in the down pillows. The bottled emotions of three long years flowed out in her convulsive sobs. She was not disturbed by Ella, who listened at the door and then left, warning the other servants that her mistress was not to be disturbed. She lay there most of the evening and into the night, alternately crying and raging until she was completely spent.

Brien had always felt she could never compete with her beautiful and delicate sister for her father's love or approval—she didn't try. But she knew he had cared for her when she was a young child; he had too often remarked that she was much like himself when he was young. Her brightness and impetuousness had endeared her to him at one time. But these last three years had robbed her of even this closeness to him. She was truly alone.

In the quiet darkness, Brien felt the moment of turning and knew that things had changed for her, irrevocably. She knew not what kind of life would please her best or make her happy, but she vowed to take up her life again, to rejoin the world she longed to explore and enjoy. She would do her best to make a good life with a husband . . . however she found one.

The heat of July was transmuted with the coming of August into a gentler atmosphere, cooler and more agreeable. By mid-month, the trip to Dunstan by carriage was almost comfortable. As they entered the gates to the main house, Brien was flooded with memories of pleasant days spent here in earlier times. Dunstan Hall rivaled the greatest estates of the whole south of England. Its massive stone walls were studded with the precious glass of another age, and the rooms were furnished in a lavish display of rich color—each one different and somehow timeless because of the grace of the elaborate panelings, moldings, and polished curves of furniture. The gardens were kept in splendid array throughout the entire year and now greeted them with a dazzling carpet of color. Brien smiled at the memory of hours spent among those paths and fountains and beautiful flowers. In spite of its formality and grand scale, she had always felt at home here.

Beside her, Lawrence Weston was also remembering
. . . a snowy-haired little imp that used to run to welcome him, nearly strangling him with the tightness of
her hug. He again saw the beautiful blueness of her
eyes, the fresh pinkness of her cheeks, and the dampness of the curls at her temples; he heard the sparkle of
her laughter. She was so beautiful, his little girl . . . his
shadow. . . .

Brien jumped as her father shouted angrily to the
driver to stop and stormed out the carriage door to
walk, before the coach had gone half the length of the
drive. What had happened to anger him so? She bit her
lip and avoided Ella's sympathetic gaze.

A scant three days later, the final fitting of Brien's
wardrobe was being done and extensive alterations
were necessary. M. Lamont and his assistants madly
ripped seams and worked well into the night for the
next several days in special rooms set aside for them.
Brien felt she was at fault somehow. Her appetite had
dwindled recently and the effects could be seen on her
body.

"M'amselle, I cannot imageene what 'as 'appen!"
the little Frenchman exclaimed. "We were zo careful
with the meazurements!" His eyes widened appreciatively as they flitted over her form. "No matter!" he
declared, tossing one hand into the air. "We will fix eet
right away. Zey will be ready as I promised." He
clapped his hands authoritatively at his assistant Chloe,
"Vite! Vite! We have work to do!"

When she heard Mrs. Herriot giving Ella instructions, her devastation was complete. "Try to do something ladylike with her hair. We're not entertaining the
parish orphan league; she's being married!"

"Dear God," she breathed, "they think me a disaster!" And she escaped to the garden to be alone awhile, unable to face one more intimation of her inadequacy. Be honest, she demanded of herself as she trod the leisurely, blossom-lined paths. As a young girl she had felt awkward in social situations, so much so that she avoided them as much as possible. But there was no avoiding them now. . . . The marriage of the daughter of a wealthy earl was indeed cause for celebration in the whole countryside. She would be paraded and flaunted and—Ah, there was no good wishing it away.

Now, if she were to succeed in this business of a marriage, she must come to terms with whom and what she was. Best to begin with an inventory of her assets. Well, there must be several: honesty, wit, education, charity . . . um-m-m. If Ella were to be believed, she being the closest thing to an expert on the relations between men and women that Brien had available to her, then certainly men cared little enough for any of these qualities in a woman. A sorry lot mostly, they wanted demure smiles, not wit; reverent attention, not conversation; and physical charms, not real beauty.

Brien sighed heavily and sat down upon the edge of the fountain's octagonal stone wall to dangle her fingers in the clear water. Her summary of men depressed her. She wanted to believe that there must be others—men of nobler spirit, like those whose eloquent philosophy and moving poetry she had absorbed into her very soul. Surely somewhere there must be men of intellect and wisdom and honesty—men that might appreciate an educated wife and count her a fit companion for their lives.

But then, a pang of realism pierced her, what if there were? Her choice was not the world of men, only one man . . . if it could be said she had a choice at all. How likely would it be for him to be of such princely disposition?

Better to plan for the worst and to not be disappointed. To achieve her end then, she must play the game fully. She must submit to the whims of trend and fashion; gowns and coiffures, perfumes and fans, flattery and persuasion. Could she go through with it? More to the point—could she carry it off?

Somewhere in her the challenge was heard. If insipid, pasty-faced girls without a thought in their heads could manage, then more so could she!

"I won't be pummeled and manipulated into an unrecognizable shape like some lump of potter's clay. I'll do this my way or not at all!" She straightened her shoulders and took a deep breath, feeling better with her resolution to take control once more.

Bit by bit, in the remaining days, Brien found herself submitting to the ministers of change: M. Lamont, a dancing master, and the formidable Mrs. Herriot. And the passage was less painful than she had first supposed as she prepared for her first meeting with Raoul Trechaud.

Three

Brien was stunned, speechless. Raoul Trechaud took her hand gently and kissed it reverently.

"Enchanté, mademoiselle."

So this was Raoul Trechaud. He was taller than Brien by several inches, with black hair, neatly gathered at the nape of his neck. His broad shoulders flexed as he bowed, emphasizing the narrow taper of his waist above long, slender legs. Dark eyes engaged hers boldly as he held her hand longer than was explained by mere custom.

"Monsieur," she managed, dismayed that her fluent French had deserted her completely. "I hope your journey was not too taxing." Her voice sounded oddly honeyed in her own ears. She stood a bit straighter in her elegant blue gown, longing for the looking glass she had spurned only minutes before.

"How lovely you are," came the perfect response. "In your presence the weariness and inconvenience of the journey are forgotten." His deep, lightly accented voice had a mesmerizing quality about it that made her want to hear more.

Strangely, Brien had not thought much about her future husband, until word came that he and his brother had been delayed and would not arrive until the day before the Hunt Ball. Feeling only a guilty sense of relief at having the extra time to herself, she was at least jolted into thinking about the man with whom she would soon share her life—her very body.

She barely noticed his pallid brother, Louis, who was introduced next; her pride was reeling from the unexpected vindication of her father's judgment. Louis seemed a well-mannered young man whose sharp features gave him a serious and somewhat melancholy look.

By design, there were no other guests at the dinner that followed the introductions. They talked of hunting, local traditions, the state of affairs in France, and Raoul's travels. Brien could scarcely mind the food or the conversation for she was caught up in her own changing thoughts and in the discovery of her husband-to-be.

By any standard, he was a handsome and worldly man, and she had to force herself not to stare. Surreptitiously, she memorized his tanned features and muscular hands; he was a hunter and a sportsman. His slightly arched nose complimented his square jaw and full, curving lips. But it was his eyes that intrigued her most . . . bold, dark, probing, as he gazed at her warmly.

Later that night, in her bed, Brien could still see his face when she closed her eyes.

The Hunt Ball initiated the fall hunting season and signaled the beginning of a vigorous and colorful social season in the country about Dunstan. Lord and

Lady Pendrake, with six less-than-beautiful daughters to marry off, thought it prudent to be generous with their hospitality and usually hosted the event. Their home had the largest ballroom in the county, though they were not the richest nobility. Adding to the usual flurry of interest in the gala was the reemergence of the Lord of Southwold from his self-imposed seclusion. All through the county there was speculation about the earl and about his marriageable daughter. Not a soul dared miss this eve.

Brien sat at her dressing table, her eyes on the looking glass but seeing little of what was before her. Ella had taken great pains with her appearance, but Brien was almost unaware of her elegant hair or her rich silk and brocade gown. Her thoughts were pulled in twain by the events of last evening and the dread of this night.

Sounds of Ella moving about in the adjacent sitting room roused her back to the present, pushing her thoughts toward the evening ahead. There would be the ride to Penworthy, the Pendrakes' house, then hours of dancing and revelry and introductions and . . . She pressed her temples with her palms and closed her eyes. She had seen almost none of these people in three years. There would be polite stares and no doubt some raised eyebrows at her appearing at her first ball with so eligible an escort. It would be a real test of her determination to build a new life.

The ride to Penworthy was pleasant, awash in the rosy glow of sunset that seemed to cast an equally satisfying aura about the company inside the carriage: Louis, Lord Weston, and the darkly fascinating Raoul. When they arrived, just after sunset, they were treated to light refreshment and introduced about generally. It was as she supposed; they were the object of polite stares and sidelong glances. In truth, she was partly to blame for the stir that accompanied their arrival. Gowns such as hers were seldom seen in the shire. Her father escorted her about the room, exchanging pleasantries and introducing her and their guests. Aware of Raoul's gaze fastened upon her, she held her chin high and tried to smile pleasantly through the interminable list of titles and relations, occasionally managing a witty retort.

Brien was glad to be able to escape their scrutiny by retiring to one of the bedchambers where servants awaited the guests. But her solitude was short-lived for the rooms were soon invaded by a drove of fashionably dressed girls and matrons who straightened coiffures, loosened lacings, and shed tight slippers for a few blessed moments of relief. For a short while at least, they were fellow sufferers in the service of fashion and the quest for beauty. The chatter rose to a din as the rooms filled with wails about lost ribbons or misplaced combs. Brien watched the goings on about her with a mixture of awe and incredulity, nearly forgotten in the others' preoccupation with their own appearance.

Two voices loudly whispering behind a nearby screen brought her jolting back to the present.

". . . and two of them, yet! It must be costing her father a fortune!"

"And think of the cost of that gown!" the second girl responded. "The yardage alone must be staggering!" They tittered.

Brien felt something inside her go cold and hard. She knew jealousy when she heard it, but her own feelings of inadequacy prevented her from dismissing their spiteful words. They stung her. Anger and hurt warred inside her, and it was all she could do to retain an outward appearance of calm. She waited until most of the women had gone and she heard the music begin downstairs; then she approached a tall pier glass in the corner.

She stared. The jealous taunts of the other girls lingered still to turn her thoughts, but she shook her head to clear it of their effect. The deep wine color of her silk and brocade gown made her skin seem flawless—creamy—in the soft light and lent a gentle pink to her cheeks. Lace was appliquéd in a panel down the front of her skirt and a stiffer lace bordered the low, square neckline and full sleeves. The gown revealed more of her than she remembered from the fittings, but was not immodest in light of the dresses she had just seen. Her breasts were rounded above the top of the bust line, but the lace offset what to her seemed a brazen display.

The image of an attractive young woman returned her incredulous gaze. It was an unreal image, just as nearly everything else seemed unreal this evening. She breathed deeply and set aside all gloomy musings. She would enjoy this night if any woman did.

Her entrance into the ballroom was marked by all present and drew Louis from conversation with several other gaily dressed young men. Pleasure lit his face at the sight of her and he claimed the first dance. When the music began she was surprised at how easily the dancing came, the promenades and whirls. She found herself smiling.

Soon the sober and sensible Brien was all but forgotten in this otherworldly place and time. Cascades of lavish sensations and new feelings flooded through her. Shimmering light from chandeliers and crystal prisms danced and glinted about the room. The bright colors and textures of the rich dress everywhere about her excited every nerve and sent her head spiraling upward. Giddy and floating about the room, she traded the arm of one partner for the arm of another and barely knew it.

The whole world seemed new to her and her spirits soared with each nod or wink aimed at her. She felt like a child confronted with wondrous treasures—wanting them all and hardly knowing where to start.

She had not seen Raoul since she came downstairs, but he had seen and watched her. She missed the calculating appraisal in his eyes and the satisfied smirk that played at the corners of his sensuous mouth. As he walked about the room, drawing admiring glances from several of the ladies, his leisurely stride bordered on a swagger, and he returned polite nods to those bold enough to smile at him from behind their fans.

When the music ended, Raoul appeared at Brien's elbow. *"M'amselle,"* he said in quiet tones that reverberated all through her.

"Oh, Raoul, you startled me." Her cheeks were pink from the dancing and hid her blushing. Under his warm gaze they became still rosier.

Undeniably a handsome man, tonight he was purely devastating. He knew how to use the color of his raiment to advantage and had chosen a rich, blue-gray velvet coat and dark blue breeches for the evening's festivities. His raven hair shone with careful attention and there was a matching glint in his depthless eyes. His skin, burnished bronze, stretched tightly over the square patrician features of his classical face. Now his generous, perfectly curved lips drew back into a winning smile made only for her.

"The party is lovely," his accent poured over her like cream. "The next dance is mine?" He faced her, standing so close that she could breathe the very warmth of him. Confused, she stepped back to check her dance card, knowing the next dance was not his, then raised her head to tell him so. Their eyes met and held for a moment. Those scorching brown-black eyes she found difficult to read she now found impossible to refuse.

"Yes, I think this one is yours, Raoul." She hoped he couldn't read her mind. What was it about him that set her on edge and caused every part of her body to tingle when he was near?, This must be the infamous "lust" from Vicar Harold's sermons. No wonder the little cleric hammered away at it from the pulpit. This "lust" seemed quite uncontrollable.

He smiled engagingly as he led her to the dance floor where the other couples were taking their places. When the music began, she noticed the warmth of his hand at her waist and the ease with which he led her through the movements of the dance. He was quite skilled, she mused, her mind wandering to consideration of his skill in other areas. Aghast at the bend of her musings, she smiled attentively up at him as if to make up for any lack of respect in her thoughts.

She was aware of the attention they attracted—or he attracted—from the ladies present. From the corner of her eye she could see them staring and whispering behind their fans. She felt a twinge of pride at having him for a partner and she nearly stumbled in the midst of a round as she realized that he was not only her partner in this dance, but fated to share her life as well. A strange calm settled over her inner self as he claimed the next dance as well. The sound of hearts breaking about the room was nearly audible.

The second set ended and they made their way toward the punch tables. Brien drank deeply from the cup he offered her, grateful for something to cool her throat. But instead the warmth of the wine in the punch conspired with the heat of the room to send her head spiraling and to bring a becoming rosiness to her face. He was charming and attentive. She was dizzy. He noticed.

"It is warm here. Perhaps the cool air of the terrace

37

would be refreshing?'' He offered her his arm and steered her through the wine-warmed room to the terrace doors. As they made their way outside into the cool September evening, Brien was acutely aware of his hard, muscular arm beneath her hand and of the faint masculine smell of him. This was not what she had imagined when her father sentenced her to an arranged marriage.

In the semidarkness of the terrace she could see several couples talking quietly or engaged in more romantic pursuits. There was a small moon drifting in and out of the high, scattered clouds. Her eyes caught the moonlight and tossed it back as a luminous glow. Raoul noticed her relaxed mood and smiled, putting his hand over hers on his arm.

They strolled out amongst the late flowers in the gardens. ''Do you miss your home in Paris already, Raoul? You are very quiet.''

He paused for a moment and smiled disarmingly. ''I do not miss my home, nor is there anyone there to miss me. I make my home wherever I am, Brien.''

The sound of her name on his lips caused a tightness in her throat and an emptiness in the bottom of her stomach. She started to walk again, searching for a subject that might interest him and distract her own unruly impulses.

''This is the beginning of the great hunting season. It will be some time before things return to normalcy here. I've never been able to fathom just what pleasure grown men can find in chasing a poor little fox, armed with heavy-footed stallions and snarling packs of dogs. Perhaps you could explain it to me?'' she teased.

He had stopped a pace from her and allowed his gaze to roam her freely. ''Some creatures were made for hunting, others to be hunted.'' His dark, probing eyes gave her to wonder into which class he had put her. She was chilled and yet hot all over.

Suddenly feeling his visual ravishment, she wondered if she should not be starting back to the terrace, or at least to the nearby gazebo. But something in her wanted to stay and see him out—to experience this new sensation of being pursued, desired.

Their eyes met for a long moment. Her breath came faster and her heart pounded in her chest. When Raoul stepped closer and put his hands on her waist, she tried to step back, only to find his strong arms held her fast. Her hands came up instinctively against his chest as he pressed her to him. Through his coat and waistcoat she could feel the hardness of it and that frightened her for a fleeting moment. She felt the press of his lean body against her skirts but before she could protest, he whispered her name, drawing her eyes to his.

She tried to read his intentions in his gaze but his eyes penetrated to her very soul while revealing nothing of himself. She felt helpless, hypnotized by the unreadable depths she saw in him. His mouth came down softly at first, then pressed harder against her own. Her attempts to pull away only brought her closer to his chest until her breasts rested fully against him. His mouth was open and his tongue traced the outline of her lips seeking passage inward and finding it.

She felt as though she were being possessed, absorbed into him. Delicious sensations warred with mild revulsion at the heat and wetness of his mouth on hers, and she remained tensed against him, a mass of confusion at what was happening to her.

When he relaxed, she broke away, trembling violently and unsure of what to do. The distance to the terrace seemed a thousand miles and Raoul blocked the way. Her chest heaved as she fought the panic rising within her. Reading her confusion, he made no move toward her, only stared at her with that scorching look

39

that left her feeling naked and embarrassed.

Was she afraid? It was her first kiss from a man and not at all what she had expected—whatever that was. It was disturbing and exciting, calling forth a peculiar feeling in the depths of her loins that frightened her as much as his actions.

"Raoul," she breathed, "we must go back."

"Not yet, Brien," his voice was husky and in the moonlight she could see his lips were parted. Smiling? What did he want with her? The answer to her unspoken question came unexpectedly: "We must be alone yet awhile, *chérie*. We must settle something between us." He started toward her but she turned and fled up the steps of the nearby gazebo. He followed, but stopped at the bottom of the steps, his eyes never leaving her, searching her.

For a long time they said nothing, though Brien sought words desperately to search him out. What did he want? Would he think her a silly, unsophisticated because of her reaction? Even now her body quivered in defiance of her attempts at self-control. The heat of his kiss still burned her lips. Was this truly the way of things between men and women?

"What is this we must settle?" she asked, striving to at least sound composed. "Have I done something to offend you? discomfort you? I assure you—"

"*Non! Au contraire*, Brien. You are a charming and gracious hostess. . . . You know the reason for my visit, yes?"

She felt her heart pounding in her throat as he slowly, sinuously mounted the steps and closed the distance between them. She found her back against a post and froze like a bird before the hypnotic sway of a cobra. One tanned muscular hand came up to trace the curve of her face, his touch achingly tender. His eyes slowly caressed her face, her tawny curls, the smooth

40

skin of her bare shoulders and the tantalizing roundness of her breasts. Then his eyes returned to hers and
he smiled gently, his dark eyes glowing at the fear and
passion he saw burning within her.

"I must know," he murmured, putting his hands on
her waist and drawing her to him. She offered no resistance as his mouth touched hers, lightly brushing it,
then pressing gently but steadily firmly. His lips were
hard and soft all at once, warm and yet cool.

Brien felt scattered, splintered by this strange, yet
absorbing encounter with the man to whom she was
promised. It was not in her power to resist him. His
strong arms crushed her breasts to his chest once more
as his hands explored the curves of her back and waist.
One hand stole upward along her side to glance over
her breast and toy with her skin above the provocative
edge of her bodice. Feebly she stiffened and pushed
against his arms with her own, then stopped as a sound
of amusement came from deep within his throat.

He raised his head to look at her and the luminous
glow in her eyes caused his mouth to curve upward
knowingly.

"Our fathers have planned a marriage between us."
He searched her depths as she could not his. "But I will
not allow it if you say me nay. I will not force you to a
marriage with me." His breathing was ragged and his
eyes betrayed his hunger. His hold on her loosened but
she made no move to pull away. In the lengthening silence he bent his head and claimed her lips again. This
time her arms slipped upward around his neck and
grasped the back of his head, forcing his mouth harder
against her own. Her lips parted to receive his darting
tongue and he pressed her back against the pillar, his
leg probing against her skirts and between her thighs.

He left her lips to trace the curve of her neck and
shoulder, his hot tongue sending little darts of fire

41

through her. She moaned softly at these unearthly sensations, moistening her dry lips, and when his mouth returned to hers, it was met with a warm willing tongue. She clung to him from desire and from a peculiar weakness that invaded her limbs.

Moments later he still held her close to him, fighting for control. He turned her chin up to him, swallowing hard, his voice betraying his inner conflict. "Let me make you a woman . . . and a wife."

The shock of the whole encounter seemed distilled in those few words. She found her voice only to echo him blankly. "A wife . . ."

He searched her intently. "Do you find the prospect odious? If so, your maiden's body betrays your heart." His jaw flexed with determination, and Brien saw a trace of what she now recognized as desire lingering in his depthless eyes. He stroked her face gently, sending a chill coursing through her. "I want you, Brien, but not only now. I would make a life with you. Do you give your consent?"

"Yes," she breathed, now all longing and confusion. She saw his look soften into a satisfied smile.

"Then it is settled. The date may be set soon. I shall speak with your father." He tenderly tucked away a stray curl of her hair, and his thumb caressed the curve and hollow of her chin. Her skin glowed under his touch and he smiled again.

"We must return." He offered her his arm and she accepted it gratefully, unsure her own limbs would support her fully. Only during the leisurely walk back to the great house did she fully comprehend all that had transpired. He had asked her to marry him! With everything arranged, he would have cast it all aside if she had denied him! She stole a glance at his striking profile as they walked and felt an overwhelming surge of gratitude for the fates' kindness to her. It seemed destiny had chosen a very special man to mate with her; she would not decry its workings again.

Fleetingly she wondered if she might awaken on the morrow to discover it had only been a dream—a beautiful dream. Yet here he was, holding her hand and walking beside her. The rest of the evening was a lovely blur.

Four

Dozens of arrangements had to be made before the betrothal was finalized and announced, not the least of which was the matter of Brien's considerable dowry. Brien understood that such matters were counted quite important and her interest was piqued sharply at the thought of what price her father would settle upon her worth. Thus she was sorely disappointed when Lord Weston informed her that the matter would be handled by the solicitors and himself and that she need not be present, or indeed know much about the final arrangements.

"It is not a matter for a woman's head," he dismissed her tersely.

Her face burned with indignation at his flat refusal. Wisely, however, she held her tongue and the realization dawned upon her that whatever else she was, she would always be a woman first in the eyes of society—and of her father. Marriage, she mused uncomfortably, was little more that a matter between men after all; it smacked more of commerce than holy sacrament. The thought lingered inescapably in the back of her mind for the next several days.

Lawrence Weston tried to appear as genial a host as could be found on that day when he sat down to the long table in the great dining room for the settlement negotiations. He had determined to be generous with his only daughter's groom and not to fret over the cost to himself. Across from him sat Raoul Trechaud, flanked by his brother and his solicitor, recently arrived from London. Weston had called upon the aid of the most able family solicitor, Mr. Poole, and the knowledgeable, at least in matters of marriage and dowries, Lord Pendrake.

After the opening remarks and pleasantries were observed, Lawrence Weston cleared his throat discreetly, calling their attention to him. "It is my intention to gift Brien and her husband with Weston Place as a part of the settlement. I thought it as good a place as any for her to begin wedded life, seeing it has been her home for some time."

Waving aside the solicitor who frowned and leaned to whisper to him, Raoul smiled thinly. "I have not seen this property, *mon seigneur,* and can only guess at the generosity you bestow."

Surprised genuinely at this hint of reluctance, Weston waved aside the whisperings of Mr. Poole. "I assure you, sir, it is a fit residence for even the most well-fixed of newlyweds."

Seeing the darkening of Weston's brow, Raoul now smiled winningly. "It is only that I had entertained thoughts of purchasing a house in London as soon as financing permitted. But we will accept the offer of the house, of course."

Weston was visibly annoyed at this man's slight of

his generous impulse and struggled inwardly with the urge to call him on the question. But he remembered just in time that Lord Pendrake had warned him that these affairs never went as planned and often ended with rancorous feelings on both sides. He would hold his tongue and his temper and see what transpired.

"I invite you to view the holdings and the lands before we continue if you would verify the value of the offer." Despite Weston's best intentions, irritation was plain in his voice.

"I have here"—Mr. Poole produced a series of long documents and presented them to Raoul's solicitor—"an inventory of the property and a reasonable and recent appraisal of the value. I think it may settle any questions as to the value."

Seeing his advisor nod and raise one eyebrow in surprise, Raoul turned quickly to Lord Weston and responded. "There is no need for a visit, *mon seigneur*. Your kindness and forethought are to be appreciated." An authoritative nod to his solicitor settled the matter with that gaunt man and the talks continued.

A large cash sum was to be turned over upon finalization of the marriage, and a generous income would see to their needs until Lord Weston's death. During the rest of the discussions, something in Raoul's smile goaded Weston. It was as though he felt Weston's generosity his due. The Lord of Southwold was still struggling with his thoughts at the very end when Raoul made an unusual request.

"Since it is your wish that we occupy this 'Weston Place,' I would see it readied properly for my bride. I have time to see to the renovations before the vows." His tone was ingratiating and a bit too charming, but as Weston glanced about the table, only he seemed to show irritation.

"I have no objection," Weston gripped the arms of

the chair hard, making his face into an impassive mask.

"Then perhaps some of the settlement can be advanced to provide for the changes that will be needed."

"Sight unseen you have decided the home I give to you, and that you eagerly accepted, is not suitable?" Weston's voice rose noticeably and all turned to stare at him.

"Mais non. I only wish to make it novel and fresh for my bride. It should be a place that bears the mark of two heritages—a blending of old and new—that is all." Raoul's dark eyes were determined as he slowly squared his broad shoulders in such a way that he seemed to grow in stature before Weston's eyes.

Wondering at the man's game, Weston felt the others' eyes upon him and was embarrassed by his own reluctance. Rubbing his chin and then toying with the lace at his cuff, he tried to hide his eagerness to be done with this unsavory business.

"I cede the sum of five thousand pounds for it. Mr. Poole will keep an account for you. It is my wish that Brien have only the best with which to begin wedded life. I deny her nothing." As the words left his lips, he felt their foul taste linger; for in truth, none of them had given thought to what his daughter truly wanted. And the duplicity of it, guarding the pennies, while making a display of generosity to a man he found he did not altogether trust, weighted his spirit heavily.

As they left the room and gathered in the salon for a brandy, Weston found himself staring at his future son-in-law. What harm could the man do him? It was only fair that the man try to better his circumstance through a financially advantageous marriage. That should come as no surprise, but Weston found it distasteful now, thinking about it in honest terms. With a girl as wealthy as his daughter, material things could not help but be a consideration in any match he would make for her.

As Weston sat alone in his study, late that night, he thought of the contrast between the recent event and his own marriage settlement. His betrothal had been made by his father and Weston had not set eyes on the girl until they traveled north to the Leighton estates to finalize the settlement. Having seen the girl at luncheon, Weston could scarcely mind what transpired at the meeting later; his eyes and mind and heart were so full of the winsome, dark-haired Emilie Garrett.

A much older Weston now shook his head fondly at the memory, then scowled deeply only seconds later. Raoul Trechaud had shown no such distraction this day. In truth he was more the calculating businessman than the smitten swain. Ah then, Weston shook his head, few marriages began as well as his . . . and fewer still lasted so lovingly through the years.

A deep, sharp pain in his chest suddenly took his breath. Confused and angered by this lapse into the well-buried past, Weston muttered a curse under his breath and slammed out of the room and into the damp chill of the half-bare garden to escape.

In the next two weeks arrangements for the nuptials were finalized amidst a flurry of social engagements Brien could not have imagined living through just a few short weeks before. Raoul made the difference. His confidence was contagious and in his presence Brien found it impossible to think that their future together would be anything less than splendid. He was like a whirlwind that swept her along in a rush of new feelings and experiences. Even at night he commanded her thoughts—coming to her in hot, startling dreams of passion and tenderness.

The anger and sense of loss she had felt when her father announced this marriage to her was gone completely. She had planned to take control of her life, to make a new future for herself . . . but one was being made for her, one that contained all a woman could ask for in life. She would have a handsome husband and children . . . perhaps the chance to travel.

She felt a certain relief that she could accept this marriage, take a woman's rightful place in the world. The old Brien would have insisted upon controlling things instead of accepting them, would have put her pride in her own intelligence and resources, even ahead of her own happiness. But she had matured past such childish willfulness now and at last was becoming a lady.

"I am anxious to see this Weston Place you have spoken of so fondly." Raoul took her hands in his, his tone almost apologetic. It was his last night at Dunstan before leaving for Weston Place and London. Lord Weston had discreetly left them alone in the salon after dinner. "If I am to see changes made there before our wedding in December, I must make plans and secure help in London."

"I understand," she murmured quietly. "Perhaps you will learn to love Weston Place as much as I. Only . . ."

"Yes, *chérie?*"

"I . . . shall miss you," she dropped her eyes, unsure of how he would respond, and she missed the brief smirk on his handsome face. He tilted her chin toward him and smiled confidently.

"The time will be quickly gone. We will not be parted for long, I shall see to that. Then you may come to inspect the changes yourself . . . you and the *seigneur*. And I will join you for the Covingtons' ball and the Masque."

"I would not expect one who is used to the brilliance and excitement of Paris to enjoy our modest local society," she observed, causing him to look at her

49

strangely. "Will you not miss it, Raoul?"

"My interests lie in other directions now. My life with you and studying the intricacies of trade with Lord Weston will be sufficient."

"The gay young blood turned country squire?" she teased. "With all the beautiful women in Paris, Raoul, why did you seek an English wife?" Her words were meant to lighten his serious mood, but she instantly regretted them. His face took on the semblance of a thundercloud and she drew back instinctively, startled and confused by his reaction.

The surprise on her face immediately caused him to check his vehemence. *"Ma chérie,* you forget, our fathers arranged our meeting." He was at once controlled, polite in the extreme. "It is no secret that our countries bear animosity for each other. But my father is a shrewd man. He is sure there will be trouble in France and seeks to have some of his family settled well away from it. There are some who think him a traitor to promote such a marriage as this."

"And what do you think of his views?" Brien puzzled over his explanation.

"I learned long ago to trust the judgement of the Marquis. Without his 'views' I would not be here . . . we would not wed in a few months time." He smiled warmly into her quizzical gaze. "But let us not dwell on the vagaries of the fates, *chérie.* What will be, will be."

Brien felt inexplicably warmed and chilled all at once.

The next weeks quickly passed, a lovely swirl of duties and preparations that left Brien little time to contemplate her future further. Raoul joined them twice for the dances and then hurried back to Weston Place to see to the changes he had begun there. He teased her

50

about her curiosity, assuring her that the house would always lack something as long as she were absent.

"Raoul, it is marvelous!" Brien stood in the great hall of Weston Place and stared in astonishment at the sights about her. Floating from room to room, she found the gracious manor house filled with delightful and surprising changes. She allowed herself to be drawn along by Raoul, who watched her delight with a knowing smile, while Lord Weston trailed behind, making his own inspection.

Stopping in the gallery along the second floor she watched Raoul furtively, amazed by the clever hand that used color to transform the sober respectability of the great stone house into warm, inviting grace. Was there anything the man could not do?

There were some new furnishings, to be sure, and new brocades at the windows, but often, as Brien paused before a piece to comment on its familiar lines, she realized that a new fabric or paint or gilt covered an old friend. New imported carpets cushioned their feet and new paper or paint covered each wall. In a mere few weeks, Raoul had managed to revive the elegance and charm of the house and to make it seem a new place to her.

"I see no structural changes." Lord Weston observed.

"There were a few, of minor significance. Would you care to see them? They are not in the family area of the house. . . ."

"No," Weston waved it aside. "I was merely curious. It would appear you have succeeded here, Raoul. You are a man of many capabilities." The lord smiled politely.

"I see what must be done and I do it, *mon seigneur.*"

* * *

In the drawing room, when her father had retired for the night leaving them alone, Raoul presented his bride with a gift, three strands of perfectly matched pearls held together by an intricate golden clasp.

"They're lovely!" she breathed.

"For you to wear at our wedding . . . they will compliment your gown?"

"Beautifully. M. Lamont has labored furiously to produce a gown like no other, and I am anxious to see it. Still, I dread the long fittings." She looked up into his face, now enticingly near, expecting him to claim her lips. When he did not, her attention fixed on his eyes, dark and unreadable. He smiled in response, but the strangeness in his eyes belied his lips. She reached out impulsively for his hand—to touch him and reassure herself of the warmth she knew must be there. Her movement lifted the imaginary veil from his face, and his other hand came up to caress the satin skin of her jaw and throat. In spite of his gentleness, Brien felt a chill at his touch.

"I must retire," she murmured. "Tomorrow it shall take several hours to reach London by coach. I do so wish you were coming with us. It seems I am ever saying farewells to you."

"Not for much longer, *chérie*. I have work to complete here. I will join you soon at Dunstan and we will not be parted again." He walked her into the hall and pressed his lips into her palm. A light flickered for a moment in his black eyes. "Pleasant dreams, *chérie*."

Ella had warmed her bed and waited to help her undress. Her bright, inquisitive chatter grated on Brien's nerves for no reason Brien could name.

"What they done to this place!" She took the pins from Brien's hair and began to brush it reverently.

"What's this?" She tapped the velvet box containing the pearls that lay on the vanity before them.

"A gift from Raoul," came Brien's thin reply and she opened the box for Ella to see.

"Lor'!" Ella exclaimed softly. "They shine like the moon. Isn't a woman in five counties wouldn't change places wi' ye in a twinklin'. You're a luck woman, mi-lady. 'E's rich and handsome. What I'd give to stand apiece in your slippers."

Brien forced a smile and ruefully thought that she might not mind the exchange, just now. Why should she feel so subdued at this, the happiest, time of her life? She was marrying a man whose wealth, status, and appearance exceeded her most hopeful expectations. What more could she want?

Surprised by a sudden thought, she shook her head. She was too clever and too practical to be taken in by the popular romantic notion of a perfect love. But her mind kept circling back to it all the same. Did she want, expect, more from him? Did he like her . . . love her? Did she love him? Slamming the door on these painful conjectures, she refused to probe further and felt an ill-suppressed pang of guilt.

Until now, in all that had befallen her, she had been honest with herself in appraising her feelings and her prospects. Now, as she surrendered to the relentless on-slaught of her "destiny," it seemed that if she questioned or examined this beautiful dream, it might melt away before her like the early morning vapors before the rising sun.

When Ella left she lay in bed a long while trying to clear her mind of the uneasiness she felt. Exasperated, she struck flint to steel and lit the bedside candle. She donned her fur-lined dressing gown against the chill of the dying fire and began to pace. Why was she so rest-less?

"If only I could be with Raoul for a while, he would make me as sure as he is," she thought, knowing full well there was more to be had in Raoul's arms than reassurance. Was this the source of her discontent—her own desires piercing her pride? Raoul had been attentive of late, she could not fault him in that, but despite his perfect manner and comments, she had detected a strange aloofness that she had not noticed before. And his eyes spoke of . . . what?

Why was he still such a mystery to her with the vows just over three weeks away? Once expressed, the question begged an answer and pressed her hard.

She found her hand on the door handle and turned it. From her chamber door along the gallery, she could see the light coming from the library door below, near the great hall. Raoul must still be awake!

Impulsively, she slipped out the door and closed it softly behind her. Just now she cared little for propriety, she needed to talk with Raoul and search him out. On bare feet, she padded quietly down the sweeping staircase and moved along the walls of the great hall, her heart thumping wildly inside her. The candles of the great chandelier were dark, and she narrowly missed upsetting a small table. She reckoned it close to midnight; the servants would be asleep. Her earlier qualms turned to determination. She would find him.

She stopped short, gasping slightly in surprise. There were muffled voices coming from the partly opened library door. Brien darted to the wall beside the double doors and listened, fighting for self-control. She had not even considered the possibility that he might not be alone. Now she could only hope to get back to her rooms without being detected.

Impulse had brought her this far, but something in the voices lodged in her mind and caused her to stay.

Who was he with? The voices were low, but with effort, she could make out what they said above the beating of her own heart.

A thin male voice with decidedly English speech wafted through the crack at the edge of the door. "Raoul, you dog, I don't know how you do it. You're very like a cat—always landing on your feet. Give you a disaster and you turn it into a triumph. By God, this is excellent brandy."

Raoul's voice was louder, his rich baritone easily recognized. "I do my best in whatever circumstance I find myself." There was a tone in his voice Brien had never heard before; perhaps the brandy affected him.

"What do you think of it?" Raoul went on.

"This place suits you well. But I never thought to see the stud of Paris turned country squire—all married and with a pack of squalling brats. Though Lord knows you've done enough to leave offspring in your wake wherever you've gone." Their laughter was harsh and raucous. Brien was frozen to the wall, mesmerized by what she heard.

"I thought to meself," the stranger continued. "he's done it this time, he has. When the Marquis bounced you out of the house, banished you, I really thought you'd packed it in. Bloody hell—was he angry!"

"Ah, he cannot be angry with me for long. I am too much like him. He could never bear to see the family disgraced. I knew he would relent. Then this plum dropped into our laps. How fares the *mam'selle?*"

"She was packed off to relatives in Austria. Hasn't returned to Paris—though I'm told your son is in the care of a gardener's family or some such. Can't say I blame you there—a fair piece of goods, that one. Even used, she'd make a prize bedwarmer."

Their laughter grew louder and more humorless, drunken. Heat rose in Brien's face and shock immobilized her. Her mind was blank except for the awful words pouring into it from the slit at the edge of the door.

"A bloody pot of jam, you've got here. Out of the stew and into a pot of jam. Sweet success." A tinkle of glasses betrayed their toast. "Your father, old boy, how does he take it?"

"He is overjoyed that I have at last realized my responsibilities to the family." Raoul's tone was mocking. "For a paltry investment he rids himself of a troublemaker and gains a financial alliance. Weston is far wealthier than *mon père* supposed, and the good earl seems eager to have a son-in-law to share it with. I have already had enough to pay my gaming debts at Madame Fontaine's. I shall be his willing and able student. *Mon père* may go hang; he will never see a franc."

"I'll have another before I go," the stranger announced. The sounds indicated that he rose and shuffled across the room to replenish his drink. "What of your darling bride? What is she like?"

Raoul's next words seared Brien's mind.

"A plump partridge, ripe for the taking." His words were beginning to slur, but Brien had no difficulty understanding this next. "I'd have tumbled her already, but I'm saving the rare piece to reward myself on the wedding night. It may not be easy—I'll swear she stirs my blood. I keep a distance now and bed the serving wenches nightly to ease the drought."

"Plump, you say? In fact?" the stranger squeaked, then belched. "Always favored them that way meself, a softer ride . . . usually have bigger tits as well. Has she?" He laughed at Raoul's silent response, whatever it was. "If you find yourself detained on your wedding night, I'd be pleased to stand in . . . my very"—another belch—"real pleas-shure."

"She's hot enough for it. They always make such a

delicious row the first time, I wouldn't miss it, my friend. She'll be especially entertaining. Give me some time to get my hands on the fortune then I may let you have her for a few nights.''

"You're quite the expert in that area, I'll allow. There'sss hardly a virgin left in Paris thanks to you. I might be tempted to sympathize with your delicious little piece.''

"Your sympathy will do her no good—but she may have need of your prayers. I intend keeping her well bedded and heavy with child.''

"Then my prayers she has-s!" the stranger declared. "I mussst to the inn whilst I still can ride.'' There was a scraping sound and a rustling noise and their voices faded as they moved toward the library doors that led onto the terrace. Raoul's deep voice was clear enough to understand still.

"You will arrive a week before the wedding and stay here with me. *Mon Dieu!* It will be good to have your wit to relieve the boredom.''

Brien's body felt numb and she held her breath to listen for Raoul's next movement after the door closed. The light dimmed in the library as he doused the candles.

His steps thudded louder and louder against the marble floor as the light of a single candelabrum edged into the darkness of the great hall. Panic welled up from the pit of her stomach and she felt a great weight pressing on her chest. The door swung open farther, stopping just short of hitting her. She gasped. But the light moved steadily onward, leaving her behind the door in the closing darkness. The light ascended the stairs and turned along the balustrade toward Raoul's rooms.

It was several minutes before Brien could breathe normally again and force herself to move. In the darkness of the hall, she searched for familiar objects to act as guideposts. Her thoughts were on the safety of her own chambers. Each step took an eternity as she forced herself to walk slowly and quietly up the stairs.

The lock clicked softly behind her and she withdrew the key, realizing how her body trembled when the key fell at her feet. The righteous anger and fear within her left her without the energy to stand. She crumpled to a heap before the glowing embers of the fire.

The first gray light of morning seeped around the tapestries at the windows before Brien could bring herself to move. In the predawn cold, she lay, wrapped in her own arms as if holding her very self together. No strength of will or logic could dismiss what she had heard or its devastating effects on her. No tears came to gather the hurt and pour it from her. There was no relief from the raging dry grief inside her.

A soft tapping on her chamber door roused her. She sat up jerkily, rubbing her eyes and trying to gain her bearings. Brien had to search stiffly for the key while Ella's near frantic cries pleaded with her.

"Milady!" she grabbed Brien's icy hand. "Ye be near frozen!"

Ella was alarmed at the rumpled form of her mistress and the glazed, remoteness of her eyes. She bustled the numbed Brien into the bed at once, tucking her in and feeling her forehead for signs of fever, then left to fetch some tea and brandy to warm her mistress.

Brien lay propped on the pillows, her eyes flitting nervously about the room, coming to rest on the velvet box on her dressing table. She stumbled out of bed and seized it, squeezing it as though she could force some of her anger into it. Bitterness boiled up inside her as she opened the box and stared at the long, delicate strands whose luster seemed to gloat and mock her.

She exploded, ripping the strands apart with such force

that the perfect orbs were flung everywhere about the room, a shower of luminous wrath. She didn't stop until all she held was the golden clasp and wisps of string.

Then something warm touched her cheek and she reached up. She looked at the wetness on her fingertips and somewhere inside her a dam burst, releasing a torrent of tears and anger and pain. She sank down beside the bed and abandoned herself to the soul-cleansing sobs that vented her anguish.

Ella found her some time later, still crying like a lost child. Putting her mistress into bed once more, she sat nearby until the young Lady of Southwold fell into a merciful sleep. The little maid's eyes widened in amazement when she beheld the empty jewel box and the white spheres randomly covering the floor. She turned back to Brien looking quizzically at her lady. Whatever happened had completely unstrung her mistress and friend. A glint from Brien's relaxing hand caught Ella's eye, and in the golden clasp in Brien's hand, she read all she needed to know.

She proceeded to the family dining room where a late breakfast was being served and announced to Lord Weston that Lady Brien was taken ill and could not journey on this day. Raoul exhibited a genuine concern for his betrothed's health, his face a perfect blend of compassion and distress. As she returned to Brien's room a growing foreboding troubled her loyal little maid.

The next morning Brien had recovered sufficiently to appear at breakfast and to journey on to London. Raoul's attentiveness shook her self-control badly, and she had to force herself to submit to his chaste parting kiss. She was secure in the knowledge that her sorrow-marred countenance was a fair counterfeit of a physical ailment. She breathed an audible sigh as they left the gates of Weston

Place.

During the long ride she had time to think. She had been afraid to question her good fortune lest it flee before her. Her own probing mind could have saved her from much of this present distress had she but used it. The insight pained her; there is no true good fortune that cannot withstand the scrutiny of cool, clear logic. The fault was clearly not all Raoul's. For so shallow a plot to succeed, the victim must be willing—and willing she had been. The price for learning to be true to one's self was high indeed.

The Westons' London house, Harcourt, was located in a fashionable part of town. It was a big, friendly house with many upper windows to let in the light and gardens that marked the seasons with Dutch tulips, summer roses, chrysanthemums, and holly. To Brien it now seemed a last refuge.

She excused herself from dinner, and while Ella prepared for her bath, she paced and fretted. "A plump partridge . . . a rare piece," she muttered. She knew the gutter-born expression, but gave it her own meaning. "A bloody mindless piece of meat I am to him. A piece of warm flesh to vent his twisted lusts upon." Her fists clenched and she shivered with a thrill of rage.

"Well bedded and bearing his spawn in an ever broader belly—never! I'll never wed that strutting cock," she declared, pleased with her play on words. "I'll find a way to end this engagement and see my dear father repayed in kind."

While she bathed, she recounted to Ella the overheard conversation and its outcome, omitting nothing. "He is not what he purports to be. His father sent him here an exile—to relieve the family of the taint of his philandering." She stared ahead of her, remembering his expert touch and arousing kisses. "It was so simple for him to impress a simple, inexperienced girl whose calculating father left her like a trussed lamb upon the altar.''

"Ah, now ye cannot think your father a party to this. Likely he's as deceived as ye.''

Brien's lovely eyes narrowed. "He saw only the gold and the title. He didn't even care to investigate my future husband—so eager he was to be shed of me. Raoul's name on the tongue of every wag in Paris and he never heard it . . . or did he?''

"The lord's a cold man betimes, but I cannot think he would do that to his only daughter.''

Brien scowled, thinking of his imperious anger when she presumed upon his authority. Was he capable of doing the thing of which she now accused him?

"I'm not sure of anything just now . . . except that this marriage cannot take place. At this late date, the embarrassment will be hard for my father to take and I shall be virtually unmarriageable. But I shall be free of his meddling and free to run my life as I want.''

"Will ye tell him what ye heard?''

"Never.'' Brien was emphatic. "He has made it abundantly clear that the words of any man are more precious to his ears than those of a mere woman-child.'' She thought hard, toying with a cake of rose-scented soap.

"Raoul's fortunes are secure enough; father knows the family's repute—there's no help for us there. So it is his character that must provide the fatal flaw.'' Like a thunderbolt it struck her. "A fatal flaw he certainly does have.'' Lifting her lovely face to Ella's intent gaze, she straightened and a determined smile came over her finely chiseled features. "The 'stud of Paris' has assaulted one too many.'' Her blue eyes were suddenly the color of steel.

"And has he?'' Ella eyed her questioningly.

Brien scowled at her maid's saucy attitude. "My father

will believe he has; that is all that matters. He will be forced to end the engagement and I shall be free again."

Settled in bed later, Brien felt the full weight of regret as she sternly banished forever all thoughts of love and marriage in her life. The pain that coursed through her, the sting of betrayal just as new and tender womanly feelings blossomed within her, went to the core of her. She brushed back an unbidden tear and steeled herself against the loss. Love, marriage—bah! Such idealistic ramblings had brought her only pain. Though the price was dear indeed, she had learned about the trap of marriage and the deceitful nature of men. She vowed to avoid both at any cost.

The next morning, Brien prepared herself with a noseful of strong, black snuff, which sent her into spasms of sneezing and brought tears to her eyes. She thought of all the sad things she could muster and was almost defeated in that attempt by the sudden, ironic thought that the feminine wiles her father had paid so handsomely to encourage in her—to suit his own purposes—would now be turned on him. Collecting herself again, she succeeded in producing red, swollen eyes and an appropriately wan face, then descended the stairs to put an end to her engagement.

Lawrence Weston's concern over his daughter's appearance turned to shock, indignation, then righteous anger as the tale unfolded. Raoul had sent for her with an urgent plea, and fearing a mishap, she had gone to him. She had been shocked to find him alone and well-soaked with brandy. She rebuked him and started to leave, but he threw her down on the library floor and fell atop her. She had struggled with all her might and let it be dragged from her how his hands on her were harsh—leaving marks that only now subsided. Had Ella not awakened and sought her, his assault would surely have succeeded.

And the things he'd said! Crude, vulgar boasts of his many bastards and his exploits in Paris. He boasted even about wrenching money from the estate already, she added in a stroke of truth she only now wondered about. It had been a living nightmare.

She had been sick at heart the next day, not in body. She finished by imploring him to break off the engagement, for she could not abide the thought of marriage with the beast! The tale was a treacherous web of truth, half-truth and lie—so intermingled that even she lost track of where one ended and another began.

Weston rose, trembling with anger, and she wondered if perhaps she had done her work too well. She had never seen him so angry. His honor, his judgement had been put to the test and found wanting in the very matter a man ought to hold most dear—the welfare of his child.

"This insult to our honor will not go unredressed. You will not marry the Frankish swine!" He flung open the parlor doors and shouted orders for his carriage to be readied immediately.

Brien paled as she surmised his course. "Father, you'll not confront him alone? Send Mr. Poole or one of the other solicitors. You're far too angry. Please let us have no further trouble over this." Her plea was genuine and struck a chord in Weston.

"There is already trouble enough, but I will not shrink from it. I'll not send another to set right my mistake."

She watched her father's carriage pull from the courtyard and felt a twinge of regret at the suspicions she had harbored against him. Perhaps he had acted in good faith after all and had been met with treachery—

like herself.

And what would Raoul think? Let him think she had learned the truth—or better yet, let him think his irresistible charms had failed. As long as he was out of her life, she little cared what he thought.

Five

The roads were dry and the weather cool. In the stylish barouche, the visible signs of Weston's anger had abated, leaving the smoldering coals deep within. He was in control now, unlikely to say or do anything rash. He blamed himself totally. He had been remiss in his duty as a father when he had failed to make inquiries as to the man's character. He had fallen prey to the myth that "successful" is the equivalent of "good." The wealth and position of Raoul Trechaud's family led Weston to believe in his integrity.

Still another thing puzzled him. The young man was handsome enough to turn any young woman's head. Society generally winked at the impassioned advances of the groom-to-be. And however clumsy or brutish the attempts, a man's fiancée would be forgiving in the interests of their future life together. But Raoul Trechaud was not a clumsy man, and in spite of Brien's anguished revelations, Weston had difficulty imagining him as a brutal rapist.

Weston had the uneasy feeling that for a second time

he was not in possession of all the facts. Brien's story had the ring of truth, especially that part about having taken money from the estate already. She could not have known about the funds Weston had provided for the refurbishment of Weston Place. Some paint and fabric—clever trappings, but hardly five thousand worth . . .'' He redoubled his determination to have this unsavory business behind him. He would see his daughter free of any entanglement with the Trechaud family.

The barouche entered the gates of Weston Place as dusk closed in on the coach. The gray air, heavy with moisture, weighted Weston's shoulders as he alighted from the carriage. He was met at the door by a surprised butler who helped him off with his cloak and directed him to the library. Raoul sat by a blazing fire, reading, as Weston strode into the room, and looked up in surprise at his unexpected and unannounced entrance.

''Mon Seigneur,'' Raoul began, rising quickly. ''This is a pleasant . . .'' But seeing the look on Weston's face, he faltered.

Stopping a few feet from where the rogue stood, Weston glowered. ''I have not come this wretched distance to exchange amenities.'' His voice was harsh but controlled. ''I am here on one account alone—to end my daughter's engagement to you and to send you from this house this very night.'' He hadn't meant to blurt it out like that, but there it was and he braced himself for what must inevitably follow.

Raoul was stunned by the bold pronouncement and his shock was clearly visible. ''This is a cruel jest, *monsieur,*'' he began as his mind raced to ferret out Weston's motivation for such a rout. ''And if not a jest, then an injustice to a man whose only desire is to spend his life with your daughter in honorable marriage.''

Once begun, the words came easily.

"Do not speak to me of your desires," Weston thundered. "You have indulged them all too often." The older man's nostrils flared and his face reddened.

Raoul took a step toward Weston, buying time with which to consider his next words. "What possible reason could you have for denying us our future together? I cannot believe you would betray your word to your daughter and the man she would marry." His mind whirled, coldly sifting all the possibilities.

Weston held his ground, his feet solidly planted and his contempt plain in his face. "It was my daughter who bade me come here this night to break off this engagement. Having seen your baser side, so well hidden beneath that veneer of courtly manners, she will not marry you—or indeed, ever see you again. And after tonight, God willing, neither shall I!"

Baffled now, Raoul shook his head. "What have I done? When have I ever been but courteous and attentive toward her?" He certainly had not anticipated this! He had assumed her full cooperation since that night in the gardens at the ball. Now he cursed himself for not paying her more heed—for underestimating her. He struggled to recall what might have set her against him and voiced these thoughts aloud.

"What has changed her mind against me in the two days we have been apart? I have the right to know!"

"Well you should know the reason, for there could be no other. Only a pig of a man would force his desires upon his own true betrothed before the vows—against her will." Weston had hoped to avoid the embarrassing details, but was prepared to press his case to the limits if need be. His fleshy jaw was set with determination and anger. Whatever he had lacked in fatherly care before, he would not fail in this venture.

"I . . . I am accused of that?" Raoul's eyes widened

in astonishment. To be accused of something he had not done when his own deeds left ample room for criticism was an unexpected twist of fate. Fighting a smile at the irony, he went on. "And what are the circumstances of this alleged attack?" A new poise stole over his perfectly carved features.

"You lured Brien downstairs the night we stayed here. The true character of men is often revealed when they indulge in strong drink. You tried to take her in my own house—very nearly under my own chambers! Had it not been for her maid, your foul plot would have succeeded. You are beneath contempt!" Weston's hands clenched at his sides, and he wheeled away to stand before the fire. The thought of his daughter pawed and abused by this high-blooded rogue sickened him. He felt a strange kinship with the heat and violence of the flames in front of him.

Raoul felt the first flicker of confidence. "She told you this . . . that I tried to force her?" His mind flew to keep pace with the pounding of his heart. All was at stake now and he could not afford to misjudge a single step. There was genuine risk in the course he now chose.

"She was ill the next day," Weston muttered, "but not from an ailment—from you!" He whirled and advanced on Raoul until only a chair stood between them. The veins in his neck were visible evidence of his inner state. The man would have youth and strength on his side, Weston judged, and experience as well if it came to blows. The sheerest of bare reason held him from striking the smug, handsome face before him.

As if reading Weston's mind, Raoul stepped back. "She said I tried to force her." His eyes narrowed with anticipation. "And did she also tell you that I succeeded?"

This was no denial! Instead, an arrogant admission

of guilt! Weston felt his belly tighten as if he'd been hit. "What are you saying?!"

"Only that your daughter's story is incorrect in several aspects—and woefully incomplete." Raoul's face was hard now and his eyes glinted faintly with satisfaction. He had launched his counterattack with stunning effectiveness. He crossed the room to the liquor cabinet and poured himself a brandy. He was in control now and he intended to relish the moments until Weston realized it, too.

Weston's silence masked his inner turmoil. "You do not deny it! Good, God, you are a degenerate!" He made a quick move toward Raoul but the younger man put a table between them. He did not intend to lose the upper hand in a physical melee.

"I do not deny bedding your daughter—but I deny that force was involved." Raoul's crooked smile distorted his handsome features. "Shall I give you the entire account? Of how Brien agreed to meet me after the house was quiet and came to me freely. We are betrothed lovers—not rapist and victim, until now, when she victimizes me!"

Barely restraining himself, Weston gripped the edges of the table until his knuckles were white. "No! This is a lie!" But suddenly he felt betrayed. Why would a man own to such a deed if it had not occurred? The nagging doubts of his coach ride now returned to him accusingly.

"Whatever else I am," Raoul said with a show of earnestness, "I am a man of truth. I would not deny that I desired Brien and made advances to her. But I cannot allow my honor and our future together to be destroyed by the feverish conscience of a fickle girl. There was no force—except that of our mutual desire."

The fire raging in Weston was dying. Cold drafts of sober reason now swept through him. Who to believe?

A daughter he barely knew or a man who would admit to dishonoring his bride before vows? And the scandal . . .

"You cannot end our engagement. She is mine now in fact as well as promise. To refuse to let us marry would be to dishonor her forever." Raoul's carefully chosen words bit into Weston's conscience. "She must marry me now or never marry. And you would die heirless . . . unless, of course, the seed has already taken root."

Rape or not—the deed was done, Weston was convinced and now forced the lingering doubt from his mind. If there were a child already? A bastard his only heir—what then? Fatigue and Raoul's cunning defense conspired to force his surrender. He closed his eyes, only to open them a moment later to a new view of the husband he had chosen for his daughter. For the first time he saw the calculating mind, the controlled, mannerly façade, the strength turned to hardness. This was bitter—to be a pawn in the hands of his own willful daughter, brought low before this rogue.

"What's done is done," Weston uttered with deadly calm. "The marriage shall go forth as planned. Whatever caused this change of heart in Brien, be it guilt or pride, you must work it out between you. In time you both may have reason to hate me for this decision."

Raoul was subdued in victory. "I am sure Brien will realize the seriousness of her plight. This has not changed my feelings for her; I still want her for my wife. In time I am sure she will accept our marriage." He poured Weston a brandy and replenished his own drink.

The lord's hand was steady as he accepted the glass. He looked squarely into the beguiling face. "Brien is all I have left. You will do all in your power to see her contented in this marriage."

In the silence that followed, each man appraised the other and wondered at the ramifications of their exchange. Weston finished first and threw his glass into the fire. His customary air of authority once more settled upon him like a cloak.

"I ride back to London at first light. In two day's time you will join us there. She will need time to adjust, but not time to brood. You must mend the rift between you quickly. Precious few weeks remain before the wedding."

A small, curious group of servants stood discreetly huddled in the passageway near the staircase in the main hall, speaking in whispers and stopping occasionally to strain their ears. The Harcourt staff had been tiptoeing about all afternoon, since Lord Weston had returned, blowing through the front doors like a typhoon run aground. He had shouted, cursed, and generally created a spectacle before closeting himself in his study and calling first Mrs. Herriot and then Mr. Poole to him. Brien had witnessed the uproar from her chamber door, and later Ella brought her a firsthand account of her father's state. Something had gone wrong . . . terribly wrong.

Brien now sat before her father in his study, transfixed by his angry gaze. She could never have imagined that such a simple plan could go so awry. Ah, perhaps she was the simple one—to believe that Raoul would withdraw in disgrace. Raoul was a man whose desires and greed made him unscrupulous and unpredictable. Only now did she realize the full force of his cunning.

The anger of betrayal blazed in her father's face. His features were hawkish and his voice bitter.

". . . and in your eagerness to be shed of this encumbering alliance, you neglected to provide me with the full details of your 'ravishment.' You neglected to tell me that Raoul's attempt succeeded!'' His face was now inches from hers, and she could feel its heat.

''Succeeded?'' She breathed in sharply. ''But, Father, I . . .''

''You told me what you wanted me to believe . . . playing upon my fatherly care to get me to act as your lackey!'' He withdrew and paced angrily. ''Running about the countryside defending your virtue like some armour-clad antique in his dotage! This marriage will go on as planned and I'll see you're made an honest woman!''

Brien's wits had fled and she shook her head dumbly. Raoul! He hadn't denied it at all! He had confirmed her story and taken it a step further—to be sure she would be trapped. He had admitted the rape and generously offered to make it right! Hoist by her own petard! Now her father would force the marriage at all costs. What kind of man would own a rape he did not commit to marry a woman who hated him enough to accuse him of it? Raoul's kind, she thought bitterly.

She sprang from her chair, energized at last by the realization of her plight. ''You would force me to marry a man who would dishonor me so? To lie to my father about my virtue? A man I now loathe and despise because he abused me?''

''Abused you?'' he cut her short, galled at her pretense of innocence. ''There can be no rape if the girl is willing—when she agrees to a tryst and offers up her body like a loaf of bread!''

The words struck Brien like the back of his hand. He truly believed it! Raoul had somehow convinced him they were lovers—that she had come to him willingly. She shook her head violently and grabbed Weston's arm as the panic bloomed inside her.

''*No!* It's not true! don't you see . . . he's only saying that to force me to marry him. He wants your fortune and will stop at nothing to get it! He never . . . succeeded. We are not lovers. I am not ruined or a whore!''

The realization trickled through to her; nothing she could say could change his mind. Raoul had done his work well. Her deception had cost her the respect of her father and had sealedh er fate—a cold, loveless, bitter marriage.

"How can I prove to you?" she wailed. "How can I make you see?"

"We shall not speak of this again." He turned away from her, wrenching his arm free. "He will be here in two days' time to see you. You will make your peace with him and the matter will be forgotten. There should be no reason to move the wedding date ahead. If there are consequences from your sin, they may well be handled later."

"No-o-o!" Her wail pierced him to the quick. "No, father . . . no!" And she ran from his towering presence.

Food was repulsive and sleep eluded her in the two days and nights that followed. Nothing could console her. Sorrow quickly gave way to a burning desire to strike back—to have revenge and to gain her freedom. Relentlessly the events paraded themselves before her, begging a solution.

She could be forced to marry him . . . but marriages could be annulled. She must make him want to end the marriage as much as she. But how? No amount of shrewishness or inadequacy on her part would deter him, he was too greedy. It must be something else . . . something to strike at his very manhood, his precious manhood.

73

A "rare piece" he had called her, being saved for his pleasuring after the nuptials. In her bed she shuddered. She would sooner surrender her maidenhead to a total stranger than that cur! He had positively reveled in the report of his conquest of maidenhood . . . was so sure she would prove "entertaining." She burned with shame and anger as she imagined Raoul's hot, possessive stare allowed to roam her nakedness on that night.

Then it was clear! Come the wedding night, he'd find no virgin bride in his bed, trembling. His manhood insulted and the marriage never consummated, she would leave the next day and he could seek an annulment.

Madness! What was she thinking? Had her hatred of him so warped her mind that she could consider such a thing? Even to have thought of so dangerous and degraded a course was evidence of how tainted she had become.

But to consider marriage with Raoul, lying beside him at night, devoured and consumed by his twisted lusts—she could not bear it. And what retribution would he take for her betrayal of him? She was not so naive as to believe that he would forgive and forget.

The night was long and sleepless as the arguments raced round and round in her head. The thought obsessed her that there was but one path for her—not to be a virgin on her wedding day and to refuse to consummate the vows with Raoul. Over and over the words beat like a chant in her brain.

This was bitter. Which was the greater sin: to betray one's betrothed and lie with another, or to live a lie of a life—poisoning each other with hatred until all around were consumed? More yet, could she bring herself to submit to another . . . a stranger? Either a stranger she would never see again or Raoul, with his twisted passions and ruthless ambition. The choice was grim at best.

By the first light of morning, Brien's mind was set. She would wrest some control of her life from the merciless fates, whatever the cost. The choice was hers and she vowed to be free of Raoul Trechaud before the marriage was a day old. All that remained seemed minor details—where and who.

Six

His Majesty's frigate *Falconer* put into the London docks before dusk, and the hands secured her before going off to revel in the attractions of the dirty and dangerous waterfront taverns. Below decks, the first mate shed his crisp officer's uniform for the breeches and heavy wool coat of an ordinary seaman. Only the costly black boots of the officer's rank would set him apart from the revelers he would join—and most would be too drunk to notice.

It was his own fault that this venture was necessary at all, he grumbled. He had allowed the ship's cook ashore with the rest of the crew and now had to foray ashore himself to quiet his growling stomach. Tucking a silver coin into his waist and a long, slim dirk into his boot, he ran a hand over the stubble of a beard beginning to show on his face. Peering into a small looking glass hanging on a peg in his modest quarters, he murmured his approval. He would pass.

The St. John's Crown lay on one of the quieter streets of the waterfront district, belying its regal name with its rough trade. Still, its clientele were the more affluent of the ships' enlisted personnel. Good food, uncut rum, and smuggled French brandy were available for the right price, and there were strong, healthy young country girls available for more fleshly pursuits in the sporting room above.

The first mate of the *Falconer* bent his tall frame through the doorway to the Crown and straightened inside to survey the lively crowd. The tavern's strong smells assaulted him—ale and sweat mingled with the odors of hot grease and tobacco. He took a seat at the only empty table, in a corner near the fire.

A plump, dark-haired girl with her skirt raised and tucked into her waist on the sides strolled over to the table. She stopped close to him and put her hands on her hips to force her breasts even further out of the dirty chemise she wore in place of a blouse. She eyed him boldly, clearly pleased with what she saw. "Wot's yer pleasure, mate?"

The mate smiled at her suggestiveness and put a friendly hand on her waist. "My pleasure'll wait. Now my belly aches wi' hunger and I be parched wi' thirst. Meat, a loaf, and a flagon of ale. We'll see about t'other later." He sent her off with a slap on the rump. He had not the slightest intention of paying for her or anyone's company later, but was not one to insult a woman, whatever her station.

In the dim light of the oil lanterns, the mate could see a group of drunken seamen telling loudly and raucously of their exploits and downing pints of bitter ale to settle wagers. At the center of the group was a younger man, who seemed to be a leader of sorts, holding their bets and making free with the wenches. The others looked to him to verify a story or order another round. His clothing was of a gentlemanly cut and the lace about his cuffs spoke of an income beyond that of honest labor. The mate studied the man quietly as he waited for his meal, musing on the qualities that caused one man to be a leader and another a follower.

Just as his meal ended, a movement in the loud corner caught his eye. The young leader had a gnarled sea veteran by the neck, backed against the wall, and was growling drunken threats the mate could not make out. The others thought this great fun and shouted taunts as the old man struggled to escape his tormentor's grasp. The old man's offense was not clear. A pickpocket . . . or just an object of ridicule made defenseless by age? The old man pleaded pitifully but the leader landed several blows about his head, and the victim slid down the wall, surrendering to pain and fear.

The mate turned his back and downed the last of his mug, a pleasant buzzing beginning in his head. He sighed heavily and rubbed his bristled chin thoughtfully. He pushed his chair back across the dirty planking of the floor.

All attention was on the painful spectacle of the old man's abuse. The tormentor had stopped to swill from a mug of ale, to the cheers of his companions. Some of the pale gold liquid ran down his cheek and onto his waistcoat. He was well on toward drunkenness.

It was a moment before the bully was aware of the tall man's presence. The rabble's leader was not as young as he appeared from a distance. His face was bloated with drink and hard lines framed his cruel mouth. The mate put himself squarely between the leader and his victim, drawing the rapt attention of the whole tavern. A good fight would be a moneymaking proposition.

A broad, engaging smile spread across the mate's face. " 'Ere now. The ol' fart's done. Ye've had yer fun—let 'im be." He stepped toward the bully with his palms open at his sides, a cajoling tone in his voice.

" 'Ow about a round on me."

"Mind yer own damn business," the bully warned. "An' get yer carcass outta my way." He moved as if to push the big mate aside, and for a moment it seemed as though the big man would allow it.

"No need fer insults." The mate swayed to one side as if to give room, but grabbed the leader's arm as he lumbered past and jerked him back forcibly to stare down into his furious face.

"Only a pussy beats on them 'e knows can't fight back."

The challenge was met and the bully landed the first blow with his meaty right fist, but it carried little real force as it connected with the mate's jaw. The mate whirled for position and jabbed a large muscular fist full in the bully's face. The leader stumbled back, stunned; and the mate seized the chance to deliver two finishing blows to the man's head and ribs. Before the body hit the ground, the mate had drawn the dirk from his boot and turned to the scurvy crew, challenging them with an amused sneer.

"Any comers? I'm jus' gettin' warmed."

The drunken lot backed away quickly. The mate seemed pleased and put the knife away so that the handle was still visible above his boot top. He stepped over the bully and hoisted up the wizened victim over his broad shoulder.

The noise of the trade resumed with shouts of "quick work mate." The crowd was not seriously disappointed by the shortness of the fracas. The mate grinned broadly at his drunken congratulators.

"The pleasure were all mine, gents!" he called, accepting an offer of a flagon of ale from the tavern keeper. He drank deeply from the musky brew then flipped a silver coin to the proprietor who nodded elegantly in return. He strode out into the cold night.

79

They were well down the street before the form on his shoulder wriggled and said, "All right, mate. Ye can put me down now." The tall man obliged him and was surprised to find him fully alert and little the worse for wear.

"Can.ye walk, then? I thot ye'd be ready for buryin' by now."

" 'Ell, no—jus' roughed up a bit. I cain't fight no more so I learned me to play daid." A gnarled finger came up to tap the temple of his grizzled head. Here was a survivor.

"Down 'ere's water," the mate gestured, putting his hand on the little man's shoulder and steering him to the well.

The cool water felt good on the mate's face and neck. He pondered the grizzled seaman beside him and asked, "What did ye do, steal 'is purse?"

A wrinkled, wet grin appeared. "Nah! If'n I had pinched it, 'e'd never ha' felt a thing."

"What then?"

"I told 'im to stop drinkin'—that's all. 'E was gettin' soused proper, and the deal meant 'e 'ad to be stone sober."

"A deal?" the mate prodded him.

"We was partners, ye might say. An' now 'e's gone and queered it for us both. 'E's like that in 'is pints—mean as 'ell." He squinted at the mate appraisingly. "Wot ship ye come off of?"

"Falconer."

"A frigate, then." There was respect in the old man's eyes and a sudden bit of calculation. " 'Ow'd ye like to be me new partner? Jus' for tonight."

"Legal or illegal?" the mate grinned. He was not above a bit of diverting adventure. He had nothing better to do with this night.

"Oh, legal as pie. The sweet deal me and 'im 'ad

could still be done.''

"Lay on.''

"The deal was for a strong, young buck to meet wi' a lady at an inn at 'leven o'clock sharp. An' 'e must be stone cold sober. Ye interested?''

"What's it about?''

"I dinna ask. A right fair young lass come to me on the street an' said she heared I could 'elp 'er. She give me five pounds when I said I'd do it. This lady 'as a job needs doin' an' wants a young man wi' a close tongue to see to it.' I says, 'Nothin' illegal' an' she says 'Certainly not—jus' private.' So I lined up ol' Jackie. And 'e went an' got drunk on me.''

"A meeting wi' a lady?'' the mate questioned. The old man produced three silver coins as proof of his story.

"They'd be fifty quid apiece for us if ye will.''

"I'm in,'' the mate slapped his thigh. "Who knows, she may be pretty.''

"Benny Stiles is the name.'' The old man held out his hand.

The mate took it, chuckling. "People jus' call me 'sir.' ''

Harrall's Road Inn was located in a quieter, working-class part of London. It catered to tradesmen and travelers needing semipermanent quarters in the city. The rooms and linen were always clean and the board, simple but tasty. The proprietor was careful about his patrons, but never pried into their comings and goings as long as their silver lined his pockets.

He had let his finest rooms two days before to a young woman who had paid for a month in advance—gold. He hadn't bothered to inquire further than the name she gave, Hastings. But when the ancient mariner and the tall seaman entered that evening and asked for the Hastings' rooms, he eyed them warily. He couldn't believe they were meant to occupy his choicest accommodations. Then he remembered that someone had arrived earlier, using the back stairs, and the same young woman had appeared to order his best cognac and a fire laid in the hearths. The old man was persistent and the innkeeper at last relented.

A young woman in a plain blue traveling dress let them in, after careful scrutiny in the dim hallway light. The mate stood near the door, once inside, and found himself feeling less adventuresome by the minute. He appraised the girl and found her attractive in a businesslike way: dark hair, slim body, erect posture, and fair skin.

The old man minced no words. " 'E's 'ere. I done my part."

"So I see." The young woman shifted her attention to the mate, boldly appraising him and walking to and fro the better to view him. She frowned as her eyes moved upward to his stubbled chin, but she seemed pleased overall. "He'll do." She handed a jingling money pouch to Stiles. "It's all there—plus five."

The mischievous eyes twinkled as he weighed the pouch in his hand. "Right smart for a night's work. Good luck, mate!" And he was gone.

The young woman crossed the sitting room to the washstand and poured a basin of water. Without a word she thrust a razor and soap into the mate's hands. His dumb look forced her to gesture to his beard. "Off with it."

"What for?" the mate eyed her suspiciously. "Wot's this about?"

"Ye'll find out soon enough." Her hands were on her waist, elbows out. Seeing him hesitate, she chided, "A shave an' soap an' water won't kill ye."

The young woman disappeared through the doorway as the mate unbuttoned his coat. There had been an irritating air of triumph about her.

He shaved carefully, wondering what he was being groomed for—or whom. The girl was pleasant enough looking, for all her bossiness. And the mate found himself wondering about the possibility of bedding her when the "job" was done. He cared not for the sex of brothel or tavern; conquest was more to his taste. Her rustling petticoats and soap-clean smell as she passed had awakened his slumbering desire, unfilled these long months at sea.

He smiled rakishly and licked his bottom lip slowly, relishing his thoughts. When he wiped the last remnant of soap from his face and rinsed it, he surveyed the job in the looking glass. The tanned face was square, divided by a long, straight nose and framed by high cheekbones and square jaws. The top of his left cheek was interrupted by a long, jagged scar running from his temple downward toward his nose. He grinned as he thought of the women who had claimed that the scar gave his face a rakish look. It added a touch of the dangerous to the otherwise pleasant handsomeness of his features.

The door to the bedchamber opened and the young woman entered again, leaving the door behind her ajar. She surveyed the mate and approval swept over her countenance. He fancied a bit of admiration there as well. But she walked to the door to the hallway and called back toward the other room. "I'll be next door if ye need anythin'." She put special emphasis on the last word and left with a parting glance at him.

Having watched the servant depart, for servant she surely must be, he was now aware of the rustle of skirts behind him. Instinctively, he whirled, coiled inside as if for an attack. A woman stood just beyond the doorway

83

in the darkened room. Here at last was the lady he had been brought to meet. Irritation at the secrecy and intrigue rose inside him, causing him to speak brashly.

"So you're the mystery lady I had to shave to meet." His hands were on his hips and his legs were spread as though he made a stand. He seemed unaware that something in his speech and manner had just changed.

The figure moved slowly toward him into the light and the mate felt as if he'd been dealt a hard right to the gut. The woman was a vision. His heart stopped—then leaped wildly in his chest as he drank in the details of her beauty.

She was taller than average and walked with a queenly grace. From the profile she presented him as she walked across the room, he was stunned by the richness of her skin and the perfect evenness of her features. Tawny golden hair was pulled back into myriad ringlets held by combs. When she spoke, her voice was so low and melodious that he forgot to listen to her words. Something about a brandy.

Hell, yes, he needed a brandy. "Yes, thank you," was all he could manage. She poured one glass and he noticed that her hands trembled. Everything about her told of breeding and wealth. When she turned to offer him the glass, his devastation was complete. Her gown was of costly dark blue silk, trimmed sparingly with pure white lace. The skin of her chest and shoulders was flawless against the dress, the way a pearl seems most lustrous when set against dark velvet. The tight bodice was cut dangerously low and he felt hot suddenly as his gaze drifted downward over the creamy mounds that met in a delicious line. Below her small waist, it was clear she wore no panniers, from the clinging flow of her skirt over her hips.

The starkness of the dress and the lushness of her

body produced a carefully calculated effect on the seaman. Suddenly aware he was gaping, he forced himself back from his reverie. Had she said something more?

"Your name? I shall have to call you something," she entreated. Her pink lips were full and moist, drawing his eyes to them.

"A-A-Allen Stewart, ma'am." It was a name he'd used before. "And may I inquire about yours?" His voice now had a gentle roll to it and his pronunciation was perfect, cultured.

"You may inquire, but I must tell you a lie; for I cannot say who I am." She smiled, he thought a bit nervously, and moved closer to the fire.

" 'I shall have to call you something,' " he quoted her, wondering if she would be affronted and caring if she were.

To his relief she smiled warmly, her eyes flitting shyly over his big frame, before dropping to her own white hands. "Then call me . . . Lady . . . and I shall strive to act the part." She seemed to relax a bit, and Allen was suddenly aware of the strain of such a meeting on a lady of her station. He wondered what dire circumstances forced her to seek out a stranger by such a costly scheme to see a "job" done. He resolved to find out soon.

Finishing the brandy, he placed the glass on the table and held out his hand to her. She accepted it hesitantly, unsure of what he meant to do. He led her to the stuffed chair near the fire, and looking much relieved, she sat down. He took the straight, caned chair opposite her.

"What is this 'job' you would have done, Lady?"

"In good time," she breathed deeply and seemed a bit more confident. "First I must know if you may be trusted. Are you truly a seaman?" Her look was clearly disbelieving.

85

"Aye. I sail on a frigate that docked only this afternoon."

"And its name?"

"How is it you question me and refuse me even the meagerest details about yourself?"

She smiled at his gentle chiding. "If things go awry, I stand to lose most. And so I must protect my own interests. I would judge you can see well to yours."

He smiled, owning the logic. "The *Falconer* is my ship." His parted lips revealed straight rows of even white teeth that drew the lady's eyes.

"Your speech is not that of a common seaman . . . your bearing has an authority to it." Her open observations surprised him. Why was she so interested in the man she hired for an errand, albeit a costly one? What more was there to this crazy scheme he had been drawn into?

"The man for this job must be discreet and able to hold his tongue. Somehow I feel you will be. Have you a family?"

Caution seized him and his eyes sought her left hand. It was bare and he was strangely relieved. Then he chided himself. Of course she would not wear a family wedding ring at such a meeting. Was she married? Why would she ask about his family?

"I have some family—but they live a distance away, outside Bristol. I see them rarely and like it that way."

"Does your ship dock at Bristol often?"

"Seldom. Lady, what is this errand for which I must yield up my life's secrets? Are you in trouble?" He realized that he cared if she were or not and upbraided himself for such chivalrous thoughts. Still, something about her unmanned him and made him want to gather her up in his arms and protect her. He leaned forward in his chair to put his elbows on his knees. At this sudden motion, she stiffened noticeably and just as quickly covered the fear that he had seen flicker in her soft blue eyes.

He found his eyes beginning to wander over her body in the lengthening pause and was torn between savoring the delectable sights and saving her from further embarrassment. She began to squirm under his warm, direct gaze and rose, leaving his mostly forgotten question unanswered.

"Would you have another brandy?"

He ripped his eyes from her and stood, leaning one shoulder against the mantelpiece. "Yes, thanks." An ache was building inside his loins, and he realized that her face appeared before him in the flames of the fire. He forced his eyes shut and saw her there as well. What was happening to him?

A motion near him caused his eyes to open quickly. The lady stood nearby, offering him a glass . . . and this time she had poured one for herself. The fire in his throat could not match the one she had started in his blood. He wanted her. It was madness to consider it.

With another woman he would have already plied his charm to render her willing. Women seemed to find something about him irresistible, and he was not above enjoying the opportunities fortune generously created for him. But she was different—indescribably, delectably so. He waited for her to move, fearing to breathe lest she detect his aroused state, but she did not leave.

She looked up into his face, studying it. The scent of fresh violets reached him, sending his mind reeling. His breath came faster and he returned her gaze warmly but he feared that to speak would spoil the moment.

When his eyes reached hers, he was stunned. Their soft blueness was not a smoky color and lighted from within by a force he himself was feeling, desire. Her lips were redder now and glistening, tempting him to claim them. Her breasts rose and fell faster as her breathing quickened. Could this be? She desired him too?

Seeking his answers, he reached out to touch her hair. She stood still and quiet before him as his whisper-light touch glanced over her curls and came to rest on her cheek. She blushed involuntarily, drawing his eyes to hers. Little could he have known the impact of his catlike golden orbs upon her, or how his broad shoulders and animal-like ease of movement fascinated her. The musky blend of tobacco, brandy, and the sea engulfed her senses and sent little tongues of fire through her limbs.

Slowly, so as not to frighten her, his arm came down from the mantel and joined the other encircling her waist. She put her arms lightly on his as if bracing for an attack—but none was launched. He drew her to him slowly, folding her close to his heart with great tenderness. She rested her cheek against his warm, well-muscled chest, listening to the tempo of his heart.

They stood, merged in a gentle embrace for a long time, each lost in jumbled, separate thoughts. For all the joy of her in his arms, something in him was reluctant to go further with her, even though she seemed willing. Why now, of all times, should ethic and conscience intervene where common sense and need had given their blessing? The higher instinct won, and in a husky voice he offered, "Lady, if you wish, I shall go."

Her head tilted back to study him. Her cool hands came up to cradle his fevered cheeks as she whispered one word. "Stay."

His head reeled as her hand curled lovingly about his neck and he claimed her lips tenderly. Her mouth was soft and unbearably sweet beneath his, and he fell— down, down, down, never finding bottom. Her lips parted slightly to admit the tip of his hot tongue, and he traced the opening with slow, hypnotizing strokes. He felt himself growing hard and pressed her closer to him. Slipping her arms about his waist and clinging to him, she met the growing force of his kisses with unleashed ardor. He felt a consuming passion to join with her—not just to have her—an urge that involved him totally: mind, body, and soul. A wild new excitement filled him, joyful, compelling. This was not like any experience he had known with a woman.

His lips roamed from her delicious mouth to her chin and downward to her neck and bare shoulder. He savored the sweet coolness of her satiny skin. But to her his lips were glowing coals, pouring fire into her very loins. She was not "Lady" now, but woman, primed and willing. She clutched him tightly, pressing her tingling breasts against him and felt him respond along the length of her. Her fingers traced the sinews of his broad back and her neck hurt from reaching up to meet his ardent kisses. But the pain was transmuted, made exquisite in the flow of passion.

He drew away to look at her and assure himself that she was real. Then he picked her up and carried her into the dimly lit bedchamber and set her gently on the bed. She made no move as he sat beside her and removed his high black boots. When he turned to her, her eyes were a curious, arousing blend of passion and sadness. They called to him in a way that shook him to the very depths of his being.

His big hands searched for the combs in her hair and put them on the table beside the bed. Unraveling her curls, he stroked them tenderly and marveled at their softness. She caught his hand and pressed its palm to her lips, running the tip of her tongue over its work-hardened creases. He smiled in awe of her. Whoever she was, she was his now.

Allen lay down beside his "Lady," stroking the smooth skin of her shoulder with his fingertips, wishing he had memorable words and finding none to express the sweet turmoil of his body and soul. Then he claimed the sweet lushness of her mouth again, pressing her back into the pillows and trying to absorb her essence into him wherever they touched. The intensity of his kisses eased and he took her into his arms, working at the lacings of the back of her gown and having difficulty.

"Wait," she whispered throatily, and slipped from the bed. Facing him she pulled the rest of the lacing loose and slid the dress downward over her hips. Layers of petticoats were soon shed, and she turned her back as she unlaced the brief corset. The chemise she wore was of gossamer-thin fabric, and the light of the single candle bathed her emerging form in gold. His eyes were transfixed upon this vision as he removed his shirt and breeches. Barelegged, she joined him on the bed, hesitating until he opened his arms to welcome her.

He pulled her to him and wrapped her in his big, warm body, sheltering her. She lay quietly in his arms, feeling the press of his hard stength all about her and timidly touching his bare chest. Then he pressed her lips hard and was met with the soft warmth of her darting tongue against his, spurring him on. His mouth moved to her neck and lower to her chest as she held her breath. He pushed back the thin garment and cupped her ivory breast in his hand, marveling at its softness and firmness. She gasped as he began to massage the creamy mound while continuing to kiss her slender neck and shoulders. She felt a crimson tide flooding her face and chest, reaching down even to her breasts, setting her nipples atingle.

His mouth found her other breast and she startled as

his tongue teased the nipple. He denied the perception and kissed the hollow between the soft mounds. In another moment he was over her, parting her legs with his own and gently lowering himself to her. Her body was cool against his skin and he moved slowly, reveling in the pleasure the contact gave him, his hardened staff probing between her legs. She clutched his back and squeezed her eyes shut, her lips parted slightly venting her short gasps.

As he entered her his body felt the resistance and it shot through him like lightning. He withdrew abruptly, shock written on his face. Her eyes flew open as she felt the change and a confusion of loss and fear rioted in her expression. He moved over her and lay beside her, watching her, searching her.

Staring up at the canopy above to avoid the disappointment she knew must be in his face, she asked, knowing the answer that would come . . . dreading it. "What is it?" The tremor in her voice cut him.

"You're . . . you've never done this before." There was awe in his tone.

Her eyes closed, shame flooding her cheeks. "No." Then a tear trickled from the corner of her eye, winding back toward the jumble of her hair. One quiet tear. He was destroyed.

Without thinking, he gathered her up into his arms and held her tightly, inwardly cursing his clumsiness. This of all things he had not expected, his "Lady" was yet a maid. The flickering of fear in her eyes, was that for him? Some moments later, he relaxed his embrace to look at her. She was not crying, but looked distant, sad.

She tilted her face to his. "I am sorry if I displease you. I wanted you. Is that not enough?" The pain in her voice and face made his chest wrench and his belly ache.

Stupid! Bungler! He had hurt her. She innocently thought he withdrew because she displeased him. His effort to do the decent thing had had the most indecent effects. He kissed her gently, starting with her forehead and working down to the tip of her nose, then at last to her fragrant mouth, missing nothing.

Her arms came up about his shoulders, pulling them to her. His passion was rekindled and she breathed fire into him once again. Her kisses had a wild sweetness that made sense to him now. The joy of her new sexuality seeped through to him, enhancing the already heady wine of her incredible beauty and gentle spirit. He traced her body from head to foot with his lips, touching her gently, stroking her with his hands and feeling her new and joyful responses in her tremors and quivers of pleasure.

He moved up over her, guided shyly by her hands as they explored his body. Her legs came up around him as he entered her slowly. Her eyes were wide and her breath came in short gasps again as the sharp pain pierced her. But then there was a wonderful, overwhelming fullness inside her and instinctively she moaned softly and moved under him.

The sensations were nearly too much for him. It took every fiber of his will to hold back as he moved between her silky thighs. When he could stand it no longer, he burst, pouring himself into her with salty sweetness.

They lay side by side at last, spent and united. He brushed her hair back from her face and she snuggled closer to his chest, having lost most of her shyness. An odd contentment filled him. Somehow the questions that bombarded his mind did not seem as important as the peace they shared.

She turned a bit and traced the muscles of his chest with a butterfly touch, wondering at their latent power and perfect symmetry. He stroked her arm and the full curve of her hip as she lay against him.

"I didn't want to hurt you."

"You couldn't," she murmured against his skin. Propping herself up on an elbow, she frowned darkly. "How can you be a seaman? Are they not a coarse, rough breed? I think there is more to Allen Stewart than meets the eye." She smiled coquettishly. "And I have experienced some of it."

His uncharacteristic blush and rakish grin told her she pleased him.

"And you, Lady, what are your secrets? Why are you here in bed—bestowing priceless treasures on a common seaman? I know you as no other man has, and yet you will not trust me with your name. How am I to live with that?"

The gentle chiding sent her up in bed with her back to him. Her hair was an inviting cascade of sand and gold down her back. Her emotions warred with common sense in a desire to tell him everything.

"Why must you question me so? Take of me what I can give—what I offer freely. I will ask nothing more of you than to be with you."

Her eyes were wet as he gathered her into his arms.

"Whatever troubles you, I want to help."

"Nothing troubles me here with you." She nestled against him so that one ripe breast pressed against his side. "Can it be that others feel . . . this? Make love as we have? Is it always like this?" Instantly she was shamed at the brazenness of her thoughts and the naiveté she betrayed.

He was intrigued and not a little amused by her question. How could he explain to her that most people search and dream for a lifetime of the kind of loving she had just stumbled upon. He shook his head. "No."

She raised her head to gaze at him and asked timidly,

"Have you known many other women?"

He smiled rakishly. "I remember only one. She has hair of sand and eyes of sky, and right now, she is mine." His lips touched hers tenderly as his hands roamed her curves and valleys freely, caressing and exploring her.

She surprised him by shifting onto her back and drawing him over her. In the movement her chemise opened and Allen grinned at her, causing her to flush hotly. He nipped the skin of her exposed breast with his fine teeth, playfully. Lying still, she closed her eyes, memorizing each new sensation. When she could bear the sweet aching no longer she drew him up to her and wrapped her legs about him. He entered her slowly, giving her time to adjust to him. This time her hips began to move, untaught, against him, drawing him further inside.

They clung to each other tightly, as if by sheer force they could merge into one being. There was no world outside their bed, no love or loving but theirs. When at last great spasms racked his body, she seemed to feel them too. Then calm, dreamless sleep overtook them, entwined in each other's arms.

When Brien awoke it was still dark outside. For a moment she luxuriated in the startlingly new feel of a warm body beside her and the weight of a heavy, muscular arm across her waist. But quickly she remembered and carefully, so as to not disturb him, slipped from their bed. Picking up her garments, she donned them with some difficulty—taking pains to be as quiet as possible. When dressed, she retrieved her cloak from the other room and went to the window to look into the narrow alley below. Through the gloom of the soot-ringed window she could make out the lines of a waiting cab. Shuddering with regret, she pulled the heavy, plain woolen cloak about her shoulders.

For a long moment she looked at the man lying on the bed and then moved closer. He was like nothing she could have imagined—animal and spirit fused. His long, muscular body was fascinating in repose, a paradox of brutal strength reined and controlled by an unexpected gentleness inside. She reached out to touch him but drew back, afraid he would waken.

She must leave now, she realized. The "job" was done, a bargain fairly met. Yet she loathed slinking away from him in secrecy, hiding from him the knowledge of who she was and what she planned. To reveal it to him would be to bear his scorn. No doubt men of his class had the same feelings as to the value of a woman's word and their right to dispose of a woman as if she were so much baggage.

She would never see him again. Her heart wrenched at the sudden realization of what she had done. A merciless fate had used her own plot to punish her audacity. The taste of sweetness in this first loving would haunt her for the rest of her days. Her punishment was most fitting.

She memorized his features, down to that roguish scar. She had forgotten to ask how he received it and knew that now she would never have the chance. There was so much about him that puzzled her. Her chest ached and tears welled up in her eyes to run over onto her flushed cheeks. From her pocket she pulled a leather pouch and placed it on the pillow that had cradled her head moments before. Pulling up her hood and tucking her hair in carefully, she turned and was gone.

When the full light of early morning sent gray shafts

of light through the dirty window, the man who called himself Allen Stewart stirred contentedly in the bed. Then, aware of a change about him, he started up, his sleep-clouded eyes searching the bed beside him and finding it empty.

He threw back the covers and bounded unsteadily out of the bed, looking quickly about the room and rushing into the next room. She was gone! He leaned in the doorway, his hand over his eyes as he sought to gain his bearings. Could he have dreamed her? He opened his eyes to scour the room for evidence of her. The silent testimony of two brandy glasses was all he could find. She had been real. He grimaced as he felt once more the sweet warmth of her lips against his, and the remembrance of the fragrance of her hair caused his throat to tighten.

He turned haltingly back to the bed and sat down heavily on the side where she had slept. Something on the pillow caught his eye, and he picked up the leather money pouch, judging its contents by the feel of it. He scowled deeply. Payment for a "job" well done? A surge of anger caught him by surprise. Had he been bought like some common . . . But, no, another part of him urged, not her. He remembered her sadness, the sweet inexperience of her lush body, the exuberance of their second loving. Perhaps a gift to see him into better circumstances?

Unsure of her motives and shaken by his overwhelming reaction to her, he squared his shoulders and set his jaw sternly. He started to get up but a glimpse of something on the bedside table stopped him. There lay the two tortoise-shell combs he had taken from her hair. He reached for them and turned the delicate reminders over and over in his hands. A flood of tenderness and longing washed over him, contending mightily with his doubts.

Determination filled him. He would see her again. He would return the pouch of money unopened and would place the combs back in her hair himself . . . however long he must wait.

Seven

The next two weeks were difficult for Brien. The gay prenuptial dinners and autumn dances were scarcely endurable. Raoul charmed the women into undisguised covetousness and the men into grudging admiration. He was irritatingly attentive and insisted on dancing only with Brien or the aging doyens of society. Each move, each gesture was calculated for effect. Brien watched with a blend of fascination and despair as he entrenched himself with the local squires and gentry. His unfailing politeness and shrewd grasp of financial dealings made strong impressions on the nobility, hard-pressed by losses in the colonies.

Lord Weston was in every way the enthusiastic father of the bride in public, but in private, he avoided Brien whenever possible, even taking meals in his chambers. She was relieved to be spared his open rancor and his presence. Once more she was isolated from the world, in spirit, if not in fact.

The long December nights were the worst. A phantom haunted her dreams. A tall, muscular man with hair like burnished copper now waited each night to carry her back to a safe, little room high above Harrall's Road. There they loved until his presence was so real that she awoke with the sensations of his heat next to her body. At times she berated herself— mewling about over a common seaman. Worst of all, she felt no shame! It was clear evidence of how jaded she had become. And then the almost tactile memory of his big hands on her skin—so gentle—and the longing in his incredible golden eyes came back to her.

Somehow, in spite of her secret and his dubious identity, she was certain their feelings and loving were the most honest and right she had ever experienced. Learning, logic, and morals against it, it still seemed right to her. To have briefly tasted such perfect union was enough. He had made her a woman in every way and whatever happened, she had that consolation.

To forget him seemed impossible and to remember him was physically painful. He had been tall and strong, but with his size was a grace of movement, a careless freedom of spirit that showed in his gestures and in his speech. The scar on his face was testimony to his willingness to fight, but with her he had been so tender—unwilling to cause her even the slightest discomfort. Another would have demanded what he took only reluctantly.

This bittersweet pain was ever with her, exacting hard penance for her sin. She found herself looking at the faces of the men in the streets, hoping and fearing that one would be he. Then moments later she would revile herself for such pointless and immoral thoughts.

Brien's wedding day dawned to a cool drizzle from a tired gray sky. Her spirits were at low ebb. The day would be long and taxing and at its end would be the dreaded confrontation with Raoul. Her only consolation lay in the prospect of ending this farce at last. Soon it would be over.

The ceremony was to be held at eleven o'clock and the household was atizzy with last minute preparations. Brien was glad to escape it all in the custom of the bride not being seen on her wedding day. As Ella helped her dress, she felt a growing coldness inside her.

"Ye needn't dread it so; it'll only take a few minutes. And the sooner over with, the better." The little maid finished tying her lacings. "Ye might even forget to tell the *mon-sieur* this eve. . . ." Her suggestion drew a cold glare from her mistress and she fell silent.

Ella had not approved of Brien's plan from the beginning. Aside from the morality of it, which she would never presume to judge, she worried that Brien overestimated her ability to deal with the full force of Raoul's cunning. He had bested her once with an unthinkable lie. Where would he stop now?

And the effect of that one night in Harrall's Road had been disturbing as well. The bloke had been handsome enough, they had been lucky in that. Ella could see the reason for the attraction. But he was a seaman and well she knew their coarse appetites and crude habits. She could not imagine a true lady like her mistress submitting to one of their breed. Yet it must have happened. In the wee hours of the morning Brien had given her a terse, emotion-laden summary, "It is done."

Ella had expected some change after so momentous an occurrence: some guilt, some sadness, some fear of lasting consequences. She thought, when the monthly course ended well, that Brien would feel it safely behind her and regain her spirit. But the lady continued to dwell on the encounter as though she had lost more than her maidenhood there. That unnamed loss worried Ella more than anything else. Brien would need all of her resources for the upcoming confrontation with Raoul.

The church was lined with boughs of fresh-cut pine and holly for the season and with rows of dignitaries and nobility. As she started the long processional down the aisle of the abbey sanctuary she was acutely aware of a collective "Ah-h-h-h," drawn from the assembly. Was that for her? She'd scarcely glanced at the pier glass before they left for the abbey. She could only wonder at the smiles and stares, feeling overwhelmed, suffocated by their speculative scrutiny.

Perhaps it was the dress, she mused distractedly. M. Lamont had outdone himself, she knew. Ignoring the fashionable wide skirts in favor of the classical lines of the Greeks, he had fashioned a gown of delicacy and supple grace that enhanced daringly the lines of Brien's own body. The soft satin was caught under the breasts and a low, rounded neckline was accented by puffed sleeves that tapered closely along her arms to points above her slender hands. The gown was appliquéd with pearls and laces and a cathedral train of lace over satin flowed from her shoulders. Her hair was a cascade of ringlets from high on her head to well past her shoulders, pearls and ribbons intertwined. A veil was attached to her hair by combs and trailed over the train. She was a vision of ancient glory—a goddess come to claim the hearts of mortals, and yet unaware of the devastating power of her beauty.

Her eyes were fixed on the altar ahead where Raoul waited to claim her. He was princely in a gray-white velvet coat and satin waistcoat and breeches. His raven hair shone and his eyes glowed with satisfaction as he gazed at her. She lowered her eyes to avoid his.

As her father put her hand in Raoul's she felt as if she were being swallowed up—drowning. It was too late—the deed was being done and in a few short minutes she would emerge to the congratulations of their admirers.

The bishop droned on, enamored of his own voice, causing Brien's mind to drift away. She remembered little of the rest of the service. Suddenly she was in Raoul's arms and was being given a proper wedding kiss at the back of the church. Her feeble protests were met with Raoul's throaty laughter and the delighted chortles of the guests pouring out of the boxes and pews.

The rest of the day whirled on about her, the bridal dinner and toasts and more toasts. The party grew loud and lively—and scarcely bearable. Brien noted that Raoul drank only moderately and murmured a prayer of gratitude.

When the coach arrived to take them to Weston Place, Brien was aching with fatigue and apprehension. The guests were quite drunken by now and pelted them with wheat and jolly, vulgar advice as they ran the gauntlet to the carriage. Lord Weston's face was flushed with drink and quite merry as he closed the door behind them. He seemed relieved to have it all behind him, and Brien envied him his good humor, however short-lived. She tried to smile and waved politely, consoling herself with the thought that they were all too drunk to notice her strained effort.

Once on the road, Raoul's hand on her arm caused her to start. She had forgotten the long ride to Weston Place alone in the carriage with Raoul. This would require utmost care.

"Madame," he began, "I fear I have neglected you." He settled back into one corner of the plush velvet seat, propping his long legs on the opposite one. He stared at her hungrily.

"I have not felt your attentions to me lacking." She was uneasy beneath his leering inspection.

"But I have not told you how ravishingly beautiful you were today . . . are now. When I saw you coming down the aisle, I counted myself a fortunate man—husband to such grace and beauty." His smile was arrogance personified. "Every man there envies me this night . . . and they have reason. You are breathtaking . . . and you are mine." His hand traced her throat and his open palm moved downward over her bare chest to rest on her partly clad breast. He cupped her breast in his hand, caressing it possessively.

Brien stiffened and looked away. To protest now might alert him to her planned resistance later. He withdrew his hand even as she was thinking this and he laughed harshly.

"Don't worry, madame. I'll not have you first in the back of a carriage, even one so fine as this." With another laugh, he lay back on the soft cushions and in a few short minutes was asleep.

Raoul had changed his elegant clothing for a simple silk dressing gown when he arrived in Brien's rooms that night. He carried a bucket of champagne and two stemmed glasses. He was in a light mood, his air triumphant.

"That is all, Ella." Brien gave her a meaningful look that Raoul did not see as he placed the bucket and glasses on the table. Ella left through the door adjoining the servant's chamber to the mistress' bedroom to wait there until needed.

Appraising her simple green muslin day dress with a petulant frown, Raoul crossed his arms over his chest. *"Ma chérie,* you might have dressed more appropriately for this momentous occasion."

Brien straightened her shoulders and spread her hands on the back of the chair in front of her. Now.

"I am sorry if my mode of dress displeases you. I saw no need for special attire."

He measured her words carefully. "Your wedding night means so little to you, then?" His tone was challenging, the lightness abruptly gone.

"Our vows shall remain unconsummated on this night and every other." Her voice was quiet but firm. Her chin raised to meet his angry response.

"I might have known you would resist to the last. It is useless. I shall have you this night with or without your consent." He moved slowly toward her, determination blazing in his eyes.

Brien moved quickly around a heavy, stuffed wing chair, keeping it between them.

"There is more," she hurried on, anxious that the whole truth be out. "The lie you gave my father is in part true now; I am not a virgin bride."

He stopped, eying her, wondering at this new tactic, judging the truthfulness in her eyes. She gazed at him evenly, openly, but he swept it away with a wave of his hand. "You are given to convenient falsehood—a bad habit I must break you of in time." His face grew darker with the passing moments.

"This is no falsehood. I would spare you the indignity of finding out for yourself. You are not the first." The pleasure she imagined when she first hatched this plan was missing entirely. Shame caused heat to rise in her face.

"This is a trick to delay the inevitable. You try me sorely, madame."

"I will never by your wife," she responded adamantly, "I detest you. And so I deny you the entertainment you had anticipated on this night. Nor will there be a marriage, even in name. I will provide a way out

. . . at considerable cost to myself. I was not virgin at our vows, they cannot bind you." The determination on her face made him admit the possibility. She continued, seeing her words find a mark. "The vows will not be consummated. You are free to seek a handsome settlement from my dowry."

His fist slashed out at the table, sending the glasses and bucket shattering, clattering to the floor. He was red-faced, his dark eyes bulging with rage.

"You scheming bitch!" he growled. "You think to rid yourself of me so easily? You think I am so weak and stupid as to swallow your lies and content myself with your leavings?" His fist came down hard on the table again, overturning it as he exploded with rage. "You conceited whore!"

"I begged you to hear me," her anger nullified the fear she felt. "You would not listen to me. I was forced to marry you and have done so. But I shall never be your wife. The conceit is not mine—but yours, in your determination to have whatever you want, no matter what the cost. Now you shall have your fortune . . . and without the cumbersome baggage!" Her heart pounded wildly in her chest as she moved to keep pieces of furniture between them.

"You have been given an honorable way out before the world—purchased at great price. I shall bear the disgrace of the annulment, having deprived you of your husbandly rights. But the real truth you and you alone must bear. I preferred another and took him to me willingly." Her voice had the steady ring of truth.

Raoul lunged forward, surprising her, and caught her shoulders in a viselike grip. She pushed hard against him trying to free herself. His eyes raked her savagely. Lies or not, bitch—I'll have you now!"

His mouth missed hers as she thrashed in his cruel and tightening grasp.

"No, Raoul! You're mad! . . . *No!*"

Suddenly Raoul's torturous hold loosened and Brien was shocked by his abrupt release. Then she realized that he looked beyond her and turned slowly to see what miracle had stopped him. Relief quickly changed to horror. Ella stood a few feet away aiming a cocked pistol at Raoul's heart. Brien was speechless.

Raoul looked from Ella to Brien, his breath hard and fast, the struggle for control evident on his face. "So this is your game," he smoldered, doing horrible violence to her with his eyes as his fists clenched and loosened convulsively at his sides. "I do not believe you had a lover. You would not lower yourself, you spiteful, prideful bitch."

It had never occurred to Brien that he would disbelieve that part of her story. It had not crossed her mind to simply make the claim and to keep her virginity. How could she prove him wrong except to give him the one thing he wanted most? The irony of it struck her, and she almost smiled.

"You accuse me of pride," she lashed out at him. "Well, look to it in yourself. You would prove your manhood by having me at any cost. A lifetime of pain and hatred is too dear a price for any man's pride."

She sighed heavily, feeling keenly the pain of regret— for what might have been and for what was yet to come. "Think of me what you will. I have told the truth. We are not—cannot ever be—truly married. Take comfort in the gold you will have and in the knowledge that because of you I am disgraced." She lowered her gaze, unable to bear the sight of him any longer.

"You have brought this upon yourself. You will pay for this treachery." He slammed the door behind him, shaking the very walls.

* * *

106

The sun's brilliant rays streaming through the leaded crystal panes awakened Brien the next morning in her empty marriage bed. She lay quietly awhile absorbing the sounds about her, marveling at their ordinary quality: winter birds outside the window, Ella bustling about in the outer chamber, the crack and hiss of the flames in the newly laid fire. Since Raoul had stormed out the night before, a curious sense of peace had settled over her, an odd admixture of relief and sadness. Most keenly she felt that she was alone.

The day passed slowly, Brien ill-at-ease with this waiting, for it was harder than she had imagined. After dinner in the evening, she sat in the library, reading the scandalous Voltaire and missing much of his shocking sense. She rose at last and paced the heavily carpeted floor, trying to understand this discontent she felt.

As she stared out into the cold, bare gardens from one of the French windows, a vague longing welled up inside her and she realized sadly that she would never again be content with the simple, secluded life she had led only months before. She had seen, felt, and done too much. The memory of a tender winter's night not long past would haunt her always, even as it did now.

This restlessness was bought dearly with her scheming and bitterly she recognized the wide swath her own pride had cut in leading her to her freedom. If she had only wanted to be free of Raoul, could she have found an easier path? Was she vengefully set against him because he hurt her pride, duped her into thinking him one of that noble breed of men for whom she longed?

Behind her the butler cleared his throat discreetly, startling her and causing her to reach for the heavy drapery beside her to steady herself. Feeling foolish for the violence of her reaction, she smiled nervously.

"Yes, Samuels?"

"I am sorry to have disturbed you, madame," he

bowed politely.

"It was all right. I thought you might be—there might be word from Monsieur Trechaud."

"There has been none, madame. Your maid suggested that I bring you some sherry before you retire." He gestured to the tray on the table, and at her nod, he poured a goblet for her.

"Thank you, Samuels." Brien found herself longing for the stern, but familiar propriety of Phillips, butler of Lord Weston's household for as long as Brien could remember. Some of the staff at Weston Place had moved permanently to Dunstan with Lord Weston and, anticipating a lengthy wedding trip, much of the new staff here had taken leave to visit families. Weston manor was left with meager staff, most of it new to Brien. Ella was kept busy seeing to her lady's needs and constantly supervising the inexperienced new servants. Even now she prepared her lady's bath and saw to the freshening of Brien's chambers.

"Will there be anything else, madame?" Samuels stood patiently by the door.

"No, that will be all," Brien dismissed him, taking up the goblet of sherry and smiling warmly. Ella, her one true friend. The little maid often suggested a dram of sherry before retiring, and Brien knew it was Ella's own fondness for the taste of it that prompted the suggestion. They often shared a glass at the end of a day. Brien warmed to her friend's gesture.

She settled herself on the settee, sipping the sherry and trying once more to involve herself in Voltaire's wit. The room grew warm as she drained the goblet, and a pleasant whirring began in her head. Her eyes felt heavy and it was harder still to make meaning of the print before her. Her eyes closed in spite of her attempts to keep them open and her head fell back against the settee. The thin volume of essays slid from her grasp to the floor.

Eight

In the darkness there appeared a light before her and she drifted upward toward it as through a dark tunnel. Her eyes flickered open and closed again in defiance of her will. She turned her head and tried to shake it to clear it, to no avail. Her whole body felt weighted and heavy as she was pressed down against something. A bed? Her eyes opened at last and she struggled to make sense of the images that swirled about her, stubbornly refusing to still their kaleidoscopic motion. Why was she having so much difficulty waking? She struggled to sit up and was puzzled greatly by what she saw.

She was in a huge stone room, sparingly furnished, and certainly not her own. Her vision slowly sharpened, and in the dim light provided by two small windows at the top of one high stone wall, she could make out a few elegant pieces of furniture and an intricately carved marble fireplace. She shook her head at the sights, and turned her inspection to the huge canopied bed in which she reposed. It was hung with rich, purple-hued and fringed brocades that dominated the room. The sheets were the finest satins and the coverlets, light down edged in Flemish laces.

Opposite the bed was a massive wooden door which was reinforced with sinister hammered-iron bands. The strangeness of it all finally registered on her returning consciousness, and she stumbled with weakness as she dragged herself from her bed. Where was she? How had she gotten here?

What did she remember last? Her head cleared quickly now. Last thing . . . the library? She rubbed her eyes. She couldn't remember going to bed or much about the library. . . . This room was not at all familiar. She made her way to the door and tried the handle but it would not budge. With growing alarm, she pulled harder and rattled the handle. The realization dawned slowly that the door was locked—from the other side. She was locked in!

She whirled about, feeling her heart beating faster. A large leather- and brass-bound trunk sat between the huge bed and the glowing fireplace—her chest! She was instantly aware of the night dress she wore. It was a thin, blue silk gauze with flounces of lace at the wrists and rounded neckline. It was part of her trousseau. Her mind raced now as she flew to the trunk and threw it open. Inside it was just as Ella had packed it—all her lovely lingerie and night robes, and nothing more!

On a small dressing table nearby were pearl brushes and a silver hand mirror, vials of scents, and a lacquered box of scented talcum. These were her things! And where were the rest? Where was Ella? The growing fear in her chest threatened to suffocate her. Where was she?

She ran to the door and pounded with her fist. "Hello!" she shouted, "Is anyone there? Can you hear me?" She listened and, hearing nothing, pounded again. "Let me out!"

She stopped pounding when her hands were too sore

to continue. With mounting anger and frustration she threw herself down in a large stuffed chair near the waning fire and buried her face in her hands, trying desperately to recall everything she could.

Think, she commanded herself. Ella had prepared her bath while she read . . . downstairs. She was waiting for word from her father about . . . Raoul! Her whole body convulsed with the recognition. Raoul! Suddenly she knew this was his doing and struggled in earnest with the panic that seized her.

Brien jumped as a key scraped loudly in the lock and the bolt was slid back on the other side of the door. A mountain of a man entered, ducking his head to clear the doorway. He carried a silver tray with what appeared to be food and a pot of tea. Brien jerked up from the chair and instinctively backed away as he approached the table near her. Putting down the tray, he stared at her, his eyes widening slowly.

She was paralyzed with fear. All thoughts of trying for the door were banished by the thought of this hulking creature catching her. She shuddered. His large, dark eyes were fastened on her as he slowly moved to the dressing table, picking up the stool and carrying it to the small, circular tea table where he had left the tray. He gestured to the repast with one massive hand. His movements were slow, but not clumsy, despite his bulk. His broad, weather-bronzed face bore scars at the chin and over one eye, and his head was shaven. Beneath his frayed, but clean clothing, massive muscles bulged ominously. Brien shivered as the odd thought occurred to her that there was little fat to his mountainous frame.

"Who are you?" Her voice sounded weak. "Why are you holding me here?"

He said nothing, but backed toward the door, unhooking the keys from his belt. In one fluid movement he was through the doorway and the huge door once more sealed her in.

She felt small and weak as the blood rushed back to her head. She was a prisoner here—and that hulk, her jailer.

Curiosity and a familiar gnawing in her stomach drew her to inspect the tray. He had indeed brought her food. The strong, hot tea was delicious. She savored the taste and smell of it. The service was silver, and the cup was the finest china. Under the plate cover were succulent roast fowl and steamed pears. This was not a breakfast meal. How long had she slept? Not even the tiny windows could provide a clue as to the time.

Her thoughts returned inescapably to her husband. . . . "Raoul," she ground her teeth in frustration. Again she had underestimated him—just as Ella had warned that she might. Now she was at his mercy completely. The full impact of her imprisonment gripped her. Raoul would have no annulment—he would have revenge. She went cold with dread at the thought of what punishments lay ahead of her. All of the wretched, loathsome quirks of his twisted mind could now vent their hostile pleasures upon her.

She paced distractedly, her body taut with anxiety. How could she resist? She had no possible weapons, not even andirons for the fire. She ran to the tray and searched, finding only a spoon. Of course. Raoul was, she was learning, a very careful man. Her heart sank.

She slumped into the chair, trying to blot out the awful images that assailed her mind. Her gaze fell on a rack of books. Something about them bothered her, and it was several moments before she could call it completely to mind. She ran her slender hand along the spines of the small volumes. Love sonnets in a prison. She looked about her with new eyes, the insight striking a spark of hope within her. She was a prisoner, true, but this was no dungeon. Does a man provide down mattresses, thick carpets, and silver service for a prisoner he wishes to degrade and torture? Or poetry and delicate lingerie? Here were clues she could not reconcile with the certain doom she had earlier forecast.

Brien sat quietly, listening in the lowering darkness for any sound. She had no candle to dispel the gloom. As footsteps sounded outside, faint and growing louder, she steeled herself against whomever, whatever it might be.

When the key turned in the lock, she jumped involuntarily and stood. Shafts of golden light entered the doorway followed by the hulking keeper carrying two large candelabra. He placed one on the table and the other on the washstand near the bed. He picked up the tray he had brought earlier and silently left.

Brien had been so occupied with his movements that she had failed to see the other figure enter. She started now at his voice and gasped.

"My lovely bride." Raoul stood with arms folded smugly across his chest, leaning one shoulder jauntily against the wall. He straightened and walked toward her with a slow sensual prowl.

Brien said nothing, hoping to hide the turmoil of fear now roweling about inside her. At least she would soon know his plans for her.

"I trust your chamber is comfortable." He stopped near the table by the light. His face was calm and the candlelight enhanced the glow in his eyes. Brien could not but admit his handsomeness, even now as a chill coursed her spine. How could he be so beautiful and yet so degraded inside?

Seeing she did not answer, he continued, "It is my wish that you have everything you need."

"Except my freedom," Brien challenged him in a throaty voice.

His eyes narrowed briefly, a cold smile spreading across his full lips. "Yes, your precious freedom—it is the one thing I shall deny you."

"Where am I?" she demanded, his civil manner emboldening her tongue.

"Where you are safe . . . and where I want you to be."

Brien felt her anger rising at his smugness. "What is it you want, Raoul? A ransom. A settlement?"

"Madame, you defame me." He put one muscular hand to his breast mockingly as if to ward off her barbs. "I claim only that which is mine by law and right . . . yourself."

"How much do you want, Raoul, a hundred thousand? . . . two hundred thousand . . . five hundred?" she taunted him dangerously.

"I have said, Brien, there are things in this life as important as money. I do not deny interest in the considerable Weston fortune, but you do injustice to my refined tastes and demean your considerable charms to suggest such is my only interest."

His sardonic tone set Brien's hair to bristling. He moved toward her and she backed away, eying him warily. But he only sat down, throwing one leg carelessly over the arm of the winged chair. She now faced him with the light at her back. The thin fabric of her night dress revealed the tantalizing outline of her lush body. Raoul's faze warmed as it wandered over her, coming to rest on her half-clad breasts.

"The peignoir is quite becoming, I approve of your taste, madame. And your hair is charmingly disarrayed . . . a most wanton effect."

Brien's hand flew to her hair of its own accord. She had not realized until now that it was loose and flowing down over her shoulders. Degrading to be so displayed before this jackal. She tried to change the subject and thwart his amorous mood.

"How long can you keep me here? If we do not appear for the wedding voyage, there will be questions."

"As long as it takes, madame."

"For what?" she demanded haughtily.

"To have you with child." His words fell about her like a steel trap. Her face momentarily betrayed her shock.

"Never," she breathed.

"*Au contraire, madame* . . . as soon as possible." His eyes now glinted as he appraised her body. "You cannot then deny the consummation of our vows, and you will be bound to me in flesh as you are on parchment. You are my wife."

"Not until hell freezes!" she blazed.

His laugh was ugly. Rising from the chair, he started for her, removing his coat in a quick, determined movement and flinging it aside.

Brien's eyes flew wide and her heart was pounding in her ears. She backed away as he advanced, trying to avoid the heat of his smoldering eyes. His waistcoat was off now and his shirt was open. His chest, tanned and muscular, came inexorably closer.

In her panic, she forgot the geometry of the room and was suddenly backed against the bedpost with Raoul only a pace away. He reached for her and her arms came up full length to hold him away. His hands bit into her arms and his face lost all trace of amusement. Only raw desire shone there now, and Brien struggled to avoid his heat, pleading incoherently for him to stop. Flashes of pain shot down her arms as he shoved her back against the bedpost with his weight, and his lips sought hers. Her head thrashed from side to side to avoid his ravenous mouth.

"No, Raoul! . . . no! . . . Stop!"

Failing her lips, his mouth found her neck and half-kissed, half-devoured it as he pinned her arms behind her. His body burned against her and his breath came fast and hard. He brought one knee up between her legs, and for an instant she wondered if he meant to take her there, standing up.

In one deft movement, he lifted her slightly and threw her backward onto the bed. Her arms momentarily freed, she pushed against his chest as he pressed down upon her, parting her legs once more. He seemed to be everywhere at once, leaving her indefensible. His sinewed hands caught her wrists and pinned them above her in an iron grip. The heavy down of the bedclothes and mattresses restricted her movement further, and his mouth found hers with bruising force. His tongue forced entry into her mouth only to withdraw as she brought her teeth crashing together. Every fiber of her body was strung tightly with rage as she thrashed and writhed beneath him.

But her struggles only seemed to fire his passion. He held both wrists easily in one of his hands now, while his free hand grabbed the thin fabric above her breasts and ripped it away to gain access to her vulnerable, young flesh. His mouth was greedy as he fastened it to her breast and suckled the rosy, erect nipples. Heat was rising in her and spreading out beneath her skin, whether the heat of passion or of battle, it mattered not.

His breeches were open and his hot, probing staff pressed against her moist flesh, tearing a ragged moan of denial from her throat. Her head tossed and her legs thrashed as he entered her quickly, harshly. He stopped at her gasping cry, then began to move, slowly, deliberately. Brien felt the pain subside and felt him move easier within her as her traitorous body accepted him. She ceased struggling and lay still beneath him as he

116

plunged and thrust harder and faster. Just when she feared he would puncture her heart, he arched against her and jerked in awesome spasms, then collapsed, spent, on top of her.

An eternity passed before he withdrew and sat up to button his breeches and look at her. Her eyes were closed and her torn gown revealed her damp, glistening body, made golden in the candlelight. Her long lashes were wet and her lips were stung red by the fierceness of his abuse. He gazed with fascination at her, his mind racing as his breath was slowing. His hand reached out to cup one tantalizingly rounded breast for a moment, then traveled down her flat stomach. Appraisal and satisfaction mingled in a sardonic smile she did not see.

"You fight well, madame. Perhaps you will learn to love as well." She felt his weight lift from the bed as he rose. Reaching for his shirt, he seemed amused by its lack of buttons.

She had not moved for some time, but now sat up slowly, drawing one soft sheet over her exposed body. Her hair was a damp tangle about her shoulders and her blue eyes were awash with hurt and anger. She bit her lip to hold back the tears.

He came to her, his eyes smoky with satisfaction as he swung his coat over his shoulder. "I do not think you will be here long, *chérie*. If you want anything, tell Dyso, your . . . attendant. He cannot speak, but hears well and has orders to see to your needs. It was he who put you to bed last eve, so you have no secrets from him." Raoul's cold smile made her shudder.

He took her chin in his hand. "You told the truth, you had a lover. You have denied me a husband's privilege and I demand retribution. I shall spend the nights with you exacting most pleasant payment. In time you will see the advantages of being a proper wife."

She jerked her head away and his face set with hard

fury.

"By the time you are free you will bear a son for me beneath your heart. Pray that your delectable body is as fertile as it is tempting. I have shown great restraint with you—but do not press my patience too far." He turned to go, but looked back at her, his face twisting into an eerie smile. "The payment will not be mine alone, *chérie*. You could have no better tutor in the arts of loving." The door closed softly and the bolt slid home.

Brien sat, stunned and hurting, bruised by his taunts and by his assault. She rubbed her lips frantically as though she could remove the taint of his mouth, then spat on the floor, wishing she could spit out the ugliness he left inside her—the disgust and loathing . . . and fear. Only then did the tears come, a hot scalding flood that unleashed the violence she felt toward him.

When she could cry no more, she dragged herself from the bed to the washstand and poured water into the porcelain basin. She pushed the ripped and ruined night dress from her shoulders, letting it fall to the floor, and scrubbed her skin relentlessly, as though she could wash away the inner contamination. Numbly she found a fresh night dress in her chest and pulled it on.

When she extinguished the candles and crawled exhausted into bed, she wondered if she would ever sleep again. But after a while she drifted into a dark, dreamless slumber. No nightmare could equal the one she had experienced awake.

The sound of a key in the lock awakened Brien the next morning, and she lurched up, heart pounding, clutching the covers to her. The hulking Dyso entered almost noiselessly, carrying a breakfast tray. Placing the tray on the table, he removed the basin and chamber pot and was quickly gone. Only then did Brien feel free to breathe again.

Stifling a rising despair, she forced herself to analyze her predicament and to decide on a course of action. There were always choices to be made, she reminded herself. There must be a way to survive this.

She swung her legs over the side of the bed and stood up. Every muscle in her body cried out in rebellion and her face felt tight and swollen. She pulled up her night dress, expecting to see bruised flesh, but amazingly, found none. Then why did she hurt so all over?

She poured a cup of tea from the tray, ignoring the food. She thought ruefully that she had Raoul to thank for her reduced appetite and weight. She had been surprised at how much the seamstresses had altered her trousseau at the final fitting. Ella had commented on her lack of appetite, but Brien was too absorbed in her thoughts to notice her own shrinking proportions.

She shivered suddenly. Anything that made her more desirable to Raoul was loathsome to her. She tried the food on the tray at once, but it caught in her throat. One buttered scone was all she could manage.

Brushing her hair and tidying up the room took only a short while. Soon she found herself with nothing to do but wait . . . and think. Raoul would come to her that night again and she must be prepared, controlled. He must not see her hurt or anger again.

His words turned over and over in her mind. "You will bear a son for me beneath your heart." How could she endure nine long months bearing a child begotten out of revenge and violence? Once the child was born, how would she bear to look at it, knowing how it came to be? Such a child would know only its mother's loathing, never understanding why. The greatest sin imaginable—to raise an innocent child, unloved and unwanted, and see him grow to manhood twisted and full of hate.

She thought fleetingly of the orphans of St. Anne's and how they crowded about her for a look, a word, a touch—hungry for the meagerest bit of affection. How they melted her heart. How reluctant she always was to leave them. Could she feel less for the poor babe that she might carry even now within her? Her eyes filled with liquid prisms. Dear God, how she wished this were over!

She repented heartily of the intrigue and deceit she had employed in seeking her freedom. Vanity, yes, vanity, had kept her from revealing the truth and setting him away from her at the start. That vanity now cost her everything.

She had not heard the key in the lock or the sound of his step, but she sensed that someone was in the room and she jerked her body upright. Dyso stood a pace away, his large, dark eyes unreadable as he stared at her. Brien shrank back into her chair, certain he meant to attack her. Perhaps that, too, was part of Raoul's plan to degrade her—allowing this beast to molest her at will. Horror spread through her and fear filled her face. Hadn't Raoul allowed him to undress her as she lay unconscious? She shuddered to think what liberties . . .

His hands reached toward her, and she gasped as the fleshy paws took one of her slender hands between them. Gently he stroked her hand; she turned her tear-blotched face toward him, disbelieving her sensations. He seemed to stroke her hand in an act of consolation. His eyes looked sad now, and Brien was shocked by the revelation of kindness in this hulking parody of a man. Confused and guilty, she realized that Raoul's violence now caused her to expect the same from others. His spiritual disease had tainted her very soul—the most damning effect of all.

She could not force a smile, as the coldness of fear lingered. Dyso made a sweeping gesture from him to her and back again. His attempt at communication was totally lost on her. Frowning in puzzlement, she shook her head.

"I . . . I don't understand."

He placed her hand back in her lap and left silently, bolting the door after him.

Shaking with relief, she sat puzzling over the encounter. Was it really compassion she had seen in his face or simply a reflection of his own misery?

The hours dragged by and Brien tried to apply some order to her scattered wits. She knew she could not endure another scene like the last night with Raoul. She was no match for his size and power. The inevitable must occur. In this contest, she was vanquished from the start. Perhaps if he seemed to win her, he might relent and allow her out of this prison. Round and round the arguments went in her head, always returning to the same unhappy conclusions; she had never felt so alone, so helpless in her life.

She lit the candles and sat down to wait for her husband. The now familiar scrape of the key in the lock alerted her to his arrival. He entered alone, carrying a bottle of wine and two stemmed goblets. He looked exceptionally striking in a coat of black satin and soft gray breeches. His bearing was supremely confident, irritatingly so; Brien had to restrain the urge to do battle again.

"I trust you fared well today. You are lovely as usual." Lifting the wine he crowed, "To toast our now consummate marriage." But when he poured the wine, she accepted it only hesitantly.

"A night's rest seems to have bettered your disposition, my beauty." He raised his glass. "To our fruitful union." He drank deeply of the amber liquid. Seeing she did not drink, he chided her. "It is inhospitable to refuse a toast to your happiness."

"My happiness was not mentioned."

His eyes flashed and he studied her before answering. "Your happiness—indeed, your life—now depends on me and me alone. You would do well to remember it." His ominous tone penetrated the wall Brien had built to contain her fear.

As she did his bidding, he seemed to relax and smiled.

Brien meant to forestall his assault and walked to the fireplace to place her goblet on the mantle. "That man, Dyso, what do you know of him?"

Raoul eyed her warily, guessing her ploy, but wondering if there were more to it. "Dyso is my servant. His family has served mine for generations. He came with me as a gift from my father." A wry smile twisted his handsome lips. "He is efficient, if slow, and quite discreet." His sarcasm was accented by a gleam in his eyes. "He is a strong fighter and agile, for all his bulk. Does he disturb you?"

"Not especially," she lied convincingly. "How does he communicate?"

"With his hands, they speak for him." Raoul grew impatient with this topic and put down his glass. He went to stand behind her and pulled her back against him, lifting her hair from one shoulder. As he pressed his lips against her cool skin, she gritted her teeth.

Effortlessly, he picked her up and carried her to the bed. She did not open her eyes or move as he removed his clothing and joined her there. She remained impassive as he opened her bodice and touched her. Resistance was futile, but he would have no response at all from her.

Her lack of response deterred him little. When it was over, he stroked her hair as it flowed across the pillow and said dryly, "Your self-control is admirable, madame, but I feel it would be a terrible waste if neither of us enjoyed it." She could hear his sardonic smile in his voice. "Be careful, lest your resistance to mortal man fall."

She turned her face from him. " 'Tis not mortal man I abhor—only you." And she made to get up from the bed.

He caught her wrist in a torturous grasp and held her back. "Perhaps your other lover stimulated you in more exotic fashion." His grip tightened cruelly, causing her to sit back quickly and wince with the pain. His face was livid. "Admittedly, my methods have been simple. Mayhap you require a more creative approach. I can provide that and more."

Her arm throbbed with pain and it flowed into her face. "No . . . no," she pleaded.

Pleased by her reaction, he released her and lay back on the pillows. She sat miserably stroking her arm, trying to hide her loathing. His cruelty and possessiveness were always just below the surface, awaiting the slightest provocation.

So it was in the several nights that followed. She endured his caresses and submitted, but forced herself to seem indifferent to his touch and to his words. It was not an easy task. His much-practiced skills in lovemaking gradually battered her will to remain aloof. She realized with alarm that each night was far more difficult than the last—especially when he stayed the whole night and took her twice before the dawn.

Then she was given respite by the cyclic course of nature. She was strangely relieved and disappointed to know Raoul's efforts to see her with child went unrewarded. The thought pursued her that this imprisonment could not go on forever—despite Raoul's boastful determination.

Seven days passed all too quickly. On the eighth day, Dyso carried in water for her bath and hair. While she stood waiting, looking at the tempting bath, he startled her by abruptly approaching her. To her complete surprise, he went down in front of her on one knee, kneeling. He reached for her hand and placed it on his balding head with a touching symbolism. His eyes were downcast, and Brien was moved wrenchingly by this act of fealty. Then he rose and left without looking at her.

That same night, Raoul was as charming as Brien had ever seen him, and she found herself wondering if life with him would be so unbearable. When he took her, she was shocked, and not a little frightened, by the rampaging desire he unleashed in her. The forced abstinence had not strengthened her against him at all . . . quite the contrary!

As he stroked and caressed her, she felt the now familiar warming in her loins and searched frantically for something to fasten her mind on—to blot out the sensations that threatened to undo her. Raoul nibbled her breasts, and his head moved slowly downward while his hands tantalized her inner thighs.

She lay motionless on her back, her eyes tightly closed. Before her mind's eye appeared two golden, catlike eyes, crinkling in a smile that evolved into a glowing and then a burning desire. Those eyes . . . *his* eyes . . . uncovered a long suppressed memory of sensation and a fresh, raw need stirred within her. She was with that most perfect of strangers again. . . .

Without her bidding, her arms came up around Raoul's shoulders and pulled him up to her. She clasped his head in her hands and responded fiercely, wantonly to his hot, thrusting tongue. They came together hard, writhing and pressing in the white heat that fused their passion into a spiraling updraft, a maelstrom of ecstasy. She felt her body throb with pleasure and she pressed him to her as if they could melt into one being. They rolled and tossed, thus entwined, until she felt at the very edge of being. Then she came—a splintering bursting outward from the center of her. Mindless, all-consuming pleasure.

They lay panting and exhausted, still joined. Shudders of satisfaction coursed through her, the aftershocks of pleasure. When her breathing slowed and she opened her eyes, Raoul's smoky gaze shocked her back to the present. This was not her lover, the tender paradox who had made her a woman. This was her husband, her captor. His face was softened now, she could find no trace of cunning or avarice there. He was supremely handsome, stirring a wild jumble of emotions within her.

Smiling at the awe he read in her face, he opened his arms to her and she crept into them, resting her head on his hard shoulder. She had not even guessed the power of such sublime fulfillment. As she drifted peacefully, his voice called to her from far away.

"My wife, I confess you are more than I imagined. Such passion is not found by many men."

She wondered at his words as she tumbled into sleep, nestled against his unyielding frame.

Awakening to the steady thudding of his heart some time later, Brien lay quietly, fearing to break the peace that had seemed to settle upon them at last. She raised her eyes to him and saw that he watched her, while giving no clue as to his thoughts or state of mind. Brien hoped he could not read the thoughts that plagued her . . . the shame and confusion caused by her body's betrayal of her heart's desire.

Perhaps here was their chance to make peace. Many women shared her misgivings about their own husbands, but without the same attraction. Was it possible

125

that in this white-hot passion they might purge away the denials and bitter memories and start again? She closed her eyes, hoping to collect herself, and in the expectant darkness came a copper-haired phantom with glowing eyes and mesmerizingly gentle touch. She nearly jumped as he reached out to her and silently, desperately, she drove him from her mind, knowing that even as she did, she could never banish him from her heart. Even in Raoul's arms it was Allen Stewart that made her respond.

Quickly, she commanded herself, it must be done quickly before you have time to retreat once more. . . .

"How much longer, Raoul, now that I am your wife in fact?"

He frowned unexpectedly as if an inner door had closed, and his eyes narrowed suspiciously as he turned them on her.

"So this is it. You learn quickly the ways of the whore, my wife." He made the title a term of contempt as he withdrew his arms from her and sat up against the pillows. "But my intentions have not changed. You will stay here until you bear my child."

She pulled herself up onto her knees, her tawny hair flowing over and about her body, shielding it from his piercing eyes. "Tonight . . . has this shown you nothing?" The pleading in her voice drew his eyes from their hot perusal of her form, and she was chilled at the coldness in them.

"You are very much a woman, Brien. But, like most women, you rate your performance on a man's loins too highly. You have shown you can please me with your body, but you still have much to learn. Others of far greater experience have found me impervious to their bitchlike wiles." He smiled cruelly as his hand reached out to possess her rosy-tipped breast harshly.

126

Seeing her wince at this touch and the genuine shock on her face, he laughed bitterly.

"I have not forgotten the sting of your denials. For all your ardor, I do not trust you—any more than you do me. When you bear my child, you cannot deny me again."

Brien's misery poured out through her eyes as Raoul rose from the bed to dress. She had been a fool to think that the hurts and wrongs of the past could be forgotten in one fevered night of passion. The hurt and humiliation came flooding back to her now, mingled with a sense of loss for what she hoped they might have salvaged here. How could she face him another night, knowing they were forever locked in struggle for supremacy?

When he left, Brien felt a consuming urge within her, a desire to call him back and surrender totally—and price to prevent their lives from being poisoned by hatred and suspicion; jaundiced by festering old wounds.

Wrapping her arms tightly about her as if to hold in the hurt, she rocked back and forth in the great, empty bed, whimpering like a child. Hours passed before sleep gave her a merciful, dark peace.

Nine

Somewhere toward dawn, Brien was awakened suddenly—startled to full awareness by something. A sound? For a long moment she sat in the middle of the great bed, clutching the sheet to her, her heart racing. When the silence and darkness continued about her uninterrupted, she sighed deeply, forcing her trembling hands to calm by grasping the coverlet tighter against her. For an instant she had thought it might be Raoul returning, and one long, shuddering breath expressed the relief of her body and soul that this last confrontation would not be resumed.

She clutched her knees to her chest and rested her cheek on them. A feeling of unprecedented doom descended on her as she recalled the evening's encounter. Raoul baffled her; she was unable to make out any of the man inside him. He seemed possessed by raging passions, with not a shred of the balancing emotions of mercy and compassion. Her one chance of appeal, that he might find her body and her willingness pleasing, was now spent for naught. Bitterly she realized that

Raoul had been right once more, and she had been naive to think that one night could turn his wrath and join them at last. No doubt that same feat had been attempted by many women, and by his own word all had failed miserably—earning his contempt in the bargain. There was no joining with this man.

Brien was fully alive now and slipped from the bed to pace the cool stone floor near the door. Her mind whirred with new and awesome conclusions. After what had transpired between them, how could he pretend that they might yet live as man and wife? He would never forget her scheming, and she would never forget the cruelty that had imprisoned and abused her. Would she ever be able to submit to him without thinking of that other . . . the one who had so reluctantly and so sweetly claimed her maidenhood?

Her heart thudded faster as the impact of her cool logic staggered her. Her situation was dire indeed. As she passed the iron-bound door, a faint change—the merest sensation—stopped her, raising the hair on the back of her neck. In the deep gloom of the chamber, she could make out the outline of the door clearly and her eyes searched it for some clue as to the cause of her rising concern. Nerves stretched taut, she approached it and touched its massive, sullen weight. As she breathed once more the identity of the sensation that clamored for recognition burst upon her reeling mind.

"Smoke!" she breathed aloud as the acrid smell seemed to grow stronger, once recognized. "A fire, there must be a fire!"

Instantly, she realized that if there were a fire her chance of escape was nil; she could not be heard if she cried for help. She was sealed in that place which would be her tomb. She would be left here to die!

Desperation moved her hands along the iron fittings of the huge door until they reached the handle, and breathlessly she pulled with all of the strength of her fear. Under the pressure, the door gave and was suddenly swinging open. She stumbled back over her own feet, unable to believe what was happening. She forced the door wider and looked for the first time into the dim, gray light of the hallway outside the chamber. Her eyes widened at the ominous wisps of ghoulish smoke in the torchlight. They confirmed her dreaded conclusion.

Without another thought, she gathered up her gown about her and ran into the hallway, looking frantically up and down for clues to an escape. Seeing the hallway end in one direction she ran quickly the other way. A few doors to what appeared to be storerooms were left ajar and the passageway grew wider as she ran. A long series of steps caused her to pause at the end of the passage, but she shook free of her incapacitating fear and mounted them quickly into a thickening smoke that now stung her eyes and burned her throat. The steps seemed to go on forever as she groped along the wall.

At last on level footing, she felt the heat grow more intense and the smoke and semidarkness made it impossible to tell whether she ran from the fire or toward it. Fear poured new strength into her air-starved muscles and she ran toward an open doorway that appeared before her in the haze. A fit of coughing convulsed her, halting her progress as she clung to the doorway for support, and bringing tears coursing down her cheeks.

She looked about her . . . was this a room or a wide hallway? Stairs! Then she was going down again to where a twisting labyrinth of terror awaited. Opening the door that blocked her path, she found herself in a wide hallway filled with smoke and hideous yellow-orange tongues of fire that licked the walls greedily. She stopped dead. In front of her was a wall on which hung a familiar painting. She rubbed her burning eyes and stared through the thickening smoke until the reality of it energized her. This was Weston Place! She gasped for air with every breath now, her labor rewarded by hot, searing fumes that ripped at her throat and lungs. Wildly, she began to run toward what she knew must be the kitchen.

Reaching the doorway to her goal, she confronted a wall of blinding, crackling flame and dry, scorching heat. For a long moment she stood, paralyzed by the fresh course of fear rampaging through her. The popping of an overheated piece of wood beyond the wall of fire somehow brought her back to her senses and she fled in the opposite direction down the burning hallway toward the dining room.

Weakness in her limbs slowed her, and she panted painfully in the smoke, growing dizzy with the effort. Against her bare feet, the polished wood of the floor was ominously warm. A burning tapestry fell in her path, partially blocking her only avenue of retreat. Beyond fear now, she was seized by a desperate determination and gathered up her gown tightly about her, stumbling against the wall and forcing herself along it and around the burning obstacle.

The carpets and drapes in the dining room were ablaze and the golden light revealed intense fire further on in the salon. Paroxysms of coughing seized her and bent her in two, pulling the last bit of fear-driven strength from her limbs. Exhaustion and suffocation overwhelmed her and she dropped to her knees, feeling as if her very lungs were being ripped from her. She collapsed into a heap on the polished floor that burned so brilliantly only a few yards away.

Unconscious, Brien did not feel the strong arms lift her up and carry her through the inferno into the cold night air. She did not hear the shouts of the stablemaster sending his son for the physician and directing the servants to a place of safety. And mercifully, she did not see the roof collapse a short while later or hear the awesome, thunderous rumble that signaled the end of the glorious old house.

   First there was darkness and a muffled pain, then an unrelenting thirst. Something weighted down her chest; it was so hard to breathe. She struggled to open her eyes but they scratched and kept slamming shut painfully. With supreme effort she forced them open for a few seconds to behold only blurred faces near hers. She could not be sure they were real.

   She heard someone calling her name, but she was powerless to respond; and the word, "Brien," echoed strangely about in her head until it died away. Once more there was blackness.

   When next she awakened, she was fully aware of someone beside her calling her name.

   "Where . . ." she rasped, her throat parched and filled with searing pain. She swallowed only with great difficulty. "Where . . . am . . . I?"

   A woman's voice came through the fog that surrounded her. "You're at Tremaine, my dear. Squire Hennipen and I have charge of you while you recover."

   As she struggled to sit up, gentle but firm hands pushed her back against the soft bed. "No, no, dear. You mustn't; you're far too weak. Just rest now. You're going to be all right."

   The kind hands lifted her head and put a cup of cool water to her dry swollen lips. Then she drifted into unconsciousness again.

   The third day she awoke with a clear head and a howling stomach. She surveyed the darkened room and struggled up, blinking experimentally. Her face felt swollen and sore, and her chest hurt terribly.

The door to the cheerful yellow room opened and a plump, well-dressed lady entered. Brien recognized Mrs. Hennipen, the wife of a squire whose lands bordered Weston Place. Her kind expression and warm eyes comforted Brien immediately.

"Thank God, you're awake at last." She felt Brien's fevered face with her cool hands. "You've given us all quite a scare."

"How long . . . have I been . . . asleep?" Brien's voice rasped and cracked.

"It has been three days since the fire." The good woman's eyes seemed troubled, saddened.

The fire! Brien started up clumsily. "Fire!" she croaked. "Where . . . "

"Now dear," Mrs. Hennipen pushed her back again. "You've had a narrow escape, and you must concentrate on getting well now." She tucked the covers in about her young patient.

"Weston Place burned?" But Brien rasped her own answer. "It burned. I saw the smoke and I ran, but . . ." She stopped, squeezing the older woman's hand. "Raoul . . . where is Raoul?" Suddenly she remembered more than she wanted.

The gentle woman stroked her face consolingly. "He's gone, dear. The fire . . ." She stopped, tears filling her eyes as the impact of her words was clearly shown in Brien's disbelieving gaze.

"Gone?" Brien grasped the woman's arm frantically. "Dead? Is he dead!" She insisted wildly, "You must tell me!"

"Yes."

Stunned, Brien released her arm. "No," she said fervently. "There's been a mistake. . . . He just hasn't been found. Perhaps he's hurt somewhere . . . he can't be dead!"

Mrs. Hennipen hurried to admit the physican who had just arrived. Brien continued to mumble about the fire and Raoul until the sleeping draught took effect. Mrs. Hennipen sat with her until Lord Weston came that evening from burying his son-in-law.

Brien awakened in the night, mumbling and tossing, until at last she sat bolt upright and screamed. It was a ragged, unearthly wail, brought forth from roiling pain and desolation. The whole household became deathly still, shuddering as she continued her raging canticle of despair. Mrs. Hennipen went to her and finally succeeded in calming her by holding her tightly and rocking her as if she were a child. Her weeping was without tears, and her face seemed vacant, bereft of emotion. She slept badly, even with a strong sleeping draught to calm her. Her father stayed by her all that night, troubled and fearful of his daughter's wild grief.

In two day's time, Brien was much herself again, tired and weakened, but able to manage some solid food and a normal mien. She sensed that all visitors to her room watched her carefully for untoward reactions, but was unable to remember the unsettling events of recent nights.

When they were alone, Brien asked Mrs. Hennipen about the events surrounding and following the fire, and was quiet as the good lady haltingly recounted that Raoul's lifeless body had been retrieved just before the collapse of the main roof. He had not been burned, but had died of smoke and heat. Lord Weston himself had identified the body and had seen to the immediate burial.

Brien was relieved to learn that nearly all of the remaining servants had escaped to safety—all but Samuels, the butler. There were conflicting stories as to the fire's origin. Some servants traced it to the grand salon, but the stablemaster identified the kitchen as the starting place. The house was utterly destroyed.

Guarding her words carefully, Brien recounted how she had awakened in the night, just before dawn, to find herself alone. Something had caused her to open her chamber door, and she had smelled the smoke. Gripped by the fresh memory of the thick, terrifying smoke, she recalled that she was confused and lost and finally collapsed; she knew not where. That was all she remembered. Mrs. Hennipen patted her hand, comforting her, and insisted that she rest. The good woman hurried down to the anxious nobleman and related the young widow's story in full.

Lawrence Weston sat with his daughter that afternoon, not sure how to comfort her, or indeed, if she needed comfort from him. She seemed calm enough, despite an occasional tremor in her voice. There was none of the hysteria of the previous nights about her now.

"I worried at first when Raoul's message about your illness came," he said, avoiding her searching look. "But he assured me that it would pass quickly and that your voyage was only postponed for a short while."

Brien was distant. "It was kind of him to inform you. What did he say about Ella?"

"He wrote nothing to me personally. I had luncheon with Magistrate Derringer and he told me the facts of the case. It must have come as quite a shock to you. Still, I suppose she must have stolen quite a bit over the years that we never discovered." He shifted uncomfortably in his chair. "All of these things happening so quickly—it's been quite trying for you."

"Yes," was all Brien could manage. Misery clouded her eyes again. Dear Heaven! Raoul had charged Ella with stealing to see her disposed of quickly. There was every chance that Ella had suffered more than she had during the past month. God only knew where she was and what had befallen her. While she was conveniently ill, no one—not even her father—had come to call on the newlyweds. Raoul's plan had been nearly flawless . . . except at the end. . . .

"Thank you for seeing to the arrangements for Raoul, father." She turned her face away from him. "Now, if you don't mind . . . I'm quite tired."

Weston rose and left, feeling lame and useless. There was much yet unsaid between them. His daughter's marriage had been against her will, even though it seemed the only course of action at the time. Now he felt responsible for her present distress. He had helped to bring this upon her. It bore down upon his spirit heavily.

With another night's rest, Brien felt much stronger and insisted on being allowed to sit by the window for a bit in the warmth of the rare winter sun. The window of her room overlooked the side yard of the neat little manor where servants, bundled against the cold, came and went about their diverse duties.

A figure in the yard below caught her attention. She could not see him clearly, but there was something familiar in his slow, rolling gait and the broad slope of his shoulders. The realization struck her like a blow— Dyso! Whatever could he be doing here? Mrs. Hennipen hadn't mentioned him. Brien watched as he stacked firewood from a cart onto a woodpile near an outbuilding. An involuntary shudder went through her as she recalled her earlier fear of him, a fear she'd never really conquered.

Mrs. Hennipen breezed in just then, carrying a vase of cut holly and fragrant winter greenery.

"Who is that stacking wood in the yard?"

Peering out the window and squinting, the plump little woman smiled. "Oh, my dear, that's your man, the dumb one. He's the one who carried you out of the house the night of the . . . that night." She stopped, seeing Brien pale suddenly. "I'm sorry, I forgot to tell you. He rode with you in the cart and refused to let anyone carry you up here but himself. He seemed quite fierce and determined, so we let him stay until the physician arrived. Sat outside the kitchen door for two days. We feared he'd freeze. My servants offered him food and shelter, but he would take none. When I told him you had awakened and would be all right, he took nourishment and seized an ax. He's cut wood enough for the winter nearly since that time."

Brien's eyes misted unexplainably. "He was my husband's servant. Dyso is his name. Thank you for your kindness to him."

"He's an odd one. But you draw breath this day because of him."

Nearly two weeks after the fire, Brien dressed and came downstairs for dinner, insisting afterward on walking outside in the snowy gardens. The air was heavy and still, saturated with winter moisture, and a serene white blanket covered the ground sharing its peace with her sore heart. Large, wet snowflakes began to fall, landing softly on wisps of her hair and melting on her warm lips. She had been forced to promise that she would not stay long and turned to start back into the house.

As she rounded the step, she was startled by the hulking Dyso looming up before her. She stepped back, staring up into his large dark eyes. He seemed to smile at her and made some hand motions. Brien knew instinctively that he inquired about her.

"Yes, I'm much stronger now. I have you to thank for that." Without quite knowing why, she continued, "There will always be a place for you with me, unless you wish to return to France—to your people." She was surprised as he went down in the snowy carpet on one knee before her.

"You will stay?" she interpreted, eyes wide with wonderment.

He nodded, looking up at her. There seemed a real pleasure in his battered face now. He rose and pressed something into her hand before lumbering away. It was cold, and she looked down to see that she held a large black key. Recognition flowed over her as she watched her rescuer's back sway gently as he returned to his chores.

Ten

Margaret Hennipen altered some of her own ample dresses for the young widow to wear until suitable mourning attire could be arranged. M. Lamont came from London himself to see to the fittings of the gowns her father had ordered for her. When the elegant little Frenchman saw her, he was speechless. Brien had not seen herself in a looking glass since before the wedding, except to brush her hair. She had noted little difference in herself, but knew that she was far from observant of her own appearance.

When monsieur began to fit the gowns he became so excited that he reverted to French totally. Of those present, Brien was the only one who could understand his bold accolades. He refused to leave several of the gowns and insisted on taking them back to London to be reworked. They would not do justice to her, he declared.

Brien could not help but smile, remembering their first meeting—his diplomacy and his unflagging politeness. She had been heavier, dowdy, but he had done his best to make her presentable and had succeeded so well that Raoul pursued her even then.

Raoul. The very thought of him filled her with an almost physical pain. How could he be dead? He had been so strong, so wilful, that he had seemed impervious to mortal banes—even death. And to die so horribly . . .

When the suspicion arose in the back of her mind, she tried to suppress it. Raoul was a passionate man, even a violent one. But he could never have done what she now accused him of in her mind. To plot to lose his bride in a fire—no! She would not believe it. But the specter once raised was not easily dismissed. She would never know if Raoul had died in a tragic accident or in a trap of his own making—a trap meant for her.

Mourning for a husband she tried to deny and disown did not sit well with her. Raoul had been her husband, technically, consummately, but not in the sense of a true marriage. She resolved desperately to suppress the memories of what happened to her as his prisoner. If she must mourn decently, then she would endure it. The world must never know the reality of their relationship—or the true nature of the cunning and mercurial Raoul Trechaud.

As the days were strung together into blissfully restoring weeks, Brien realized that her situation had its more positive aspects. The Hennipens and their household, the physician, and even her father seemed to hold her in almost reverent regard. The few visitors who ventured to Tremaine in the forbidding weather displayed ill-disguised curiosity mingled with an exaggerated deference to her slightest wish. She was a widow now—deprived of a virile young husband on the threshold of their life together. No one would dare intrude upon her grief. After a while, she would be forgotten and free to do as she wished, to make a new life for herself without the interference of anyone, even her father. Bitterly, she realized that she had what she had schemed and sinned to achieve—her freedom.

At night in her borrowed bed, she wrestled to turn her thoughts away from that small stone prison where Raoul had inflicted his desires upon her. This part of the past was far harder to lock away than the rest. Remembering his use of her and the way he made her feel, she colored with shame even in the darkness. Her own body had betrayed her at the last, responding to him as to another lover she had once taken freely. And even then Raoul's treachery was apparent. He had used her body for his pleasuring, enlisting it against her in their battle of wills. She shuddered, thinking of his well-practiced touch and the cruel smile on his sensual lips as he took her. She closed her eyes and steeled herself against the cold lingering fear that threatened to bloom anew at this remembrance.

It would not be hard to remain in mourning and to be content with her widowhood. She would never be able to bear the feel of another man's hands upon her. Ella's coarse observations on the males of the species were again borne out . . . men wanted but one thing from a woman. And no man would ever have that from her again.

Dunstan Hall was breathtaking in verdant spring dress. Brien drank in the sweetness of the air and peace suffused her—her first in several months. Lawrence Weston himself met her at the door and kissed her dutifully on the cheek, casting an appraising eye over her elegantly attired black figure.

"You seem quite recovered. I am glad to have you home where you belong." He did not see Brien bristle at his words and continued. "I have instructed Mrs.

Herriot to take Monique from her household duties and to have her see to your needs until you can find a suitable maid. She has already prepared your rooms."

"That was kind of you, but you needn't have bothered." Brien was annoyed by his authoritative manner and presumptions. "I have already engaged a new maid from London. She will arrive this week." Removing her gloves as they entered the drawing room, she decided this was an appropriate time to set matters straight between them.

"Father, I wish Mrs. Herriot to remain completely in charge of the house. You may count on my help for entertaining, after a decent interval, but the rest of my plans are not certain. I wish to disrupt your routine here as little as possible." She had removed her hat and dark veil, using the action to avoid his astonished gaze.

Weston eyed his daughter warily. "You speak as though you will not be staying long here. What other plans could you possibly have?"

"Perhaps some travel . . . I am not sure." She smoothed her severe coif in the mirror above the fireplace. "I may purchase a house in London and make my residence there."

Puzzled and growing irritated, he rubbed his chin roughly. "What is wrong with Harcourt? You know it is your home as well as mine. You're welcome to live there if you find country life too dull." His sarcasm caused her to turn to him with cheeks flushed and eyes snapping.

"All of my life you and others have dictated to me and decided for me. From now on, I shall do the deciding for myself. My own decisions can hardly end worse than those forced on me in the past." Her reference to her ill-fated marriage struck a chord in Weston.

"If you refer to your marriage, Brien, then you must share the credit for that decision. Your conduct left no other course," he stormed. "I trust you will observe a proper widowhood, out of respect for convention, if not for the man." His tone was one of command, and Brien's indignation was fanned anew.

"My marriage and my widowhood are my business! I shall not embarrass you, if that is what you fear. I must rebuild my life and put the past behind me." She hoped her contempt was as plain on her face as it was in her heart. Then she answered the question he had been loath to ask.

"I have no heir for you from my short marriage and you may not look for one from me—ever—of that you can be sure. I shall never marry again."

Her words struck him with tremendous force, turning his own anger into insight. A shocked silence spread between them, and Brien opened her fan, plying it briskly to avoid looking at him. Weston was now more moved than angry, without knowing just why.

"Was it that bitter for you?"

Brien felt a large lump in her throat and something in her stomach lurched downward. "I'd rather not"—she swallowed hard—"discuss it. It is over now." She looked at her fidgeting hands.

He moved toward her, speechless, and powerless to stop the hurting inside her. What had befallen her at the hands of Raoul Trechaud, he could only guess, but she had revealed much by her determination to avoid the course of motherhood. He put out his hand to touch her, but dropped it to his side.

She had not seen the genuine concern in his face or his gesture. She was tired from the journey; her whole body felt exhausted. This was neither the time nor place to air her plans, but she thought it might be good to give him something to think on.

"I've a mind to study commerce with you. I have a quick mind, and it would be good to put my 'expensive' education to practical use.''

''Given time, I am sure you will find more suitable pastimes. You have only just arrived and are tire—''

''I shall spend my time as it pleases me!'' she declared hotly, whirling on him. ''I am a woman . . . that was nature's cruel jest on us both, but I'll not live a life of misery because of it. I have strength and wit aplenty and a bellyful of womanly duty!''

Weston was aghast . . . thoughtless and speechless.

''I am a thinking and feeling person and I'll not be sold again at any price.'' Her scathing glare withered any reply before it could form fully in his mind.

After a long, painful moment, her rigid stance softened and her chin lowered. She closed her eyes and the sorrow and fatigue showed itself plainly in her young face.

Lord Weston walked away to stare out the window, his hands shoved deep into his coat pockets. He was a study in bewilderment. His daughter hated her very womanhood—and likely him as well.

A hard-won civility returned to her voice.

''I must apologize. I had not meant to say all this to you now. But perhaps it is as well that we set things aright from the start. I am weary, it is true . . . and rootless. I do not know what I want.'' She looked down at the simple band of gold upon her left hand. ''I only know I do not want what I have had.''

Weston went to her and took her hand between his, compassion filling his face and heart for the first time in years. He realized with a pang that he knew little of this woman-child of his. And now he had been given a second chance with her. She needed him.

''Rest now, before dinner this evening. We will talk more about the future later.'' His voice was thick and caused Brien to look at him, searching his face. She nodded and started to leave, but his voice called her

144

back.

"Brien, I only want your happiness."

She studied his face for a long moment without reply, then left him.

Eleven

Monique awakened Brien the next morning at seven o'clock and handed her a folio of documents with instructions from Lord Weston that he would discuss them with her over luncheon. Uttering quite unladylike phrases, Brien bounded out of bed, smiling triumphantly.

Each document she perused raised more questions than it answered. She hurried to her desk and took quill in hand to make notes to herself in the margins of the pages. When lunch was served to them in the south parlor, she felt quite prepared. For every question she raised, Weston thought of three more for her. When the barely tasted luncheon was cleared away, Brien realized dismally that they had only begun for the day. The rest of the afternoon she spent in close attendance on his every word. By dinner, her head ached and she was beyond comprehending more. After dinner, she excused herself and retired early.

Lawrence Weston smiled to himself quietly, confident his wilful daughter had "learned" enough commerce to last her a lifetime. He poured himself a large brandy and set his mind to conjuring up possibilities for her future. There must be something a woman of her intellect and position could do with her life. But for the life of him, he could not think of a single honorable alternative. Marriage seemed the only thing . . . and she had rejected it entirely. He retired early himself, deferring further thought on the matter.

The next morning at nine o'clock, he was surprised to see his daughter, fresh and eager to resume her lessons, across the breakfast table from him. She had listed their holdings in mines, lands, ships, and commodities—and had questions about all of them. He rose to the challenge diligently. By the evening, Brien retired before dinner.

The third morning Weston was decidedly less enthusiastic about his course of action when, promptly at eight o'clock, Brien arrived for breakfast armed with ledgers and more questions. One thing he had already learned about this woman-child of his; she would not be easily dissuaded—and he was increasingly reluctant to try.

Brien proved a bright, capable student and by summer Weston found himself hard-pressed to best her in knowledge of the family's assets and financial matters. He took great pains to see that his daughter was informed of all major business transactions and, finding himself curious about her opinions on matters other than business, sought every occasion to find them out. She possessed a logical, facile mind—was well read and concise in expression. Weston winced openly to think how his daughter's depth and richness would have gone undiscovered by him had it not been for a tragic accident.

He had occasional misgivings about allowing his daughter to escape her "womanly responsibilities," whatever they were. But in truth, there was little for her to do otherwise. Mrs. Herriot ran the house with the precision of a Swiss movement, grateful for Brien's policy of noninterference; and her maid saw to her personal needs and clothing. That left only the ladylike pursuit of needlework, or entertaining, which was limited by her status. Her devotion to the orphanage of St. Anne's and the poor of the district filled some of her time, but he had to admit that her quick mind soon would be restless and resentful with any course other than that which they followed.

More truthfully, he enjoyed watching her as she plied her unique blend of charm and logic in the matters of their business and commerce. By incisive questions and demure flattery, she could best their most experienced captains, clerks, and solicitors—and make them enjoy it at the same time. With no small pride, he realized she matched and bettered his own considerable wit and persuasion.

It was only in the matter of marriage that she ran counter to his will, and he had not given up hope of steering her back toward more sensible attitudes regarding giving him grandchildren. She could not keep her heart hidden forever, and try as he might, it seemed Raoul Trechaud had never captured it.

Unknown to her father, Brien had set their solicitors to work on a private matter, conferring with them about it only in his absence. She hoped to learn the whereabouts of her friend and loyal servant, Ella. They discovered that she had been sentenced without appearing before the magistrate in person and had been packed off to a constabulary to await a prison ship bound for Australia. That was the last anyone had ever heard of her. There were problems with the records; some had been destroyed in a fire. Mr. Poole warned her that the chances of finding her friend were slim at best, but Brien would not abandon the search, even though she privately despaired of finding her. A debt of gratitude kept the search alive when common sense poured disdain on its chances for success.

Brien had decided to observe a full year of mourning, though a shorter period would have been acceptable for so short a marriage. Originally, the idea had been to give her as much time as possible before the gossips and meddlesome peer watchers began their speculation and intrigues. But of late, the drab black of mourning and the solitary life had begun to weigh upon her. She began to consider shortening the year and accepted the invitations of a few local squires' wives for tea.

It was painfully clear to Brien at these small gatherings that she was *the* object of intense curiosity in the county. The ladies asked thinly veiled questions about her marriage and the tragedy that ended it. Brien was unflaggingly polite and demure in answering, catching their sidelong glances and furtive nods. Unwittingly she held Raoul aloft to them as the prince of manly virtues and grace, more by her studied omissions than by her words. These ladies remembered all too well his dark, probing eyes and sensuous mouth, his broad shoulders and charming accent.

But their curiosity did not stop with Brien's marriage. Although they were annoyingly sympathetic, Brien felt they measured her very body with cold scrutiny. And they did. A young and beautiful widow was far more to be feared in the ranks of dowdy matrons than any comely maid. The possibility for temptations, once having tasted the forbidden fruit of marriage, was everpresent. Feeling a responsibility to the sanctity of

149

the homes of the community, they investigated all threats, however remote or highly placed.

Brien perceived this element early on and let it slip that she was not eager to remarry and would remain close by her father—in London. By her sedate actions and elegant manner, Brien added fuel to the already scorching legend springing up about her ill-fated marriage to the French nobleman. She, quite unknowingly, was becoming the romanticized heroine of an idealized love match. Everyone had quite forgotten the quiet, dowdy maid who had sat demurely by her father in the family's box at mass and was never seen otherwise. By all accounts she was a beautiful woman, tragically bereft of a handsome, virile young husband. She bore her overwhelming grief bravely. Her very desire for a year of mourning seemed all the gossips needed to verify the tale.

In September they moved to Harcourt House in London, eight long months of mourning past. Their move came just as the plans were being drawn for the fall social season. She was relieved to be able to decline the generous offers of hospitality for a while longer, dreading the speculative glances and innuendos about her future she feared she must face. But then, London was a huge city, full of important people; she would draw little attention here.

As the sultry summer gave way to the enlivening crispness of autumn, the city came back to life. Brien watched the people, horses, and carriages in the streets and markets and found herself thinking more and more of music and laughter and social events. Paradoxically, she longed to escape the very solitude she had once clung to so ferociously in her mind. Perhaps she could end the mourning business a bit early. . . .

It was M. Lamont who provided the spur that set her into action. He insisted she visit his shop for the final

150

fittings of her new wardrobe, there to view his wonderful creations in the wall of mirrors created for such elegant occasions. Brien agreed reluctantly, more in deference to the man's feelings than from any desire to be fashionable.

Her personal maid for the past several months had been Jeannie Trowbridge, a sweet-faced young girl of seventeen, daughter of a tailor who had died leaving a houseful of children and a mountain of debts. As the oldest girl, Jeannie was let out to work in the milliner shop of a family friend as soon as she turned fifteen. She had proven adept at the trade and found herself called on for advice in coiffures. The milliner, having fallen on hard times himself, had had to let her go, just as Brien began her search for a new maid. From the start they had gotten on well and a true feeling of friendship had developed between the lady and her adoring attendant.

The little maid had taken great pains with her hair the morning of the fitting and had commented that she had never seen her mistress looking lovelier. Brien had put it down to the girl's gratitude and awe of her mistress' station.

But when Jeannie finished lacing her into the first of M. Lamont's creations, Brien was dumfounded. The deep décolletage of the ice green and white silk barely contained her. The gossamer sleeves were snug on her arms their entire length, revealing while not binding them. The bodice was tight and the full skirt flowed over a small hoop and into a slight bustle in the back. She paced the fitting room in front of the massive mirrors, fascinated and scandalized by what she saw. As she whirled, the skirt wrapped intriguingly about her legs.

"Is this all there is?" she gasped to the beaming M. Lamont.

"You blend in a symphony of movement, the dress and you."

She tugged upward on the neckline. "But after every dance I shall have to be restuffed into it. And no panniers? How would I dare wear it in public? She grinned mischievously. "Wouldn't father die to see me in this?"

"The gown was not designed with fathers in mind," M. Lamont sniffed defensively, injured that his creation might be seen only as a tool of rebellion.

Brien repented, seeing his wounded pride. "It's clear you mean to show me to the world—all of me!" With a long sweeping glance at the mirror over her shoulder, she crowed, "It's marvelous!"

By the end of the fittings she was exhausted. Left alone in the carpeted and mirrored room for a few moments, she walked closer to the mirrored glass, looking closely at her visage. The young woman she saw, had seen all afternoon, jolted her. Gracefully tapering legs led upward to provocatively rounded hips and a narrow waist. Her breasts bulged defiantly above the corset, creamy mounds that met in a warm line. Her skin was smooth and silky across her bare chest, and her cheeks were now pleasantly flushed with pink. She stretched her arms above her head, turning slowly to inspect all sides of this new creature. She arched and moved, fascinated by the grace and flow of this new body. Then she moved close and made faces at herself: coy, pouting, tempting, haughty. She leaned even closer and fluttered her long, dark lashes slightly. A small smile bared her white teeth behind full, peach-hued lips.

Like a thunderbolt, the mystery of Raoul's persistence was swept away. He had wanted her because she was desirable! His remarks about her beauty were not malicious taunts; he meant them! He really did desire her! And M. Lamont, in his own way, paid her the highest compliment he could, he created for her clothes that would enhance her unique beauty daringly. His designs trod the narrow lines of propriety with aplomb. She felt a delicious pleasure course through her body and whirled about, reveling in the wonderfully free sensations.

In another moment she was taken aback, unnerved by this new view of herself. Why had she been so unwilling to see the changes that had taken place in her when most girls scrutinized their looking glasses daily for improvements? Was it only that she had considered herself dowdy and plain next to her stunning older sister? What else had she been unwilling to face in herself?

Jeannie returned just then to help her dress, but on the way home, those thoughts recurred and persisted well into the evening. She had much to think on. . . .

Twelve

A slow trickle of invitations appeared at Harcourt and on the first of December, Brien beleaguered her father with questions about which to accept. Under his careful tutelage, she at last selected a dinner party given by Lord Randolph Hazelett for her debut into London society. Mercifully, she was only partly aware of the true meaning of her acceptance of this coveted invitation. Lord Randolph was a former Chancellor of the Exchequer, wealthy, and politically powerful. To be given an invitation to one of their sparkling affairs was to receive the invitation of all London.

She was noticeably nervous as Jeannie did her hair and helped her into a gown of mist blue velvet, festooned with a tableau of embroidery that began at the waist and curled lovingly upward over her breasts and downward over her panniered hips. Ecru lace and puffed sleeves adorned the tight bodice that showed her magnificent breasts to stunning advantage. Jeannie had taken special pains with her hair, creating a flow of ringlets and ribbons in a swirl over her head and down her back. A simple ribbon adorned her perfect throat and cream white pearls dropped casually from her ears.

Lawrence Weston's jaw dropped as his daughter floated down the staircase toward him. Appreciation and fatherly protectiveness struggled silently within him. She did not appear to be a woman who recoiled from the ideas of love and marriage. In fact, her daring gown and flawless beauty would fairly invite the attentions of any male—even the most disinterested or infirm.

As they entered the elegant drawing room of Lord Hazelett's opulent home, they were both keenly aware that every eye was on Brien. Curiosity about her had spread to London with the story of her ill-fated bridegroom, romanticized and enhanced by her seclusion and the rumors of her great beauty.

Fairly, it could be said that no one in the room was disappointed by a comparison with her fame. She was indescribably beautiful and possessed a natural grace that put people at ease immediately. And with her abundant charms, there was an earthy, physical aura about her. Hers was no pale ethereal beauty. She compelled a physical reaction in the men she was near without coquetry or guile. Her gentle, throaty laughter and sparkling blue eyes had captivated them all by the time dinner was served.

Weston watched as his daughter made conquests of the men and confidantes of the ladies. He was bemused by the transformation and by her obvious pleasure at being the center of attention. She was no tepid, sighing bride; she was fully, irresistibly woman—perhaps her only legacy from the virile, passionate Raoul Trechaud. Weston smiled quietly to himself. A marriage that did that for a woman could never be called a total failure.

The evening was made all the more memorable for

Brien when she retired to one of the ladies' rooms on the upper floor where dozens of ladies repaired curls and noses and availed themselves of the chamber pots hidden behind screens. Brien was straightening her skirts behind one of those screens when she overheard the excited chatter of some young girls.

". . . never seen anything so elegant. That dress must have cost a fortune!"

"I've heard her husband was deliciously dark and handsome—French, too. They say he was a rake before he met her . . . gave it up for her."

A third chimed in, "It's not hard to believe. Not a man here has seen aught but her tonight. It's not fair—all that money and beauty too."

The first voice resumed. "They say when she heard he was dead, she howled and wailed like an animal for days—nearly mad with grief."

The second girl had clear reverence in her voice. "I wish I could have a love like that."

"I heard she vowed she'd have no other man," the third giggled. "He must have spoiled her for all others."

"I wish someone would spoil me like that," the second girl dreamed again.

Their voices faded as they exited and Brien crept out from behind the screen, amused and intrigued by the overheard gossip. She wondered how many other whispered conversations about her were even now taking place. The absolute irony of it; the most painful thing in her life was now the cause of her overwhelming social success. She smiled weakly and shook her head. They believed her marriage to be a blazing love match.

But there was a brighter, more practical side to all this. If this gossip was any indication, then she might yet be spared the matchmaking that plagued young widows. Let them talk, she determined. She'd not spoil their fun. Neither would she pretend to that which was not. People seemed to believe what they wanted without her help thus far; they could carry on without her aid.

When the evening was ended and they were again in the coach, Brien sighed with satisfaction, leaning back luxuriantly into the red velvet upholstery. "I had no idea it would be so lovely."

"You enjoyed the dinner then?" her father teased.

"Of course," she declared, turning to him in surprise, but smiling at the teasing in his eyes. "Do you think they liked me?"

"Liked you?" He pondered it. "I am sure you enchanted every person there. Tomorrow we shall have to hire a secretary to manage the flood of invitations we shall receive."

Brien laughed contentedly, that low, throaty noise that Weston had just seen entrap members of parliament and peers of the realm.

News of the beautiful young widow spread like flames from sparks in dry grass. Discreet questions about her to old family friends elicited the tantalizing story of her handsome, lusty, young husband and of their great love, smitten in early flower by his tragic death. When it was learned that she had accepted the New Year's Ball at the Duke of Hargrave's, half of London made discreet inquiries about attending.

Even as Brien launched her new life, Lord Weston received mixed tidings concerning his business dealings in the colonies. The local economy, inflated with nearly worthless paper script, was sagging badly. Defying the terms of the 1783 treaty, several colonial assemblies had declared debts owed to British merchants null and void. Merchants who had speculated heavily by allowing liberal credit in the postwar buying spree were now driven to the edge of bankruptcy by the failure to collect on the notes they held.

The new "congress" in the colonies was quite slow to take action of any kind and in any case was still occupied with matters of a "constitution" and consolidating its own power. Still outstanding war debts pressed the beleaguered new government hard. Complicating matters, communication with the colonies was slow and awkward; documents were often subject to close scrutiny by several pairs of eyes before they reached their destination. Most dealings with British merchants were conducted in an atmosphere of suspicion, despite mutual needs for continued commerce.

Thus far, Silas Hastings, Weston's agent in the colonies, had forestalled legal difficulties, but reported increased problems with collecting outstanding debts and insuring the safety of the stores and warehouse. Weston decided to withhold this disturbing news from Brien until after the holidays, for he was more eager to see her reenter society than undertake his business woes.

With the arrival of the holidays, Brien decided that their lives needed a change of pace. It would be the first time in many years that the Westons entertained, and Brien threw herself into the festivities with all her heart.

Holly, candles, ribbon and pine boughs decorated Harcourt and new friends were frequent guests, drinking toasts and eating heartily to celebrate the season. Harvest had been good and trade was brisk. A feeling of calm, as before a storm, settled over the political scene, and there was less talk of the difficulties with France and the economy.

Brien was well contented with her life now and found much to be grateful for: new friends, the excitement and fascination of commerce, and her deepening relationship with her father. These past months they had drawn very close, and she recognized now that she cared deeply for this man who indulged her so shamelessly and tutored her so expertly. At last, she had everything a woman could desire.

Thirteen

The ball that welcomed the new year would be a fitting climax to so perfect a holiday season. It would be large, noisy and flowing with champagne. Her pulse beat faster when she thought of the stir she would create in the gown M. Lamont had created for the occasion. Addlepated as a girl before her first dance, she slept badly the night before and could eat nothing that day.

As Jeannie did her hair she fidgeted nervously and was relieved to step at last into the sea green velvet that made her eyes into tidal pools. The front of the gown was low cut and made as a false lacing that would not meet. A panel of flesh-colored satin behind saved her modesty. At a distance it did not appear to be there, and the effect was most delightfully shocking. An emerald of no small value graced her ivory throat, and ribbons and emerald pins graced her almost classical coiffure. Her dark green velvet cloak was lined with the finest beaver to block out the winter chill.

The palace of the Duke was at the edge of a fashionable part of London—nearly an hour away. They talked easily during the ride, Weston avoiding the topic that weighed more and more on his mind—their finances in the colonies.

The massive house was ablaze with lights and the yard was nearly full of carriages and milling servants seeing to the horses. Once inside the great carved doors, they were both awed by the grandeur of the massive marble columns and double staircase. The grand hall itself was as big as a ballroom, but the ball consumed the entire first floor of the house. Double doors separating the rooms had been thrown wide to permit the free flow of guests from one room to another.

When they were announced, the reaction to her presence was immediate—heads turning and necks craning. The ladies whispered animatedly behind fans and the men stared, open-mouthed, in appreciation.

As they glided forth to greet friends, Weston muttered for her ears only, "It's you and that damned dress!"

Brien only smiled, rather like the cat that had gotten the cream.

After a pleasant chat with the Duke and Duchess of Scarborough, the ever persistent Charles Medford was there to claim her for a dance. Much of the attention in the room was focused on them as they danced, so striking a combination they made.

Flushed and exhilarated at the end of the dance, Brien used her fan briskly and parried the advances of Edward MacLeod, member of parliament and most eligible bachelor. Before Charles could object, Brien was once again swept onto the floor, this time by MacLeod. And the next dance went to Reydon Hardwick, heir to the fabulous fortune and title.

With Reydon, Brien left the ballroom to seek refreshment, but they were stopped along the way by acquaintances and friends well into their spirits. When

Reydon finally retrieved glasses of champagne Brien was parched with thirst and downed it as quickly as propriety permitted. Then Reydon refilled it for her willingly. The heat, excitement, dancing and champagne conspired to lift her head into a dizzy spiral.

Then it happened. As she laughed with Reydon and some of his old school chums, her eyes flitted across the crowd into the next room. And something—someone— there caught her eye. He was tall and broad shouldered and as he moved, turning slowly in her direction, something familiar in his strong jaw and fine, straight nose struck a chord of remembrance in her. She laughed absently, no longer hearing what the others said. Her attention was on the hauntingly familiar features outlined in the dimmer candlelight of the next room. The man talked casually with his companions, making gestures with his broad shoulders that caused Brien's breath to stop in her throat and quickened her heart.

Then, as if responding to her intensifying gaze, he looked toward her and her knees grew weak as their eyes met. She was transfixed for what seemed an eternity. Her companions were now aware of her withdrawal from their merriment and expressed concern as they watched her face drain to ghostly white.

Those blazing golden eyes seemed to scorch her across the distance, and she slowly sank beneath the impact of recognition. Reydon Hardwick caught her as she fell and, in the commotion that followed, carried her upstairs at the insistence of their hostess, the duchess.

A swooning lady was not uncommon at these affairs, but the Lady Brien was not just any lady. Much concern and some speculation swept through the crowded rooms at the sight of the dashing Reydon Hardwick carrying the delectably unconscious Lady Brien up the staircase, albeit he was closely followed by her father and Dr. Jared Samuels.

When she was safely deposited on a great canopied bed in the duchess's suite, Dr. Samuels ordered everyone out of the room except Lord Weston, and then proceeded to examine her. He quickly concluded that her condition was not serious and rolled her over onto her side to loosen the lacings of her dress. Chances were, with room to breathe once more, she would revive quickly.

Weston stayed only long enough to see Brien stir and exited to confront a desperate Charles Medford and an anxious Reydon Hardwick. He assured them that her condition was not serious; the heat and excitement had simply taken their toll. He personally ushered them back to the other guests, covering his own concern convincingly. Brien was not of dainty constitution. To his knowledge she had never swooned or fainted in her life.

Downstairs in the grand salon the cause of Brien's discomfort leaned his shoulder casually against a marble mantelpiece and sipped from a crystal goblet. His attention was fixed on a young man beside him, absorbing every word the young nobleman spoke.

". . . Breathtaking, that's the word for her. There's not a man here, including the Duke who wouldn't give a year of his life for one night with her."

"You say she's a widow?" the tall man asked, a smile spreading slowly across his rakish features.

"Indeed." Edward MacLeod drew deeply from his glass and continued, "Not a merry one, however. She was only a bride of a month or so before her husband died. He must have had quite a month; she's not overeager to replace him." They laughed.

"Perhaps she developed a distaste for that side of wedded life." The tall man raised one eyebrow, grinning.

"Cold, you mean?" Edward squinted and pursed his lips in thought. Then he shook his head. "No, I hardly think so. Just one dance with her in your arms and you'd see; she's so warm she fairly melts. Her husband was the son of a French nobleman—had a reputation for getting whatever, or whomever, he wanted. To hear the ladies tell it, he was quite handsome. Rumor says it was a great love. Whatever it was, she hasn't got it out of her system yet. Here, Aaron, you're not thinking of having a go at her are you?" Edward first seemed incredulous, then amused.

"You never know," tall Aaron answered dryly.

"Well, now," Edward watched him with unconcealed fascination, "that would be a match I'd pay to see—the Lady Brien and the rake of Wiltshire. I'll even introduce you, by God!"

"Tempting offer, Edward, but I won't be staying long enough to give the project my full attention. I have a new ship due to be christened at Bristol. I must return this week." Aaron straightened his muscular frame and gestured toward the food tables with his empty glass.

"Aaron," Edward said taking him by the arm and steering him toward the food, "I'll never understand your desire to risk your neck at sea when you could be sitting home inheriting a fine title and dallying with countless maids."

Aaron laughed wryly. "As for women, I have all I can handle in port. The other I care little about."

Edward turned to him, a slice of ham dangling from his fork. "And your father, have you seen him of late?"

"No." Aaron's flat reply closed the matter, and he moved down the table filling his plate.

Edward looked up, coming to stand beside Aaron. "What's this?" He looked through the doorway and beyond into the great hall. Brien, wrapped in her emerald cloak, was being carried down the stairs by her father. They moved through the parting guests on a course for the front doors.

"Well, it's more serious than I thought. Sorry, old man." He thumped Aaron's arm. "You won't meet the beauty of London this night." And he turned back to fill his glass.

Aaron stood looking after them in the doorway. His sun-bronzed face was tense with concern that was soon covered with a rakish grin as he joined MacLeod for a toast.

The crisp night air revived Brien greatly as they entered the carriage. Her father tucked a fur lap robe over her as they began to move.

"Are you warm enough?"

"Yes, thank you," Brien breathed, staring straight ahead.

Weston took her hand between his. "What happened, Brien? Is something wrong? It's not at all like you to—"

"No," she interrupted, seeing his concern. "I was just foolish . . . no food all day, dancing, and too much champagne." She forced a weak smile. "You'll see. I'll be fine in the morning." She drew her cold hand from his and shoved it into her muff.

They rode the rest of the hour home in silence.

She went straight to her rooms when they arrived at Harcourt. And after she was in bed, Jeannie returned bearing a warm brandy and orders from Lord Weston that Brien must drain the cup.

The warmth of the liquid flowed through her pleasantly. When Jeannie left and the room was dark, Brien gave way to the panic that had felled her earlier.

He was there at the ball! Those eyes—those golden

eyes! And there was even the scar! And he saw her too; she was sure of it. What would a common seaman be doing at the duke's ball?

Her common sense rebelled. He could not have been the same man! That man only resembled Allen Stewart. Her fatigue and the champagne conspired to make her see Allen's face, Allen's eyes, instead of those of the stranger. There was a resemblance—only a resemblance. She said it over and over to herself. "Merely a resemblance."

But as the night dragged on her mind would not dismiss entirely the possibility. *If* he were the same man, how could he be there, dressed as a nobleman? Did he know who she was and where she was? What if he contacted her? She groaned to think how famous she had become. If it were Allen Stewart he would have no difficulty in finding her. Only time would tell if the man she had seen truly was Allen Stewart—and if so, what price he would exact for his silence.

She finally drifted into a fitful sleep full of dreams. She relived each embrace, each kiss of their night together, and awakened twice in the night with an ache in her loins that she recognized all too clearly. Moaning softly she realized that the passion she had thought locked away forever was free once more. Not even the taunts and assaults Raoul had made her bear had dimmed it. For a year she had safely, sanely denied her soul's and body's needs and now they raged vengefully in her, twice potent because of their long deprivation. During her year of mourning she had convinced herself that all men were the same underneath and that a taste of their kind, their lust and brutality, was all she needed to cure her of all desire for men forever. She had even come to credit Raoul with removing that fleshly thorn from her side. With near horror she realized that it had only been dormant . . . and she was again susceptible to its temptation.

She wanted to cry but no tears came. Her mind returned inescapably to Allen Stewart; his strong arms and rolling speech defied his background, and his copper hair and golden eyes drew her soul to him and seemed to offer his in return. He was magnificent. Her breasts tingled at the memory of his warmth pressed against them. She was nearly panting now, just thinking of him and how he made her feel.

The swine! She turned violently on her stomach and pulled a pillow over her head as if to block out the sight of those burning, catlike eyes. They tortured her and in the end robbed her of the peace she thought she'd earned these past months. She hated them most of all for that.

Three days later, Brien felt quite herself again and was convinced that the champagne and her own imaginings were to blame for the whole silly episode. At night in her bed, her dreams told otherwise. A pair of golden eyes teased her, then were slowly transformed into the eyes of a horrifyingly beautiful leopard that sinuously stalked her. She held her breath as it came closer and closer, but it never attacked her. Then she was transported to that room, that bed in Harrall's Road; and Allen Stewart was there, loving her, completing her. She awakened with a satisfied, languorous feeling that infuriated her moments later.

God and the devil! What must she do to rid herself of this obsession? There was no one to ask, no one to send on a search for the truth. If it had been him, surely he would have contacted her—or would soon. Again she was reduced to waiting. Another two weeks passed before she ventured out into public again. After a pleasant dinner party, she was convinced she had nothing to fear.

* * *

Weston noted his daughter's periods of distraction, but, seeing her overall good spirits, assumed that the vagaries of the female condition afflicted her. The word from the colonies was worse each fortnight, and he resolved to hold it from her no longer. She took the news hard, outraged by the injustice.

"The cheek of those scoundrels!" she prated. "Biting the hand that feeds them!"

"I was afraid you'd take this hard," Weston chided her. "But you must realize that this is not a vengeful act. Their economy suffers terribly, and they could not raise the funds if they tried. Daughter, there are times when the wisest counsel is that which urges nothing. This is the game." He opened his hands and searched them. "We must be patient. Our claims will wait."

"Patience is a dear commodity," she growled lifting the ledger sheets, red with default. "Is there no way we can force them? Attach their property?"

His eyebrows shot up. "This does sting. Who would you take to the courts? Shopkeepers? Farmers? What would you do with wooden cabins and steel plows? What magistrate would counter a colonial assembly, even for a handsome fee?"

Brien's face colored sharply. "I never meant—"

"No, no," he silenced her. "I dislike bribes myself. But there can be no argument that they grease the wheels of commerce admirably at times. If I were a colonial, nothing would enrage me more than the offer of money from a wealthy, 'opportunistic' English lord. No, we will wait."

Brien was totally dispirited. She had been so enthusiastic about their prospects in the colonies. Somewhere she had developed an affection for the recalcitrant provinces and had needled her father into risking more investment than he thought prudent. Now she smarted keenly at the impending failure of the venture. The thought of sitting powerless, while a vulgar mob destroyed her pet project, went against her grain.

Weston sensed her dissatisfaction with his advice and determined to forestall any planning of her own. "Things are moving fast now. In a month or two this may well have passed." He hoped he sounded more confident than he felt.

Life at Harcourt was now a double vigil; hoping for word from America and fearing word from Allen Stewart. Through it all she curtailed her social events little. She reasoned that the more she acted as though things were normal, the more normal they would become. And no word came from either source.

All was well until mid-February. Lord Weston was brought home from his offices quite fevered and chilling. He had a racking cough and was unable to keep food down. Brien watched him weaken day by day as the fever persisted and slowly worsened. Dyso helped her restrain him when the delirium caused him to thrash and rave. The long nights beside his bed blurred into a flow of fatigue and pain for her. She feared she would lose him just when she had found him.

Dr. Samuels came daily and stayed several evenings, for Brien would not leave her father's bedside unless the doctor were present. The good physician saw the toll it took on Brien to care for her father day and night. He declared she would be the fever's next victim if she did not rest and care for her own health. And he stayed several nights in her stead at the nobleman's bedside.

Somewhere in the night, during the third week of his illness, the fever broke. A relieved Dr. Samuels ordered continued cold compresses and assured Brien that her father would recover. For the first time in years, Brien prayed—a prayer of intense gratitude.

That week, the beginning of March, saw a turn in her father's health and news arrived from America.

Silas Hastings sent word that he had collected a percentage of the debts, but better yet, had seized a goodly stock of merchandise for nonpayment. He awaited instructions on how to proceed.

Brien's heart warmed toward the tall, gaunt man whose eyesight caused him to wear a continual frown. Silas had gone to the colonies as a young man and had prospered as Weston's agent, marrying the daughter of a wealthy merchant. Through the years, his first allegience was to Weston Trading and his second to his adopted country. Brien knew the conflicts and war of revolution must have oppressed him terribly.

She held the news from her father until he was well enough to sit up and was at last eating well once more. She would deal with this herself.

She developed a plan to take her out of London for a while and solve their colonial crisis as well. She would personally travel to America and use every weapon in her considerable arsenal of charms to find a cash buyer and liquidate their American holdings. They should at least recoup their costs in the venture.

Lord Weston was mending quickly for a man of his age. When Brien presented the news and her plan to him, he was at first adamantly opposed to it. But Brien sent inquiries through her solicitors and began making arrangements for the voyage in spite of his disapproval.

And as usual, Weston finally had to agree on the soundness of her plan and on her ability to carry it out. Her own excitement was the factor that tipped the scale in her favor. With no small guilt, he realized the strain of his illness had drained her as well. She had always dreamed of travel; the trip would refresh her and serve their business needs as well.

Lord Weston arranged for her to be given his power

of attorney and sent a letter to Silas Hastings requesting suitable accommodations be arranged. Brien accepted the invitation of Lord and Lady Devon of Bristol, old family friends, to be a guest at their home while awaiting her ship. And lastly, they arranged passage on one of Weston's own ships for early April, sailing from Bristol.

As their departure neared, preparations increased at a frenzied pace—with fittings and shopping, packing and farewells. Brien reveled in it.

When at last Brien set forth in the coach for Bristol she was more tired than excited. Lord Weston came downstairs to see her off, and she extracted a promise from him that he would rest and take care of himself in her absence. They agreed that she should send progress reports on the regular packets that traveled back and forth.

Jeannie and Dyso accompanied her on the trip. Weston had asked dryly if she would feel safe, traveling with such a small retinue. He knew of Dyso's devotion to his daughter and was confident of the man's ability to insure her safety. To be sure, it seemed an odd entourage as they stopped at a country inn for the night: the lady, her maid, and their hulking protector.

Fourteen

On the third of April, the coach drew up in front of the impressive Devon House in Bristol. Lady Angela Devon greeted them warmly and led Brien to her room, chatting enthusiastically. Brien's first reaction was to wonder if she would be able to bear a full week of the woman's chatter, but she soon regretted this harsh judgment. Lady Angela was true to her name, with warm, dark eyes and such a sweet spirit that Brien found herself feeling quite at home in a short time. The woman was lonely and delighted to have a lady of such quality as a house guest.

After a warm bath and light tea, Brien was introduced to the Devon children, three of them. They were delightful creatures, full of energy and curiosity. They nearly overwhelmed her with questions and hugs and raw enthusiasm. They were censured and ushered out good-naturedly, but Angela's exasperation could not belie the pride in her eyes. Her children were wonderful. Brien felt an unwelcome stab of envy at the dear woman's domestic bliss.

At dinner that first evening, Lord Emery Devon brought disturbing news. The ship *Libertine* on which Brien was to sail had not yet left the Azores. When she had put into harbor there to make repairs on damage caused in a storm, a fever had felled the captain and crew. Most would live, but it would be months before the *Libertine* would see home port again.

Brien's spirits sagged terribly under the news. Her host promised to personally seek passage for her on another vessel. His fleshy pink face and sparkling blue eyes made Brien believe he would not only try, but would succeed.

Time lay heavy on her hands the next two days, so Lady Angela arranged a tea one afternoon in her honor. Brien was surprised to find the Bristol ladies well acquainted with her tragic story. They chatted pleasantly, between sidelong glances, and Brien was glad to see them go.

Angela giggled as she took Brien's hand and drew her upstairs to dress for dinner. "You charmed them all! They'll talk about nothing else for months."

Brien solemnly hoped they would all lose their voices.

That very evening, Lord Emery announced that he had, by the barest of chances, secured passage for Brien's party on a new ship making her maiden voyage to America at week's end. He was quite thrilled.

"She's a new design—lighter keel and draft and fuller of sail. They say she'll cut a full week or more off the best time. Better yet, she's built for passengers as well—with cabins! Dash it all, Lady Brien, you have phenomenal luck!" He was justifiably proud of his good news.

"Perhaps I only borrow your good luck, Lord Emery. 'Twas you who found this remedy for my distress. I am most grateful.'' Brien's gratitude was indeed heartfelt, for her longing to continue her journey grew with each passing minute.

Lord Emery patted his pretty wife's hand affectionately. ''My dear, I took the liberty of inviting the ship's captain and owner to dinner tomorrow evening —along with the Clermonts and Wiltons.'' Seeing her frown in dismay he continued, ''You'll forgive my impertinence when I tell you that the ship's master is none other than Aaron Durham.'' His eyes twinkled with satisfaction at the shock on the dear woman's face.

''Oh, Emery,'' she breathed. ''Aaron Durham? Are you sure?''

''I spoke with him myself this afternoon. He was reluctant to take on passengers, this being her maiden voyage. But I explained Lady Brien's predicament and he said he could hardly refuse a lady in need.'' Emery's chuckle caused Brien to shift uncomfortably.

''Such gallantry,'' Angela remarked dryly. She turned to Brien. ''Forgive us, dear Brien. But it seems you will be sailing with the redoubtable Aaron Durham. He's . . . well, he's . . .'' She couldn't find words and looked to Emery to finish for her.

''. . . interesting, fiercely independent . . . and infamous with the ladies.'' He appraised Brien over his wineglass.

''And tomorrow he'll dine with us,'' Angela continued. ''I don't know whether to feel honored or scandalized.'' She touched Emery's arm. ''Do you think it wise—Brien's sailing with him?''

''My dear,'' Emery indulged her, ''the man honors his word greatly; none deny that. And Lady Brien has brought her own ample escort. She will be as safe on board ship as she is in our own house.'' He laughed. ''And I'm sure you will warn her sufficiently before she sails.''

Brien's gratitude waned measurably during the discussion. She had no desire to spend the lengthy voyage fighting off the advances of an amorous captain. But she needed swift passage to America and must take it as she could find it. It might be a month before she could find another suitable vessel. The Devons had been so kind; she would not let them think her ungrateful.

"I am sure the arrangements will be fine, Angela. I am not, after all, a vulnerable maid." She laughed with them. "And Dyso is a formidable deterrent."

The next day Angela was aflutter making arrangements for the dinner. Brien was relieved to be spared her constant chatter and excused herself after lunch to rest before dressing for dinner.

Before she could begin her nap, Jeannie was determined to tell her of the gossip she had heard in the servants' hall.

"Gwen, the house parlor maid says he's devilish handsome." Seeing Brien could not be interested in her tidbit, she returned to that task at hand. "Which gown will you wear this eve?"

"I care not. You choose one." Brien held her head with one hand and closed her eyes. All of this bother just for passage to America. She suddenly doubted whether the whole trip could be paid for from the meager profits she hoped to obtain for Weston Trading. Perhaps she would have been wiser to have stayed home and written off the loss, the Weston fortune would be affected little one way or another.

The whole trip seemed pointless, somehow . . . just like everything else she did these days. She had been sure this trip would break the routine of her London life—be a true adventure. And now she grew dissatisfied with the "adventure" almost before it had begun. Just what did she want?

Curling up on the bed and drawing a light coverlet over her she tried to rest. Her mind kept turning the last question over and over. She had no answer . . . only a list of things she wished to avoid. And she told herself it did not matter. She would find her way; she would recognize what she wanted when she saw it. And she drifted into a fitful sleep.

When Jeannie returned that evening with her dress, Brien was aghast. The sweet-faced girl's eyes twinkled. "You said for me to pick one."

Brien looked despairingly at the wine-coloured silk that even without her in it provoked curiosity. "Yes, but . . . I have no desire to be consumed as the main course this evening. I shall have to wear something else . . . something more modest." She frowned half-heartedly at the girl's downcast expression.

"But, Lady Brien, there's no time to press another. One carriage has already arrived." The plea in Jeannie's face was real.

Brien thought a moment, then removed her dressing gown. "Very well, help me into this man trap."

Jeannie grinned slyly as she removed the gown from its hanger. "I wish I could see their faces."

"Bristol society is not as tolerant of the whims of fashion as is London. And the colonies will be even less so. Aboard ship I shall have to restrict my wardrobe to the simple muslin traveling dresses. After tonight, see that this one is packed on the bottom of the trunk. I'll use it only if heavy artillery is needed to persuade a buyer." She was not truly angry. "Perhaps it will be interesting to see what a taste of naughty Paris does to Bristol."

Jeannie stepped back to admire her. "You're a vision! You could call warmth from a dead man's

176

bones.''

Brien laughed impishly. "I shall remember that if I meet any bones this evening.''

Brien entered the drawing room after all the other guests had arrived—or most of them. Every eye turned to her, widening with astonishment and pleasure. The gown was starkly, sparingly cut, and its main effect was to make the viewer want to see more of the lady. Their attention sent delicious waves of heat through her.

Lord Emery, ever gallant, was moved to eloquence in his introduction of Brien to the Jeremy Wiltons and the Richard Clermonts.

Brien smiled demurely. "Lord Emery is too kind. He and dear Angela have saved me from a most desperate fate and have taken me into their hearts." She reached up for Angela's hand and squeezed it. "I shall never be able to repay their kindness."

Lady Evelyn Clermont eyed her appraisingly. "I'm sure they do it out of love for you and your father. How is Lawrence these days?''

Brien sat down opposite her on a settee, ignoring the saccharine tone of her comment. "He is just now recovering from a serious illness. We had planned to make this trip together, but he insisted that I come ahead—without him. This is my first trip since . . . my bereavement." She lowered her eyes and paused. "I have always had such curiosity about the colonies.''

"I can hardly believe they will afford the civilized society you are accustomed to in England, Lady Brien." Lord Jeremy Wilton tilted his nose with disdain. "Personally, I find them crude and noisy.''

"You have been there then?" Brien was annoyed by his superior attitude, but interested in anything she might learn about her destination.

"During the conflict, I was there briefly," he sniffed.

"Jeremy was in His Majesty's Foreign Office and traveled there once." Lady Charlotte Wilton was clearly impressed by her husband's worldliness.

"How interesting. What colonies did you visit, Lord Jeremy?"

Before he could answer the butler appeared at the door to announce, "Captain Aaron Durham." A tall broad-shouldered man swung into the room, pausing at the door to casually survey the gathering.

Brien gasped involuntarily. Her eyes were riveted on the impeccable black broadcloth and gray-blue vest that covered his broad chest, fearing to behold his face. Forgetting herself momentarily, she jumped up from the settee, causing the men who were seated to do the same—consternation registering on their faces.

Brien watched horrified as the man she knew as Allen Stewart greeted these people as old acquaintances. She fought a rising tide of panic as he drew inexorably nearer. The room grew hot and charged around her.

At last he stood in front of her. taking her extended hand in his and barely missing it with his lips. She desperately hoped that her face did not reveal her distress, because every eye in the room was fixed upon them. He straightened and his golden eyes caressed her as his sensuous mouth curled in a languorous smile of recognition.

"Delighted to meet you, Lady Brien." His low tones sent a shock through her, and she withdrew her hand hastily.

She nodded slightly, hoping to retrieve some semblance of composure. "And you, Mister Durham, or was that Captain Durham?" She hoped that her tone would pass for cool civility.

"Whatever you prefer, madame." The warmth of his gaze gave the reply a seductive quality.

She moved away to stand by Angela's chair, painfully aware of the others' attention. "Well, Captain, I understand we are most fortunate to be sailing with you, especially on such short notice." As she spoke she avoided his direct gaze, her heart pounding in her ears with panic. Would he betray her?

How could she explain her acquaintance with this rake if he insisted she must know him?

"Lord Emery related your predicament, madame, and I am ever quite accommodating to ladies in need."

His double entendre caused Angela to laugh aloud—briefly. A sour look from Lady Evelyn silenced her.

Brien at last looked him squarely in the face and went weak at the impact of his handsome angular features and tanned skin. His face was just as she remembered—even that scar—and his golden eyes seemed to penetrate her very soul. She felt as vulnerable as if she stood naked before him. Her fan fluttered upward to her bare chest, shielding it from his rapt attention.

After an uncomfortable silence, Lord Emery relieved the situation. "This ship of yours, Aaron, tell us about her. I hear she's quite remarkable." Brien was surprised to hear Emery call the sea captain by his given name—according him the deference due an equal.

"Yes, quite remarkable," Aaron mused, still gazing unabashedly at Brien.

She could hardly miss the double meaning of his words and was sure the others had caught them as well. He seemed to be enjoying this torture—and she was instantly angry at the presumption.

Aaron tore his eyes from her and continued, "She has three main masts and a shallow draft—by British standards. Her hull is V-shaped. I designed her with cabins for passengers as well as cargo holds."

"You think there will be increased trade with the

colonials, then?'' Lord Jeremy raised one eyebrow skeptically.

"Undoubtedly." Aaron leaned one shoulder against the mantelpiece as he appraised the affected young man before him. "With common language, heritage, and goals—the two nations stand to gain far more by cooperation than by conflict."

"Ah-hem." Wilton cleared his throat and assumed an indignant posture. "Nations? I should hardly call that motley consortium of farmers and shopkeepers a nation."

Brien was relieved that this thinly disguised challenge relieved her of Aaron's scrutiny. He seemed in no hurry to embarrass her by recalling their former acquaintance.

Aaron smiled sardonically. "They have promise. They fight and sail exceedingly well for shopkeepers and ignorant farmers. I was on one of the ships taken down by their John Paul Jones and his elusive bark." But then his hand went up in a signal for truce, just as Wilton drew breath for a hot reply. "The battles have been amply fought; let us not presume to rejoin the conflict here. There are more entertaining pastimes available." He flashed a disarming smile at Angela, who flushed coquettishly.

"Quite right, Aaron," Emery agreed and the subject was closed.

"About your ship, Captain Durham," Lady Evelyn broke in. "I understand she was christened of late. What name does she carry?"

Aaron smiled and glanced briefly at Brien before answering. "*Lady's Secret.*"

Brien had to stop herself forcibly from gasping aloud. She bent her head and plied her fan vigorously to hide her reaction. No one but Aaron seemed to notice.

"My goodness," Angela teased, "what a provocative name. However did you come to choose it?''

Brien's own voice startled her. "Have you many ladies' secrets in your keeping, Captain?" What possessed her to challenge him so openly? But she must know his intentions now or suffer unbearably the entire evening.

"Every true lady has some secrets, madame." His smile had faded, but amusement lingered in his eyes.

"How cryptic you are, Mr. Durham," Charlotte Wilton observed. Turning to Angela she crooned, "Angela, we must investigate this further. Mr. Durham seems to invite speculation about his own secrets."

Everyone was quite amused, except Brien.

At dinner, Angela had seated Brien opposite Aaron Durham. Brien was sure Angela intended no malice, but found it hard to forgive her meddlesome intrigue. Under Aaron's thorough inspection, she had little appetite. Each witty remark was less bearable than the last. She longed to be anyplace but this, seated across from the one living man who knew her intimately, passionately. Her irritation increased as he continued to make comments that had obvious double meanings—much to everyone else's delight.

This must be further punishment, she decided, exacting atonement for her sin, to be so effectively tortured without being able to utter a single retort. Yet his remarks troubled her less than the tactile, ravaging looks he pressed upon her. He well enjoyed her only partly concealed discomfort.

Brien could see Angela's delighted, knowing look and realized that she revealed too much by her silence and avoidance of Aaron's gaze. She could not shrink from this challenge and live with herself. She drew a deep breath, straining the wine-colored silk nearly to the breaking point.

She sat straighter, meeting Aaron's eyes boldly. She knew now he was not ready to betray her. She refused to consider why, but drew confidence from the conclusion.

"How came you by that intriguing scar, Captain? Forgive my impertinence, but it has puzzled me for some time." She smiled sweetly as she read the surprise in his face. She too could play at double meanings.

His hand went to his left cheek, and he shrugged nonchalantly. "A memento of the colonial conflict, madame."

She smiled more sweetly as she drove in the thrust. "And in whose favor did you win it?"

Lady Evelyn's gasp was quite audible. Every eye turned to them expectantly.

A spark in his eyes told her that she touched a sensitive nerve. But he charmingly replied, "In the right cause, madame."

Touché. She nodded, a knowing smile playing at the corners of her luscious mouth. Then quietly she began an equally frank appraisal of him.

His copper hair was given to a slight wave. She allowed her gaze to roam his torso and come to rest on his hand as he reached for his goblet; it was his left hand. She wondered about his conquests since that night in Harrall's Road. A pang of envy struck her, and she was suddenly appalled at the licentiousness of her thoughts. The man called up her baser side!

Her attention was drawn back to the conversation by Angela's voice.

". . . is a widow." They were discussing her!

"My condolences, madame." Aaron nodded politely, his face unreadable.

She flushed, wondering what he must think of her marriage.

"That was some time ago, Captain. I am content to

live with my father now and to care for him.''

Sir Richard, well into the wine, retorted, ''More's the pity!'' and received an ill-concealed jab from his wife.

''Lady Brien is hardly a recluse, Sir Richard. She is quite busy in London,'' Angela crowed. ''Busy evading suitors.'' She giggled, and Brien realized that the wine had taken its toll on her as well.

Aaron Durham turned to her. ''Lady Brien, have you any children?''

Brien weighed his question and found it lacking in duplicity. ''No . . . I . . . we had none.'' She lowered her eyes.

''Now there's the pity,'' Emery Devon declared. ''From such a match the children would have been the envy of Venus herself!''

Angela shushed him and turned to Brien with a knowing look. ''She has plenty of time yet for children.''

''Ah, but has she the inclination?'' Sir Richard blurted out. And the ensuing laughter brought heat to Brien's face as she tried to show a humor she little felt. She could not look at Aaron Durham, but was sure he must have enjoyed it.

''Such speculation is pointless, Sir Richard.'' Brien tilted one brow provocatively. ''Fate is fickle and enjoys a jest on us all now and then. I refrain from testing her favor whenever possible.''

''A philosopher as well,'' Aaron studied her with fascination. ''Lady, there is more to you than meets the eyes.''

''Be careful, Aaron,'' Emery warned, ''or you may find out how much!''

The others laughed raucously, delighted by this tête-à-tête at her expense. The beauty and the beast paired and evenly matched.

Brien was vastly relieved when Aaron Durham declared he must leave early owing to pressing business the next morning. Her hand was the only one he failed to take before departing. She thought it crudely obvious of him to omit so civil a gesture.

He had no sooner departed than Lady Charlotte scoffed, "Mr. Durham certainly lived up to his reputation this evening." She turned to Brien. "I do hope he didn't embarrass you too much, Lady Brien. He is such a rake."

"Charlotte!" Jeremy Wilton scolded. "Lady Brien need not hear such gossip."

"If indeed, it is gossip," Angela put in. "Forewarned is forearmed, they say."

After the guests had departed, Brien made her way upstairs, numb with fatigue and the constant tension of the evening. Aaron Durham had behaved within the bounds of convention, barely. But each suggestive remark and lascivious glance had promised that he would be harder to rebuff without an audience.

She wondered briefly if she could arrange to be called back to London on some pretext or other to avoid sailing with him. Her scheming and planning had nearly ruined her life before; now she was loathe to deal falsely on any level.

Aside from the dishonesty of such a ruse, he knew who she was and where she was now. She would have to deal with him sooner or later; it may as well be now.

She opened the door to her room as she rubbed the back of her aching neck. Jeannie had been ordered not to wait up for her. Now she faced the arduous task of her evening toilette alone. Eyes downcast, she plopped tiredly down on the stool before the vanity and flung her shoes off one at a time.

She sighed, closing her eyes briefly.

"Would you like me to rub it for you?" A rich, deep voice, behind, shot through her.

She whirled about, eyes wide with astonishment. Aaron Durham lay sprawled across her bed on his side, staring lewdly at her.

"You!" she exclaimed. "What are you doing here?"

He shook his head dourly. "Is that the way you greet an old . . . friend?"

She was livid with indignation. "Out of here or—"

"You'll scream?" he finished for her and went on quite impudently. "I have something to say to you. I'll not leave without saying it. But if you feel the need to explain me to your friends, I'd love to watch." He sat up.

"What do you want?" Brien felt alarm growing inside her. She rose, facing him, mentally measuring the distance to the door.

A slow, sensual smile spread across his features. "I looked for you—after that night." He threw something up into the air and it jingled slightly as he caught it once more. "To return this to you." He tossed the leather pouch to her and she caught it by instinct.

She looked at it wonderingly, angry now and moved all at once. She remembered well. When she looked up, he was standing by the bed, the smile gone from his rugged burnished features.

'I'll take no pay for what I did that night." His voice had a bitter edge, but his eyes glinted strangely.

She looked down at the pouch, aware it was harder to see for some reason. A tightness filled her throat and she was unable to speak.

"I found you at last in London. But, hearing you were a widow, decided to let the past lie."

It had been him!

185

"But fate has seen fit to throw us together again—and I meant to see this restored to you by my own hand."

Brien looked at him, her eyes clearing as she fought to control the warmth that rose inside her. Why did he do this to her?

She looked so miserable and so sweet standing there, he fairly ached to hold her. She seemed so much like the girl he had loved in Harrall's Road. For all her money and position, she still needed what he longed to give her.

She took a deep, shuddering breath and was once again in control.

"It was not meant as payment," she breathed. And again she gritted her teeth to stem the tide of emotion breaking upon her resolve. "It seemed . . . all I could do for you. I thought you a penniless seaman." She looked at him accusingly. "The deceit was not all mine, Aaron Durham."

His laugh had a strange timbre to it that made it all the harder to stay angry with him.

"Lady, I yielded up every secret I had to you that night." His eyes began to glow as they wandered over her—aided by remembrance. To her dismay he sat down once more on the bed.

"Except your real name—and other such insignificant details." She now wondered what else he had in mind this night. In her anger, she had stepped closer to him and just realized how dangerous that was. His presence seemed to envelop her, overwhelming her senses, causing her heart to pound faster. What was happening to her legs? They felt like water!

In the lengthening silence she stared at him and he at her. Their eyes met and Brien felt he pulled at her very soul with those large golden eyes. They were unlike any color she could name, just as the jumble of emotion he

186

stirred in her defied terms.

Shocked and suddenly frightened at the longing spreading through her, she declared, "What's past is past. We shall forget it."

"How, sweet lady, do you propose I forget the sight of you almost naked, bathed in the gold of candlelight. How do I erase the memory of you warm against my skin and soft—"

"Stop it!" she ordered, wishing she could stop herself from feeling warmer and more willing by the minute. "If you have any thought of tumbling into my bed because of our mutual history, you can forget it now!"

"Madame," he said patting the bed beside him, smirking, "I am already there."

Rage filled her. "Get out of here before I call for help." Her eyes flashed and her palm itched to smack his smug face. But that would only bring her closer to his heat.

Thoughtfully, he stood and walked to the window. "There will be plenty of time at sea." He raked her body visually. "Several long weeks," he continued, making an arch overhead with one hand, "with a canopy of stars overhead. And the gentle sway of the ship under your"—his hand moved to suggest her lower contours—"bed." His wolfish grin brought sparks to her eyes.

He sat on the window ledge and swung his legs over effortlessly. Turning back a moment he went on. "And since you value your honor so highly, I suggest you leave that dress at home. It has a stunning effect, as you must know. Wear it on board, and I'll not be able to answer for the conduct of my crew." With a throaty chuckle, he was gone.

Brien stood fighting for control and lost. Seizing pillows from the bed she flung them against the far wall fiercely.

"Bastard!" she spat, "You conceited jackanape! How dare you!"

But in truth, she knew not whether she raged because she despised or wanted him.

At morning tea the next morning, Brien found Angela flushed with the success of her dinner party and eager to press her about the unforgettable Captain Durham.

"Brien, dear, you must tell me what you thought of him—or I shall die of the curiosity." Angela's childlike delight made Brien forgive her unabashed prying.

Brien measured her words carefully. "He is a man of glib tongue and roguish eye. I'm not at all surprised at his reputation with women." She sipped her tea watching the other woman drink in her words. "But I was surprised to hear Emery extend such familiarity to a sea captain. He allowed the man to call him by his given name."

Angela nearly burst with wanting to tell her about him. "Oh, he's not an ordinary sea captain," she offered. "He's the eldest son of the Count of Wiltshire, Count Thomas Durham. He is in every way my Emery's equal." She realized her pun and giggled, "You see, he has even me doing it."

Brien was clearly puzzled. "If he is heir to an estate and title, why does he captain a vessel?" The man was a perplexion.

"He seems to do so because he loves it! He has always strained at his father's strict rule—or so I hear. When he was eighteen, he ran off to join the navy—without benefit of commission or anything. It was some time before Lord Durham found him—and so finally let him be. In the colonial war, he distinguished himself and was given a field commission. He served on the fin-

188

est of his majesty's ships.'' Angela leaned forward and lowered her voice. ''He seemed determined to flaunt his father's rule—and to debauch half the maids of Cardiff and Bristol. He doesn't force himself; women just seem to find him irresistible.'' She eyed Brien coyly.

''But I'm sure that is obvious to you by now. He simply couldn't keep his eyes from you last night. And you were so charming.'' She laughed quietly. ''I hope you'll forgive me for putting you in such a delicate position.''

Brien studied her and found her utterly irresistible. ''I forgive you.'' She patted Angela's hand.

''There's more—most of it rumor,'' she said eagerly.

''Forewarned is forearmed,'' Brien quoted her. ''Lay on.''

Angela related how, after six years at sea, he returned home suddenly, a year ago. He seemed to have struck a truce with his father, but eventually had to move and make his home in Bristol. His reputation as a sailing master continued to grow, and to it was added that of having an excellent business sense. The men found his word scrupulously true and the ladies found his charm devastating. He dallied, though not seriously, with several young girls of quality—all properly arranged by his father.

Delicious rumors spread that he had been earlier disappointed in love and would never propose to any woman. His father was furious and their relationship grew more strained with the passing months. One story said he had denounced the title he would one day inherit—telling his father to pass it to his younger brother. But, of course, it was only rumor.

Brien was thunderstruck. To think that by mere chance such a man had come to her bed in Harrall's

189

Road—totally unknown to her. His speech, his looks, his gentleness—it all fit now. She found herself warming dangerously toward Aaron Durham. She could little afford such sentiments and sternly chastised herself for them.

In her room later, she tried to convince herself that she only felt kinship with his rebellious spirit. They shared a common hatred for the social system that twisted peoples' lives so cruelly in the service of privilege and the social order. In their own way, each had waged and won a battle against it.

Then she thought of his look, his touch—and had to admit there was more. Refusing to consider any but the basest of motivations, she concluded that her reaction to him was that of a healthy young woman for a man—any woman and any man. He was a rutting animal in his prime, one who used women as playthings, discarding them when they became tiresome. Well she remembered the pain of being used by one just such as he. She would not be owned or used by any man—ever again—not even by one as fascinating and enigmatic as Aaron Durham.

Fifteen

The morning they sailed, Brien dressed carefully in a dark blue muslin dress with a high, square neck and large cuffs at the wrists; it was made less severe by pale blue embroidery upon the bodice. She wanted to appear as sensible as possible in her approach to this voyage—to seem a seasoned traveler. As their carriage neared the docks, she felt her stomach lurch and seem to flip. She was frightened and admitted it freely to herself. Jeannie, riding quietly beside her, was pale and wide-eyed as she clasped her hands tightly on her lap. Glimpsing the tightness in the maid's face, Brien realized that she was responsible for far more than herself on this trip. And once the voyage was over her work would just begin.

Lord Emery supervised the loading of her trunks aboard ship and then escorted her on board. The vessel was a blur of activity: a maze of crates, barrels, ropes, and men in motion. They were met by a pleasant young man in a crisp dark blue uniform and shining black officers' boots. The first mate, Robert Hicks, was of average height and stocky build, with unruly brown hair and inquisitive blue eyes. He bowed politely and took Brien's proffered hand with open reverence.

"We are honored to have you as our first passenger, madame. When the Captain related to me that we would have a passenger this maiden voyage, he neglected to mention that she would be the very embodiment of loveliness." His gallant manner and smooth speech belied his boyish countenance. Brien liked him in spite of her suspicions as to his motives.

"Thank you, sir, but I am sure your captain has far more important things to occupy him. Might we walk about on the deck until it is time for us to be underway?" Her smile was dazzling, bringing the desired result, a smile in return and an affirmative answer.

"Yes, ma'am. Perhaps on the quarterdeck the view would be better. . . ." He grinned impishly as a burly seaman swung perilously close with a hoisted barrel. Hicks doffed his hat and swept it toward the steps to the upper deck.

Emery Devon strolled with her and Jeannie until the boatswain called the all ashore, but Brien's thoughts were not on his words. She glanced furtively about for a glimpse of the ship's master, and, disappointingly, found him absent.

While Brien strolled the deck, the very eyes she missed took in her every move from a vantage point atop a stack of crates on the dock. The odd, golden orbs narrowed in thought as they flitted over her womanly form, so annoyingly hidden beneath the dark blue wool of her traveling garb.

One corner of his generous lips lifted in a wry smile. What did it matter how she dressed? The image of her ripeness spilling lusciously over a wine-colored silk was burned into his brain. For over a year she had tortured his dreams and thoughts—nameless, tender, sad,— until she obsessed him as a wraithlike presence. He realized with a frown that he had allowed her to twine about his imagination, making her into what he would: a princess, a goddess, a sprite. Seeing her in London had been a shock—one to send a man's senses reeling— seeing the focus of all his dreams in fleshly form arrayed. And still more of a shock it was to find that she had a name and that other men now openly gazed on and hungered for the beauty he had come to think of as his own—or as the invention of his troubled mind.

And yet—he rubbed his chin—this was not the gentle maid of his remembrance. When he faced her in the Devons' drawing room he had nearly gasped at the physical impact of her upon his starved senses. The rise and fall of her creamy breasts seemed to beckon him, to invite him to pour his heat, his breath into her, with their maddening rhythm. It had taken every ounce of self-control he possessed to keep from setting hands to her there and then, in spite of their noble audience.

But the pure pain of being near her was shockingly pleasurable—setting fire to his loins and racing his heart. Every turn of her mouth, every sweep of her lashes, every bend of her waist, or wave of her hand enticed him to the rapture he had known with her lush and fragrant body. His wraithlike lady, the sweet tormentor of his dreams, was at once swept from his memory, replaced demandingly by this tantalizing woman of earth and warmth.

Even now his chest rose and fell with telltale quickness and there was a perceptible tightening in his loins. He had thought of little else but her since Emery Devon casually noted a friend's need for swift conveyance to America. They had been in a goodly tavern near the docks, where Emery and two associates lifted a mug. One of Emery's companions spotted Aaron and called him over to join them. He had first resisted the idea of any passengers on this maiden voyage, but then Emery had let fall her name, "Lady Brien." And Aaron had found himself strangling on that bitter brew.

Again the corner of his mouth drew up as he thought of her, standing there so near him in her dimly lit chamber. Two years of waiting behind, he had vowed to shame her for callously paying him off for the "job" he had done, as though he were some dockside whore. Confusion clamored in his chest at the thought. He had long since separated the gentle maid who yielded him all from the calculating bitch who cast a casual coin in his bed. They could not have been the same woman. His confusion mounted furiously as he recalled her reaction to finding him in her room. She was truly both women; disturbingly vulnerable as her eyes glistened and she swayed under the memory he forced upon her, and yet haughty, demanding, as she imperiously ordered him from her room, and panted fire at him when he dallied.

Aaron was roused from his musings by a cry from the deck to prepare to get underway, and he began a slow descent from his perch. Blood rose under his bronze-hard cheekbones as he realized the unprecedented concentration he bent on this woman. It unsettled him to admit his confusion and, yes, the eagerness he felt for her. His face hardened at the thought; then a knowing look crept over his taut features. This was no great mystery. She'd stirred his blood mightily. She was—to use Edward McLeod's word—breathtaking. Another slight bend of his lusty thoughts and he could see her, feel her beneath him, sighing, responding, pleading. As he lingered over the image of her passion, another rose to darken his face abruptly: her—with eyes flashing, posture regal, and ripe lips haughty with disdain.

His tongue toyed at the corner of his dry lips. God,

how he wanted her! She was more than he could have imagined and she would challenge his every move, his every word. But ultimately he would be victor in this earthy game in which fate had always given him favor. He would see her humbled and in his bed ere they set eyes on Boston harbor—of that he was sure. Then a flicker in the back of his mind caused him to falter in mid-stride before he could dismiss it and continue. What more would he get in the bargain?

Sooner than Brien wished, Robert Hicks came to show the ladies to their cabins. Carrying a small case, she lifted her hooped skirts slightly as she followed the mate to the narrow door of the hatchway. Her thoughts were still annoyingly on the whereabouts of the ship's roguish captain, and she chided herself severely for it. She barely noticed the approach of the narrow hatchway and bent her head slightly as she had seen Mr. Hicks do when she entered. Steep stairs descended into a lantern-lit passageway that broadened little at the base of the stairs. Belatedly, Brien found herself trapped halfway down the narrow steps by the hoops under her skirts. She was appalled by her predicament and by the fact that Mr. Hicks, already at the landing below, must be enjoying quite a view. She pushed hard on the sides of her skirts and managed to free them temporarily by forcing them to billow strangely in front and back. But the bottom hoop dragged ominously onward, rising slightly toward her waist with each downward motion. She paused twice, kicking the bottom hoop farther down the passage while thinking murderous thoughts.

Having fought for every inch of progress, she breathed a sigh of relief as she reached the landing at the bottom and turned to proceed down the few remaining steps. She could see that the passage widened considerably once down and was thankful it would soon be over. But a tug from behind grabbed her backward unexpectedly. Her hoop had caught on the round wooden knob at the top of the railing on the landing. Her face was now scarlet as she struggled to maintain a semblance of dignity while trying to extricate her obstinate apparel. From the corner of her eye, she could see Mr. Hicks in the passageway ahead, trying hard to suppress his mirth. Jeannie stood helplessly by, horror-struck.

Brien paused, closing her eyes to regain her composure, and she released her hoops so they billowed out to the sides once more, though tilted askew by the offending post. She pulled up sharply on the skirts to free the snared hoop, but it held. Then she stepped backward and gave a mighty tug. Up it came, filling the passageway behind her and binding her legs in front. She tried to turn and force it down, but was soon trapped in the twisting fabric.

Mortified now, her rear completely exposed and her movement hindered by the twisting fabric about her, she heard an amused chuckle from the top of the stairs and she recognized it immediately. The chuckle grew to rich, deep laughter as Aaron Durham descended the steps behind her.

He pushed down the recalcitrant hoops and laughed even harder at her scarlet face.

"You find strange amusement in others' misfortunes, sir!" she retorted hotly. And she turned, struggling down the passageway toward the guffaws of the red-faced first mate.

Fighting her way through the narrow door to her cabin, she found it large enough to permit her skirts to billow out once more. She was burning with shame when the once-more sober Hicks entered. His eyes were moist and his mouth twitched uncontrollably.

"This will be your cabin, madame. I hope you will

be comfortable here." He turned to Jeannie. "If you will follow me, miss, your cabin is at the end of the passage."

As they turned, Brien asked angrily. "Why is her cabin not by mine?"

"The Captain assigns cabins, madame. He is in charge." And they were gone.

She moaned in frustration. Just then Aaron Durham, clad in a partly open white shirt, dark breeches and tall black boots, bent his tall frame through the doorway.

"Lady, if you continue to wear those hoops aboard this vessel, my men will be highly amused. And you will be most uncomfortable. I suggest you pack them away until we dock in Boston."

His presence filled the room and pressed her almost physically. She drew her shoulders up sharply.

"Thank you, Captain," she said hatefully. "It is clear I have already begun to learn of life at sea. And while you are here—why cannot my maid have the next cabin, instead of one at the far end of the passage?"

"Because, madame, the next cabin is the captain's." His mouth curled in amusement and he ducked quickly through the door.

The captain's? He had arranged to have her isolated from her servants in a cabin beside his! Outrage at the presumption filled her. How dare he?

She slammed the door shut and jerked up her skirts. Seconds later the hooped petticoat lay in rings about her feet. She gave it a kick of contempt.

"Oh, to be a man! I'd wipe that smirk from his face!"

The gentle rolling of the ship as they got under way calmed Brien's ruffled nerves. But as they met the churning waters of the Atlantic, the swaying increased and Brien learned the true meaning of the term *mal de mer*. She was grateful for the small windows that admitted fresh air and light. She lay down briefly on the narrow bed and found it only made her feel worse. It occurred to her that she might be sick the entire voyage!

When Mr. Hicks knocked discreetly on the door to call her to dinner in the common room, she could hardly reach the door to answer him. She declined as gracefully as she could. Her pale, drawn face and tight lips drew a sympathetic look from him as she closed the door.

After a terrible night of heaving and roiling and sleeplessness, Brien was thoroughly miserable and regretted every greedy, prideful impulse she had ever harbored—especially those responsible for this trip. Hicks brought the devastating news that Jeannie was ill as well. His promise to look after her was small comfort for Brien. She thanked him for his gentlemanly courtesy and concern.

The second day and night were even worse. But on the third day she awakened, hungry and much steadier on her feet.

Dressing herself clumsily, she cursed vilely the rapacious demands of fashion that prevented a lady from dressing herself. Again, men had the better of things. They only required a shirt and breeches and boots.

She appeared at the commons room looking pale and forlorn. Mr. Hicks helped her to a seat at the long oak table and pronounced her a fit sailor. Brien consumed the simple fare with relish and felt all the more steady for it.

At Hicks' suggestion, she proceeded to Jeannie's cabin to check on her. She had not eaten for three days and was quite ill. Brien was struck by the acrid smell of sickness when she entered the cabin. One small window admitted little air or light. Brien poured water and washed the girl's wan face, then helped her change into a clean night dress. Jeannie smiled weakly as Brien sat down on the narrow bunk to brush her snarled hair.

"Jeannie, what ever will I do without you? This very moment I must look a fright. Well, don't you mind; just concentrate on getting well. I'm sure this will pass soon. We'll take care of you."

As Brien left the cabin she prayed a fervent thanks that they were not both so ill. She went directly to the commons room where Hicks was drinking a cup of coffee.

"I need a flagon of strong rum, Mr. Hicks . . . and quickly."

He was startled. "Madame . . . I . . . I really don't know. . . ." he faltered.

"Really, Mr. Hicks," she was suddenly up to her ears in propriety. "The rum is for Miss Trowbridge. She is quite ill and in need of a strong sedative to help her rest. Now will you get it for me, or shall I find the Captain?" Her face was set with determination, and in the end Hicks nodded and soon produced a large pewter tankard of potent uncut rum.

Brien picked up her skirts and moved carefully down the passage. As she opened Jeannie's door, the ship pitched suddenly and she spilled some of it on her dress. Undaunted, she poured some for the girl and helped her to drink it.

This had been Ella's remedy for an upset stomach. A liberal dose of whiskey or strong brandy—and sweet sleep. Perhaps it would work on Jeannie.

She stayed in Jeannie's cabin a few minutes until the girl was asleep, then crept quietly down the hallway to her own room. Just as her hand touched the handle, the door to the next cabin swung open and Aaron Durham stepped into the passage.

"Lady," he addressed her and she looked up. "Tsk, tsk. At this hour in the morning—to smell as though you've bathed in rum." He grinned wickedly.

She closed her eyes and let out an exasperated sigh. In a moment, she was safely inside her cabin, leaning against the closed door. He meant to torture her with verbal thumbscrews.

That afternoon she ventured up on deck for the first time since sailing. She had put her hair up simply, in a braided loop at the back of her head. Her skirts were now too long without the hoops and she had pinned them up under the sides into false panniers. They showed a bit of lace on her petticoats, but even that was far preferable to tripping over them constantly. With a woolen shawl about her shoulders, she could have passed for a country girl on market day.

The bright sunlight caused her to squint at first, but she soon smiled at the friendly warmth on her face. She surprised herself at how steadily she could walk on the deck.

Above her, by the wheel, Aaron Durham watched her drink in the crisp April air and stroke the rail gingerly with her slender hands. Her hair was a tawny gold in the sunlight, and in her plain, blue dress and knitted shawl, she seemed fresh and genuine. He felt a stab of regret at his earlier taunt. She had fared better than most women did at sea—especially pampered ones. She had even found a way to stylishly surmount the problem of those bulky skirts. He smiled lazily.

"Hicks," he called. "Take over." And in a minute he was down the steps to the main deck and making straight for her.

She watched the sea, fascinated by the rising and falling of the waves and the endless stretch of sky above.

He stood beside her a full moment before she realized he was there.

"How do you like my ocean?" He leaned one elbow on the rail beside her.

"It is magnificent." She ignored his cheeky attitude.

He was silent for a moment, watching first her and then the sea. "I'm glad to see you're feeling better, Lady."

His continued use of that particular name grated on her. "My name is Lady Brien Trechaud, Captain. I would prefer you address me that way."

"Gladly." He nodded. "What takes you to Boston in such a hurry?"

She thought a moment, then turned to study him, leaning against the rail. She would tell him the truth. He could hardly think less of her than he must already.

"I have urgent business there. A venture I backed has proven unprofitable. I shall find a cash buyer and divest Weston Trading of its American holdings." She searched his face for a trace of mockery or a hint of disbelief. She found only appraisal there, and she was glad he did not dismiss her story out of hand. This seemed to fit the slowly assembling puzzle of Aaron Durham—fairness.

But the puzzle of Brien Trechaud was suddenly jumbled by this new piece of her. He had thought her spoiled and vainly feminine. Just now she seemed anything but.

"You take part in your father's business, then?"

"After Raoul—Since the death of my husband, my father has taught me commerce and finance." She smiled timidly, wondering if she had revealed too much to a man who might one day use it against her. "My father indulges me shamelessly. I am all the family he has left, and I am his only vice."

Suddenly she wanted to tell him everything. "We

201

. . . were not close for several years. But in these last two we have come to—" She stopped, aware that he stared at her strangely.

"I am sorry," she flushed, embarrassed and angry with herself for being so vulnerable to those probing golden eyes. "I'm sure you have far more important things to do." She moved abruptly away from the rail.

Frowning at her sudden withdrawal, he stared after her. Turning back to the bridge he realized that his legs felt weak. The sadness in her eyes had reached into him, stirring him. He swallowed hard. Why did she do this to him—confuse him so? She was just a woman, like any other woman. But no! She was a beautiful woman and more—a person to him now. It confounded him that he should care.

From the wheel he watched her cross the deck to sit on a crate beside the hulk, Dyso. The massive arms and hands made motions, and Aaron saw her smile in recognition. She fascinated him.

The next morning Brien rose early to walk on deck in the damp chill of early morning. Opening her door, she gasped. Dyso lay on the floor just outside her door with a blanket as his only comfort.

He jerked up as the door opened and looked at her, then got up slowly, wrapping the blanket into a ball.

"Dyso, have you been there all night?"

He nodded, looking down—whether from fear or embarrassment, she could not tell.

"Why don't you sleep in your cabin?" She feared she already knew.

One of his massive hands gestured toward the next cabin—Aaron Durham's cabin. Then he brought his fists together in a pounding motion and swept them open toward her.

She knew. "It's all right, Dyso. No one here would hurt me." She put one hand on his arm. Something in him called to the gentler side of her. "Please sleep in your cabin where you'll be more comfortable."

But he shook his head sharply and moved quickly up the passageway to the steps.

That night after Brien had gone to bed she heard a quiet thump on the floor outside her door. Dyso had resumed his vigil. She smiled bittersweetly. There was such a thing as too much protection.

Jeannie mended slowly and the color revived in her face. After a week she was able to go on deck for fresh air and sun. Brien was relieved to have her companionship at last. They adopted the habit of walking about the deck just before retiring to their cabins for the night. Brien claimed she found it useful in inducing sleep.

In truth, she had found it difficult to sleep the entire first week they were under way. Her mind kept recalling glimpses of Aaron; she saw him in the sunlight on deck with the sun setting fire to his copper hair, or his perfect teeth flashing her a lecherous grin. And just as she expunged these images from her mind his eyes appeared before her—glowing, hungry—and a familiar ache spread through her loins. There seemed no escape from his torture, even in his absence.

In the quiet darkness of her cabin, she let herself wonder what it would be like to sleep nestled against him once more. Too well she remembered the warmth and the work-hardened firmness of his body against hers. She wondered what he would think of her now—and if she truly stirred him as he did her. Ah, but dreaming of Aaron Durham was one thing; allowing him to share her bed was quite another.

Many men had made overtures to her in the past months. They panted and fumbled, or were arrogant and adroit. All had been disappointed, and all had failed to strike even the smallest spark within her. It had not been difficult to rebuff them.

But this man was different. She dreaded the time when she would be alone with him. And she was sure he would arrange it somehow. She remembered his parting remarks as he slipped from her room at the Devon House. She could still see the twinkle in his eyes as he talked about the roll of the ship beneath her. And in her bed now, it seemed the rocking of the ship took on a sensual quality. Dear Heaven! Must every roll or yaw of the ship remind her of that stud?

One evening as she strolled the deck alone, she noticed him gazing at her, one brow raised in a lusty appreciation. She recognized the source of the light in his eyes and the lazy smile spread over his sensual mouth. Rather than dismay, she now felt a new sense of control and straightened her shoulders, pushing her breasts harder against the straining muslin. She would give him something to ogle. The graceful sway of her hips increased slightly and as she turned she glimpsed Aaron's expression. His face was redder now, and his impudent smile had faded to a hungry stare.

How truly predictable of him, she thought smugly, suppressing a smile. Let him taunt and threaten her. He would find she was not without an arsenal of effective weapons in this battle of wills. Whatever caused his reluctance to expose her past, she would use it to good advantage. It never occurred to her to wonder why he had not pressed her or made demands on her.

She stopped by the bow and watched the play of the fading sun on the waves. He crossed the deck and stood beside her, almost unnoticed.

"Lady Brien, your evening strolls are an inspiration to the crew. Pray do continue."

His mocking tone caused her to turn to him with a hard brilliance in her eyes that belied the sweet smile she affected.

"Why, Captain, I was not aware that your crew lacked inspiration for keeping fit. Walking about on deck is the only exercise available to me. Would you have me curtail it?"

"Not at all, milady. Though I am certain your nightly promenade has far less to do with keeping fit than with the chance to impress us all with your lovely figure." Again his white teeth flashed in a rakish grin.

"Oh?" She barely could contain her temper and tossed her head back haughtily. "And are you impressed, Captain? Surely you of all men must have ample basis for comparison. I have heard you are quite expert in such matters." She folded her arms so that they pushed her breasts higher and her eyes took on a seductive, smoky hue.

Her movement registered its effect in his face, his eyes now glowed like golden embers. "Of course a year is a long time"—he stroked his chin and perused her body boldly—"but if anything I'd say there was improvement."

Her face was hot with indignation at being bested in the game she had started! "Your vast experience with women no doubt makes your judgment quite expert. It seems a shame that you shall not be able to carry your comparison further!" She whirled and with long strides, crossed the deck to the safety of the hatchway.

Aaron stood leering after her until she disappeared from view, then smirked triumphantly. Leaning his tall frame against the railing, he crossed his arms and his tongue played at the corner of his mouth. She certainly pushed his self-control to the limit. And he wondered if they both might enjoy having it snap.

MacLeod was right; she was warm and physical. A shrug, a toss of her head, or a sweep of her long lashes could compel a wave of heat through him. It seemed worse for having tasted an enticing sample of overwhelming ecstasy with her. Could she have forgotten? Had he recalled only what he wanted to recall?

No. Something told him it had been just as he remembered—clearly as yesterday.

And now her low, musical voice enmeshed him even as her eyes blazed at him. He wanted to pull her to him and cover her rounded, pouting lips with kisses. His eyes devoured the ripe curve of her breasts, and he recalled the feeling of their cool firmness pressed against him.

As he leaned against the rail, his heart was pounding and his loins ached. How long could he stand not having her? Something told him that it would be worth the wait. The game was tantalizing, but his cooler side cautioned him to seek the game's conclusion soon—before she slipped away again when they docked.

The next afternoon Brien found Jeannie on deck engrossed in conversation. When she spoke, Jeannie started, and both she and Mr. Hicks were quite redfaced.

"Jeannie," she said, wondering what had been developing here under her very nose, "I wonder if you'll come by my cabin when you have finished your discussion?"

"Of course, milady. I'll come now if you wish." Jeannie began to rise from her seat on a barrel.

"Nonsense. Stay and enjoy the . . . sunshine awhile longer."

Brien went to her cabin feeling delightfully impish. Mr. Hicks and her own Jeannie Trowbridge. Not a bad match for a lady's maid. Mr. Hicks was kind, boyishly charming, and, from all appearances, quite capable. Under a more responsible, settled captain he might do quite well.

Her own thoughts caused her to wince. Here she was playing the matchmaker when she loathed the thought of anyone arranging her life for her. Perhaps she only imagined something between them. She would ask Jeannie about it.

Her thoughts then drifted as she stepped out of the cumbersome shirts and stretched luxuriantly on the bunk. She lifted one shapely leg and turned it slowly, judging it with a critical eye. Had she truly improved in the year since Allen Stewart made love to a nameless lady in Harrall's Road? There certainly had been changes—both outside and in.

She tried not to think of Raoul now and the time she spent as his prisoner. But somehow she sensed that the earthy charm that drew men to her came in part from a sensual confidence that had to do with her marriage. The bungling and blatant attempts of the courtly swains to gain her favors had surprised her. To her dismay, she found herself comparing their ineptness to the wantonly exhilarating seduction Raoul had played against her so deftly. One searing look from those black eyes and her legs had gone weak.

His very restraint and smooth, animal-like presence had at one time driven her to seek him out in the middle of a sleepless night. Raoul had known well the value of his unique gift with women. He had told her, not modestly but honestly, that she would reap the benefit of his vast experience.

Smiling, Brien turned over on to her stomach. It seemed now that Raoul had taught her all too well. She

207

could never be content with a sweet, fumbling Charles Medford or an aggressive, arrogant Reydon Hardwick. The man she would warm to must be tantalizingly gentle and doggedly persistent, supremely confident and unexpectedly vulnerable. He must be big and handsome, and his eyes must speak—

Heaven above! She was describing Aaron Durham! That swine! He invaded her thoughts at every turn. She frowned and jumped up from the bed to stand with her hands on her hips in ineffectual defiance.

What if she could warm to that rake? After all, she was human. But she would never submit to his wandering lusts. That strutting cock! Taunting and leering at her. She'd not be ordered or managed by any man— ever again. She had vowed never to marry again and meant it fully. If keeping her freedom meant foregoing a few of the more licentious pleasures in life, then so be it; she would willingly make the sacrifice.

Besides, the thought crept into her mind, with a man like Aaron Durham, there could never be more than a few stolen moments of guilty pleasure—and possibly a bastard child to remind her of a momentary weakness for a lifetime. Why was it her fate to be paired only with infamous philanderers?

When Jeannie's soft knock came at the door awhile later, Brien was filled with a new determination to avoid any entanglements with Aaron Durham.

"Ah, Jeannie," she greeted the girl more as a friend than a mistress. Pulling her to a seat on the bunk she inquired, "Whence comes this new interest of yours in sailing?"

Jeannie only blushed and studied her hands in her lap.

"Or is it more an interest in Mr. Hicks that causes

your rapt attention to his every word?''

"He only talks to me on deck—or at meals, when he can be there." Jeannie defended him. "He was very kind to me when I was sick, and gentlemanly too." Her face was so hopeful that Brien nearly laughed. But such tender emotions needed guidance, not scorn.

"It's all right, Jeannie. I couldn't fault you for following your heart. You do care for Mr. Hicks, don't you?"

"Yes, Lady Brien, I do." She reddened.

"And does he show the same interest in you?"

"I . . . I think so." The girl squirmed under Brien's questioning.

"Well, then, I feel it my duty to caution you. I have some experience in matters of the heart." Jeannie's wide eyes displayed a healthy respect for her mistress' worldliness.

"Mr. Hicks seems a capable young man, kind and honorable. I think you would make a good match—if things were to go that way. But hold a bit of your heart in reserve. Aboard ship in the middle of the ocean it is easy to mistake attention for love. The test of any such feelings will be their endurance—especially in port, after the voyage has ended."

Brien noted dismay in her maid's sweet face. "You mustn't let that dishearten you. If you grow to truly love one another, there will be no threat in a temporary separation. And better that you find out soon—before you have reasons to regret."

"I understand, Lady Brien." The girl nodded solemnly. "I promised me long ago I'd warm no man's bed before being proper wedded."

"Of course not. Now let's get on with my hair, shall we?"

Brien felt genuine warmth for the maid. Her sweet disposition and even temper balanced well her mistress' more extreme nature. And Jeannie enjoyed Brien's fame and reveled in Brien's account of the exploits and scandals among the nobility.

Being Brien's maid gave Jeannie a certain status from the start. And she repaid Brien's many kindnesses with true loyalty. Now, Brien felt responsible to look after the girl's happiness.

"How about if I do it up high for once?" Jeannie proposed, brushing her long silky tresses.

"Whatever for? The commons is hardly a place for elegant dining. There's no reason to expend such effort for appearances here." The implication of Jeannie's suggestion rankled her for no identifiable reason. But perhaps she misread the girl's tone.

"I just thought it might be nice to fix it up a bit—to boost your spirits." That did it. She was tiptoeing around the obvious.

"Jeannie, what are you trying to say?"

"Only that . . . I've seen the way Captain Durham looks at you. And you hardly ever give him a civil word. You haven't been out of traveling clothes since we started, and you don't want me to fix your hair fancy."

"And?" Brien sighed. "Just what are you getting at?"

"Just that you go out of your way to avoid him—and his notice. I just been wondering why."

If Jeannie had noticed—well more had Aaron Durham. No doubt he enjoyed her futile attempts at escaping his attention. He must think she crouched in fear of his awesome manhood. Her lips drew into a thin line and her eyes narrowed sharply. The worst of it was they were absolutely right!

She had hidden behind the practicality of traveling clothes and plain coiffures at least in part because she feared tempting his seemingly boundless lust. Well

. . . no more!

"Why not do it up, for once?" She flourished one hand. "I have been forgetting myself lately. An occasional whimsy is good for the soul!"

But something had stuck in her mind. "Just how does Captain Durham look at me?"

Jeannie paused, weighing her words. "Like his heart is in his eyes," she said wistfully. Obviously Aaron Durham had another conquest to his credit.

"Don't you mean his lust?" Brien said sourly.

"Lady Brien!"

"Don't sound so shocked. I've caught him looking at me as though he'd devour me in a second if I gave him the least encouragement. He's irresistibly handsome and slippery as an eel. He has a terrible reputation with women, and from observation, I'd say he earned it. Don't let that charm fool you, Jeannie." Her voice was overly vehement.

"Ah, but it's not me he plies with charm," Jeannie giggled.

"Count yourself lucky in that!" Brien smarted from Jeannie's insightful remark.

At dinner, Brien was later than usual and Mr. Hicks had already gone topside to take his watch when she and Jeannie entered the commons. Aaron, dressed in the usual shirt, breeches, and boots, rose from his seat as she entered. His eyes lighted at the sight of her with open admiration.

Her emerald green dress of cotton batiste was cut low and square and had caps over thin voile sleeves. The tight bodice tapered into a deep V in the front, made all the more provocative by the absence of hoops.

Brien was irritated by his close scrutiny, but was determined to be gracious at all costs. He would see that his incessant lechery daunted her little.

She took his hand and he helped her to the table which was set with cloth as for a special occasion.

"You are indeed lovely this evening, Lady Brien. I hope you enjoy this special dinner to honor the maiden voyage of the *Lady's Secret*. The fare may not be so refined as that you are accustomed to, but will provide a welcome change." He smiled broadly at Brien, produced a bottle of wine from a cabinet along the wall, and snatched four pewter wine cups before returning to the table.

"I hadn't realized you planned a celebration this evening, Captain," Brien said accepting a cup from him.

"I thought it my secret." His eyes twinkled. "But seeing you have dressed for it, I kept that secret badly." The undercurrent of meaning in his tone was unmistakable.

Brien threw a withering glance at Jeannie. "Your surprise was safe from me, Captain. It was pure coincidence that I chose to dress for dinner. I could bear the garb of travel no longer." Her nose tilted haughtily.

Aaron's eyes twinkled as he raised his cup. "The good ship, *Lady's Secret*. As fine a lady as I have ever . . . sailed."

Brien nearly choked on the wine at those last words. The man had no shame! She glowered at him, then raised her own glass.

"May the *Secret* roam the seas all her days freely, without fear of pirates or privateers—or others who would molest her." The pointed entendre caused Aaron to arch one brow.

"You seem uncommonly preoccupied with freedom, madame. Can it be you harbor dangerous Whig sentiments; or is your interest in freedom of a more personal nature?" His golden eyes probed hers, causing her to shift in her chair to avoid them.

"Both, I think. I wish freedom for myself; can I wish

less for others?''

"Most interesting sentiment from a woman who makes men slaves to her charm.''

"Captain,'' Jeannie broke in uncomfortably, "would you mind if I took a cup to Mr. Hicks?''

"By all means,'' Aaron nodded, never moving his eyes from Brien.

She felt a sudden panic at being left alone with him, but had no pretext for making Jeannie stay.

As Jeannie quitted the door, she bounded up and turned away from him.

"Must you stare at me so? As if I were meat and you a starving mongrel?'' She was annoyed by her own reaction as much as his.

"But I spoke only the truth. You are incredibly beautiful. Would you deny me a portion of that which you bestow gladly on all other men? To look at you and caress you with my eyes, to taste and drink deeply of your beauty? Um-m-m. Be fair, milady.'' His voice had taken on a low, seductive quality that sent a tremor of excitement through her.

Her heart beat a little faster in defiance of her will. "It seems there is little I can do to stop your gaping if you are not gentleman enough to control yourself.'' She had to struggle to find the words to lash him with! The swine! He enlisted her own body against her!

"I heard rumors, in London, that Madame Trechaud will not think of marrying again. Is there truth to that rumor?'' He approached her from behind.

"For once the gossips do me well. It is true; I shall avoid marriage at all costs.'' She turned to find him staring down at her, warmly.

"At all costs?'' he grinned wolfishly. He shook his head. "Brien, you are too warm, too womanly to forego the contenting pleasures of wedded life at so tender an age.''

She stomped her foot in defiance. "Your presumption is astounding! You have no right to pass judgment on my life or future! I have tasted those 'contenting pleasures' and found them not to my liking." Her cheeks were scarlet now and her eyes flashed sparks at him.

"You forget, Brien, it was I who first introduced you to those pleasures. I remember well your reaction; it was not at all unfavorable." His hand come up slowly and wrapped around her waist. A thrill went through her at the touch.

She was mesmerized by his eyes and the sensual, low roll of his voice. She wanted desperately to strike him or berate his lustful intent, but every part of her was responding to this call to arms . . . her heart and body partners in mutiny.

"You were wonderful, Brien," he tantalized her, "sweet and warm and soft in my arms. You poured against me, eager and yielding." His arms were both about her and he pulled her to him slowly.

His lips claimed hers tenderly. Then he pulled away to look at her face. Her eyes betrayed the passion he had unleashed in her. Her arms came up around him as he bent to kiss her once more.

Now his lips parted, and his tongue traced the fragrant outline of her wine-warmed mouth. The barrage of dizzying sensations was exhilarating and temporarily blocked all thought of retreat. And she responded, pressing against him, feeling a curious relief that it was happening at last, that which she had dreaded. She met his kisses with equal ardor, wishing she could drink in the very essence of him—join with him.

Suddenly she pushed back from him, as if shocked back into reality by her own passion. They stood, panting for breath, devouring each other with their eyes. Panic seized her and she whirled, trembling, away from his rave.ilous gaze.

A movement in the doorway startled them both. Brien gasped as Dyso thrust his bulk through the opening. Stopping just inside, he surveyed them both, puzzled by what he saw and clearly disturbed. His scarred face darkened and with two swift hand movements he asked the questions.

"No, Dyso," Brien said firmly. She had regained her breath and some of her shattered composure. "We were about to have dinner." Both men noticed that her hand trembled as she pointed toward the table.

"I'm really quite hungry, Captain. Could we see this festive meal you've promised?"

It was several minutes before Brien could bring herself to look at Aaron. His expression was one of gentle amusement, instead of the self-assured taunt she had expected. She blushed slightly at her guilty thoughts. Jeannie had rejoined them and relieved the tension with her constant chatter. Dyso ate heartily, showing no signs of his earlier suspiciousness.

Brien relaxed enough to think. The outer walls of her fortress had been scaled and breached. Gone were all fears of a man's touch. She felt defenseless against this phantom of her dreams now made flesh and blood. She must contrive never to be alone with him again. The danger of lasting consequences from a night's encounter with him were too great to risk—even for the ecstasy she would find in his arms. Miserably, she admitted that ecstasy it would most certainly be.

It was nearly dark when she and Jeannie followed Dyso on deck for a breath of air. Brien was relieved that Aaron had excused himself from their company to study charts in his cabin. The wind had a dampness to it as the clouds darted past the face of the moon. Before long, Brien shivered and suggested they go below to avoid the worsening weather. She needed the sweet release of sleep to give her perspective on what she felt was a disturbing change in her—an uncertainty that she felt all too often of late.

She pulled her damp shawl from her shoulders as she stood before her cabin door. She glanced furtively at the next door, wishing it would open. No! She must put all that from her mind immediately! And with one determined turn of her hand she was safely inside her own darkened cabin.

The oil lamp swayed darkly from its post above her as she reached for it. The light warmed her when she replaced the globe and hung the lamp back on its peg. Why did she feel so empty—so lonely?

She sat before the desk and removed the combs and pins from her hair. Since Jeannie's illness, she had grown used to doing this for herself and found the nightly ritual strangely comforting. Strange that she had ever considered this thick tangle of softness a burden, she pondered as she brushed. Hair and gowns and invitations—she had come to relish the attention they brought her. But in part she felt a stab of guilt at their exorbitant cost and the underlying suspicion that she used them to avoid the emptiness of her hours.

She lifted the mirror to be sure she'd covered all of the locks and gasped. In the corner of the mirror she glimpsed the sensual face of Aaron Durham—leering at her. She whirled to face him, indignant at this second invasion of her privacy.

"What are you doing here?" she demanded, jumping up.

His lean frame was stretched out lazily on her narrow bed, his arms crossed behind his head. He smiled, luxuriating in the sight of her tawny hair cascading about her shoulders.

"Your hair is every bit as enchanting as I remembered." He allowed his gaze to drift over her boldly.

"Out! Out!"

She flung her finger at the door and gritted her teeth. "Dyso will be here any minute," she threatened. Her heart was beating faster. His long, muscular legs were covered by tight woolen breeches and those high black boots. His white linen shirt was open partway and revealed a coppery thatch on his muscular chest. Her gazed wandered, taking in the details of him even as he studied her. Then she realized where he sat—and that he made no move to leave.

The rutting rake! "What are you doing here? Get your bloody great body off my bed!"

"Perceptive wench, as well. Thank you, milady."

" 'Twas no compliment!" she raged. "What are you doing here?"

"Why . . . watching you brush your hair, milady. And it was a delight to behold." The wide-eyed innocence was replaced by a worldlier glint. "Pray, don't let me interfere with your toilette." He studied her and rubbed his chin. "What would be next? The dress! Shall I help?"

"I shall call Dyso to remove you," she said starting for the door.

In a twinkling, Aaron's muscular frame was spread resolutely between her and the portal.

"No offense, milady, but your protector has very little humor about him and I have no desire for burial at sea." He bowed sardonically.

"Then remove yourself or I'll scream," she uttered through clenched teeth.

"Scream, then, if you must, and prepare to navigate to Boston safely by yourself." His face had lost most of its cockiness, but there was a lingering trace of amusement that Brien found irksome.

217

No scream split the air. Each eyed the other warily.

Brien closed her eyes and sighed sharply. "What is it you want of me?" The question was more of a complaint. "You taunt me, mock me at every turn, ogle and leer at me; you separated me from my servants and now you invade my cabin!" Her voice rose in a crescendo of indignation.

He started and pulled away from the door, putting a finger to his mouth in a gesture for silence. Instantly, Brien realized that Dyso had taken up his vigil outside her door. She quickly weighed the possibility of calling to him and recognized all too clearly the logic of Aaron's survival in getting them to the colonies safely.

Aaron pulled her, struggling silently, to a seat on the bunk beside him.

"Please keep your voice down and I shall keep my distance." Seeing her move as far away on the bunk as possible, he grinned.

Her lips pouted, and she looked up at him through a canopy of long, dark lashes. Her hair was tossed about her, and she seemed so unconsciously alluring and filled with a recalcitrant sweetness that he ached to hold her.

"Why have you come?" she insisted, fearing she already knew.

He seized first one clever retort, then another, discarding them all. He surprised himself when he said, "I wanted to talk with you."

She surveyed his face and weighed his words. "You could have spoken to me on deck or in the commons. You had no need to lurk about in my darkened cabin."

"True." He leaned back, propping himself on one elbow. "But would you have me confess in front of my crew that the thoughts of you abed only a few feet away robs me of sleep, that the sight of you on deck with the sun in your hair sends an ache through me, that the scent of you as you brush past me in the passage pours fire into my blood?''

Brien's jaw dropped. This was a most unusual assault. He was as good with words as he was with kisses. Should she feel flattered or offended? He was not mocking or taunting—simply describing his feelings—and in doing so, was giving voice to the selfsame misery she endured.

"I cannot be held responsible for your reckless lust, Aaron Durham.''

"Ah, but you are, madame. Tonight when you kissed me—''

"I kissed you?''

"You kissed me back,'' he countered. His eyes drifted over her as his hands could not. "I wanted you as I have never wanted anyone else.''

The huskiness in his voice caused Brien's eyes to widen with alarm. Her heart pounded as she braced for the attack that never came.

"Much has happened since our night together. But I have not forgotten the joy of you in my arms. Were it mine to choose I would take you in my arms now and love you with all that is in me.''

"Love is a word that rolls easily on your tongue.'' She was confused and growing upset at this disarming seduction. She searched her heart for a wisp of real anger. "No doubt you have learned to ply it well to your advantage. But I am not fooled. Once bedded, I would soon be forgotten. Such was the fate of scores of unwary maids if only a small part of your renown be based in fact.'' A good hard knot of anger was forming in her stomach and she welcomed it.

"Your conceit is beyond belief, Captain. Just because you want me, I am to roll over like a bitch eager to have her belly rubbed.'' Her eyes snapped. "Tell me, how many little copper-haired bastards now bear

219

your face and shame, from how many tender lasses whose names and faces you've forgotten?'' Her own vehemence surprised her.

His eyes narrowed with a harder gleam than Brien had seen there before. ''I have no bastards, madame,'' he growled. ''If truth be told, there is not a woman alive to say honestly that I forced her or that I promised anything that I did not fulfill. Or do you only listen to the gossip that suits your purpose?'' He sat up, searching her face, unaware of the murderous effect of his burning stare and his strong maleness on her will to resist.

''Is it my reputation you hate, Brien, or is it me?'' His voice had the ring of cold steel to it as he strained to control his temper.

She looked down, unable to bear the truth of his words as they hit at the core of her only real complaint against him—his reputation with women that uncannily paralleled her husband's.

''I . . . do not hate you.'' She relaxed her rigid posture and closed her eyes. ''But I have learned well the ways of men.'' The touch of sadness that often surfaced when she thought no one could see was now plain in her face.

His own anger melted at once into unexpected tenderness. He reached inside his belt, drew something out, and put it into her hands.

She stared at two tortoise-shell combs, her mind whirling now with a slow recognition. They were hers. Her fingers caressed them and explored the brown and amber smoothness. She turned to him, confused and beyond speech.

''Don't you recognize them?'' he said softly. ''They are yours. I took them from your hair that night. It was all I had to prove to me that you were not a phantom of my mind—a sweet delusion. I vowed I would put them

220

back into your hair myself, if ever I found you.''

He had looked for her as he'd said! Warmth flooded her and she looked up to find him standing by the bunk.

She rose and turned so that he could not see the mixture of fear and longing that filled her. She squeezed the combs tightly to blot out the temptation that beckoned to her now—having him.

He stepped closer to her and one bronzed hand hovered over her shoulder before caressing the satiny skin. He felt a tremor—or was that his imagination?

Taking her silence for consent, he pulled her back against him, gently.

She could hardly breathe. Her bones seemed to have turned fluid and she had not the will or power to move from his strong arms.

His shallow breath moved a wisp of hair near her temple and she closed her eyes, battling fear and reason to remain there.

The low rumble of his throat called her back. ''Brien, if you want, I'll leave.'' He had felt the first hard stirrings of passion, and they warned him that to have her now might be to lose her again.

Jolted by this offer—just as she had begun to surrender—she summoned all her strength and moved away, feeling the warmth of his hands on her waist as he released her.

There would be another time, he thought, when she would come to him gladly. He wanted her joyful, eager, and free of doubt. With fresh insight he knew that was all she asked—the freedom to choose, to give. And he must give her that freedom now.

Without another word, he stepped up onto the bunk and flung open one of the small windows above it.

''What are you doing?'' she exclaimed, whirling about.

He paused, one hand on the window and one

gesturing toward the door. "Well, you could hardly expect me to exit over your besotted protector."

The sound of the sea drifted in through the small opening. Alarm filled her. "But you can't go out there—you'll be killed!"

"Ah"—his face was merry—"we do make progress. The lady cares whether I live or die. Fear not, madame, 'twas I designed this ship." And in one fluid movement, with a twist of his muscular frame, he was through the window.

Brien climbed up to close the window and leaned her head out into the darkness to look after him. But all was darkness, and she was thoroughly drenched in the process. She pulled in and latched the window, mortified at the danger and her own horror of it.

Moments later, a gentle, but unmistakable, rap on the wall from the next cabin caused her to smile and breathe easily once more.

Sixteen

The next night, after Jeannie left her she sat on her bed dangling her bare, slender feet above the smooth floor. She had much to think about. No matter how she turned she came back to the same starting point—Aaron Durham.

A chronicle of his assets and defects could be of little help, but she listed them all the same. Tall, lithe, handsome, clever, tender, exciting—was stubborn an asset or a flaw? She threw up her hands in despair; the man defied classification!

She thought of his ease of movement and his square, determined jaw and the glint of passion that seemed everpresent in his fabulous eyes. She felt an aching in her stomach, and below, that no nostalgia or curiosity could explain. Her skin burned under his eyes and her throat tightened each time his lips curled into a roguish smile. Something in him called to her, consuming her thoughts by day and her dreams by night.

Most devastating, he knew her secrets and her passion—and he did not use them against her for his own selfish ends. What did he want from her? She smiled ruefully; That was plain enough. He wanted her beneath him—both in bed and out. Didn't he? Confound him! Why hadn't he pressed her harder last evening? She had needed no further persuasion to make her tumble helplessly into bed with him. With her primed and pliant next to him, he was reluctant. It was as though he handed her all control as he placed those combs in her hands.

She bounded off the bunk to probe the side pocket of her open trunk. She held the twin prizes of her search up to the light, the plain tortoise-shell combs.

Desire hit her with gale force and she shuddered. She closed her eyes, feeling a tingling in her breasts and a warmth spreading in her loins. She could not deny these feelings any longer. She wanted him.

She could not know about the future and what was in store for her—for them. But she must have him—be with him now. If it was only passion, she would find it out in the cold light of morning. Then she would be free of him. And if there was more? She would deal with that when the time came.

Her satin robe billowed around her as she whirled out into the passage. Dyso, lying across the narrow passage, sat up quickly, blinking at her with sleep-clouded concern.

She smiled briefly and put forth one hand, motioning him to stay. The hulk watched as she gathered her robe about her and moved to the door of the next cabin. Without knocking, she turned the handle and disappeared inside.

Dyso rubbed his face slowly. A faint smile flickered about his mouth as he heaved himself up and lumbered down to his own unused cabin.

* * *

Aaron Durham sat at a large desk at one end of his spacious cabin. His boots were off and he wore no shirt, as if half-prepared for bed. A stack of charts absorbed his attention until the movement of the door jerked his head up defensively.

His jaw dropped at the sight of Brien standing there in night clothes. The glibness of a lifetime deserted him as she floated forward into the soft light of the single lantern. There was a radiance about her and a glow in her eyes that transfixed his very soul. His heart stopped, then thumped wildly.

She paused before him and knelt, tucking her feet beneath her. Looking up at him, searching him, she pressed something into his hands.

Tearing his gaze from her face, he saw the two small combs in her hand and he found it hard to swallow. He could not speak, but words were not necessary. She sat meekly before him and he touched her flowing hair tenderly. His hands shook as he tucked the combs into locks of hair she pulled back from her face for him.

When she tilted her face to his once more, she rose to her knees and timidly touched his bare chest with her fingertips. Her hands flew to the ribbons of her robe. It slid down her arms and fell around her on the thick rug. Underneath, she wore a gauze-thin night dress that clung to her body, revealing erect nipples and the enticing curve of her body below. The skin of her bare arms and chest was as smooth as fresh cream and he yearned to sample it.

Her faint, roselike scent wafted up to him, sending his head into dizzy spirals. But her eyes, soft and very blue called him back to her fragrant body.

"Are you a dream, come to tempt and torture me in my lonely bed?"

Her throaty laugh sent a chill of excitement through him. "I am no dream . . . only a mortal woman who comes to you freely, asking only to be with you."

His hands on her shoulders pulled her to him and she wrapped her arms around his muscular body. He held her softly against him and felt his blood rise against her soft frame.

In one swift movement he scooped her up into his arms and carried her to the large bed at the other end of the cabin. There he lay down beside her, looking at her.

Her arms opened to him and he entered them, possessing her lips softly. His big hands traced the ripe curves of her body through the gossamer fabric, even as her fingers explored the expanse of his muscular back. The warmth and lean, naked power of his chest against her left her breathless.

His hot mouth left hers to trace the hollow of her throat. She arched against him pressing her breasts toward him as his mouth neared them. In a second, he pulled back the fabric and gazed in awe at the creamy mounds. He pressed his hot cheek against her tingling nipple and gently nuzzled her breast. The delicious sensations caused her to moan and clutch him to her tightly. His tongue lingered over the rose-colored nipples.

Brien felt herself soaring. When she closed her eyes she could still see him, and he engulfed her with rapturously loving sensations.

She took his face between her cool hands and lifted it to her own. His eyes shone with hunger. Wantonly she pushed him back and sat up.

He leaned on one elbow, wondering what she would do. Was this some new torture she had in store for him?

She drew the filmy night dress over her head and threw it on the floor by the bed, shaking her hair so that it spread about her shoulders. She sat on her knees before him, naked, her eyes shining with desire and pride.

He swallowed hard, trying to drink in the details of

her beauty: the soft tumbled hair, the full, round breasts; the smooth round hips, and silken thighs.

She was far more beautiful than he had remembered, and the sight of her flushed with passion and naked before him overwhelmed his senses.

She smiled seductively and slid down to lie beside him, pressing her long, tapered legs against his bulging breeches on the way. In a moment, his remaining clothes were discarded and he rejoined her.

Now his mouth was fierce upon hers, demanding a response and receiving her darting tongue willingly. At length, he rolled on top of her, searing her skin with his heat. Soon he was inside her, moving to meet the rhythm of her undulating hips.

They seemed to move together a long time, hanging on the very edge of ecstasy. Then a thunderous spasm of passion fused them into one soaring, splintering entity.

Brien gasped for air, shuddering occasionally as the peace of fulfillment seeped through her. Aaron moved over to lie beside her, his own expression mirroring the smoky contentment in hers. She snuggled against his big, firm body, awed by him and amazed at her own wanton pleasure in their loving.

Aaron's mind whirled above them in lazy contented circles, marveling at this woman who lay curled against him. Her passion surprised and delighted him. Not even their first night together could match the splendor and excitement he now knew.

"Brien, Brien . . . Brien." Her name rolled sensually on his tongue.

She thought her name never sounded so sweet as on his lips. "Yes, Aaron?"

"I only wanted to say your name." He shifted his chin so that it rested on her forehead. "For so long I called you 'Lady'—it seems strange to call you by a real name."

Something in her heart quivered. "You thought of me then?"

His laugh was heavy with irony. "Too often for my own peace of mind. I was so driven by want of you that I named my ship for you." Tucking his chin he gazed lovingly down at her. "Does it please you to know you unhinged me so?"

Her eyes sparkled. "It barely compensates for the nights I have awakened hot and shaking, pursued by a phantom with burning golden eyes that haunted my dreams."

"Can it be that women share such dreams of passion?" He looked at her wonderingly.

She propped herself up on one elbow, amused. "I can only speak for one." She traced his long straight nose, then let her fingertips drift to the scar on his left cheek. "Can it be you know women so well and yet do not know how they dream, how they desire?"

His face colored slightly. " 'Twas you proclaimed me expert with women. I make no such claim."

"You may rightly claim expertise with one," she smiled coyly.

His white teeth bared in a satisfied smile. "At you, Lady, I am only beginning." With one hand he grasped the back of her hair and pulled her head to him, claiming her lips roughly.

New warmth flowed through her as she met the ardor of his kisses with renewed desire. When they broke apart at last, she snuggled against him and nibbled his shoulder with her fine teeth.

The low rumble in his throat told her he enjoyed her wanton play. But soon she turned her back to him and drew his arms about her. Sleep overtook them at last, Brien cradled by Aaron's big warm body.

* * *

A loud banging on the cabin door awakened Aaron just at dawn. He started and sat up quickly, glancing about the rumpled bed. It was empty and he frowned. The meaty fist at the door was persistent and growing louder. Mumbling a curse as he ran a hand through his hair, he bounded out of bed and drew on a pair of breeches.

"Save your strength—I'm coming!" he barked, buttoning the snug white wool.

"Captain," Mr. Hicks called from the other side of the door, "we've hit a fog. You're needed on deck, sir."

Aaron jerked open the door. "Did you strike sail?" he growled, pulling on a boot. He returned to the side of the bed for the other boot and his shirt. Mr. Hicks stepped in and peered about the cabin curiously. "Aye, sir."

Aaron caught the man's scrutiny, and it angered him suddenly. "When did you take the last sighting?" he demanded, shoving one arm into the shirt.

"Three bells, sir." Hicks regarded him respectfully. His captain was in foul humor and he pondered the possible reasons. He could readily think of one, but there was no sign of her here. Perhaps that was the short of it. The woman had gotten under the Captain's skin, that was plain enough to see. And his Captain was not one to take no easily—especially from a woman.

"I was on deck myself when we ran afoul of it. Posted watches right away and struck canvas."

Aaron finished tucking the band at his waist. "Good enough, Hicks." He motioned to the door as he shot a parting glance in the looking glass above the basin. The stubble on his face would have to wait.

"Tell the cook to send up some coffee—wake him if you have to." His tone was less harsh now. He looked at Hicks' tired face. "Then get some rest; you'll need it, Hicks.'' He clasped the other man's arm briefly, then with long strides was up the steps and on deck.

The cool, damp mist in the air clung to his face and clothes. The sun was well up by now, but the air seemed dark and heavy. From where Aaron stood on the bridge at the wheel, the bow of the ship was lost in the fog.

Hicks had posted experienced hands at the bow and they strained eyes and ears, searching the oppressive cloud.

A fog like this in mid-ocean meant the mix of strong currents of warm and cold—and a danger of icebergs drifting south with the cold, arctic flow. With no wind, the fog might stay for two or three days; or it could lift that very afternoon. There was no way to tell how long it would last or how dangerous it might be.

Now in command of his ship and of himself, Aaron had time to think. Where was she? Had she really come to him last night, or was it a dream? No, he mused, feeling the press of her fragrant mouth once more, it was no. She had left him in the night again. He frowned, not sure why that should trouble him. And his irritation at Hicks' insinuating curiosity—that was not like him. Did he fear for the lady's reputation? Certainly she could see to her own interests. But now he felt responsibility—to or for her? He would regret any action that might cause her the slightest pain or discomfort.

A smile played at the corners of his mouth. She was enchanting; by turns coy and playful, then sweet and yielding. She had made love with him directly, passionately. It had been better than his many dreams of her, for she brought to his bed the wild sweetness of her own spirit, exciting in ways he could never have imagined. She was truly a woman, not the wistful girl who had charmed him so in Harrall's Road. With an intense pang of envy he wondered about her marriage and the handsome Frenchman who had called her his wife.

" 'Tis the route to madness. It has nothing to do with me," he muttered, trying to put it from his mind.

Looking out over the deck and off into the swirling mists, his mind kept going back to her. A fresh longing took hold of him. He wanted her again—now—but more than physically. He wanted to be with her, watch her, talk with her, share with her. He longed for her and this insatiable new feeling shook him to the very core. Having her in his bed, loving her last night, had not eased his body or mind. Having tasted such exquisite closeness, he found he desired it all the more. She was in his blood and he found he didn't mind admitting it. What would MacLeod think of the rake of Wiltshire now?

He straightened behind the wheel at the thought. His renown with women had always been a source of mixed feelings for him. Earlier, as a young officer, he had reveled in the amorous games of conquest in which fortune had given him an edge. But the ease of conquest made quantity the only challenge.

Suddenly, a year ago, he could no longer ignore the emptiness and futility of the game he played . . . of the life he led. He had resigned his hard-won commission and returned home to his father's estate.

He had tried to reconcile with his father, even to courting two young girls his father had selected. But in the end, he had had to leave Wiltshire and take up residence again in Bristol. He knew he could never live as his father would require him to. No small part of that decision was the haunting sweetness of a tender December night; it had prevented him from enjoying any night with a woman since.

Now the vague discontent he had lived with for many months became a focused, sharpened dissatisfaction that prodded him mercilessly. And he understood that somehow Brien was the cause and the solution. This longing he felt for her was much akin to the restlessness that caused him to flee his father's control.

· And what of her? Why had she come to him last night? Passion, yes, but was there more? What did she feel, think? As his ears strained toward the muffled lapping of the water at the sides of the ship, he frowned again. The sea demanded his attention like a jealous mistress.

Brien awakened late that same morning, and sent Jeannie off in search of breakfast while she luxuriated in bed. She smiled and stretched extravagantly. Anyone seeing the satisfied glow on her face might easily have guessed the reason.

She thought suddenly of the cause of this pleasant languor that possessed her. Where was he now? She would need time to think, that was clear.

She bounded out of bed, pulled her night dress over her head, and discarded it. Pulling a chemise over her head, she relived the exhilaration of removing her gown in Aaron's bed—the astonishment on his face as she sat before him on her knees, framed in a wild jumble of soft tawny hair. She chided herself for the lasciviousness of her thoughts.

But she had loved being with him. In his every move, every touch, she found surprises. He was a curious man; brutally strong and remarkably tender. Each passing day in his company meant greater danger to her now that she had known the splendor of a night with him.

She hadn't expected to feel this way toward him. She had succeeded in convincing herself that she was only curious about this man whose reputation with women rivaled her husband's. One night and she would be over this madness. But one night had only validated the dream she had lived with since their first loving. It would be harder to resist now, knowing what she would miss.

A strange satisfaction lingered inside her. Not even shaking her head sharply would rid her of it. It stifled the feeling of alarm that tried to grow inside her. What if she were with child now?

The calmer part of her mind took control. Nearly a month with Raoul's virile husbanding had left her childless. Perhaps she could not have children. The thought impaled her! Surely it was not true!

A sardonic conscience, hard pressed and long denied, rose up to taunt her. Wasn't that just what she wanted? Cold, loveless, childless freedom? She had planned and schemed toward it, and now as it seemed thrust upon her, she found the possibility appalling.

The true impact of her desires seeped through to her. In rejecting marriage and its subjugation, she had unwittingly rejected two of the things that gave life meaning—love and children.

"But I have love now—my father. I know he loves me." But the transparent futility of the argument caused her to wince. Lawrence Weston was not a young man and his health was further weakened by his recent illness. When he was gone, who would she have?

Adamantly shaking her head, she refused to pursue the logic. She would be different. She would have a good, useful life. She might not bear children, but she could help care for those abandoned by others. And she would run the business ventures her father had begun. She would find ways to use her time.

And what of Aaron Durham? She shivered unexplainably. Fortune had thrust them together twice now. How could she deal with this man-phantom that reminded her of all she would sacrifice to run her life free of others' expectations? No ready answer came to her quandary. But she knew that she must never warm his bed again—however strong the temptation, however compelling her need for him.

The fog remained until the next afternoon when the sun burned some of it off and rising winds carried the rest away. Aaron had been on deck almost continuously, and Brien had kept to her cabin, both relieved and disappointed to be deprived of his presence.

The cool white of the sun seemed distant through the high clouds but was a welcome sight all the same. Jeannie put down her needlework, declaring she would bear it no longer. Brien joined her, glad for an excuse to be up on deck for a while.

One furtive glance told Brien he was not on deck. Jeannie brightened considerably at Mr. Hicks's presence.

"The fairest flowers of God's beauteous garden," he declared.

"Are you well acquainted with the gardener, Mr. Hicks?" Brien teased.

"I am every ready to give credit where it is due, madame. A man would be a fool indeed to live in this wondrous world, never allowing proper respect to its Master."

Brien was impressed. "Men of such persuasion are rare. We must hear more of your views another time. Might I walk about on the quarterdeck?"

Receiving an affirmative nod, Brien made her way up the steps to the railing on the bridge. The view of the long ship from there was commanding. She was properly awed. She watched the sailor at the wheel as he touched it reverently. She could see why men loved the challenge and power of the sea and risked life and fortune to test themselves against it. It was exhilarating just to watch. A pang of envy swept her. She would love to have shared in this feeling—this communion with the elements of nature. It was truly enough to lure a nobleman to sea, forsaking title and comfort. At least one nobleman.

Him again! Was there any topic she might name where his name and face did not appear? Her face darkened. Where had he been these past days? Was he really so busy? Or was he avoiding her? She had not even seen him since she'd left his bed a night ago. Not a look, a smile, a nod—nothing.

Her lovely eyes crinkled with suspicion. He had not even been to meals. Something was very wrong. Her heart beat faster. At first she was relieved by his absence; it saved her from the embarrassment of rebuffing him after so abandoned a night of loving. But suddenly it irritated her. Was she being scorned herself? She was not as sure of him or his motives as she had been even a short while before.

Now her own words came back to haunt her. "On board ship in the middle of the ocean, it is easy to mistake attention for love."

Shame flooded her cheeks. She had been played for a fool. She had offered herself eagerly to him, and now he scorned her with silence—just as she had predicted. Once bedded, soon forgotten. The thrill of conquest was her chief allure. With that gone, the rake need not bother with her again. Still, she was stunned at how quickly it had happened. She might have expected it once they docked—but the very day after?

Tears brimming in her eyes, she ran down the steps and into the hatchway. Once in her cabin she gave way to tearing sobs as she lay on the narrow bed. Her own special misery seemed to be to read men wrongly —to trust them and ennoble them in her heart, when in reality they were quite different. Later she washed her face and applied rice powder to hide the redness around her eyes. She would have no trouble ignoring him for the rest of the voyage. She would never let him see that it mattered to her. If he could forget so easily, then so would she. She would blot out every sensation that linked him to her.

That evening, there was a hard knot in her stomach as she entered the common room for dinner. Aaron was there, freshly shaved and wearing a dark blue uniform trimmed with gold braid at the shoulders and collar. His high black boots gleamed. She accepted his hand in escort to her seat, but ignored the slight pressure of it.

Hicks had seated Jeannie beside her and Dyso took up his usual place at the end of the table. Aaron watched her, aware of a change in her manner.

"You are lovely this evening, Madame Trechaud."

His use of her married name startled her. She had thought him above such a mean taunt as that.

"Thank you, Captain." Her voice was icy.

"Mr. Hicks no doubt told you why I did not join you for meals of late." Aaron was irritatingly charming. "Fog in this part of the ocean could well hold hidden dangers. I was obliged to be on deck."

"So Mr. Hicks explained," Jeannie assured him, smiling affectionately at the first mate.

"Your devotion to your ship and our safety is commendable, Captain," Brien said saccharinely. Her eyes were mocking and Aaron was disturbed by their transformation.

He went on pleasantly. "It is my job to see to your safety and comfort."

Annoyed by his unshakable calm, Brien knotted her

hands into white fists and fixed a polite smile on her face.

"I had an opportunity to read some interesting essays during these dreary days," Brien continued, turning pointedly to Mr. Hicks. "There were interesting quotes from the sermons of John Wesley. Have you heard of him, Mr. Hicks."

"Yes, Lady Brien. Who in England has not heard of Wesley?" Hicks sensed the strain between them and did not wish to be used to ignore his superior officer.

"What do you think of his 'methods of piety'? I warned you I would know more of your views." She flashed him a dazzling smile.

Even knowing she must do this to pique him, Aaron found himself angry with her. Her coolness was unexpected and puzzled him greatly. Was he never to be sure of her motives or feelings? She seemed as capricious as the wind.

The rest of dinner saw a dreadful sparring between Brien and Aaron, with Jeannie and Hicks looking on uncomfortably. Only Dyso ate the meal with good appetite. Aaron excused himself early to check the watch on deck, and a heavy silence fell over the group. Then Brien withdrew to leave her maid and the first mate to their own company.

In her cabin, Brien paced in the dull glow of the lantern, unaware that on deck Aaron paced as well. It would be hard to say who passed the more miserable night. Neither slept well and both awakened in foul humor. When they met at lunch, Brien was unusally quiet, and Aaron was uncharacteristically sharp with the cabin boy—and with Hicks.

Jeannie and Robert Hicks exchanged wondering glances as the animosity between the captain and the lady grew. And Aaron took his dinner on deck that evening.

In her cabin, dressed for bed, but unable to sleep, Brien paced again, trying unsuccessfully to turn her thoughts from Aaron Durham to anything—anyone—else. Why did he matter to her so? She should be relieved to no longer be the object of his lust. They had had a splendid night, and now her guilt and his disinterest had revealed the shallowness of such encounters. She should be grateful to learn so important a lesson so cheaply.

The turning of the door handle caught her attention suddenly. She looked up to find Aaron filling the doorway, his face set with determination. The soft click of the latch was the only indication of the passage of time for her. Her heart had stopped at the sight of him.

"Your cabin is one further, Captain," she said weakly.

"I think we should talk."

"I'm really quite tired, Captain. Can this not wait till morning?" Brien stifled a false yawn.

"No," he said firmly, putting hands on hips and spreading his legs in a gesture of resolve. "This will not wait. I would know two things from you, Lady."

"If it is so urgent a matter, I shall do my best to answer."

Her exaggerated civility produced no change in him. Her mind raced to deduce his reason for coming.

"Why did you come to me two nights ago?"

"I . . . I . . . I . . ." she stammered, unable to tell him and not sure if she knew herself. "This is hardly a matter for discussion, Captain." It was hard to feign ladylike surprise at his boldness when she considered the topic under discussion.

238

"Nevertheless, it will be discussed." His critical gaze did not miss the trembling of her hands as she pushed back her hair, absently.

"Your memory is indeed short. Only the night before you visited my cabin to restate your persistent invitation. Why should you be concerned with my motives? You got what you wanted." She struggled to phrase it delicately. What did he want from her now? Had he no couth at all?

"I must know from you why you came." His big arms folded across his chest, making him seem immovable and stern.

"Then I shall answer the only way I can. I am not sure why I came—unless from curiosity. I am human. You are handsome and enigmatic."

"You came because you were curious?" His voice had a hard, angry ring to it.

"And why have you hounded me from Bristol on, lurking in my chambers and leering? Will you tell me it was for a great and noble ideal—or more truthfully lust and that same curiosity!"

Her words bit deep. He growled, "I wanted you— I'll not deny it. And I enjoyed it too. I thought you woman enough to admit that as well."

"Oh," she taunted, "did you come for a testimonial to your skill, Captain? Surely there are others, of more varied experience, far better qualified to flatter you than I."

The cords in his neck stood out and his jaw flexed as he strained to control his rage. "My apologies, madame. For a while I mistook you for a lady I once knew. But I see now how mistaken I have been."

His words struck her like a fist in the face, and she whirled away from him. Her eyes brimmed uncontrollably. She could not break down in the middle of a good fight! How dare she behave like a simpering female!

But the tears burned streaks down her inflamed cheeks.

Aaron's arms dropped to his sides. He felt uncomfortable as his last, taunt lay burning on the air between them. He could not leave on that cruel thrust. This was not like him. She seemed to pull passions from him that surprised even him.

"I am sorry, Brien. I had no cause to say that." Seeing she did not respond, he went on. "I do not know what changed you toward me, but I am sure you did not come to me from idle curiosity."

Her shoulder slumped slightly and her head bowed. Her hair veiled her face from him as he moved to one side. He ached to touch her.

"I do not wish any bitterness between us." His voice was thick. Unable to gain a response, he walked slowly to the door and was gone.

The new day dawned bright and cool. Brien went on deck after breakfast—eager to escape the stifling cabin and anxious to appear as normal as possible. The breeze ruffled her skirts and made her pull her cloak tightly about her. Dyso had accompanied her on deck and stood looking out to sea, a strange peacefulness on his fierce features. Brien left his side and strolled to the bow.

She did not hear Aaron approach and lean on the rail behind her. His voice startled her.

"It won't be long before you'll glimpse America for the first time."

She was glad to have a neutral topic to talk to him about.

"Is it very beautiful, this new land?" She searched the horizon that his hand had indicated while her mind whirled. She felt a need to set things right with him and this might be her best opportunity.

"Some parts are magnificent. But there is poverty and hardship as well. I admit that it fascinates me as much now as when I first set eyes on it." He turned to her with a new light in his eyes, a passion unlike any she had seen there before.

"The place has such vigor. It throbs with life the way Britain did a century ago. In this country a man is just that—a man. No more, no less. There is no privileged elite—except that of courage, skill, and cleverness."

Brien surprised herself with the observation: "You love it, don't you—this new land? It is in your face as you speak."

He frowned thoughtfully and answered, "I suppose I do. I never considered it that way." Her insight unsettled him and he looked away. "In America a man's sons can make their own lives—become whatever they can become, instead of stifling under centuries of tradition."

Brien knew he revealed a very personal part of himself in this statement.

"And daughters?" she asked. "Are women there still bought and sold with dowries and not taught to read, lest they learn how little of the world they may have?"

Aaron was jolted by her question. Before her, all women were . . . women. He never considered they might have dreams, ambitions, or curiosity, except in social or domestic ways. Now with a single thought, she turned his neat "modern" view of the world upside down.

She answered for him, reading his answer in his silence.

"No, it will be the same there for women. Men will cast off the bondage of class, privilege, and tradition. Even so, they will press it cruelly on the women they claim to love so well." Her countenance was sad,

241

wistful.

He was shaken by her words, and by how surely they fit her life. How could any fair, honest man fail to see what she had said? He felt awkward suddenly, and very ordinary.

She turned to him, unsure of what to say. "I apologize to you for the terrible things I said to you last night." Her words were low and earnest. He stared at her numbly.

"I had no right to be angry with you. Pride and stubbornness are my greatest faults. It seems you ran afoul of both at once. I came to you because I wanted you—that was all." She looked down at her hands as they clutched her cloak tightly. "You bear too many of my secrets now." She raised her eyes to him and the misery in his face jolted her.

"I have made a mess of my life thus far. I shall try not to tangle you in it further." She touched his arm timidly, walked quickly to the hatchway, and was gone.

Aaron stood frozen by the rail. A sweet confusion of longing and misery welled up inside him. He wanted this extraordinary woman more than anything in his life. He knew now he would never be content without her.

Nothing in his life had prepared him for the wealth of new emotions she laid bare in him. It frightened him, but—Dear God—how he wanted to savor them. It was like being reborn. The whole world outside him vibrated with new color and texture and meaning.

He had avoided entanglements at all costs; from youth he had disavowed all claims made on him. And now in a few moments, the pattern was so totally reversed that he reeled from it.

He needed Brien. She haunted his every moment, waking, sleeping. He hungered for her laugh, her look, her kiss, the sound of her voice. He had joined with her, and she had become a part of him—as necessary to his life as breathing or eating.

For the first time since he was a lad of seven he knew real despair. How to make her his, without forcing her—possessing her? He must have her with him, willing, loving. What would it take for her to need him as much as he needed her?

The rebellious pragmatism of his spirit reasserted itself. He would have her, be with her. He would find a way. She had wanted him, too; she had admitted as much. She would want him again; he would see to that. His shoulders straightened purposefully as he strode to the quarterdeck.

Dyso, watching from the rail, had seen it all. Their words were withheld from him by the distance, but he read their faces well. A smile crept over his scarred face. He walked to the bow with his rolling gait, watching the determination on the captain's handsome face.

Seventeen

The *Secret* docked in Boston on a drizzly gray afternoon. It was not long before Lady Brien's message to Silas Hastings bore fruit, in the form of a stately enclosed carriage dispatched to greet her.

A sense of loss swept over Brien as they descended the gangway toward the dock where the carriage waited. She tossed her head defiantly and ignored it. She had come with a mission to fulfill and now she must succeed.

A tall, gaunt and graying man stepped forward to greet her as she neared the carriage. He wore a pair of spectacles and Brien was struck by the oddity of their appearance. Only then did she recognize Silas Hastings plus fifteen years.

He bowed reverently, taking her hand. His face changed remarkably as it warmed with a genuine smile.

"Lady Brien," he said affectionately, but with a tinge of deference. "I can hardly believe my eyes! What a beautiful young woman you have become! I believe I saw you last as a bright and inquisitive six-year-old child.''

"And you, sir, were a clever-minded and most tolerant clerk. You managed to conduct business and occupy my father's 'shadow' at the same time.''

Aaron stood by, amused to think of her as a troublesome, precocious child. He stepped forward and cleared his throat discreetly.

Brien turned her head toward Aaron, not taking her hands from Silas' grasp. "Oh, Silas, this is the captain with whom we sailed. Aaron Durham.'' She conquered her irritation at his presence. She would have preferred to greet her host alone and to start fresh in this venture, with no haunting reminders of the past or her journey.

Still, Brien managed to appear charming, even gracious.

"Ah, then 'tis you I've heard of,'' Silas proclaimed as he extricated his hand to extend it to the handsome captain. Seeing Aaron's puzzlement, he went on, ". . . Your ship—she's a new design and all that Harold Caswell can talk of.''

"Ah, yes. You know Harold, then?''

"We dine together whenever I am in New York. He sings your praises loudly. I would be pleased to see your ship in detail.'' He glanced past Aaron to the sleek hull behind him.

"I cannot be held responsible for Caswell's boasts, but I shall be pleased to show you my ship, sir.'' Aaron leaned back jauntily on one leg as he basked in the older man's admiration. Brien thought he looked far too smug for her liking.

"Forgive me, Captain. Permit me to complete the introduction. This gentleman is Silas Hastings, my father's agent in the colonies, and my host.''

They nodded politely before Silas turned to Brien once more.

"Helen, my wife, was distraught to miss greeting you here, but she will soon bear our child and I could not allow her to risk it. I thought you would understand."

"Of course," Brien smiled, slightly surprised that this efficient, modest man had enough passion in him to father a child at his age. Somehow he had seemed a singular feature of her father's business. She reproved herself for such unfairness. He was not ancient or infirm; why should she be surprised that he had a life of his own—and a family?

The trunks and bags were soon loaded on the carriage and they were on their way through narrow cobbled streets that hummed with activity. Brien watched the city from the carriage window, absorbed by the activity and surprised by the familiar scenes and dress of the people. She had expected more exotic sights and now realized the wisdom of Aaron's statement that the two peoples had too much in common to be separated by petty grievances. Still, there was a difference she found unlabelable.

She realized that she gawked like a six-year-old once more—and truly, she did not care. In this new place, she felt a freedom to do, be, whatever she pleased. She turned to Silas and saw unconcealed pride in his face, delight in her fascination.

"So much activity! It's wonderful, Silas!"

"I thought you would enjoy it. I was not terribly shocked when your father wrote that you were coming as his 'partner.' Even as a child you had a head for business. We were devastated at the news of your bereavement, Lady Brien." He squeezed her hand gently, unaware of the familiarity of the gesture.

"Life goes on, Silas. Father and I have become much closer since my widowhood. I plagued him mercilessly to make me his protégé. Now I must not let him down." Her face took on a somber look. "Tell me, do you think we'll be able to find a buyer soon?"

Studying his hat in his hands, Silas smiled. "On that issue I do have a bit of good news. The details can wait, but a Dutchman named Van Zandt has recently made inquiries into purchasing Weston Trading. He is apparently a wealthy man—and shrewd in business. I have shown him the warehouse and shops, but have delayed discussion of any price until you arrived. He stated interest in the lot; however, I'm told he drives a hard bargain, Lady Brien."

"Just Brien will be fine, Silas." She flashed him a dazzling smile. "I have it on good authority that titles mean little here now." She gazed once more out the window at the houses they passed.

"Mr. Van Zandt will find me a ready match for his bargaining."

Silas smiled quietly. If he had doubted Weston's wisdom in sending his daughter to conduct the business, he forgot it now. She was clever, most charming, and quite determined. He was heartened at last and looked forward to the first meeting between buyer and seller.

Helen Hastings was in the parlor of their three-story brick home when they arrived from the ship. The house was not imposing from the outside, but had an eye-pleasing solidity about it. Inside it seemed much larger, comfortable, and was tastefully decorated in blues and dark reds.

Helen waddled into the front hall, pink-faced and a bit out of breath. Her bulging middle gave evidence of her advanced condition and Brien marveled that she could walk at all. One look at the woman's pleasant, round face and Brien liked her already.

"Oh, Silas," Helen breathed, "Is this your Lady

Brien?'' She took Brien's hands and squeezed them. "She's lovely!" Her open admiration drew scarlet to Brien's cheeks.

"Brien, this is my wife, Helen." His proud, indulgent look made Brien want to giggle. Snatches of his usual sober, proper manner reminded her of days long past.

"I am delighted to meet you, Helen. But I fear I have come at a most inconvenient time for you." Brien's eyes lowered to Helen's monumental middle.

"Heavens, no!" Helen laughed. "This is our fourth; I'm an old hand by now. I'll be glad of the company. This last waiting is the hardest."

Helen gave the servants orders as to the trunks and rooms and led Brien in to the parlor. The room was bright in the late afternoon gloom and Brien felt more at home here than in her own chambers at Harcourt.

Helen sat down heavily on the stout sofa and sighed with relief as she propped her feet up on a stool.

"And your voyage, Lady Brien, how was it?" She was breathless with the exertion.

"Fascinating . . . and tiring. I had never been at sea, well, not in my remembrance. This is all truly an adventure for me." Helen drank in her words.

"And what do you think of us colonials?" Helen grinned mischievously.

"My first impressions were from a bumpy carriage ride," Brien disclaimed, "but I admit, I'm fascinated. It's so much like England, yet different in a way that is hard to pinpoint. And your speech—it's enchanting."

Helen smiled, well satisfied with her guest's response. "Silas said you were ever the adventuresome one as a child. He's always spoken fondly of you and Lord Weston. I hope we can make your stay enjoyable as well as profitable, Lady Brien."

"Just Brien, please, Helen." Brien entreated. "My

only regret is that it took a crisis to prod me to come. Father would have loved coming too, but for his health. I shall have to enjoy it for us both.''

A stout, older woman entered with a tea tray just then, and Helen gave orders for a bath to be drawn for Brien.

Brien's eyes were wistful. A bath. "Oh, I'd be so grateful. After so long at sea, I can think of nothing I'd like better than a long soaking bath.''

"Would you mind pouring tea? I'm afraid I shan't reach.'' Helen's plea was real, as she soon demonstrated.

Brien laughed. "Delighted to.''

After tea with Helen and a luxuriously long bath, Brien was treated to sumptuous dinner with full service, accompanied by excellent French wines. She wondered wryly what Jeremy Wilton would think of these "barbaric" colonists. After dinner, she retired early on her first day in America. She had no trouble sleeping in the bed that did not sway beneath her suggestively.

By morning a refreshed young woman rose well after dawn and gazed at the neat garden beneath her second-story window. Brien felt more relaxed and at peace than she had for months. Flowers blossomed in spring profusion in the walled garden below her window, wafting up sweetened air through the slightly opened window.

The release of tension pointed to the strain she had felt during the entire voyage. And now her spirits soared free, unpinioned by the newness of the land and the adventure that lay before her. New confidence filled her. She was determined to strike a good bargain and see the best of America—this exciting new world—to boot.

At breakfast, Brien joined Helen and Silas and met their three children. All three had curly brown hair and clear blue eyes. The youngest, Robert, climbed onto Brien's lap as soon as she was seated. Despite his mother's remonstrations, he would not be dislodged, and in the end, took his breakfast on the fairest seat in Boston. The lad's cuddly roundness fascinated her, and she squeezed him affectionately several times before he left her to play in the garden with his brother and sister.

"Helen, your children are wonderful."

"Thank you, Brien, You are so kind. But you must not indulge Robert too much. He already thinks rules were made for other people." She smiled wanly. "He is in for a surprise when this babe arrives. He'll no longer be the center of the world anymore."

Silas laid his large, thin hand over his wife's. "He'll adjust, I'm sure. The others have had to."

Brien thought how lovingly Silas looked at his plump wife. It was clear Helen adored her tall, rail-thin husband whose graying temples told of a difference in their ages. They were domestic tranquility. Finding herself staring at them, she was quite annoyed by her reaction. She should be delighted that Silas had such a vibrant young family. But Silas drew her attention from these musings.

". . . I hope you won't mind touring the offices and warehouses on Saturday. I thought you would like to rest and see some of our city before taking on the business."

"Very thoughtful, Silas," Brien mused. "I'd love to see more of Boston. Would it be possible for me to walk about—perhaps visit the market?"

"Of course, dear," Helen put in. Then she turned to

her husband. "Why don't you take the morning and show her some of the city, Silas. Then, later, she can return to visit places that interest her." She smiled impishly. "She's brought her own protector."

Brien felt sheepish, suddenly. "I suppose you must wonder about him."

"I meant no offense," Helen entreated.

"None taken," Brien assured her. "Dyso was my husband's servant. He is dumb, but hears well and can speak some with his hands." She lowered her eyes and voice instinctively. "The night of the fire that claimed my husband, Dyso carried me, unconscious, from the burning building. He has been with me since—and is invaluable. He will be glad to help you in any way he can while we are here."

"Brien what was your husband like." Helen's face was wistful as she raised one hand to silence Silas' objection before it was pronounced.

"He . . . he was not an ordinary man. Raoul Trechaud was the third son of the Marquis de Sanier of France. He was dark and quite charming. My father found him a quick and able student of commerce." She paused to word the next part carefully. "We were only married a month. We did not have time to make ours a proper marriage. I was only beginning to know him when the fire occurred." Every word carried the weight of truth.

Helen sighed heavily. "Not even a child to comfort you." Her eyes were moist.

Brien now squirmed uncomfortably in her chair. "It is less painful now. Time does heal wounds. I have decided to devote myself to my father's business and to charity work."

"Ah, but you will marry again," Helen declared. "There will be plenty of time for babes and such."

Brien thought to forestall any matchmaking Helen

251

might have in mind.

"I fear not, dear Helen. I am reluctant to ever marry again. I enjoy my life now far too much—and the freedom it affords."

"Not marry . . . ever?" Helen was incredulous. "Oh, no, Brien. You cannot mourn such a short marriage forever."

"Helen!" Silas roared in exasperation. His startled wife turned to him, paling. Obviously his ire was seldom heard in this house.

"Brien has candidly informed us of her reluctance to marry—and to discuss marriage. We will abide by her wishes." He waggled his finger at her comically. "No prying and no plotting!"

He turned to Brien with an unaccustomed redness in his gaunt face. "Helen is loathe to let any unmarried person pass under our roof without attempting to remedy what she considers to be God's great oversight."

"Silas!" Helen flushed, pouting some.

" 'Tis truth, Brien. I maintain she could find no one to pair me with and so she married me herself, so as not to spoil her record."

Brien marveled later that Silas and Helen were so unlike and yet so well suited to each other. Her early impressions of America were the same: many people, quite unlike in dreams, background, and aims, yet living together as though they belonged there. And so they did, she reckoned.

The sights and smells of the city were a blend of the familiar and the foreign. Just when she would find a street that she vowed to be a duplicate of a Bristol lane or a Cambridge street, she caught a glimpse of a deerskin shirt or heard a rolling accent that reminded her of the comparative newness of civilization here. She was in a different country now, but it was tantalizingly easy to forget.

Not long after her arrival an invitation was delivered to the Hastings' household which included their lovely guest. It was to be a party, Brien's first social in the new world.

Brien felt a surge of exhilaration at the thought. She grasped the tops of her knees and hugged them to her as she sat on her bed, clad only in her plain silk wrapper. She was supposed to be resting, as the rest of the house surely was, in preparation for a night of merriment and delight held in her honor. Even though the affair was to be held in the home of a friend, the Hastings household was charged with anticipation. Brien was infected massively with the contagion. Even Helen would join them this eve, in spite of Silas' stern advice against it. He feared her slightest exertion would hasten the babe's entrance into the world—or harm it.

Anticipation prickled up Brien's spine as the carriage drew up in front of one of Boston's finest homes. As they stood in the hallway, waiting to be announced, she was astonished at the elegance about her and her gaze roamed the new Hepplewhite lowboy and chairs that were all the fashion in the best homes of London. The round carpet beneath their feet was soft and richly hued and above her head a leaded crystal chandelier poured forth golden light to bathe her in splendor. She smiled secretly at the memory of one braying ass who decried these people as savages and beasts. Would that he might see her now, she chuckled.

At their announcement a modest but increasing wave of attention and admiration swept through the throng of brightly clothed guests. Brien was now doubly conscious of the light green silk taffeta she wore which sported no panniers, but a bustle and bow behind, over her hips. Lamont had assured her this new style would flatter her excellent figure far more than the panniers which even now began to wane in popularity on the continent. She had remained unconvinced and only agreed to the one gown of that style to appease his artistic sensibilities. Only now did she realize the full extent of her daring in trying the new fashion here.

But she needn't have worried at all. She appeared a goddess, a conquering queen—an apparition of flowing grace, unbounded by trend or artifice. Her tawny hair cascaded with flowers down the back of her head and over one tantalizingly bare shoulder. Her gown was cut low in front, as was the common fashion, but everywhere followed the luscious curves of her own winsome form. The light green and white of the dress cooled the heat of her revealed shape, taming the effect—making her quite approachable.

Her eyes, great blue pools, vied with her womanly curves and her generous peach-hued lips for the viewer's gaze. Not a man in the room escaped entrapment in the snare of her dazzling charms and sparkling wit. When she looked at a man it was with directness and interest in his words, rather than the cloying, insipid adoration of the other young women. Here was a woman who truly listened to a man and more, understood the affairs that concern him greatly: land, finance, and trade. And she was all the more desirable for it.

The string quartet wound up and handily delivered a set of lively country dances, into which Brien whirled and skipped as though she had danced them all her life. Toward the end of the set she found her partner suddenly withdrawing, bowing courteously to his replacement. And she stifled a gasp as Aaron Durham put one warm hand to her waist and took her left hand in his, drawing her back a bit too close to him. She quickly remedied the situation, pulling abruptly away, her consternation plain on her face.

The maneuver and her reaction to her partner was not missed and a few polite guffaws from onlookers tamed her display of indignation. He had not even spoken to her, the cad—only set his roving hands to her eagerly and in front of a whole roomful of people. She steamed inwardly each time they returned to their partners, as is the way of country dances, and he sought each time to add some new affront, some fresh indignity to the boiling pride within her. He held her too tightly, brushed her breast with his arm as they turned, or breathed into her ear as they promenaded. She was being ravished by degrees in the middle of a crowded dance floor!

By the end of the set she was quite red-faced and hoped that a demure smile would let it pass for the effects of exertion in the lively dance. She could scarcely restrain herself from lifting her skirts and running away from the cad when the music ended. But Aaron took her hand as if reading her thoughts and, holding it quite captively, planted a moist and most ungentlemanly kiss upon it. She jerked her hand away only to have the other captured in its place and found herself being forced along into the other salon where wine and punch were freely dispensed.

"How dare you!" she muttered for his ears only as he held her unseemly close to him along the way. "Who let you into this good man's house?"

Aaron smiled confidently as he nodded to an acquaintance along the way. "You did not enjoy our dance, Brien? Pity, I found it quite the most enjoyable I have had in a long while."

"How could I enjoy it with you pawing at me?" she snapped. "Had I known you would be here I most certainly would have declined the honor—I would not have appeared.'' She lied, she knew, but her injured dignity bade her wield some retort.

Without relaxing his grip on her, he handed her a cup of the cold punch and she accepted it, careful to keep her face averted and to smile convincingly at those other guests who even now watched them expectantly. As he reached for a cup for himself, he loosened his grip on her and she seized the opportunity to fly, turning quickly away. She heard her gown give a sickening rip and she stopped dead, finding herself caught fast by her skirt, the longer length of the graceful bustle trapped by something. Looking down she found the culprit—Aaron's tall, polished boot. She stepped back quickly, hoping no one else heard, and still not looking at him, muttered for his ears only, ''Sir, you are standing on my gown. Is it your intention to disrobe me here, in front of witnesses?''

''Indeed, I do seem to have caught some bit of fluff underfoot,'' came the reply with a tinkle of amusement to it.

She looked up, aghast at his coolness and brashness. He had trapped her with her own garments and held her to his side forcibly. She searched for a stinging retort, but found her anger cheated by a wave of other sensation. She now realized why she had refused to look at him, she had been afraid of this very feeling.

He wore a hunter green velvet coat, cut away at the front to sweep gracefully toward the longer ''tails'' in back. His vest was of cream velvet and his breeches, of the finest light wool, matched the vest in color. Plain linen ruffles graced his wrists and an emerald cravat bound his handsome throat. He was magnificent, filling her head in an instant and soon her lungs as well with his manly smell of sandalwood and soap. He overwhelmed her with his looks and his proximity. She had never seen him so arrayed.

"Will you please remove your oafish foot from my gown?" She affected a sweet smile for the benefit of the onlookers.

"If you promise not to flee like some trapped sparrow," he grinned. "I would spend some time with you this eve . . . and give you a proper welcome to the colonies."

"Some time? With me?" she demurred spitefully. "Am I to feel honored by your interest? Your heavy-handed—nay, footed—tactics are more than enough to disenchant even the coarsest maid, sir."

This was not going exactly as he had planned. With all these nitwits gawking about them, he could hardly make progress. Ye gods! What had possessed him to step on her skirt?

"Then come with me to the garden and I will promise faithfully not to tread further on your apparel."

Her eyes flickered brightly as she gazed up at him and she affected a smile. There was great temptation in his handsome eyes, but she thrust it away from her as if it were poison. The rake! Demanding her obedience to his whim!

He mistook the momentary softening in her face and moved his foot from her gown, confident now of victory. It took him a full minute to realize she was moving away from him and definitely not toward the gardens. He cursed himself for seven kinds of a fool as he watched her ripe curves sway gently further and further from his grasp. Damn the clumsy beggar he felt! How stupid of him to think she would surrender to him so easily. Had he learned nothing of her?

His eyes roamed absently over the guests as he re-filled his cup, waiting for his anger to cool. A smile registered on his mind and brought slowly into focus two large brown eyes and shining dark hair draped alluringly over smooth, clear skin. A girl, a lovely girl, peered delicately over a punch cup at him and now blushed becomingly as she found he returned her look.

The evening might not be a total waste, Aaron thought, smiling openly at the girl's boldness. So he would disenchant the coarsest maids, eh? Well that was yet to be seen. And he moved toward the inviting eyes of one of the many true conquests he had already made that evening.

Brien's indignation cooled quickly at the sight of Aaron whirling a local, dark-haired beauty onto the dance floor, especially since she had just declined several earnest offers for the same. She had made her way to Helen's side and now sat by her friend on the settee, arranging her position so that she had a partial view of the dancers—not that it made a whit of difference to her, she thought stonily. Let him strut and prance, she burned inwardly, it made her no difference.

But again and again her eyes were drawn to the dance floor where Aaron's tall form bent and swayed about and over the little dark maid who gazed up at him as though he were the angel Gabriel, come to save. She noted that Aaron's hands lingered at the girl's waist and that he gave her over to another partner reluctantly. Brien's cheeks grew crimson as her conversation grew nonexistent. Helen cast a doubtful glance her way and slyly watched the room to see what sight caused her lovely guest to frown when she thought no one watched. But her search was fruitless.

"Brien, dear, you must not feel you need keep me company. Do go and dance and enjoy the evening to the fullest!" Helen patted her hand and then plied her fan earnestly to hide her searching gaze.

Tearing her mind from the dancing figures, Brien answered what she had heard with only half an ear. "Of course nothing is wrong; why, should it be? I am so enjoying the soirée, Helen." But her face and manner bore no amusement and she turned to see Helen's open puzzlement.

There was no help for it! The wretched man was spoiling her evening completely! The cad—recklessly plying the same irksome techniques on that poor innocent girl as he had only minutes before tried on her. Her face colored with shame to think how effective those loathsome touches and whisperings had been.

Just then, the set ended; Brien was again besieged by swains seeking her as partner and this time she accepted with a gaiety to her manner she little felt.

To her outrage, Aaron again took the floor, this time with a willowy maid who looked to be no more than seventeen. And in a few short steps and turns, Brien glimpsed the poor besotted girl gazing up at him with huge, cow-brown eyes beaming adoration. Disgusting!

And so it went for several dances, each choosing lively partners and stridently ignoring the other until the floor was charged with the friction between them, as tangible as smoke on the air, if less visible. The other dancers sensed it, not realizing from whom it emanated and its cause. At the end of the set, Brien withdrew discreetly to another room, stopping to chat with several new acquaintances along the way.

Then as she made her way to an open French door leading to the portico outside, she felt her elbow gripped tightly by a large hand and felt herself hurried along into the cooler night air and friendly semidark outside. She knew resisting was futile, just as she knew without looking who owned the viselike grip. Her heart leaped suddenly at the knowledge.

Anger rose inside her at this new indignity, but it was anger mingled with triumph; her ploy had succeeded. And had she time to delve further, she would have found delight hiding beneath it all.

Out of sight of the doorway now, she was jerked

about forcibly and slammed against an iron-hard chest which forced the breath out of her with a little "woof." Before she could draw breath again, big hungry lips covered hers and roughly bent across them, commanding a response from her innermost depths.

At the instant of contact with Aaron's big, hard body, Brien had lost the struggle, giving up even her need for breath under the onslaught of his enraged passion. Now weak with a peculiar hunger in her loins, she could only pour against him for support and surge upward to meet his hot, demanding mouth. All thoughts of conqueror and vanquished were gone now, lost in the searing of their coming together.

Just when she thought her air-starved lungs would burst—and that she would gladly endure it, Aaron lifted his face from hers to delve deeply into the closeness of her now-dark eyes. His face was hidden in the shadows above hers and she could not see the tension it contained.

"Don't ever do that to me again," he commanded hoarsely.

Her arms had wound themselves about him and now abruptly withdrew, as if scalded by his heat.

"Do what?" she demanded, swallowing hard to alleviate the choking in her throat. She pushed hard against his chest, freeing herself unexpectedly from his unwary grip. She backed away from him and soon found herself against a balustrade and most grateful for its support.

His arms twitched convulsively with the urge to grasp her again and hold the cool sweetness of her against him. But he knew the moment was gone. Now only words would win the evening, and invariably, in dealing with her, he chose the wrong ones.

"Don't toy with other men in my presence, Brien." It was a command and Brien's mouth dropped open in a surprised "Oh."

"In your pres—How dare you speak to me so! How dare you!" He talked as though he owned her!

"How dare you, milady, flaunt yourself about half-naked and ask the men of the world to remain sane and courteous—and at a safe distance. If I hadn't taken you from there, some wine-maddened swain in rut would surely have."

"Flaunt myself!" She saw everything suddenly in shades of red and crimson. "And what pray are you? Saved from one rake by another with the same intention! And you presume to dictate decorum to me, when this evening it is you who have lusted and panted after and pawed over every woman here capable of walking!"

Having cooled some, a feat of mightiest will, Aaron paused at the retort and threw back his head and laughed heartily, a clear, free rumble from his depths. And in his laughter, Brien found a balm for her own peevish pride, a glimpse of the irony run full tilt. They had played the same game, both with unimaginable success. And how silly, how wasteful a game it had been.

Brien laughed now at the absurdity of it, her throaty musical tones seeping through whatever bastion of resolve Aaron had wrought around his true affections.

Brien stopped laughing, eyes moist and glistening. "Then we have both played the game well, Captain. I fear as time goes on we may find we have other unsavory habits in common. I pray not."

Aaron shifted in the light so that his eyes glinted, revealing his pleasure in her admission. "There is one more thing we have in common, my love. . . ."

The casual endearment caused Brien to breathe in sharply. "And what might that be?" she sparkled. Even in the dim light, she glowed, inviting his touch on

261

her pale skin.

"We want—need each other." He smiled, reaching for her hand, which was yielded to him reluctantly.

Brien was one to honor an honest remark and found herself surprised indeed that she felt no anger at his blunt appraisal of their relationship. But how then did one rebuff so honest a man, when rebuff was not uppermost in one's desires? One need not dispute the statement at all—only redirect the thoughts into more rational channels.

"Such sentiment need not impair either of us, Captain. As I have seen tonight, you enjoy the game too well to be confined to wanting what you cannot have. You soon will find easier game." She smiled directly and confidently into his face, once more in control of her reeling emotions.

He chuckled and took her chin in his hand. "But I'll find none livelier, that is sure." She made no move to free herself and he studied her intently, feeling that warmth again rising in his veins. Instinct told him a softer tact was now required. He released her chin and his hands sought hers. He flashed a perfect smile, softening his features with an almost boyish charm. This clearly was no time for sparring.

"Dance with me, Brien, and in all respects, I'll show my most courteous self." His gaze held the warm promise of a new experience that Brien yearned to have.

A momentary frown flitted across her lovely brow. The request was too courteous to suit her and she found the old suspiciousness on the rise again. She knew him to be a man of his word; still she did not trust him, or was it that she did not trust herself? That unruly sentiment she so feared seized her and bent her to a softer response than she would have liked to hear from her own lips.

"If your word is true, then I'll have you for a partner." She looked down as if to hide the anticipation in her face, and moved toward the door.

Inside, the set of dancers were reforming and Brien paused to take Aaron's arm as he led her onto the floor. She was surprised at the ease now between them and at the graceful flow of their movements. His every step carried her with respect around the floor. When she glimpsed his face she saw there undisguised adoration, mingled with deference. It shook her to the very core. This was less bearable than his frontal assault. She found herself losing ground with each second that passed. Others looking on could tell a truce was struck, if not a real peace made.

Near the end of the first dance, Brien saw Silas motion to her from the doorway, and as the music died, she hurried to him, leaving Aaron standing, talking to another exhausted dancer.

Silas indicated that Helen was feeling quite tired and he wanted to take her home. He insisted that Brien stay and that he would find her a proper escort home.

Brien glanced nervously, longingly over her shoulder to where Aaron had just found her absent and now looked about for her. "No, Silas, I wouldn't dream of it. Besides, I'm quite tired myself. I shall go home with you now." And she took Silas's arm hurriedly, turning her back just as she saw Aaron start toward her.

But as they approached their evening's host, Silas was stopped by an acquaintance begging introduction to his fair guest. Brien smiled engagingly but her anxiety mounted furiously with her need to be gone. She was unsure of herself because of what had passed between her and Aaron just now and longed for time and distance to quell her fears. She felt control of her own unruly emotions slipping from her grasp.

Then a familiar voice rolled beside them. "Your pardon, Mr. Hastings.''

They turned and Brien gasped, startled by the depth of her reaction to him. But she quickly covered her reaction behind her brisk fan, wishing with all her heart that she could shrink from Aaron's penetrating gaze and knowing that to live with herself, she must face him.

''Ah, Captain Durham, I believe.'' Silas extended his hand in greeting. ''A pleasure, sir. I did not realize you were here this eve. A pity that we are just leaving . . . my wife, Helen, is quite tired and must go home.''

Brien felt Aaron's searching gaze upon her and colored in a rush of confusion. Why must she endure this torture? Then a thought struck her as she realized that Aaron's eyes lingered longer than was prudent upon her, under Silas' perceptive regard. Dear heaven, what if Aaron offered to see her home?

'' 'Tis a shame.'' Aaron's words held an irritating duplicity that stung Brien sharply. Then he tore his gaze from her and continued in a much lighter vein. ''I wonder if you would care to see the *Secret* tomorrow, sir. You had expressed interest in her before. I have the afternoon free and would gladly escort you myself.''

A light frown flitted across Brien's brow at his sudden shift in moods. It was as though he swept all consideration of her aside in an instant, and it piqued her no small amount.

''I would like nothing more.'' A schoolboy's delight showed in Silas' face. ''I've been fascinated by ships since I was a lad. Yours, I'm told, harbingers a great change in the craft.''

Aaron pushed back his elegant green coat and put both hands on his hips in a fashion more suited to a seaman than a gentleman. He leaned back on one leg, grinning his pleasure, every inch the proud, cocky male that Brien had sworn to avoid—mostly because he was so irresistible.

264

"I'm no prophet, sir, but our first run was better by far than even my own estimates. As to her smoothness, you must ask your guest." He turned those disturbing eyes once more on Brien.

Silas turned to her. "The Captain desires a testimonial, Lady Brien."

Affecting a coolness she little felt, Brien drew herself straighter. "I have traveled little, and thus have nothing to compare it with. The crossing seemed smooth enough and the captain and crew were most diligent in the performance of their duties. Beyond that, I am unqualified to render judgment."

Noting Brien's change of mood, Silas studied the pair before him, wondering briefly how well acquainted they might have become on the voyage. It did not seem likely that Brien could have avoided or ignored the rakish good looks and self-assured ease of the man who captained the vessel she sailed. In ten day's time he had seen her smile and sparkle and only now, confronted by this dashing ship's officer, did she show reserve and assume the superior air common to her class. Silas, ever perceptive, wondered why.

"Two o'clock, then?" Aaron's clear voice rumbled forth, drawing him back from his musings.

"Splendid!" Silas answered. "I shall meet you at the dock then."

Aaron turned again to Brien and bowed with irksome extravagance. "Madame Trechaud." And he was gone.

Striding to the door, without taking leave of his host, Aaron felt a rush of annoyance, and he drew a heavy breath as the servant swung wide the heavy door to permit him to exit. Once in the cooler, fragrant air, his thoughts turned darkly to the one who beset him mercilessly, both in her presence and away from it.

Capricious witch! One moment she berated his lust and the next she spurned his courtesy. But as his horse turned out of the yard and set a leisurely pace along the dirt and cobblestone street, his face softened as he remembered that last dance with her. She had responded to his every touch and blossomed delectably beside him. And he had not missed the secret little smile she aimed at him. Nay, he had made progress this eve; he would bet on that.

How much progress, he would have been overjoyed to know, for Brien was in turmoil during the long coach ride home. The knowing look on his face as he made that mocking bow now rose again before her mind's eye to taunt her anew. And she was at a loss to explain her own feelings as they reeled and tumbled and roiled about inside her. This last experience with him was unlike anything she had experienced with him before. She felt honored and held with respect. He was more than attentive—almost . . . loving—as he held her and touched her waist and hands. There was no assumption or arrogance in his manner, no taunt to remind her of his secret knowledge of her body and desire. He was, she realized, all she feared he could be . . . all that she wanted in a man. How could he have so reversed her thinking in so few minutes? Aye, he made more progress this night than he knew.

She sighed sharply, causing both Helen and Silas to look at her wonderingly. But she was absorbed in thought and making firm resolutions to herself and missed entirely the glances they exchanged.

Dear heaven, must she contend with that rake in the new world as well as the old?

The following evening, as they dined, Silas announced they would have a guest for dinner on Saturday, apologizing to Helen for having promised without consulting her. Brien was enthuiastic, but the mention

266

of Aaron Durham's name poured over her like a pail of icy water. Helen noted well her response but was too polite to comment, though her curiosity was at full flood. Throughout the rest of the elegant meal, Silas' unceasing praise of the man and his foresight and ingenuity were like salt in an open wound to Brien.

The time until Saturday passed all too quickly for Brien. She enjoyed the quiet mornings with Helen and her children and her afternoon walks about town, escorted by Dyso and occasionally her little maid. They drew curious stares, due to her elegant dress and beauty, and Dyso's size and formidable appearance. News of her, her wealth and beauty, spread quickly through the city and everywhere people were anxious to greet her and to see for themselves if the stories were true. Her warm smile and even-handed pleasantness endeared her to many who had expected more noble airs from one of her wealth and station.

Eighteen

Brien had never completely comprehended the space needed to store three hundred barrels of oil or one hundred fifty bales of cotton. Most of the decisions involving a direct inspection of cargoes or warehouses, her father had reserved for himself, occasionally leading to a flaring confrontation with his headstrong daughter. But usually, his blend of authority and logic prevailed and Brien stayed behind, poring over books while he went to the docks or warehouses. Now she felt the thrill of discovery as she contemplated the huge brick structure before her. This was her warehouse, her business—her adventure.

A gray drizzle weighted the morning air that Saturday and muffled the sound of the horses' hooves against the ill-paved streets. Now she would have time to inspect the business first hand and she vowed not to miss a single detail. Inside, Weston Trading was a fascinating jumble of smells and sights and workmen bustling about moving crates on small-wheeled carts. Brien paused often to ask questions about the contents of an exotic-looking crate or barrel, or to seek the market price of a given commodity. Her thoughtful gaze and penetrating questions both impressed and challenged Silas, who proved a worthy source for all her inquiries.

At last they made their way to the office, where Silas presented her with tally sheets and manifests and pointed out the salient features of their record-keeping system. Brien was glad now to have found time to study the ledgers Silas had brought home for her. She was at last drawing a fair idea of their predicament. For two hours more, they discussed the properties, goods, debtors, and stores. Brien was convinced that Silas had done everything possible to forestall the crisis that loomed upon them now. Only two things remained to be settled.

"Silas, what will you do when it is sold? Will you work for Van Zandt?"

"No. I don't fancy working for another this late in life. Helen's father left her most of his estate and we've made prudent investments with the profits. Over the years I have gleaned a generous share of Weston Trading's profits and have put them to good use as well. We'll be well fixed, no matter what comes to pass with this business. My only regret is that it must be sold to strangers. If I could have put hands on all my investments, I'd have purchased the company myself. I've put much of myself into this business."

"You'll receive a share of the price it brings." She raised one hand to staunch the protest. "That is our wish—father's and mine. And nothing is so immovable as the decision of a Weston."

Silas shrugged in surrender. "You've always been more than fair with me and I know Sir Lawrence is taking a walloping on this one. I know there's nothing to do but sell—but I haven't accepted it yet."

"There's the last of it, Silas. What price shall we ask

for your life's work?'' It pained her to reduce it all to a level so impersonal as money.

"Um-m. The whole lot for twelve thousand sterling—and not a whit less. It would be a bargain for any buyer at that price."

"And what will Van Zandt offer?"

"He is shrewd, by repute. He might begin as low as eight thousand. I'm told that bargaining is first his sport, then his livelihood."

"And is he trustworthy?"

"I have heard nothing to say he is not. But I know he is not a well-loved man, for all his money."

"Well, at least I have a place to start." Brien sighed. "Arrange a meeting for us next week if possible. And cross your fingers for luck."

Dressing for dinner Saturday eve was more worrisome than usual. Jeannie fussed interminably over her hair and the emerald silk that was sewn with lace in each seam had to be pressed twice before it looked properly done. Helen had said nothing about other guests and Brien had been reluctant to ask, lest she seem overly anxious. Helen's pointed comments and prying questions had convinced Brien that to say anything about Aaron Durham would be tantamount to an admission.

Aaron had arrived when Brien swept into the drawing room. He leaned casually on the mantelpiece, engrossed in conversation with Silas. No other guests were present. Brien now knew there would be no others.

"I hope I haven't kept you waiting," she said charmingly. She would permit nothing to interfere with an amiable evening.

"No, dear Brien, not at all," Helen crooned, patting

the settee beside her.

"For such a delightful vision we would gladly have been kept waiting." Silas had noted that Aaron stiffened noticeably at the sound of her voice.

Standing by Helen now, Brien blushed becomingly, acutely aware of Aaron's roving eyes.

"Silas, you are ever kind. I would not willingly detain anyone—but the whim of fashion is a merciless mistress and women must pay homage daily." Turning to Aaron she said simply, "Good evening, Captain."

He bowed slightly at the shoulders, that irritating air of amused appraisal apparent once more in his relaxed posture.

"The way Brien talks, she'd see us all in breeches and boots if she could," Helen quipped.

Silas raised one eyebrow. "Surely not, Brien. And deprive us of the unceasing delight of femininity in extravagant array?"

"Delight for you, perhaps, for you do not have to be laced and powdered and weighted by folds of cumbersome, useless clothing. But I assure you, you men have the best of it in clothing, by far," she teased.

Silas gasped as if scandalized. "Fortunately few women share your sentiments. How dull it would be to see only breeches and boots in the streets and at parties."

Aaron cleared his throat. This chance was too rare to miss. "I see you have resumed wearing hoops under your skirts, madame." His impertinence caused Helen to gasp and Silas' jaw to drop.

Brien was aghast! Thinking quickly how best to explain, she tried to ignore the anger he was starting inside her.

"Yes, Captain, I have." She turned to Helen with great aplomb. "On the ship, the narrow passages would not admit my hoops and I was forced to abandon

271

them while on board to save my modesty." Then she turned to Aaron, eyes snapping. "How perceptive of you, Captain. I did not realize you followed ladies' fashion closely."

"Not all ladies' fashion, madame," he grinned rakishly, "only that of a few ladies."

Helen laughed aloud and Silas was chuckling in spite of himself.

Brien was reduced to silence and glared at him openly. How dare he be so impertinent in front of her friends!

During dinner, Brien was seated across from Aaron and had little appetite, even though she had been ravenous but an hour before. She noted that Helen picked and fussed with her food and ate little. Her hand went to her middle and lingered there periodically.

Conversation was light, spiced by generous double entendres aimed at Brien. She was vastly relieved when Silas plied Aaron with queries about ships and their construction. He said he had heard Aaron planned a line of fast cargo ships and pried mercilessly into the details of the venture. Brien found herself unsettled to think of her "phantom" as a clever businessman.

"And your business, madame, have you succeeded in finding a buyer?"

Noting Silas' consternation at the comment, Brien said cautiously, "There is an interested party, but we have yet to fix a price."

"And who is this buyer?"

"That should remain—" Silas began.

"There can be no harm in divulging the gentleman's name, Silas. The Captain no doubt will be discreet." Brien smiled coyly at Aaron, meeting his warm gaze full on.

"As always, madame," Aaron rolled.

"A Dutchman from Pennsylvania by name of Horace Van Zandt is near making an offer for our entire holdings."

"Van Zandt?" Aaron seemed surprised, and not pleasantly so.

"You know of him?" Brien was now uneasy; this powerful, exciting man impinged on every aspect of her life! Now, even her business. What had she done to deserve such torture at fate's hand?

"Aye, I know him well enough." Aaron's gallant mood changed perceptibly and he frowned.

Brien was disturbed for no reason she could name —except that she now realized that Aaron's opinion was counted of some worth by her friends and by others well versed in trading. "You do not make your acquaintance sound a happy one."

"Van Zandt made much money running the blockade during the war. It is rumored that even now his ships are privateering in the Indies. He is not a man of integrity. I can only caution you to see the color of his gold before signing any property over to him."

Aaron pursed his handsome lips and shifted in his chair. "I would far rather that Weston Trading continue its American trade. This country is growing; the need for goods will soon surpass our ability to supply them."

"Tell that to your colonial assemblies," Brien said dryly. " 'Twas they forced us to this."

"This, too, will pass with time," Aaron gazed at her evenly, but with an unidentifiable glint to his eyes.

Helen turned their attention once again to their meal. "Shall we take coffee in the parlor? The seats there are far more comfortable."

Murmuring agreement, they rose and followed their swaying hostess.

Brien began to notice that Helen's face was pale and she had served coffee and had taken none herself. In a flash, the quirks of her behavior fell into place. She was in labor already and was too polite to spoil the evening. Brien marveled at her friend's self-control and winced inwardly at her own ignorance in such matters. No doubt another woman would have read the signs with the greatest of ease. But many of the secrets of womanhood eluded Brien.

"Helen, who is your midwife? You must come upstairs now and we will send for her." Brien rose and put her arms gently, but firmly about Helen's shoulders.

Silas jumped as if he'd been shot. "Has the time come?" he asked anxiously.

"I fear so," Helen smiled wanly.

Silas wrapped her small hand in his rail thin one. "Dear Helen, you should have said something!"

"There is plenty of time," she smiled up into her husband's concern-lined face. Then a sharp contraction caused her to draw breath in surprise. She clutched her stomach instinctively. "Oh . . . things are moving along. I suppose you'd best fetch Mrs. O'Grady, Silas."

"But will you be all right until I return?" Silas was ashen now.

Helen struggled up with Brien's help and, supported by Brien and Silas, started for the stairs.

Aaron stepped forward. "If I may be of assistance, I can fetch the midwife if you will tell me where she lives."

Silas shot a grateful glance at his guest. "The little house at the end of Walpole Street. Mrs. O'Grady." And they heard him depart as they moved slowly up the stairs.

It seemed a long, tedious wait for Mrs. O'Grady. Brien roused the servants and set them busy with water and linens. Then she helped Helen undress and get into bed. Silas paced outside the room and raced down the stairs to meet Aaron when his knock sounded on the door. After he showed the midwife upstairs, Silas was dismissed brusquely and told to wait downstairs.

Dejectedly, he entered the parlor and asked Aaron to stay and keep him company.

"There doesn't seem to be much a mere man can do in these things," Silas said sinking into a large winged chair. "This is our fourth and if we had a dozen, I should never get used to it." His hands hung limply over the arms of the chair.

Aaron poured the man a stout glass of brandy and sat down beside him. Strange, he mused, how this quiet, capable man was rendered useless by the pain of his wife's childbearing.

Brien had never felt so useless or inadequate as now when she tried to be useful at this birthing. Mrs. O'Grady issued orders with military precision. The midwife knew well the signs and stages and expected immediate, unquestioning obedience.

Two hours of slow writhing pain were followed by a sudden release and Helen almost smiled as she strained mightily, resting and gasping for breath between efforts. When at last the squalling red infant was free, Mrs. O'Grady smiled warmly, changing her whole countenance.

Brien held the babe in clean linen while the cord was tied and severed, suddenly realizing that she had difficulty seeing. Awe filled her as she wiped the wriggling form and wrapped it snugly. The peaceful glow of Helen's face as Brien placed the babe in her arms, made Helen seem the most beautiful woman on earth. The exhilaration of the moment swept over Brien; she trembled, scarcely able to comprehend the wild mix of emotions and feelings that possessed her. As she gazed upon them, she felt privileged to have been a small part of the most important event in the history of the world—or at least her world. She felt a closeness with Helen, with all women, as though she had been admitted to their society at last.

Brien bathed Helen's face and helped her change into a fresh nightdress. "Shall I get Silas now?" she asked. The woman nodded and Brien went downstairs, still wearing the damp apron that had protected her expensive gown.

Silas, now bleary-eyed and coatless, jumped up at the first sight of her. The strange radiance about her startled him.

"You can go to her now, Silas," Brien told him in a reverent whisper. "Don't scowl so. Helen and the babe are both fine—and the babe is beautiful." She smiled broadly at him.

Relief spread instantly through his tense frame and he squeezed Brien's hands wordlessly before bounding out of the room and up the stairs.

Brien watched him go, laughing softly at the incongruous sight of the rail thin legs and arms flailing as he took the steps two or three at a time.

Then she was aware of another presence—behind her. She turned quickly and found Aaron staring at her strangely.

"I didn't know you were still here." She smiled dazzlingly at him, for no reason she could name pleased with his presence.

"Could I have left Silas in his harried state? He felt the need of companionship; I was happy to oblige." He smiled and reached for her hand, leading her to the sofa.

She sat down wearily, her face glowing. Aaron

brought her a glass of sherry and as she accepted it, their hands touched briefly. A small shock of pleasure ran through her at the contact.

He sat down beside her drinking in her warmth and beauty. She seemed so womanly, so pliant and mellow that he felt an ache spreading through his chest and down into his loins.

"It was wonderful, Aaron." There was a soft remoteness to her gaze and voice. "I've never attended at a birthing before. It's . . ." She shrugged in wonderment, unable to go on.

When she looked up at him, her large blue eyes were luminous with nameless beautiful feelings. There was a poignant sweetness to her half-smile that stirred his heart wildly.

She reached out for his hand and felt him start at her touch. Before she could withdraw, he had taken her hand between his large warm ones and raised it to his lips. He kissed each fingertip tenderly, then held it gently against his chest.

Deeply shaken by his tenderness and moved by her recent encounter with the earthiness of nature, she felt drawn to Aaron Durham as never before. She reached up and touched his face, tracing the squareness of his jaw as she had done so often in her mind. Feeling now completely vulnerable under his great golden eyes, she lowered her head and closed her eyes.

"If you could have seen him—the babe. He is so tiny and warm and helpless. Something in me wanted to hold him and love and protect him." She shook her head. "I cannot describe it. Helen was so strong and so beautiful. Already she loves the babe dearly."

Aaron pulled her to him slowly and held her in his arms. Far from resisting, she laid her head on his chest, feeling not the slightest twinge of guilt or inclination to move. He smelled of soap and brandy—a musky, spicy

277

scent that seemed to fit his excitement and strength. Under the broadcloth of his vest, she could feel the fast beat of his heart—keeping pace with her own.

He only held her. Brien felt he wished to share this awesome experience with her. And she realized that there was no one on earth she would rather be with at that moment—sharing.

It was some time before they heard Silas' footsteps on the stairs and broke apart. Brien jumped up shakily, smoothing her dress, and turned to greet him.

"I have another son!" Silas strode in, grinning broadly. And now he positively roared, "And he is beautiful! Let's have a brandy to celebrate!" He was across the room in a flash, opening a decanter and flourishing it with boyish glee.

Brien stole a look at Aaron. He was truly a remarkable man, one worth caring for—loving. His strong face and broad shoulders fascinated her still. She wondered if in a lifetime a husband and wife would tire of seeing each other. It did not seem so with Silas and Helen.

The drifting of her thoughts disturbed her. Too much had happened this night to see it all clearly now. And she was so tired . . . so terribly tired.

"Thank you, no, Silas," she declined the glass he proffered. "I cannot, or I shall spend the night in a chair. I must retire now." Her eyes grew heavier as she spoke.

Silas' disappointment was short-lived and gratitude shone in his eyes. "Of course, Brien." He put down the glass and took her hands in his. "How can I ever thank you for your help?"

"Ah . . . 'twas little enough. The payment was the joy on Helen's face. Good night, Silas." She turned to Aaron and extended her hand. "Good night, Aaron." With a quick squeeze of his hand, she was gone.

Silas studied his companion as Brien quit the room. There had been something here; something had passed between them, he was sure of it. And the lady had called him by his given name . . . a small slip—but a telling one. Helen had said as much, but then she always seemed to know about these things first.

He regarded the captain closely as they raised their glasses. Aaron's rapt attention to Brien had not been casual desire for a beautiful woman. Silas marked that he would give Helen her due—in due time.

Nineteen

The next weeks were difficult for Aaron, knowing Brien was in the city and that he could find no pretext for calling on her except his growing feeling for her, a reason that would have laid his pride open fully to her coolness and possible scorn. Thus tortured, he fled for a few days to New York, hoping to ease his aching head with thoughts of a new venture, shipbuilding. He met and bargained with his friend Harold Caswell, persuading him to invest modestly in another ship of the *Secret's* design and to make the arrangements for a likely spot in a local shipyard for the construction to take place. After his next run to England, he should have the capital to begin construction.

While in New York, he stayed in a modest inn near the waterfront district, where the lodgings were pleasant, though far from genteel. But hunger and boredom drove him out nightly to a nearby tavern, the Golden Spar, the food was ample and tasty and the trade was lively enough to provide entertainment as well.

Seated alone at a small rough table in the corner

watching the flow of the trade as was his wont in establishments of this kind, Aaron took his evening meal there once more. It was the early part of the dinner hour and the place was soon filled with regulars, noisily greeting each other after another day's labors and consuming food and drink gustily. The service seemed too slow to meet the satisfaction of two burly patrons, backwoodsmen from their rough, handsome deerskin shirts and wrapped leggings. They swilled the dark ale quickly and felt its effects strongly before their food was brought, pounding their heavy mugs against the coarse plank table impatiently.

The harassed tavern keeper disappeared behind a thin, tattered curtain and soon returned, shoving a young woman through the opening ahead of him, snarling an order.

"Move yer carcass, wench! Yer not bought to laze about all day in the kitchen when there's customers fer servin'!" Seeing her narrow-eyed glare of contempt as she rubbed one arm that had crashed against the doorway, he drew back one hand and laid it hard against her cheek. "Yer a proud bitch, ye are . . . too fine fer honest work." He halted both speech and upraised hand as the young woman straightened defiantly before him, her hand soothing her savaged jaw as her look poured disdain on the coarse, sullen master of the establishment.

"Get to it 'fore I lay you flat," he growled, again threatening her with his fist.

Hesitating long enough to strain the man's control, the girl gazed evenly at him, then turned slowly toward the barrels behind the counter to fill the heavy metal pitchers standing ready nearby.

In the noise and press, the scene was ignored by most of the patrons. But Aaron had taken it in with interest and now shifted slightly, watching the serving wench who seemed to hold her own with her master. The young woman's carriage was erect, and her dark hair was pulled back severely into one long, thick plait that hung nearly to her waist. As she swayed and bent to dodge the eager hands that greeted her filling of mugs, she seemed well learned in the necessities of survival in this trade. Yet, as she approached the frontiersmen, Aaron noted a wariness in her manner, as if she were not accustomed to their looks and was unsure of dealing with them.

One of the woodsmen, who had black, coarse hair sprouting from seemingly every inch of his body, laughed drunkenly and grabbed for her with both arms, upsetting his precarious perch on the three-legged stool. Recognizing a familiar move at last, the girl pulled away just in the nick of time, sending the horny beast sprawling on the floor instead of against her. And though the trapper's companion howled his derision at his clumsiness, the embarrassed woodsman came up, red-faced and sputtering with rage. "You up-pity bitch! You need learnin'!"

The girl clutched the empty pitcher in her hands to her breast and began to back away, toward the corner and Aaron Durham. The other patrons laughed and wagered amongst themselves, some shouting vulgar encouragement, but all watching intently. Those whose sympathy might lie with the girl were not ready to defend her against the burly woodsman. Even the surly tavern keeper swallowed hard as he looked on, already anticipating his own losses to come from this incident.

Aaron was on his feet as the woodsman made his move, lunging at the girl and grabbing her about the waist with both arms. He had caught her in mid-step, off balance, and brought her crashing to the floor beneath his bulky torso. In the fall, the girl's arms had flung wide, instinctively still clutching the pitcher. And now as the cursing woodsman rose above her to better his position on her, the heavy pewter serving piece found the brute's head with crushing force.

For a stunned second the whole tavern was quiet then near bedlam ensued as raucous laughter rocked the room, mixed with hoots and calls and more vulgarity—all focused on the remaining trapper. Pride was at stake and the man moved slowly forward, sobered by his companion's fate, and now determined to mete out justice to the one who caused it.

The girl dragged herself from under the inert form as if it were a vile thing and stood up shakily with the help of a strong arm from behind. Before she could brush the damp sawdust and grime from her skirt and hair, the remaining woodsman charged her like a bull with bloodlust in his eyes. His enraged howl froze her on the spot, her eyes wide with horror as she stood defenseless against her descending doom.

There were some lessons Aaron had learned at the hand of his lordly father that he found it impossible to repudiate. And this was one—that all women, whatever their station or lot, were to be afforded respect and protection. Few times had he challenged the teaching and now it descended upon him with a vengeance at the sight of the wench's impending, and undeserved, doom.

The woodsman was surprised at the large body that suddenly intervened between him and his target, but he was committed to the action and his head found Aaron's rock-hard stomach. They crashed back against the nearby table, sending patrons and ale mugs flying as they struggled to regain their footing on the damp floor. Losing to the force of gravity, the woodsman went down on one knee, grasping desperately at the tumbling table on the way. Aaron's years at sea on rain-soaked decking gave him the advantage in agility and he maintained his footing, seizing the opportunity to land a knee up under the trapper's chin and send him sprawling on his back.

The room had exploded inside the trapper's head and when he came to rest he failed to rise of his own power. The drink, as much as the blow, was to blame and Aaron gasped for breath gratefully as he grabbed his aching stomach.

The catcalls and jeers were slowing now with the finish of the fight, so soon after it was engaged.

Panting heavily, Aaron turned to the girl, who stood cowering in the corner, and grinned broadly at the surprise in her large dark eyes. The others jeered and jested now about his reward to come; for at least the wench owed him a good tumble for his trouble. The girl's chin trembled as she watched him warily and edged out into the lantern light.

For a moment, Aaron's gaze was riveted on her young face, and all the noise and motion about him hung suspended in time. Somewhere in the recess of his memory these same features were etched, the same proud bearing, the same lively eyes. Then it hit him, harder than the woodsman's blow and he sucked in his breath sharply at the recognition. Now his only thought was to have her alone.

Further in his cavalier character of the moment, he whirled and tossed a gold coin to the tavern keeper and called that it was to pay for the romp he'd just had—and the one to come. The girl was instantly hoisted up and over his broad shoulders, and in a moment her squirming, squealing, cursing form was mounting the narrow stairs rump first, heading for the meager sporting rooms above. The tavern keeper now glowed with satisfaction and enlisted the help of some half-sober patrons to remove the vanquished woodsmen before they regained their senses.

Ducking low into the first dingy cubbyhole that passed for a room, Aaron straightened, allowing his eyes to become accustomed to the darkness while his nostrils strained against the fetid smell of the place. The wriggling form on his shoulder rained down devastating curses upon him as she beat ineffectually on his broad back with her fists.

Answering none of her abuse, he spotted the tinderbox and meager candle near the low straw pallet that passed for a bed and struck flint to steel awkwardly, while juggling his angry passenger. Only in the weak glow of the candle did he allow her to slip from his shoulder and slide down his front so that her back was to him. He bound her arms to her sides with his own as a precaution.

"You slimy, back-stabbing bastard!" she raged. "Do yer worst while 'e can 'cause I'll kill 'e before dawn, as God is me witness."

"Not likely," his breath came fast as he fought to maintain his advantage. "I've no taste for the skin of a tavern wench—if indeed that's what you be."

The sense of his words finally penetrated her anger, and she slowed her struggles a bit. But her silence told him she might reconsider her threats, upon hearing more.

"You're new here—to this tavern and to this life, eh? Perhaps you were of another station not long ago . . . say . . . a lady's maid?" The amusement in his voice renewed her struggles, then abruptly they stopped and he heard her gather breath as if questioning this big stranger who held her in an ironlike grip.

A long, productive moment passed before he continued, his eyes twinkling now with victory. "If I let you down, do you promise not to flee? I'll treat you well. I only have need of information—and that of the type I feel sure you can give me. Will you see it my way, or

285

must I hold you captive awhile longer?''

She nodded slowly, but no sooner had he released her than she flew to the questionable haven of a far corner. They stood appraising each other, her heart beating nearly out of her chest as he raised the candle and stepped nearer to inspect her. She struggled to remember this well-dressed man with cultured speech and authoritative bearing and how he might have knowledge of her and her past. But she drew an empty slate for her efforts.

"Yes." He seemed satisfied. "You're the one. Though I believe you could do with a wash. . . . 'Soap an' water won't kill ye' '' His mimicry brought forth a rush of anger in her, but with it a crystal clear recollection and her mouth dropped open in astonishment.

"What's your name?" he extended his hand to lead her near the stool and low pallet that served as the room's furnishings.

"E-E-Ella." Her voice seemed small as she sat down on the straw, still seeming as if a puff of air would send her flying out the door. He took the stool beside her, making a show of putting both hands in plain sight.

"You were a lady's maid in England just over a year ago, is that not so?"

She nodded timidly, gathering herself for possible flight. "Yes, sir."

"And was your lady not Brien Weston Trechaud?" She nodded tersely as the realization came fully now, breaking over her as a tidal wave of relief.

"The same, sir. An' now I've a clue who ye be." She mused aloud, "The clothes are fancier, but the scar's the same. Ye be 'im at the inn the night . . ." She stopped, her expression brittle with resolve. "I don' know where Lady Brien is, nor will I help ye find 'er." Ella's proud little chin came up determinedly.

Surmising the threat she perceived in him, he smiled

286

genuinely. This telling would take a bit of doing and more to get her to reveal what she knew of Brien's marriage. Instinctively he sought her story first and thought to slip into the rest.

"That is not what I seek. I know where Lady Brien is, Ella. She's here in the colonies, this moment, in Boston. I've seen her and she now knows me by my true name, Aaron Durham. I captain a ship and have wealth of my own. You need not fear for her safety from me. I would do nothing to hurt her."

Her manner was openly mistrustful, but she wanted to hear him out.

"Tell me about you first. How came you to this low estate?" he asked wryly, flashing her a dazzling smile that caused her to send one hand up to preen her disheveled hair.

"I'm an in-den-ture." She had difficulty with the word but the meaning was plain enough.

"How is that?" His interest was sincere as must have been the truth of her statement. No woman of good upbringing would choose this life willingly. She'd been sold.

"It was that Raoul's doin' . . . 'er husband." Ella tossed her head in reference as she studied her chore-reddened hands. " 'E said I stole things an' 'ad me carted off the very day after they were wedded." She eyed him surreptitiously, the urge to know growing unbearable in the silence. Then she blurted out, " 'Ow is she? Is she all right? I mean, 'er and 'er husband?"

"She's fine," Aaron nearly chuckled, but reined his humor so as not to give her cause for affront. There was her trust to win before he'd know what he wanted. "As to her husband, I cannot say—nor can any mortal." Seeing her frown, he leaned a bit closer, counting it a score that she did not flinch away. "He's dead. More than a year, it seems." Seeing her surprise and growing delight, he continued with his meager facts. "They were wed only a month or so before a fire claimed him."

"No . . ." The girl stared in amazement, then instantly her eyes snapped angrily at Aaron. " 'Twas no more than 'e deserved, the 'igh-born bastard. Cruel and greedy, 'e was—insisted on marryin' Lady Brien even though she didn't want 'im."

"Go on," Aaron urged gently when she stopped. But she shook her head and he tried another route. "Then tell me what happened to you."

"Like what?" she asked desultorily.

"How came you here as an indenture?"

"I was sold into it by a greedy-gutted gaoler. I was to be sent aboard a prison ship for some 'ell 'ole of a penal colony—Austra-ler or some such. But I guess the turnkey figured to make a fair coin on me an' a few other women. So 'e sold me an' them onto a ship bound 'ere." Aaron waited patiently for her to continue and his patience was soon rewarded. "I only been 'ere a few weeks. Before 'im," she threw a disparaging tilt of the head toward the door to indicate her present master, "my papers were 'eld by another innkeeper, out a ways from the town proper—on the road. But a fire near wiped 'im out an 'e had to sell my papers—to that rotter down below. I been 'ere four weeks now an' 'e's mad as hell I don't take my turn up 'ere with the two others." She raised defiant eyes to his. "But I won't . . . I'll run first an' take my chances."

"Hold now"—Aaron laughed—"with that mutinous talk. It can't be all that bad." Raising his open hand to defend against her hot reply he hurried on. "So you were sold illegally as an indenture. And what did you steal?" He drew back sharply as she exploded with rage before his eyes.

"Nothin' . . . ye cold-'earted—Nothin'! 'E 'anded

288

me over to the magistrate an' 'ad me sentenced without even a say or a witness . . . just 'is word. As if I'd take aught from my lady. 'E just did it to be rid of me an' get at 'er!'' She snorted contempt and stomped up and down before him, throwing caution to the wind in her urge to have her say.

"Ye must see, she never wanted to marry 'im. An' when she told 'im she'd not truly be 'is bride . . . 'e might have killed 'er if I 'adn't o' been there with a pistol.''

Aaron's eyes widened in astonishment. "Not be his bride? Were they married or not?''

Patient now with his slow-wittedness, Ella sighed sharply as she appraised him through narrowing lids. "She refused to bed 'im on their wedding night. You might well guess the reason she gave 'im, the jackal. 'E left all right, but swearing revenge all the way. An' 'e returned the next day wi' some men an' packed me off to prison.'' Her eyes and voice lowered again with a simmering hatred. "Lord Almighty knows what 'e done to 'erself, the brute.''

"She told him then . . . about me.'' Aaron's face hardened as the pieces of the puzzle fell together in awesome fashion.

Ella searched him. "Yes and no . . . She told 'im there was another an' asked 'im to annul their marriage.'' She stopped at the sight of Aaron's darkening face.

"That was her plan, then . . . to use me and spite him.''

Reading his thoughts plainly, Ella confronted him with hands on hips and certain fire in her eyes. "Ye think what ye will, mister! She doesn't answer to the likes of ye. She suffered enough because of what ye done that night, to be sure.''

"If I read her plan right, she got only what she deserved.'' Aaron's face reddened now at the full impact of his suspicions confirmed.

"Yer pride is dealt sore—is that it?" Ella mocked. "Well, if it's any comfort to ye, she thought of naught save ye right till 'er weddin' day. Even not knowin', I'd wager that blackguard made 'er pay well for yer night on 'er." She tilted her head with a show of scorn, unmindful of her station or personal peril. "And now will ye wring yer price from 'er as well? Gold? Or is it another toss ye fancy? She was sold once by father, no doubt abused by a husband she despised, and now to fall prey to yer slimy . . ."

Ella's eyes were murderous now and Aaron felt himself flush under her heated accusations. Was that what he wanted now? Vengeance for some imagined wrong? The bargain he first agreed to was well met, once with gold and now twice with sweetest pleasure. And still he made demands on her as though she owed him something more. But what? His own jealousy had ridden him hard at the thought that she took a husband to her willingly; was he relieved to find that she had been forced? She only dared take her pleasure as men are wont to do—where they please, instead of where duty dictates—as he himself had so often done.

He sat with his hands folded in his lap limply, staring intently at the stubby candle. He had much yet to settle, and this frank appraisal of his own motives was an unsettling start.

Ella watched and pondered his expressions that broke and changed with the inner conflict he felt. Her lady had truly lost more than her innocence that night and now the maid saw why. The man was ruggedly handsome and yet smooth of limb and with gentle manners. Her anger cooled rapidly as the sense of his words came back to her. Her former mistress was here, in the colonies . . . in Boston. Had she already talked too freely to this man who might yet seem harm done to her

lady? And yet he did not seem the type to . . . He said
Brien knew him as a man of wealth—so they had met
again. And now he sought information about her marriage, a union that he clearly found disturbing. Why
else would he bother . . . unless he . . . Ella found
herself warming toward the drift of her thoughts. This
man would mean no harm to her lady; she was sure of it
now and she smiled knowingly.

Aaron slapped his thigh with one hand, causing Ella
to jump a bit and glower at him in surprise. He
searched her form appraisingly. "Ella, I have a mind to
take a house in Boston. I have an offer, but it would
take some staff and more time than I wish to spend running it. Loyal as you are to your previous employer, I
feel you could be trusted. Have you the skills and tal-
ents to make a good housekeeper?"

Surprise at his abrupt shift in topic silenced her for a
moment, the shock plain on her face. "Ah . . . I think
. . . I am sure I could if it were a modest house. I learn
quick." But still her look was less than trusting.

"Then if I bought your papers back for you, would
you come to work for me . . . with wages?"

Astonishment plain on her, she could only nod
dumbly, fearing to even think what else might be required in the bargain. Whatever befell, it could be no
worse than the indignities of labor and degradation in
this wretched hole. And she would have her papers. . . . Her mind raced now to ferret out his motives.

He rose before her, bending slightly to avoid the low
ceiling. Nodding politely in a gesture that flattered her
no small amount, he murmured, "Then, it is done."

Twenty

Horace Van Zandt strode heavily into the office of Silas Hastings and stopped short, appraising each shelf, book, and chair on some mental tally sheet. He accepted the offer of Silas' hand with ill-concealed disdain.

"Lady Brien," Silas called her from the window where she watched the harbor below. As she approached, Silas saw Van Zandt's bloated face and bilious eyes light from within.

"May I present Mister Horace Van Zandt." He turned to the obese man to complete the formalities. "Lady Brien Trechaud, daughter of Lord Weston and part owner of this enterprise."

Brien fought a wave of revulsion to extend her hand to the man. She nodded, acknowledging his name as he took her hand and pressed his bulbous, wet lips against it. His ponderous weight shifted about his frame as he bent before her. And as he moved away toward the seat Silas offered, the flaccid jowls of his face jiggled hideously. Brien was glad to have him as far away as possible and actively suppressed a shudder as she took the chair by Silas'. If he was unloved, she mused, it was not entirely the blame of his business practices.

He sat eying her as one would a potential acquisition. His red face and thick lips had a cruel cast and he breathed in quick snorts, as if fighting his own bulk to draw air.

Brien lifted her head to avoid his leering, now glad to have chosen a modest dark blue dress for the occasion.

"Mr. Hastings has supplied you with a list of holdings and inventory, I believe." Brien effected a cordial, but official tone.

" 'E hast indeed," the fat man grunted.

"Then have you any questions about them?"

"Nein. I know all I need," Van Zandt assured her, his beady eyes narrowing.

"Then all that remains is that we fix a price," Brien said firmly, hoping her determination would be taken for confidence. "Have you an offer?"

"I haf," he growled. "But you vil get it at dinner tonight."

Brien bristled at his arrogance, but bridled the rising anger within. Instinctively, she knew that charm would ply this bulk where indignation or resistance would fail miserably.

"A charming invitation." She smiled winningly. "But if I have your offer I may think on it today and we may be agreed this evening."

His eyes were narrow slits now as he appraised her. Her erect posture and guileless expression lent credence to her seeming acceptance of his invitation.

"Ah, vell. For dis varehouse and goodts, stores and stock, I give seben t'ousand—sterling." His tongue curled around the final "g" drawing it out obscenely.

Brien's heart sank, but outwardly she showed no sign of disappointment. She felt herself smiling wryly. "I

293

shall need no time to consider that offer, sir. The answer is no." She threw a smoky look at the bargainer from beneath a thick fringe of dark lashes.

"Unless you would care to better that offer—more toward the fair worth of my holdings . . ." She ended by studying him openly, as one man would study another—an adversary.

Van Zandt pursed his lips and squinted one eye. This woman dared bargain with him. The game took on new interest, and his broad smile was a fair counterfeit of geniality.

Silas was wide-eyed at the exchange and he looked, bewildered, from one contender to the other.

Van Zandt slapped one elephantine knee with his hamlike fist. "By Gott, den vat vould you haf me offer?"

Ignoring his profanity, Brien calmly stated her price. "More toward eighteen would fit their worth."

Silas was stunned and sought Brien's gaze. Her eyes were now like the cold blueness of fine steel.

"Den you vill not zell." Van Zandt lost all pretense of humor. But Brien marked well that he made no move to leave.

"On the contrary, sir. I shall sell at a fair price." Brien spoke as charmingly as if he had paid her a compliment on her hair or dress. "Now, would you care to make another offer at dinner this eve? By then you may have had time to reevaluate the property."

An ugly smile laid bare Van Zandt's yellowed and decaying teeth. "*Ja.* By dis evening I reevaluate." He pointed a fat ringed finger at her knowingly. "I make you another offer, den. Who knows? Mebee you soften dis heart of mine." He patted the broadcloth-covered expanse that engulfed what at one time must have been a chest.

"What is good for the purse, may not delight the

heart, Mister Van Zandt. And the reverse may well be true. I shall see you at dinner this eve. Mr. Hastings will arrange dinner at the Braithwaite Inn. Seven o'clock?" She rose and extended her hand to him across the desk.

He struggled up, panting with the effort. He bent his head to kiss her hand once more, failing to note the determined set of her face behind the pleasantness.

"*Ja,*" he grunted and then swayed out, the floor groaning in protest under his bulk. Two hard-looking men joined him as he made his way to the door.

Brien stood serenely until he was well onto the street. Then she grabbed her handkerchief and rubbed her hand viciously where his foul mouth had made contact with her skin.

"At least it was short," she gritted out through her teeth.

"Brien, the man is no fool. I see plainly that he is cunning and undoubtedly lacking in the nobler virtues. It is not prudent to bait him—or underestimate him." Silas reproved her gently.

A strange, hard gleam showed in her eyes as she faced her friend. "I know well the force of cunning—and I do not fear it, his or any other's. I shall have fourteen thousand and not a whit less. Paying a fair price is his cost for having dinner with me. I think he knows that."

Silas was aghast. "You can't mean that. You believe he is thinking only of dinner?"

"He will," she smiled coolly, "when he sees Dyso as my escort."

Silas was speechless. He wondered if she could extract her price from that miserly mass without far greater cost to herself. She had triumphed in this first encounter, and shown herself a worthy adversary. But he feared that Van Zandt would be the ultimate victor on other ground. He seemed unhampered by convention or morality.

That evening, Brien, accompanied by Dyso, went by carriage to the Braithwaite Inn. The inn belied its modest name with an elegance that rivaled some of the excellent restaurants in London. The establishment catered little to local trade; most wealthy families entertained in their homes. Visiting wealth and dignitaries often used the dining rooms to entertain, lacking their own facilities. Brien was anxious to see it, though less than enthusiastic about the circumstances.

Brien would never have considered asking Silas to entertain that beastly creature in his home, even in so important a cause. Something about him polluted and despoiled whatever he touched. Yes, neutral ground would serve well in dealing with him.

Brien arranged that Dyso be seated at the table beside hers and that he be served the same as herself. Her protector's concern was plain in his face. Brien had told him enough to ask for his alertness, but advised him to show restraint, whatever befell. He indicated clearly that his strong arms were her defense. And she felt relieved.

Van Zandt arrived shortly and drew poorly veiled stares from the other patrons. If Dyso's scarred, fearsome countenance and size had shocked them, Van Zandt's appearance revolted them. The irony of these two associated with the most beautiful woman in the room was clear in their surreptitious glances.

"Ver *ist* Has-tings?" Van Zandt demanded crassly, looking about for him.

"Mr. Hastings was needed at home," Brien said demurely. "But Monsieur Dyso accompanied me." As she indicated her loyal servant at the next table, Van

Zandt was treated to a chilling glimpse of the cold, ruthless potential of the lady's protector—and the contempt that showed plainly in the hulk's face.

The fat man regarded his lovely companion closely. For all her charm, she possessed a flintlike determination inside that he grudgingly respected. She had planned well.

"Dis offer now . . ." the buyer began.

But, Brien's raised hand cut him off sharply. She perused the menu. "Please let us order first, I am famished. Then we shall talk."

Van Zandt found no way to object, and ever eager to consume the sustenance of his girth, he fell to reading the menu, mouth watering.

Brien managed to be polite through the courses of excellent food—even as this revolting bulk chewed and mauled huge servings of beef and downed quantities of wine and bread. When she was tempted to be sick at the sight of his feeding habits, she remembered resolutely her mission, and forebore.

He began to boast of his ships and their ventures, relating some gruesomely detailed accounts of battles during the war. Her longing to conclude all dealings with this pig grew with the passing minutes. She now ripely despised him.

When their food was finished, Brien could forestall it no longer.

"*Und* now . . . dis biz-nesss," he proclaimed, wiping his greasy fingers on his vest. His porcine face was redder due to the wine, and Brien could not but think of a great sow she had seen at the town fair at Dunstan when she was a girl.

"I trust you have evaluated the properties fairly," she began the bargaining.

"*Ja,* I haf t'ought on it. I mebee offer ten t'ousand." His beady eyes now glowed as he watched for her reaction.

She was careful to conceal her distaste. "Certainly that is fair for the goods and stores. Now on to the warehouse. What of it?"

"*Nein.*" His shaking head sent reverberations through his fleshy jowls. "Ten t'ousand for all."

Now Brien fought the urge to do verbal battle and produced instead a mental ledger sheet. "Currently in stock, we have merchandise and commodities that are worth far in excess of that figure, sold at a reasonable profit."

"If you value dem zo highly, den zell dem yourself," Van Zandt challenged her squarely.

She struggled for every ounce of composure she could muster.

"As you well know, we cannot collect outstanding debts now—due to the vindictive assembly's action. We cannot continue to sell without recourse for payment. But as we shall not give the merchandise to our customers, we shall not give it to you." She paused, giving her words time to sink in.

"Mebbee ve meet agin—mitout dis friend of yours," he leered, indicating with a toss of his head Dyso. The implication of his words was clear. Silas had been right; the man would demand more for his money than honest goods and property.

She pushed back her chair suddenly and smiled icily. "Good evening, Mister Van Zandt."

He grabbed her arm in a viselike grip, his greedy fingers eating into her soft flesh. He had pushed the bargaining too far, not his usual style.

Dyso was instantly at her side, his face murderous. Van Zandt released Brien's arm and cowered back as Dyso leaned over him. More than anything else in the world, Brien wanted to let Dyso chastise him properly. But she restrained him with one hand on his sleeve;

their movements had created a stir in the room. Her face colored with embarrassment mingled with indignation.

"Please zit, madame. I am sorry for dis unpleasantness. Not to happen agin." For no discernible reason, he seemed to want to make amends.

Brien felt the coolness of advantage now. "I will not. If you should wish to make a suitable offer—say, fifteen thousand—then you may transmit it to me through my agent, Mr. Hastings. Good evening, sir."

She turned from the slack-jawed and red-faced Van Zandt and walked with great dignity to the door—and the cool sweetness of fresh air.

The next several days were a confusing mixture of waiting, exploring the city and pondering the strange and unsettling turn of events of the last days. Brien felt changed somehow and it frightened her. She steadfastly, pridefully, refused to examine her heart for the truth that she knew she would find there.

Had she but looked inward, she would have seen the opening of the full blossom of womanhood, stirred up from the primal seed borne in every fiber of her being. She was irresistibly being drawn to those very things which in her youth and anger she had spurned. And the opening of this new flower had begun on that sweet night when she had felt the throb and pulse of new life in her arms. The vague longing that possessed her deepest thoughts at night went unrecognized by her intellect, while her heart echoed its haunting call . . . her need for the love and loving that only this man could give her, and her need to nurture, suckle, and protect a babe—her babe.

But, by day she seemed content to be in the company of Helen and to venture out amongst these new people in this new land. In this short space of time she had felt more at peace than at any other time in her life. And curiously, she felt a sense of freedom here—a release from the strictures of a class- and rank-conscious society. Here she was not Lady Brien, wealthy patrician, but Only Madame Trechaud, lovely and charming and capable. It was with chagrin that she authenticated Aaron Durham's view; this place was special—liberating and invigorating all at once.

Nearly a week had passed without word from Van Zandt, and Brien was surprised to find that it concerned her less with each passing day. She had adopted an optimism which presumed that all would work out for the best. And she remembered and heeded her father's advice that time often resolved problems too complex or overwhelming for mere humans to deal with.

Brien sat reading in the quiet of the new July morning, mulling over the words of a poet when sturdy Alice appeared at the parlor door with a puzzled look on her face.

"Lady Brien," she awaited acknowledgement.

"Yes, Alice, what is it?"

"There's a woman come to the kitchen door with a basket of fresh fruit and she says she has a word for your ears only, ma'am."

Moments later, as Brien entered the kitchen, her gaze was drawn immediately to the slender, blue-clad form of a young woman near the open kitchen door. Hearing footsteps behind her, the woman turned to greet Brien with joy and certain relief in her face. But Brien was frozen to the spot where she had paused upon entering. Raw astonishment stunned her every nerve and choked the very words from her throat.

"Milady!" the young woman exclaimed, and instantly tried to choke back the words with a stifling hand, lest they might give her former mistress offense.

The word broke through Brien's benumbed mind and she held her arms out to her friend and former servant as she found her voice. "Ella!"

For a long moment the high-born lady and young woman in servants' garb shocked the kitchen staff with their long, tearful embrace and joyful exclamations.

Some time later Brien glimpsed the cook's puzzlement and quickly glanced about to find that the entire kitchen staff had stopped stock-still and was staring at them. Coloring markedly, she felt a need to explain her exceptional behavior. "This woman is a dear friend of mine. We have been parted for a long while and at last are reunited. Alice," Brien turned to the stout serving woman, "could you bring us some tea in my chambers? We have much to discuss and must not bore the rest of the house with our reminiscences."

Alice bobbed stiffly in agreement while casting a dubious glance at Ella, who was being whisked away upstairs to the lady's chambers. She turned to the rest of the staff and shrugged her disapproval. Who knew the whys and wherefores of the lady's mind. These titled folk from England were a queer lot, at best. The others, while not all harboring the same sentiments, returned to their work whispering and wagging their heads.

Once in the privacy of her room, Brien grasped Ella's hands and held them out from her sides, appraising every inch of her friend as if she could ferret out the mysteries of the lost years just by looking.

"Let me see you! Oh, Ella, you've hardly changed a bit! How came you here? How ever did you find me!"

Ella laughed patiently. "I learned ye were 'ere by accident. Me new employer let drop yer name an' I asked 'round as soon as I 'eard ye were 'ere. Oh, milady, ye

301

look so beautiful, I scarce can believe my eyes!''

Brien pulled her to a chair beside the tea table and in a second had taken the other chair herself, pulling it around to face her long-sought friend.

''Now tell me how you came here . . . to America. All of it! I want to know everything that has happened to you since . . .'' Brien stopped, remembering all too vividly the last time they were together and the nightmare that was wrought from those circumstances for them both.

''Then ye'll tell me about yerself. Ye being a widow and all?''

''So you've heard that much.'' Brien sighed. There were things she could tell and, alas, things she could not. A light melancholy threatened to settle on her mood. ''Yes, Raoul died little more than a month after that horrible scene in my rooms at Weston Place.'' Ella nodded sympathetically and Brien realized that her status as a wealthy and eligible widow must be noised about Boston freely for Ella to have heard of it. And for once she was grateful for so fleet a chain of gossip.

''But first, tell me of you!'' Brien insisted. ''I've pressed our solicitors hard for more than a year for word of you. It seemed you'd dropped from the face of the earth.''

Ella smiled and warmed to her tale, suddenly feeling the warmth and closeness they had shared years before in the lord's house in England. She poured forth a wondrously complex story of intrigue in which she was saved from the perils of a prison ship by the nefarious dealings of a greedy gaoler. The choice, to be sold into indenture or die of disease, or worse, in the hold of a prison ship bound for a God-forsaken wilderness, was easy to make and she related that she had little reason to regret it since. Her papers were first bought by a goodly innkeeper who until a short while ago had provided a

302

clean, honest living for her in return for honest labor. Then her papers were sold when a fire ruined the man's business. After a short stay in an unsavory tavern, she had had the good fortune to be sold to a merchant of Boston who had found her in that tavern and taken it into his heart to be kind. He had thus far proven a fair master, agreeing to set her time aside in half the usual years. And she had been advanced to housekeeper of late, a position she had always coveted, even though it was a modest house.

Brien shook her head in amazement at the story. "Of course we'll buy back your papers, now that I've found you. And we'll set you up in a shop of your own—or a small inn—or whatever you fancy!

Her enthusiasm was contagious, but made Ella squirm under its unbridled generosity. "Oh, no, Lady Brien. I could not allow it." She shook her head firmly. "I owe the man a debt an' I'll pay it fair. I'm happy now in my new master's house an' I'm not anxious to leave." The words were dry and unpleasant in her mouth, as lies often are. But it was in a good cause that she withheld from Brien that she was already a free woman and already knew some of the story that Brien would relate. But to tell of her freedom without revealing the source of the true generosity of her benefactor and the cause of it, could not be done. Best to let the matter lie as it would.

In the intervening two weeks since her rescue from the tavern, she had seen first hand the worth of the man who had bought her freedom. Mostly she had seen his effect on others and the even-handedness and wisdom with which he treated all. She had assumed the role of his housekeeper and found herself now loyal to his cause as she had once been to Brien's. But perhaps their causes were not so separate after all. The two times he had spoken of Brien since that night in the tav-

303

ern, it had been with a softness that in Ella's eyes marked him as a man whose heart was already given. Contrary to her fears he had asked nothing of her with regard to Brien, only that she refrain from telling Brien her present employer's name and the circumstances of how she came to work for him. It was a promise that exacted more in the keeping than Ella had first imagined. This was hard . . . to hold back the hordes of questions she longed to ask and the incidents she longed to tell.

Plainly puzzled by her maid's reluctance to accept a just recompense for the trials she had suffered, Brien continued, "But you must let me do something for you. You've suffered much on my account and I cannot live with myself knowing you in wrongful bondage when money would see you free. Ella, you must let me!"

Fearing to press the case further, Ella smiled sheepishly and hoped her reluctance would be seen as another aspect of her loyalty to Brien and her desire not to impose upon her friend's good graces. "That I could allow, an' I'd be grateful. It's just that—I know ye must have another maid now an' I feel beholdin' to me new master. . . ." She could find little logic in her own statements and stopped before they led her into deeper waters.

But Brien, seeking to see her friend in the noblest light, picked up for her with a glint in her dancing eyes. "So you're reluctant to leave your new master, eh? And just how good has he been to you, Ella? Have you taken a fancy to him?"

Ella's downcast eyes and crimson face revealed her confusion in a way that seemed to validate Brien's assumptions. "So, that's it!" Brien's laughter was sparkling with delight, and she clasped her hands together.

"Not exactly 'im . . ." Ella squirmed anew. "But there is someone in 'is house. . . ." And it was not altogether a lie. There was a man who came often to do

304

business with Master Aaron . . . and he had cast a lingering eye upon the new housekeeper. Ella knew from the looks that there would be further business brought to the house, and she found the thoughts pleasant, to say the least.

"Then you must take the money for your papers and, by all means, stay on in your new master's house. What is his name, by the way?"

Snatching desperately for a name, Ella chose the last one on her thoughts. "George, Anthony George."

Brien went to her chest and threw it open, pulling from beneath a stack of lacy lingerie a leather pouch which contained a goodly sum in gold coin, the better part of three hundred pounds. She returned and put the pouch in Ella's hands.

"There, will three hundred do? I can arrange more—"

"No! That will be more than enough!" Ella nearly strangled on her words and looked up at Brien with a mixture of pain and bewilderment. How had she gotten so enmeshed in this web of half-truth?

"And you will give this to your master, Mister George, and bid him see you a free woman again?"

"Yes." Ella's eyes were moist and she hastened to change the subject lest she give in to the temptation to tell all she knew. "I'll be ever grateful." She smiled wanly. "But now ye must tell me yer story. I cannot bear this curiosity a minute longer."

Before Brien could begin, a knock came at the door and Alice entered with tea and sweets on an elegant tray. Brien thanked her for her trouble and escorted her to the door hurriedly, eliciting an indignant stare for her odd behavior.

Settled once more opposite her friend, Brien began her story of her abduction and her life with Raoul. Only with Ella could she have felt secure in telling that her husband held her against her will, much as a prisoner. She left to Ella's vivid imaginings the lurid details of her days and nights in Raoul's possession and hurried on to the fire and her amazing rescue. Her description of Dyso's role in her salvation brought forth a shuddering recollection of him from Ella. He had been one of the men who had bound her and taken her to the constable. But Brien reassured her that the man meant no malice and went on.

Again Brien relived her year of mourning and the new closeness to her father that it brought. Ella's doubtful looks were soon laughed away as Brien related an incident or two that dealt with her becoming her father's protégé in business. Then on to her social debut and her life since, including her reasons for her trip to Boston. But one thing remained and in a reckless moment, Brien plunged ahead.

"Ella there is one thing more I must tell you. You have been a better friend than any and I could not hold this from you if I tried." She drew a great breath to steady herself and went on. "The man we knew as Allen Stewart, that one the night in Harrall's Road . . ." She paused clasping her hands nervously, reading Ella's fascination in the young woman's eyes. "Well . . . we . . . met again."

Ella's expression was one of shock and she struggled to maintain an appropriately astonished demeanor.

"You'll not believe it, but he was truly no seaman . . . at least not what we thought. He is of noble birth and captains his own vessel now. Aaron Durham is his rightful name. He is a man of honor and has kept my secret well." She managed a thin smile, unsure as to her story's reception. "I think I have little to fear from him."

"Well, that's a stroke o' luck deserved," Ella quipped. But she could not resist an urge to delve further and squared it with herself in the name of authenticity. It would be natural for Ella to be seething with curiosity, as she was. "How did ye meet?"

"He captained the ship that brought me to America." Brien knew as soon as the words left her lips that the statement would raise more questions than it answered. To her relief, Ella provided a way out.

"Well, then, 'e 'ad time enough to try to get a price from ye. It's naught short of a miracle that 'e turned out a decent sort. Ye might have been sore set upon." Ella hoped her words were convincing, for she truly felt them. But she smiled a bit at the knowledge of the true reason for the man's gallantry—and it had little to do with noble spirit. Seconds later, that same knowledge pricked Ella's conscience sorely.

No less was Brien nettled as her friend took her leave some time later. She had wanted to tell all and share her innermost feelings with someone, for in the telling she might have made some sense of them herself. But in the end, she knew it was right that she entangle her friend's loyalty no further in her life. And she knew certainly that were their cases heard fairly, hers would fall ignominiously before Aaron Durham's. Few of her associations with the man were to her credit, while all of his to her bespoke only his praise.

Just past dinner that evening, Ella entered the dining room of the house she managed now for Aaron Durham. He sat alone, thoughtfully savoring a glass of brandy. She planted herself before him, and when he raised questioning eyes to her, she pulled a heavy object from her apron pocket and handed it to him.

Surprise at the act, the object, and her next words was written large in his expression.

"I saw milady today. She bade me give this to me

new master—to see me a free woman.'' The bright grin on her face was matched by the one dawning on his as he realized that for things to so transpire, his house-keeper must have kept his confidence well.

As he gazed at the worn leather pouch in his hand he found cause for greater amusement and threw back his head with resounding laughter. When he sobered some he turned again to Ella's bemused frown.

''Twice paid with the same gold. Shall I make the same vow?'' He chuckled grandly, setting his shoulders trembling again.

Ella shook her head at the man and dipped slightly before turning to leave. Just before the door closed behind her, she heard Aaron's deep voice rumble forth, calling her back.

''Ella, how much is in it?'' he hefted the pouch so that she could see.

'' 'Bout three hundred pounds, gold.'' Seeing his laughter begin anew, she shut the door softly and smiled, shaking her head.

Aaron sat, bemused still, sometime later, gazing at the bag of coins. A not unwelcome warmth welled up inside him. ''Three hundred for a night's romp . . . I'm flattered. But milady's generous nature must not be abused. She should have fair worth for her money. And she will.''

Twenty-one

Dressed for bed that very evening, Brien paced her room. The night was unseasonably warm and she wore only a thin nightdress. The sweet night air wafted in through the open French windows, setting her mind buzzing with the events of the past weeks—the birth of Helen's babe and her meeting with Ella. They would soon baptize the babe "Brian" for her and "Lawrence" for her father. Her dear father would at last have a namesake, but she was disturbed that a friend had had to be the one to supply it.

When her father lay ill, nearly dead with the fever, she had regretted her vow never to marry again. She had wished bitterly that Raoul had succeeded in getting her with child. At least Lord Weston would have had the comfort of an honorably born grandchild—and she would have had someone to fill the void that would come when her father died.

Why was freedom so important to her? Why could she not be like other women, content to bear children and sew and . . . But this was madness! She was not like other women—and wishing would not make it so! There was an independence in her and a strong will that would not let her yield to anyone as master. And yet there was this longing. Could she ever find a remedy for this restlessness in her breast? Had she ever truly felt at peace?

With a pang of conscience she realized that she had felt just that way—peaceful and fulfilled—as she lay in Aaron's arms that night on board the *Secret*. Something about him and his loving reached inside her to her very soul and calmed her. It was as though they joined in spirit as well as body.

A surge of heat and longing welled up in her loins. To dwell on him was sweet torture. He was a man of great strength and tenderness, vision and common sense. A casual movement of his shoulders or the light pressure of his hand on hers could start that fearsome fire within her. She secretly enjoyed the way his eyes caressed her body whenever they met. His impudent, easy manner intrigued her, and his wit and lascivious double-edged conversation challenged her to be at her best—to best him if she could. Of all men in the world, she cared what only two thought of her—her father and now Aaron Durham.

She paced with increased vigor to blot out the physical longing that thoughts of him had conjured in her. She envied those nameless, faceless girls he had courted and plied with tender persuasion. Even more she envied those who shared their nights with him. To lie beside him all night and to face each new day beside him . . . No! One more night with him, loving him, would undo her completely. And yet there was such temptation in his every look, his sensual stride, his hawklike golden eyes. She must now be ever on guard against both him and herself.

She felt a chill come over her, as if warning of another presence in the room. Turning quickly, she sought the window with her gaze and her eyes widened in alarm as she discerned a tall pair of black boots in the shadows of the drapes.

Gasping sharply, she looked up to see the tall, muscular frame of Aaron Durham leaning against the window frame. His face bore a blend of amusement and admiration. Her long, thick hair cascaded over her shoulders and her thin night dress clung to her body in places, revealing tantalizing clues to her nakedness beneath.

"What are you doing here?" she whispered hoarsely, afraid that somehow he would be able to read her thoughts.

He pushed away from the window with his shoulder and stepped forward into the warm flood of candlelight. Brien nearly gasped as a wave of longing seized her at the sight of him. He was every inch the powerful male, strong and compelling.

Feasting his eyes on her soft form he said softly, "I could not resist you any longer." His voice had a strange husky quality that sent a shiver through Brien's heart.

"Resist me?"

He smiled rakishly, eyes now searching her mercilessly. "You beset me at every turn, milady. My ship is haunted with your memory. The image of you naked in my arms is burned into my mind and flesh. Every thought, every word has new meaning to me because of you. I can resist you no longer."

Under his probing gaze, Brien felt as though he had read those words from her own mind. Confused and shaken, she turned away from him and, seeing her dressing gown lying on the bed, became aware of her exposed state and grabbed it up to hold in front of her. Her thoughts raced.

"I have made no demands on you," she answered defensively. "What is it you expect of me?"

His face was a shade redder now. Her heart quickened as he took one step nearer.

"I need you, Brien, I can say it no plainer. I walk about a shell of a man—my heart stolen from me by a fair and charming thief. I am loath to ask for its return, even though I speak now to the culprit."

"Aaron Durham," she scowled, feeling her very bones growing fluid with desire. "It is near midnight at the least! This is no time—and no place—to play the overheated swain!"

His big hands spread wide, leaving him defenseless. "True," he agreed, " 'tis not the usual manner of paying court—but then, you are not a usual woman. A good case may be made for an inventive approach where more commonplace efforts have failed." He was now within arms reach, his powerful maleness, causing Brien to sway.

Steadying herself against the bed, she found no resistance to him inside her—despite her recent resolution against him.

"Paying court? Do you claim to invade my rooms in the dead of night to pay me court?" She tried to sound incredulous.

"I find it hard to believe myself; yet, here I am." His tongue played at the corner of his mouth and his eyes glowed intensely. His breath came fast.

A feeling like an insatiable hunger swept through her, and she admitted to herself how much she wanted what he came for. In one last valiant effort at distraction, she tossed back her long hair with one hand and taunted him.

"And what are your intentions, swain? To have your pleasure in my bed, surely. Then what?"

He reached for her and drew her to him easily, his

hands burning the flesh of her waist even through the gown. His next words seared into her bedazed mind.

"Then I am yours, whenever, wherever you say. Whatever conditions you impose I shall willingly meet. Be mine, Brien. Give my body and soul rest in your arms." The soft entreaty in his eyes and voice melted her will.

His lips closed over hers and she soared upward against him. Eagerly she met his tongue with her own, reveling in his saltiness and the feel of his big, hard body against hers. Whatever happened, she would not regret being with this exceptional man, loving him. For she certainly did . . . love him.

His big hands roamed up and down her back, tracing the curves of her waist and hips through her gown and setting her nerves on fire with each stroke. She squirmed with pleasure as his lips nibbled at her ear and at her silken neck, half tickling, half devouring her. Her hands came up against his chest and found the buttons of his shirt. Eyes aglow, she pushed back unexpectedly, and her fingers worked at the buttons. Soon, his jacket and shirt were a heap beside them on the floor.

He folded her to him against his bare chest, feeling her nuzzle against the light furring there. His heart nearly leaped and he picked her up suddenly to place her gently on the bed. Her hair rippled across the pillows and her night dress twisted tightly over her breasts, exposing the tops of those creamy mounds and revealing the outline of erect nipples beneath. She was woman now, ready for love and smoldering with a long-denied passion. He bent to touch her breast and she closed her eyes, moaning softly and calling his name in a husky voice that excited him beyond fever pitch.

In a moment, his remaining clothes were on the floor and he came to her, scalding her with his kisses and melting her against him with his heat. Somewhere in the next moments, her gown was removed and for a sweet eternity time was suspended as they lovingly explored each other, hands and lips tracing, memorizing, beloved curves and mounds and erotic hollows.

Then he came to her as she spread her legs languidly to receive him. He filled her, completed her with his hot, thrusting maleness. This passion was different from that on the ship. Now they arched and joined without reserve, knowing each other's pleasure and wildly indulging the long denied desire that drew them inevitably together. Their last soaring rush pushed them both into an updraft, wrenching every fiber of their bodies in a prolonged spasm of ecstasy.

They lay joined for a long while and slowly the room stopped spinning and the thunder in Brien's ears receded. Aaron moved to lie beside her and she felt a sense of loss, as though he took a vital part of her with him when he removed his flesh from her.

She was soon comforted by the feel of his hand stroking her face. He propped himself on one elbow to watch her, eyes closed and body moist and flushed with fulfillment. She was most beautiful now, he thought, warm and openly loving.

Her eyes flickered open to gaze at him. He was shaken by the smoky, amorous look in them. As she wriggled nearer to him, one lock of her tangled hair fell casually across her rose-tipped breast. He put out a hand to tame the straying lock and she caught his hand and put it to her breast. In her eyes, the faint, but unmistakable flicker of passion still glowed.

He rolled over onto her and covered her face with light kisses, lingering over her closed eyes and moist lips.

"You are wonderful, Brien," he murmured against her mouth. "One night with you is worth years of torture."

Her eyes flickered open. She frowned a bit, stroking his face gently and running her fingers through the coppery mass of his hair.

"Years of torture? You make me sound a cruel and heartless mistress. Yet it seems whenever you wish you romp casually into my bed—and I find I have little defense against you."

"I do not 'romp casually,' Lady. 'Tis not lightly or from mere hunger that I touch you." He moved his hand along the ripe curve of her hip. ". . . But from caring for you, and needing you."

Her face clouded. "But you must not," she protested, putting her fingers against his generous lips.

"'Tis indeed late for saying nay, Lady."

"No." She pushed him away from her and sat up, drawing the sheet over her as if drawing a veil between them once more. A curious, sweet stab of pain shot through her heart. Before her better sense could censor her tongue she blurted out, "What you said . . . about caring for me . . . is it true?" Her smoky, gray-blue eyes searched him. Her heart nearly stopped.

"Aye, it is true enough. I care for you as none before and none after." He took her hand and kissed each of the fingertips in turn. "To be near you, and never touch you is pure pain for me, Brien."

She closed her eyes sharply so as not to reveal the shock that his admission generated in her. The realization penetrated through her carefully planned defense and confusion filled her. He did care for her!

"You do care for me." She stated it wonderingly.

He lay back, grinning, tucking his arms behind his head. "That, I think, puts it mildly."

She sat up on her knees, clutching the sheet to her, but it slipped as she turned to him, revealing one ripe breast and rosy nipple to his warm appreciation.

He pouted outrageously. "And you, milady, have you no words of comfort for me?"

She smiled slyly, tilting her head so that her hair hid her naked breast from his marauding gaze. "I should think you had been comforted enough for one night."

He reached for her and drew her to him roughly. "But the ache goes deep. It would take many such nights and many gentle words of endearment to assuage it."

"Then would you hear my sad tale—of the restless nights I have spent, haunted, pursued by a phantom with golden eyes and hair that glows like fire in the sunlight."

"A phantom that stalks the daytime?" he frowned.

"My days and my nights," she said wistfully. "I am ever at his mercy—and he enjoys well my discomfort."

"The scoundrel," Aaron growled. "I shall teach him manners if ever I happen upon him."

"Be not cruel to this phantom of mine. For all my discomfort, I have grown quite fond of him." She smiled lovingly into Aaron's hungry eyes.

"You care for him? This one who devils your peace and threatens your virtue?"

"My only complaint is not his loving . . . but his leaving." And instantly she regretted those candid words.

He sat up in a flash and grasped her arms. "Twice before you have left me to a cold empty bed at dawn. Why?" His face was sober and there was no pretense of dreams.

"Aaron, I . . . I could not stay," she pleaded, caught in an agonizing crush of conflicting emotions. "I did not wish to feel for you. . . . It is not wise, it makes no sense." She pulled away to hide her face from him.

"What is it you feel for me, Brien? I must know."

His gentle command forced the truth from her, but not before she could dilute its strength.

"I . . . I care for you," she said haltingly. It would bind her to him to say she loved him. And what did she know of love? Was this madness she felt continually on his account really love?

He turned her face to him tenderly and pressed her lips with his own. When she opened her eyes she saw no disappointment, no reproach in his face.

"You cannot say it now, but you will soon. We were meant to be together, Brien, and we will be."

Catching his confidence like a contagion, she circled his neck with her arms and drew his lips to hers. They loved and slept together till dawn crept in through the open windows.

Brien awoke suddenly to the faint light, heart pounding. She turned and Aaron was there beside her, sleeping peacefully. She reached out to touch his muscular, browned arm, remembering the first night they were together and how she had longed to touch him the next morning, daring not to.

He stirred at the warmth of her hand and raised his head sleepily. Seeing her, he smiled contentedly and reached out his arms for her. She crept into them, wondering at the strong feelings between them that lingered through the coolness of dawn.

Could anything in life compare with the joyful intimacy she now shared with him? After a night of hot, intoxicating loving, to awaken to the cool sweetness of dawn to a tender closeness of body and spirit. Surely life could offer no more sublime experience.

She kissed his stubbled chin lightly. "You must be off, before the household stirs. Jeannie will come to awaken me soon."

"And what if I refuse to move—stay here in bed until she comes?" His eyes twinkled.

"You would ruin my good name," she was scandalized by the realization that he really was tempted to do it. "And sully my reputation as a heartless widow."

"Or perhaps confirm the suspicion that you are not. No man under eighty could fail to see the warmth in your breasts." His eyes were flecked with glowing specks and Brien blushed scarlet at his openness.

"Such talk."

His big hand cupped around one generous breast and she gasped at the contact. He leered shamelessly at her.

"They are such magnificent ones. The talk of all London—or of the male population."

She slapped his hand away gently. "I cannot be held responsible for the idle conjecture of old reprobates." But she turned to him wide-eyed. "Do men really talk of such things?"

He grinned, sitting up and gazing appreciatively at her nakedness. "Only if the woman is worth talking about. For a widow, Brien, you know very little of men."

Her face clouded suddenly at the mention of her marriage. "I was married only a month—hardly enough time to become expert in the vagaries of men's gossip."

"About your marriage—" Aaron began, but was cut short.

"If you tarry longer, you'll be found here for certain," Brien said sharply. Then she softened it with, "I'll help you dress." She tilted her head coyly. Any guilt she felt at employing her charms so was buried deeply beneath the pleasure of the next moments.

Slipping naked from the bed, she donned her dressing gown, neglecting to tie it as she pulled her hair from beneath it. Next, she gathered his breeches and stockings and carried them to him where he watched her

318

from the bed. She felt his eyes on her every move and she gloried in this new-found ability to tantalize him. He would not soon forget this night, she vowed, knowing full well it would haunt her as well.

While he buttoned on his breeches, Brien picked up his tall, black boots and hugged them against her as she leaned against the bedpost. When his shirt was tucked and his sash in place, he turned to her for the footgear.

She was smiling seductively, and his eyes fell to where her partly bare breast was pressed hard against the top of his boot.

The sight set off an explosion in his blood. His face washed crimson and his breath came faster. "My boots, Lady, I'll have them now." He took a step forward and she backed away playfully, daring him to come for them.

"Your boots, sir?" she asked coquettishly.

"I'll have the boots and you!" he threatened, stalking her as she backed from him.

"Such promises!" she purred impudently. Turning quickly, she ran to the bed and was on and over it before he could grab her. The battle was joined and deftly; he stalked and chased her about the room until she found herself between corner and wardrobe with no place to run. He closed in on her, laughing softly, his breath ragged with excitement.

Her breath matched his and her eyes glistened. The game was over, the sweetness of surrender lay ahead.

He took the boots from her unresisting hands and tossed them behind him. His big hands slipped inside her open gown next to her bare skin and he kissed her hard as he crushed her to him possessively.

For a moment Brien thought he did mean to take her again, but soon he released her. He swallowed hard as he turned to pick up his boots, every fiber of his body crying out in protest.

319

Brien had lost all desire to see him gone—whatever the price. She leaned, eyes closed, against the wall, her gown open alluringly in front.

When she opened her eyes, Aaron stood nearby, boots on, caressing her with his eyes.

"I should go now . . . it will be full daylight in another few minutes." His voice was husky.

Finding her will at last, Brien moved toward him, her eyes betraying her.

"What am I to do with you?"

He smiled roguishly. "You can marry me—or not." He leaned back on one leg, resting his hands on his waist. "But never ask me to do without you again, Brien. I will have you as part of me; you have only to name the conditions."

Awestruck, Brien stood speechless before him. He proposed? To her? For Aaron Durham to propose marriage willingly—even urgently . . .

Seeing her confusion, he laughed, a charming, deep rumble. "You will need time, I see that." And he gathered her up into his arms, staring down into her sweet, troubled face. "Can you not give me a single word of encouragement?"

"Oh, Aaron," she wailed.

"It's all right," he crowed, "your body encourages me enough for your heart as well."

Flushing deeply, Brien realized that she had molded herself to his frame and even now trembled with passion.

"No excuses," he chided. "We will be together, Brien. Until then I shall court you openly and honorably. This is fair warning." His eyes crinkled with mischief. One quick, hard kiss and he was gone.

In the purple shadows of the early summer dawn, a

lone figure, leaning against the wall at the end of an alley, rubbed his eyes and ran a coarse hand through a ragged mane of hair. His long vigil ended with the appearance of a booted figure on a window ledge several houses away. He straightened, a yellowed sneer spreading across his grizzled face. He rubbed his chin speculatively and turned his collar up against the morning chill. Shoving his hands into his pockets, he slipped away quietly along the fences and buildings to the street.

Twenty-two

Brien drifted pleasantly through the morning, a lingering contentment pervading her whole being. She sat with Helen awhile and admired little Lawrence when the nurse brought him for his feeding. When the babe was filled and sleepy, Brien held him for a moment before the nurse took him. She cuddled and cooed to him and stroked his downy cheeks. Then she stroked his tiny fingers and kissed his yawning mouth. At last she surrendered him up to the nurse.

Helen chatted on about babes and pregnancies and families. Brien was not bored at all and listened with new interest to the intimate feminine matters that she could never have thought to even ask about. There was much to being a woman that she seemed not to know.

During her seclusion at Weston Place, Brien had little contact with other women. Most of her knowledge of men and marriage came from her stern nurse's lectures and the authoritative, if ribald, accounts volunteered by her dear Ella. It had been quite a task to reconcile the disparate views. And Brien had finally settled the question with characteristic common sense. This business of marriage and the duties of a wife to her husband must be neither all bad, nor all good. A great deal must depend on the man and the woman. Since there existed no consensus on the matter, and owing to the dearth of written material on the subject, she came to discount its importance and to ignore its application to her own life.

Inexperienced and not a little confused, she had found it easy to avoid the entire question, being the plain and plump daughter of a reclusive English Lord. Then her father had unwittingly thrust her into the hands of a worldly, lustful man whose only thought was his own pleasure. And at Raoul's hands she had learned to distrust any man who claimed to want or need her.

But Aaron Durham was not just any man. And now she was pursued again, pressed again, however charmingly. She could not make logic of anything about their relationship—least of all why she wanted to believe him when he said he cared for her. She had thought herself beyond such feelings.

If nothing more, Aaron Durham had given her back that part of herself that would risk caring, feeling, again. He could excite, calm, comfort, or even hurt her the way no other ever could . . . even Raoul. On the ship when she thought he'd rejected her, she had felt despair such as Raoul's degradation had failed to produce in her.

And now she felt a guilty sense of excitement that he wanted her enough to court her openly, to risk rejection in pressing for her love. She could not turn aside his assault on her heart, and she wondered if surrender would be so terrible.

That afternoon, a small box containing a lovely blue

porcelain vase arrived, addressed to Brien and bearing the sender's bold signature, Aaron Durham.

Brien smiled, gingerly tracing the cool procelain with her slender fingers. Helen's eyes widened as Brien presented the vase and named the sender.

"Of course I shan't keep it," Brien said casually.

"But it is lovely, Brien. And it is not overly personal." Helen studied her friend carefully. "But to accept it would be to approve the captain's attentions to you. Just what do you think of the Captain?"

Brien's mind was flooded instantly with replies, but she contained them and drew forth a careful response.

"He seems a man of integrity and strength. His manner, however direct, is disarming. He has wit and persistence in abundance."

Seeing Brien pause, Helen picked it up, "And his tall, rakish good looks are enough to warm your blood every time he comes near."

Brien's mouth dropped open. "Really, Helen—"

"Oh, Brien, do you think us all blind? He looks at you as though he were dying of thirst and you are cool water. And when he is near you stiffen and become proper beyond belief. And you blush when he looks at you. My dear, even Silas has commented on it—and Silas is always the last to know such things."

Brien's heart nearly stopped. Did they suspect the true nature of her relationship with Aaron Durham? She pushed the thought from her mind as she studied her hands nervously.

"I admit he interests me. And I am not indifferent to his manly grace or handsomeness. But there is no room in my life for a man now—especially a sea captain with a roving eye."

"I doubt his eyes have roamed an inch from you since he first saw you. Or is it his lack of a title that bothers you?"

The insinuation of snobbery caught Brien off guard. She stared at Helen. "My husband had no title."

"But he was of the nobility," Helen persisted. "If he were Lord Durham would you receive him differently?"

"Helen, there is simply no room in my life for anyone, seaman or nobleman." Apparently Aaron's background was not known in the new world. Brien wondered why. Still, he was respected.

"How can that be, Brien? I have seen you hold my little Lawrence and love him tenderly. You deny that you need the comforts of love and family, but it is plain there is a part of you yet unconvinced. You have such love to give, Brien."

Brien rose and strode to the window. Her eyes were moist with the truth of Helen's argument. Then why did she resist it so? As time dulled the memory of Raoul's treachery, she had less and less reason to avoid marriage. Aaron had erased all doubt that she could again enjoy the pleasures of marriage. But in a month of Raoul's incessant phyiscal demands, she had failed to conceive. And now as she was truly tempted to a new future, the past reached out to crush her hopes. She probably would never bear children. What kind of wife would she make for a man who deserved strong sons and daughters to carry on his name, his goodness?

Each day for the next week a small box arrived containing a perfect lover's gift for Brien. Each gift was accompanied by a card bearing the signature of the captain of the *Secret*. Lace, hair combs, a silk and ivory fan, a crystal decanter for rose water. Helen and Silas exchanged knowing glances as they watched Brien's heart soften before their very eyes.

At the end of the week a note arrived while Brien was

reading in the parlor. Helen, who was now up and about, delivered it to her and stood by as she read it.

" 'Lady Brien Trechaud is invited for an outing and picnic this afternoon at one o'clock. A carriage will call. A. Durham.' " Brien blinked uncertainly. "This is no invitation . . . it is a command! How presumptous. . . ."

"It would be unseemly to go out into the countryside with him alone," Helen agreed, judging her reaction. "But, I trow Dyso would make an excellent chaperone."

Brien rolled her eyes and donned a mischievous smile. "Helen, how long has it been since your dear children have had an outing in the country?"

Promptly at one o'clock a carriage drew up in front of the Hastings house and Aaron Durham was ushered into the center hall. Brien entered soon with the three Hastings children in tow. Dyso appeared at the door with a large hamper and Aaron's face registered the growing realization of what would transpire that afternoon.

"I should have brought two carriages," he observed glumly.

Brien smiled graciously. "We shall have plenty of room. The two smallest ones can sit on our laps. This is so good of you, Captain. It's been quite awhile since any of us have been on an outing. I'm burning with curiosity about the countryside." And she put on a broad-brimmed hat and serenely ushered the children out the door and into the carriage.

The ride into the country was quiet except for polite remarks about the scenery or flowers. Brien was slightly regretful of such a large retinue, but soon forgot it in her wonder at the beautiful country. It was so like her own land about Dunstan Hall.

When little Robert began to squirm on Brien's lap, Aaron wished silently that she would feel the discomfort keenly—'twould serve her right.

The driver turned onto a tree-covered lane which followed the course of a meandering stream. The rutted path was covered with grassy evidence of its disuse. At Aaron's order, the carriage stopped by the stream at an area well carpeted with grass and clear of brush.

Once out of the carriage, Brien stared wide-eyed at the scene. The trees lent cool shade in the noon sun and the grass smelled sweet. The stream was clear and rushed over rocks strewn as the marbles of an angry child.

"This is beautiful," Brien breathed. She turned to Aaron and found him watching her. "Will the owner mind if we lunch here?"

"Not at all. I know him well. He would be delighted to have you here."

The children crowded about her begging to remove their shoes and to wade in the water. Seeing Aaron nod approval, she reluctantly agreed and they bounded off.

Dyso retrieved the hamper from the carriage and placed it on the ground near a great oak tree. Brien asked him to keep a watch for the children in the stream and he nodded agreement and was quickly down the grassy slope to where the children were already entering the water.

Watching Dyso briefly before she turned to her own task, she mused aloud, "The children seem to understand his hand language better that most adults. They're not at all afraid of him."

"Children are sometimes more accepting because they see what is really there and not just what they want to see." Aaron took a seat on an exposed root.

Unsettled by his remark, Brien knelt on the cool

grass to unpack the hamper. Spreading a large coarse cloth on the ground, she unwrapped loaves of fresh bread, cheese and cold slices of ham, raisin tarts, and two jugs—milk and ale. She turned to Aaron.

"I forgot to ask Dyso to put these in the stream to keep cold."

"I'll do it," he bounded up and took the jugs from her. His hand touched hers briefly.

She pretended not to notice the contact but was inwardly glad there were so many people around to constrain her actions.

When Aaron returned minutes later, he removed his coat and sat down in the grass at the edge of the cloth. He reached for a slice of the bread Brien was cutting. The sight of her at so domestic a task was strange to him. An unruly, damp curl of hair at her temple enchanted him and the moist pink of her skin warmed him inside. Every time they were together he found new aspects to her and he loved her all the more for it. A life with her would never be dull.

"I must thank you for the kind invitation, Aaron. But you must have known I could never have come alone."

"Perhaps," Aaron conceded, "but must you have a full regiment for an escort? You have little to fear from me, Brien." His eyes roamed her casually.

"It is not you I fear, Aaron—it is us. I would do nothing to embarrass Silas and Helen. Another chance like—We simply must not be alone together again."

Aaron frowned. "You did not seem to mind our privacy a week ago. What has brought about this sudden interest in propriety?"

Brien's face lost its huomr. "It is neither sudden nor false. I have much to think about and you complicate things terribly."

Aaron was genuinely pleased. "Good. Then at least

you think about me.'' He grinned roguishly. "And I think you are most charming when most improper.''

Her face flushed with deep color. "And I suppose it never occurred to you that another such night might see me with . . . a babe beneath my skirts. But then it would not be your life ruined . . . only mine.'' She taunted him.

His grin disappeared. "You must know little of me to suggest that I would not own my responsibility to you in such a matter. The child would be no bastard.''

The remark had been more cutting than she intended, and she closed her eyes to gain her bearings. "I only know that I cannot continue to tumble into bed with you at every opportunity.''

"Twice in two months is hardly a record for frequency,'' he grinned, relaxing once more. "If you were with child I would be delighted—and we would be married immediately.''

"Married?'' Brien took her breath sharply. "But I don't want to get married!''

Aaron sighed and shook his head. "I warned you earlier, I will have you—and I shall. But I will live with you honorably and openly. That can only be in wedlock, Brien.''

"Oh, no,'' she said firmly, getting up and brushing the leaves and grass from her skirt. And she whirled to walk stridently to the stream and call the children for lunch.

Aaron tried to be angry with her, but it was no use. Pushing is a poor way to lead, his captain had once said. He must be patient; she would come about.

During lunch, Brien teased the children and promised to wade the stream with them later. Aaron agreed it would be safe to explore further up the lane and their afternoon was set.

After finishing off the delicious food and packing

away the remains, Aaron and Brien walked up the lane with the children. As the young ones explored and ran on ahead, Brien and Aaron walked slower and slower, putting distance between them and their charges.

It was so peaceful here, strolling under the old trees. Brien found herself wishing frevently that they were her trees . . . that this was her place. She frowned slightly. She was becoming too attached to this land and to the man who walked beside her.

Aaron noted her pensive state and plucked a daisy, handing it to her with a smile. "You're quiet, Brien."

"I'm sorry. . . . I was just watching the children. They're marvelous—so full of vitality and curiosity. Silas and Helen are so fortunate." Her tone carried a hint of sadness.

Aaron reached for her hand and squeezed it gently as they walked along. "Tell me about you, Brien. About your family."

"My father is Lawrence Weston, earl of Southwold, and my mother was Emilie Garrett of the House of Leighton. She died when I was twelve. I had one sister, older, named Denise. We were very close but I lost her too; she died when I was fifteen. My father and I are all that's left. We have few relations—not even a male cousin for the title, after my father."

Aaron watched her grow pensive once more, feeling as though there were a secret barrier between them that kept him from her.

"There's not much more to tell, really."

"Were you close to your mother?"

"I suppose not. She was so beautiful and so gracious—"

"Like her daughter," Aaron broke in.

"No," Brien stopped and looked at him. "At least not this daughter. My sister, Denise, was very like her. Their beauty was rare and delicate."

She started onward, but was stopped by his un-moving grip on her hand holding her back. "And you?"

"Me?" she shrugged self-consciously, "I was plain and plump and bookish. My father engaged a tutor for us when I was nine years old. M. Duvall was my closest friend for years—until his health failed and he retired. He taught me the world, spread it all before me like a banquet. And I yearned to sample it, experience it all. I heard my father once say that I should have been a boy. I suppose he was right."

Aaron stopped her with a jerk. "Then he is a fool." His face was suddenly sharp and determined. She'd re-vealed more than she knew.

Not sure whether to take offense, she went on. "No . . . I think he was right. I am restless and stubborn and interested in things unseemly for a woman—business for one. When I was little, I despised dolls and tea. Father indulged me and took me with him often to his offices. Poor Silas was but a clerk, but he bore my harassment splendidly. I think I would have made a better man than woman."

"And what makes you think that interests and per-sistence are a measure of men and not women?" Aaron gazed deeply into Brien's pool-like eyes, easily reading her confusion.

Brien was jolted by his words. Such sentiment com-ing from a man—even a very special man. Her heart thumped wildly in her chest. And in her mounting anx-iety she sought to turn the topic away.

"Now, as a widow—" she tossed her head—"I may pursue my interests unhindered by the expectations of society." His release of her hand turned her toward him, unsure of what transpired between them and now regretful of the peace they had just shared.

"So, you would continue living a lie?" His voice was

very calm, too calm.

"A lie?" Brien puzzled.

"Your widowhood." Aaron plied his cheek with his tongue. "You use it as a guise to suit your purposes, when, in fact, yours was no marriage at all."

Blood rose under Brien's skin. "My marriage is none of your affair. I might have known . . . sooner or later you had to use it against me." Her eyes blazed now with hurt, more than anger. "You are true to your sex after all. Treacherous and unfeeling." She turned toward the children but he caught her shoulders and held her in a viselike grip.

"We will settle this now," Aaron demanded.

She struggled against his grasp, horrified at the turning of the afternoon's events. She hoped that the children did not see.

"You didn't love him, did you?" he demanded. When she did not answer he continued.

"You thought to embarrass him on your wedding night—so you used me!"

"No!" she exclaimed, horrified at this twisted version of her past—that skirted so carefully the truth.

"A man of your husband's reputation could hardly have failed to notice that his bride was not a virgin, Lady!" Aaron growled, his face red and terrible as he gripped her harder. "That is why you came to me in Harrall's Road that night. That was the job you wanted done. Just to find a suitable stud for your plot!"

"No," she wailed, struggling so hard her breath came fast and she quivered with hurt and rage.

"What did you want, Brien? Money? Revenge?" Aaron yelled at her now, venting all the jealousy he had long denied. Then he released her abruptly.

"No!" Brien screamed at him, "No! Freedom . . . That was all! Freedom!" Her whole being was agonized at his wrongful contempt for her. To bear this

332

from him . . . Then anger bested the hurt and she faced him to set the record straight. It took all her energy to control her trembling body and voice.

"My father saw only his family's money and arranged for me to marry him. He was a rogue, cunning and deceitful! Because of his lies my father forced me to marry him—thinking he would set my honor right. Raoul convinced him we had been lovers when I tried to break the engagement. I thought when he learned his lies had come true, he would annul our travesty of a marriage. But his greed and lust exceeded my worst fears. He insisted the marriage stand!" Her voice was hoarse now and she shook visibly. But it purged her somehow to scream out the burden she had carried for so long.

Aaron was stunned, horrified by the pain that ripped through her. And he had caused it by probing too deeply at the secrets that separated them.

She was agonized now and sank to her knees, burying her face in her hands and wailing, "Don't you want to know what he did for revenge?" When she lifted her face the tears spilled down her cheeks, burning them.

"Hear it all and then hate me—but at least know the truth! Raoul imprisoned me in the very house where I spent my girlhood. And nightly he came to me and forced me to submit to his twisted lusts, punishing my body for my depriving him of his husbandly rights!" She spit out the words as though they burned her tongue, each a fresh agony bound to call more abuse upon her. The torrent of hurt that poured forth next pierced him cruelly.

"Now do you find pleasure in knowing what hell my marriage was for me?" Her voice was hoarse and her breath came in sobbing bursts.

The hurt and fear in her face tore through his guts

like white-hot pincers. He sank to his knees beside her and gathered her into his arms.

"My God, Brien, I—" He couldn't continue. How could he have been so stupid, so clumsy . . . and so blind? She had suffered much already and now he prodded her mercilessly to bare her soul to him. He had only meant to make her see how foolish it was to go on hiding from life—from the truth.

Ironically, now it was he who found the truth unbearable. His chest ached at the thought of anyone abusing this sweet, strong lady. And now he knew she had been abused. He was angry with everyone who had ever caused her a moment's pain—especially himself. Small wonder she fled from involvement with men and possible marriage.

Unable to find words to comfort her or excuse his conduct and jealousy toward a dead man, Aaron was silent. He held her close until her crying sounds stopped and she pulled away from him.

She released a long shuddering sigh. She felt lighter somehow. The horrible truth was out, and it did not seem so terrible or fearsome as it had inside her alone. Aaron must hate her, but he would have had to know the truth sooner or later. It was best he knew now—before he knew how much he meant to her. He was the only one in the world she could have told. Even his scorn would be easier to bear than carrying the burden of her past alone.

Then he took her chin in his hand and tilted her face to his. Brien was staggered by the misery in his face.

His voice was hushed. "I cannot ask your forgiveness, Brien. I am not worthy of it. I would give years of my life to take it all back. I could not bear the thought of you in another man's arms—even if you were his legal wife." His expression was bleak.

She couldn't believe her senses. He apologized? Felt

he had wronged her? She reached out to touch his ruddy cheek.

"You don't hate me?" she wondered aloud.

"Hate you? 'Tis you should loathe me. I had no idea how terrible it had been for you. I only meant to remove that barrier that always seems to be between us. I wanted you to stop pretending to be loyal to the memory of a husband you could never have loved." He paused. "I should have left you alone that night in Harrall's Road. It might have gone better for you." His misery clutched at Brien's heart.

"No, Aaron," she cradled his face in her hands. "I never regretted that night with you—not for one moment. Thoughts of you and your gentle loving made it . . . bearable for me." A little smile brightened her tear-blotched face. "How we came together did not, does not, bother me. It seems the fates find us an interesting combination; they have brought us together again."

Calm returned to him as he drew her into his arms. She nuzzled against his strong chest, reveling in the clean, masculine scent of him and the strength of his arms about her. She felt free for the first time in two years.

When she raised her face to his, he claimed her lips lovingly. When they parted, Brien traced the squareness of his jaw and the firm fullness of his generous lips.

At length, he rose and helped her to her feet. Brushing the grass and leaves from her dress she muttered, "I must be a fright." She wiped her eyes with the handkerchief he offered and turned for his inspection, "Am I presentable?"

"Enchanting."

Embarassed, she fumbled with her skirt. "We must find the children. I hope they're not lost by now."

He grabbed her hand and drew her farther up the

lane. "We'll find them; they can't have gone far."

The little Hastings were wading in the stream once more and it took a bit of doing to gather them up and herd them back to the meadow. When they returned, Dyso had packed the hamper and quilt, and waited patiently for their return. They were soon on the way back to Boston.

A pleasant weariness settled over Brien as she sank back against the smooth leather seat, cradling Robert in her arms. The tyke was soon cozily snuggled down into sleep, despite the excited chatter of his elders.

Aaron stole a glance at Brien and found her cheek resting on Robert's curly brown head. How sweet and loving she seemed, as though she belonged there with a sleeping child on her lap.

Knowing that Aaron watched her, she cared little to hide the peace and contentment she felt all through her.

As the carriage drew up in front of the house, Brien felt a stab of regret that their time together was over. Aaron carried little Robert into the house and deposited him in the nurse's arms. The older children bade Aaron a solemn farewell and were promptly marched into the kitchen for a thorough washing.

Brien put her arm through Aaron's as she walked him to the door. "I enjoyed today immensely. Thank you for it, Aaron."

"Will you come for tea on Sunday?" she asked precipitously. She was loathe to let him leave without knowing when she would see him again.

He grimaced. "Tea?" Then he raised one brow and glanced furtively about the hall before slipping one arm about her waist and pressing her to him.

"I'll endure it if it means a chance to be close to you."

She slipped away from him. "You'll have to comport yourself in more seemly fashion, Captain." Then she lowered her eyes demurely. "We would enjoy your company, I'm sure."

"We have much to talk about, Brien," he said seriously when he caught her gaze.

"No, Aaron . . . I need . . . time. . . ." She floundered under the onslaught of his fabulous eyes.

"Very well, you shall have it. Tuesday I sail for New York to see about a shipyard. I shall be gone a week or so. Then you shall not be able to put me off so easily."

And he was gone.

At tea on Sunday, Aaron could hardly take his eyes from Brien. Painfully aware of his blatant attention to her, Brien tried to be gracious, but had difficulty concentrating on the conversation. She wanted to believe he did it out of feeling for her, but somehow she knew he enjoyed the embarrassment he caused her.

Helen finally excused herself from the room and asked Silas to help her in the dining room. After a puzzled silence, the realization struck home and he agreed enthusiastically to aid her. Helen drew the parlor doors together behind her discreetly.

Brien groaned in frustration, hopping up from her seat. "Now see what you've done."

Aaron smiled lazily, leaning back in his chair to better appreciate the sight of her. "Your hostess is a perceptive woman. I doubt her leave-taking was all my doing. After all, 'twas you invited me to tea."

"In a moment of weakness, I assure you."

"Let us not disappoint dear Helen. Come sit and let me woo you properly." He patted his lap, grinning. His eyes glinted and Brien swayed under them.

She plopped unceremoniously onto the sofa opposite

him, in defiance of her own impulses. Tilting her chin up she remarked, "I would Van Zandt were as eager to deal with me. I should be on my way back to England this very moment, a richer woman."

Aaron shrugged, not overly disappointed at her reaction. Nothing ventured . . . "If you will not favor me with your charms, then favor me with your busineess news. Van Zandt is proving a hard man to win, is he?"

"He has made two offers, both insulting. I told him so." She shuddered involuntarily. "I'm not at all sure I wish to sell to the swine—even if he meets my price."

Observing her regal bearing and disdain, Aaron frowned. "I warned you that Van Zandt was not to be toyed with. I ran across him during the war. He has no morals, no principles, no higher nature you could appeal to. He seems to desire a modicum of respectability now and perhaps thinks that the purchase of Weston Trading will afford some of that. But, just as easily, he could turn his considerable resources against you viciously." His seriousness shook Brien to the core.

"Do not underestimate him. Your air of nobility may charm others—even me. But to Van Zandt it will be an irksome goad. Be careful you do not spur him too hard."

Brien's large eyes told him his message had struck home. Yet there was not a trace of fear there. Aaron's lips tilted in a wry smile. That was his woman! A formidable opponent herself.

"Thank you for your advice. But if Van Zandt makes another offer, it shall be in Silas' office—and in the presence of a raft of solicitors. I have no wish to confront that pompous mass more than is necessary."

"Ah, that's good to know. Hearing you dined with him, I wondered at your taste in men."

She flushed, but suppressed her indignation and walked to the window, sweeping provocatively by his chair in the process.

"Well you should know my taste in men, Aaron Durham, for if ever there was . . ." She stopped. What was she saying?

Aaron was on his feet and beside her before she could blink. He took her hands in his and stared into her face. "What, Brien?" His voice had a curious husky quality now as he breathed in the fragrance of her.

"If ever there was man to embody them it would be you," she whispered. Her breath came faster, and she waited for his lips to claim hers. But the sweet expectation went unfilled a moment longer.

"Brien, there is something I must tell you," Aaron said somberly, fighting the consummate urge to drown his reason in the warm sweetness of her mouth.

"Let it wait, Aaron." Her arms came up about him. "Let us not disappoint our hostess."

Brien's head lay on Aaron's shoulder as they sat on the sofa. They talked.

"What is your father like, Aaron? You've made reference to hard feelings between you. Surely it has not always been so."

He was silent a moment. "My father is a rare man, keen of mind and of great integrity. I respect him for that. But I could never live as he has. From the time my mother died, when I was seven years, until this day, I cannot say I have seen him smile. He is as hard as the granite walls of Wiltshire."

In the pause, Brien watched his serious expression. He seemed so distant from her suddenly. She wished to reach into his thoughts and draw him back to her.

"When I left over a year ago to make my home in Bristol, he swore to disown me if I did not return to beg his forgiveness."

Something in his voice alarmed Brien. "Will you go to him, Aaron?" She thought of her own father and of how narrowly she had missed knowing him, loving him. Aaron's reply startled her.

"No." His response was resolute. "I do not want his money or title . . . or anything else from him." The strong edge of his words was honed fine with bitterness.

"You cannot mean that surely." She sat up to face him.

The disbelief in her face bothered him for no reason he was willing to name—but it nagged at the border of his consciousness.

"Ah, but I do mean it, Lady. I shall never be a count. I have left that all behind me now." He shook his head.

"But, your duty . . ."

"Is to live my life as I see fit. I am not proud of some aspects of my life, Brien. But I have been honest in all my dealings with men and women. I prefer to make my own way—and to make my own wealth. I do not ask favors or privilege—only to be given the chance to live my own life as I see fit. I want to be what I can be."

Brien felt for the first time the real impact of his rejection of the class to which she belonged. Her heart floundered in her chest. Until now she had harbored a secret dream . . . marriage to this noble son of England. He needed time . . . time would see that he was reconciled with his destiny . . . his duty. He was the one true match for her in every sense, even to the noble rank of his house. It had seemed so easy. . . . His voice brought her back to him.

"Brien, I must tell you. This trip to New York—the *Secret* will bear American colors." He waited for the impact of his words to be felt.

Her face drained of color as her eyes widened in astonishment.

"But, no! Aaron . . . that would mean . . ." Her voice trailed off. Aaron was declaring his intention to leave England permanently. Registering his ship as an American vessel would mean declaring himself a citizen of the rebellious provinces.

"No," she breathed as the realization overwhelmed her.

"Brien, I intend to make Boston my home." His golden eyes probed hers deeply for her response, even as she searched her own heart.

Both found only confusion. This of all things she had not expected. She had felt that she understood his rebellion against tradition and his father—but this! To give up his citizenship—his homeland—as a final stab at his father's position and authority. To cast away every tie to his land . . . his people!

She stood up, wordless from the shock, and walked away from him.

"I thought you should know." His voice was steady behind her.

"When did you decide this?" Brien fought with the growing despair in her.

"It has been my plan for some time." He ached to touch her and bridge the gulf that each moment widened between them.

For some time? He had planned it all alone! From their talk on the ship to that night in her chamber. And her? What did he expect of her?

A lump in her stomach began to twist and burn in the growing silence, fomenting righteous anger. It was clear now; he expected her to choose—him. She must choose him over her father, her position, her country— her whole way of life!

A sardonic voice rose inside her. If she chose him what else did she choose? Poverty? Lonely months with him at sea, plying his carefree trade? An inner door crashed shut at the sting of this new betrayal, sealing away newly wakened feelings and trust.

The long silence became unbearable and he drew the final curtain on their future. "I love this country—you said it yourself. So I will make this my home, my people."

"Do you not see what this must do?" She shook with emotion and tension.

He saw more than she realized. "Now, without promise of a title, you will not have me."

She wheeled on him, eyes blazing. "I never thought of you as a title. It's not like that at all." But his words echoed strongly in her brain.

"The future is here, Brien. And my future is here."

He left unspoken the part that might have included her. And she would not finish it for him. By his choice he had put an ocean between them.

Did lack of a title mean that much to her? Or was it the rejection of her beloved England? Or more still, the arrogance that assumed her need for him would see that she capitulated to his demand for his own freedom. How could she have misjudged him so?

"All I have is yours, Brien. But all I have is in America, now."

There it was. The ultimatum she dreaded was delivered with staggering effect. She must choose now between everything she knew and loved and this extrordinary man who owned her heart and body.

How dare he do this to her!

He read in her face the conflict of her heart, and his own bearing wavered under the press of his feelings.

Her battle against the terrible onslaught of pride finished quickly, and vanquished hope crept back into the recesses of her heart. Her face hardened as her eyes lit with the anger of betrayal. She turned away from him and felt a pricking in her eyes. There was no swooning or grief now—only a cold self-reproach.

Aaron scowled, the corners of his mouth turned down sharply with disappointment. He had lost the only battle worth winning. His chest wrenched and for a long, excruciating moment, he wavered. Then he turned on his heel and strode quietly out of the room.

At the click of the door Brien whirled and glimpsed only a part of his shoulder as he departed.

How could she have been so blind? Aaron Durham was a special man—but he was just a man. He expected the weaker, emotional side of her to acquiesce to his plans—all for the privilege of sharing his bed in this raw new land. It never occurred to him the price he asked her to pay. The sardonic twist of her thoughts vented the hurt she struggled to contain.

She wanted to be angry, to rave and call him vile names, even hate him. But the fairness of her mind prevented it. There was blame enough for both . . . and pain.

Sinking onto the window seat she stared unblinkingly into the street below. Her hurt and anger were well met, even bested, by her feeling for him. She felt only fatigue and blessed numbness, for all her energy was consumed in the battle of emotions.

"He taught me I am capable of caring. And now, caring for him, how could I ask him to sacrifice his dreams and principles to return home to a title and a tradition he despises. He never would ask it of me . . . he didn't ask it of me. He left it to me to offer. Was it conceit or love that made him hope I'd say yes?"

Enough! 'Tis done! A sterner voice rose inside. You will pay dearly for each lesson, but at last you will learn of men. You look for the impossible in a man and are disappointed when you cannot find it. Content yourself with the life you will have—are meant to have.

And slowly the tears came.

The parlor maid brought a message to Silas at the breakfast table and he put down his cup to devote full attention to the contents.

Brien was lost in thought and barely noticed the grave expression on his face as he finished the communiqué. Paling, he turned to Brien.

"It's burned. The Cambridge shop . . . it's burned. Last night." He lifted the paper in silent testimony.

"What?" Brien was jolted back to awareness. "Burned?"

Silas looked at the message once more before handing it to his fair employer. "The cause of the fire is unknown. The stock was destroyed, but the building is repairable." His hands dropped helplessly onto the arms of the chair. "Thank God no one was hurt. Harrison, the shopkeeper was unharmed. He's a good man—and honest."

A chill spread through Brien at the realization of the danger that narrowly passed them.

"Will there be an investigation, Silas?" Brien was disturbed for no reason she could lay name to.

"In a small town like Cambridge, the local magistrate may make inquiries, but I doubt much will be learned. There are myriad reasons for a fire in a store with such varied stock." He looked at her warily, disturbed at her question and the suspicion that it planted in his own mind.

"I don't like it. This is suspicious timing for a fire. That shop was our largest. It will mean a real loss." Her lips drew into an uncharacteristic thin line as she stared at the paper in her hand, and rose.

"What can we do now but wait? If another of our shops should suffer a similar fate, it might frighten away potential buyers. We should take steps to protect our investment." Determination sharpened her lovely features.

"We could post a night watch at each of our shops. Could you see to it, Silas?"

"But, surely, you can't think . . ."

"I don't know what to think. But we will not allow the chance that it may happen again, accident or not. Will you see to the watches, Silas?"

Brien's coolness and resolve were remarkable in view of her recent distraction. It was as though a metamorphosis occurred before their eyes.

"Of course, Brien," Silas acquiesced.

As if reading their thoughts, she straightened.

"I have allowed this business to languish of late. It shall not happen again. We will find a buyer, and soon."

In the three days that had elapsed since Aaron's hurried departure from the Hastings House, Brien had been quiet and distant. Exchanging worried glances, Silas and Helen had tried to act normally and pretend they did not notice.

At last, Helen had tried to talk with their friend about what had happened, but she met with stony silence, and in the end, withdrew, leaving Brien to her own company.

Now she seemed once more in control of herself, and the situation led to relief on Silas's part and sadness in his dear wife, who had hoped to see the blossoming of the sweet relationship between the captain and the lady.

That very afternoon, a message arrived by courier

for Lady Brien Trechaud. The courier awaited a reply and Helen hurried the message upstairs to her guest.

Hoping against all reason that it was from Aaron, Brien tore into it in most unladylike fashion. The coarse scrawl and improper English left no doubt as to the authenticity of the signature—Horace Van Zandt. Her disappointment at the authorship gave way to pleasure at the contents.

". . . to make you final offer. Send confirmation by messenger," she read the finish aloud. Raising her head thoughtfully, she frowned. The timing of this new offer, so soon in the wake of the fire, was strange coincidence. There was nothing left to her in the colonies, but to make as good a bargain as possible for the sale of the company and to return home, where she really belonged.

"Van Zandt wants to make another offer," she informed Helen. "Will Friday be too soon for Silas to arrange a meeting with the solicitors in his office?"

So it was that on a sultry early July morning, Brien sat once more in the offices of Weston Trading, awaiting the final bargaining for property she was increasingly reluctant to sell. Silas and two of their local solicitors were present to witness the agreement and bind it with appropriate contracts.

The groan of boards and the scraping of chairs in the outer office announced the arrival of the obese buyer.

Van Zandt sleazed through the doorway by a narrow margin and stopped just inside to survey the woman he had come to vanquish.

"Welcome, Mr. Van Zandt," Brien said confidently. She refused to offer this creature her hand and sat down behind Silas' desk, indicating with a wave of her hand the stout chair on the other side for Van

Zandt.

"Goot day." His awkward bow was more of a nod and his ugly yellow smile caused Brien to shudder in spite of herself.

"May I offer you some tea, Mr. Van Zandt?" The service was on the desk before her, ready to pour.

"*Ja*, tanks," he nodded, setting his jowls reverberating.

Taking a cup to pour, Brien commented on the recent loss of the Cambridge shop. She noted that Van Zandt showed no surprise. "Of course, we shall adjust the price accordingly." Her hand was steady as she offered him a steaming cup of tea and she noted well the tremor in his as he accepted it. What could he have to be nervous about?

She took a cup herself and as Silas poured his own, she settled back to study the sweating hulk before him.

"You English must haf your tea," Van Zandt snorted. "Zo very civilized."

Brien's chin tilted upward and her eyes narrowed almost imperceptibly. "Thank you, sir. We do prize civility. But not at the expense of profit." She forced a winning smile. She would not rush this time.

Downing the hot liquid in quick gulps, Van Zandt deposited the cup with finality on the desk in front of her.

"Now, " he declared, "ve talk."

"Yes," Brien agreed. "We have considered the inventory of goods at the Cambridge shop and adduced it to have been worth two thousand."

"Ja, ja, perhaps." He waved his hand disinterestedly.

Brien's composure was strained to the limit. "Then have you an offer, Mr. Van Zandt?"

"I gif you offer . . ."—his bilious eyes became fat-framed slits—"privately."

Brien was relieved to be able to show incredulity. "These men are my advisors. They are privy to all my affairs, sir. You may speak freely and in confidence before them."

"Vat I zay—I zay to you alone." The determination of his face struck a chord against the memory of Aaron's warning.

Brien's resolve to keep Silas beside her wavered. Turning to her supporters, she convinced them with her confidence that she would not need them.

"It seems Mr. Van Zandt desires to make the offer in private, Silas. Would you mind?"

They quitted the room reluctantly, Silas commenting that he would be just outside. Brien felt a wave of gratitude to her host.

Cynical amusement played at Van Zandt's mouth as the door closed on them. "Now ve talk."

Brien put down her cup and folded her slender hands patiently on her lap. He was enjoying this buyers' market far too much to suit her.

"You vill zell to me for seben t'ousand pounds," he hissed, his watery eyes gleaming strangely.

Stunned by the unexpectedly low figure, Brien stared at him. "Don't you mean seventeen? Quite a generous offer." Brien had heard him correctly, but bought time in which to react carefully.

"No," he proclaimed. "Seben t'ousand. And you vill zell to me for dat."

"Never." Brien's coolness surprised them both. "Your last offer of ten was unacceptable. What makes you think I should ever agree to seven?" Her eyes flecked with sparks from the abrasive combination of her anger's flint on her will's cold steel.

"You agree because your noble name can not have scandal." Seeing her frown, he continued, leering shamelessly at her shapely form. "You haf visitor at

348

night in your room—all night. Dur-ham, is not?" His sneer sent chills over her.

" 'Ow vill Bos-ton tink of dis English slut who parade around high and mighty—and spends nights with lovers?"

"Lovers?" Brien was incredulous. How could he have known about Aaron's visit? Her mind raced to match his moves, his intention now perfectly clear—blackmail. But he had chosen the wrong victim. Just now she cared little for public censure and even less for the sale of her property to this blackguard.

"How dare you confront me with such degraded fabrications?" Her face was tight with rage and she clenched her teeth, "You call me foul names and think to bully and frighten me into giving you what you want?"

"You haf no choice," Van Zandt snarled. "For all I know, you haf many lovers of low character who tell every-ting for little silver." His porcine face was menacing.

He meant to disgrace her by bringing forth a throng of false lovers to attest to her debauchery. What of her friends, Silas and Helen? They would know it for a lie—but what would they suffer from others? And Aaron?

Her eyes narrowed as she answered his threat. There was only one course.

"Then bring them on, you swine! There is no man living to truly swear to what you spew. I fear not your sick, loathesome threat one bit!"

She jumped to her feet, drawing upon every scrap of dignity she possessed. Van Zandt matched her.

"I would not sell to you now at any price," she ground out through gritted teeth. "Now get ou tof this office and never again disgrace Weston property with your revolting bulk!" She flung one hand regally toward the door.

In a flash, his hamlike hand grabbed her outstretched arm and pulled her partly across the desk toward him. As she struggled to be free of his killing grip, she felt the pot of tea beneath her and instinctively grabbed it up, flinging the stinging hot liquid full in Van Zandt's face.

Bellowing in surprise and rage, he grabbed at his scalded face and released her in the same instant.

From the side door, Dyso burst in and, seeing Brien unharmed, rushed to pound a heavy fist into the howling face of the flesh mountain. The outer door swung open and Dyso shoved the panting, cursing mound through the doorframe and into the outer office. Van Zandt ranted and cursed in English and his native tongue. Brien caught only snatches of his ravings. But one word stuck in her mind and disturbed her heart . . . burn!

Twenty-three

As the *Secret* lay berthed snug against the dock that next night, a large figure, moved stealthily, emerging from the shadows to challenge the watch on the gangway. Before the watchman could shout for help he was knocked unconscious by a huge, leadlike fist. The figure paused over the unconscious heap, picked up the seaman, and carried him onto the deck. Depositing his burden carefully, the intruder silently made his way to the hatchway and entered without hesitation.

Aaron Durham sat pouring over manifests in his cabin when the door slammed open. Instinctively, he reached for a nearby sword, baring its cold blue edge effortlessly. Already out of the chair, Aaron blinked unsurely as he recognized the face and form that pushed through the door before him.

"Dyso?" he puzzled, without relaxing his coiled muscles.

The hulk, stopping just beyond the naked point of

the blade, nodded in response.

Aaron shifted his stance without lowering the weapon. He was unsure of the hulk's intention and wished to keep the momentary advantage.

"What do you want?" Aaron growled. "How did you get past the watch?"

Dyso's hands pointed to Aaron and arched in a sweeping motion toward the door, then back to himself. Seeing the puzzlement on Aaron's face, he repeated the sequence, more slowly.

Aaron frowned, lowering his sword and easing the tension in his arms and legs. "You want me to come with you?"

Dyso's quick nod was the only affirmation; the man's huge face was impassive.

"Did Brien send you?" Aaron sheathed his blade and regarded the man speculatively.

Dyso shook his head and one massive hand pointed to Aaron, then closed in a fist that tapped his chest above his heart. Then the massive hands waved together asymmetrically downward, tracing curves Aaron well understood; they could only mean Brien. Dyso clenched his fists to flex the bulging muscle of his right arm and made a pounding motion on the arm with the other fist.

Aaron's mind raced to decipher the cryptic message of those violence-hardened hands. Then it came to him. . . .

"Brien—is she in trouble?"

A subtle relaxation of tension in the big man's face as he nodded confirmed Aaron's guess. In an instant, he thought how earlier he had seen this hulk as an adversary, an impediment to being near his lady. But the man was far more perceptive that Aaron realized. He had seen that Aaron cared for his lady and now came to Aaron for help. Dyso needed his words to protect

Brien.

Aaron smiled wryly at the twist of events and reached for the long knife that lay on the desk, tucking it into his boot.

"Take me to her, my silent friend." He clasped Dyso's mighty arm and started for the door.

But massive arms shot out to restrain Aaron, and he whirled with a darkened face. Had he misread the hulk?

Dyso's fearsome face showed a deep frown and he shook his head vigorously.

Aaron's muscles were again taut as he searched his potential opponent for clues to this obstinance.

"You won't take me to her?"

Again the hulk's head shook with determination.

"If she is in trouble I want to help, but I must know the cause."

Dyso's hard glare softened and he nodded, retaining the talon grip on Aaron's arm. His free hand flew in a series of gestures that indicated a belly grown large.

Aaron was intrigued by the puzzle the man presented and slowly relaxed, producing a noticeable easing in the pantomiming hulk.

Then a thought flashed in his brain, nearly staggering him.

"Is she with child?"

To his absolute surprise the hulk smiled, then shook his head slowly, allowing the amusement to fade from his face. No, she was not pregnant. And again he repeated the gestures, adding an almost comical puffing of the cheeks to the routine.

It seemed an eternity before the insight came. Van Zandt!

"Is it Van Zandt?"

A terse, relieved nod told Aaron much.

"Damn," he muttered savagely. "I warned her!

Have they quarreled?''

Another nod. The large black eyes burned now as the two massive fists pounded together. Aaron's gaze was drawn to them and he wondered at their awesome potential.

"Has he tried to hurt her?" Anger was rising inside him. When Dyso shook his head, Aaron went on. "He's threatened her?"

"Of course." Aaron paced the cabin anxiously under the protector's gaze. "I feared such—and I tried to warn her." Remembering his lady's regal dignity and the determination that bordered on arrogance, he laughed aloud. Turning to the puzzled Dyso, he mused, "I'll wager the confrontation was most interesting. I'm surprised we didn't see the fireworks two days out of port!"

Propping one long, muscular leg on the chair, he rested an elbow on it. "What shall we do with her, my friend?" He smiled in spite of himself, remembering her pride. He thought of her outrage if she were to discover Dyso came to him for help. "That stubborn pride of hers will not let her admit a need for help."

Straightening, he said quietly, "Shall we pay a late call on Mr. Van Zandt?" Grabbing the scabbard of his sheathed sword, he motioned to the door. "Let's go."

In the night breeze on deck, Aaron found his first watch slumbering peaceably. Stooping briefly to reassure himself of the man's condition, he winced at the sight of the dark swelling of the man's jaw and glanced at the once more impassive Dyso.

"You do neat work, my friend. He'll be fit by morning." Dyso had used the only means available to secure access to Aaron's cabin. It was clear from the seaman's state that a careful amount of force had subdued him. He would sleep soundly until morning and would awaken with little more than a sore jaw.

The streets were quiet now that it was well on toward one o'clock. An occasional dog barked or the leaves of a tree rustled to punctuate the dark stillness. Straining his ears, Aaron heard only one set of boots, his own. A quick glance beside him revealed the silent, rolling stride of his companion, setting a pace that Aaron's long legs were hard pressed to match.

Dyso gestured suddenly to an alleyway and was moving quickly down it into the closing darkness before Aaron could utter a word. Aaron followed dumbly and Dyso led him through a maze of alleyways and streets until at last he paused and slipped through a partly opened gate. Dyso's ironbound arm thrust Aaron back against the fence and a second later, Aaron saw the reason.

The rear door of the large brick house before them was guarded by a burly seaman armed with a brace of pistols, no doubt loaded and ready for mischief. There was no doubt as to the occupant of the house. Dyso had led him unerringly to Van Zandt's residence. How the hulk had known the way—and that it was guarded—mystified Aaron. There was obviously more to the man than he could ever have guessed.

Slipping past the guard would be impossible. Aaron judged that even a swift assault would rouse others with its noise. There must be an evening of the odds. Reaching out with his foot, he pushed the bush in front of him several times, creating a rustling sound. Drawing no response, he repeated the movement more noticeably. Dyso, watching first Aaron and then the guard, sensed the plan and moved stealthily off to the shelter of a tree across from the shaking bush.

Calling out unsurely and straining into the darkness outside the lantern's dull glow, the heavy seaman moved toward Aaron's hiding place. As he passed the tree where Dyso hid, a fist thudded down on the back of his neck with awful precision, sending him sprawling unconscious on the ground.

Aaron heard the thud and crept out from behind the shrubbery of the garden to inspect his companion's handiwork.

The house was not difficult to navigate even in the semidarkness. Up the stairs, they tried only one empty bedchamber before finding the one where Van Zandt slept, propped up on pillows in a huge bed—snoring loudly.

Aaron lit a candle as Dyso drew the drapes at the window. Then he approached the sleeping figure, pulling the steel stiletto from his boot and testing its razor-sharp blade with his thumb. He motioned to Dyso to stay near the door.

Touching the point of the cold blade to the wattle of red flesh overlying Van Zandt's neck Aaron said boldly, "Waken, Herr Swine. We have business, you and I!"

"*Vas?*" Van Zandt started up, but, encountering the point of the blade, blinked dumfoundedly and sank back under its sharp pressure.

"*Vas meinst du?*" he rasped.

"Do you not remember me, *mein herr?*" Aaron's exaggerated politeness gave evidence that this task was not altogether unpleasant for him. He smiled coldly.

"Shall I refresh your memory, Herr Swine? I was mate on a brigantine you ran afoul of during the war—the *Challenger*. Aaron Durham is my name."

A flash of recognition crossed Van Zandt's face at the name. His bilious eyes narrowed hatefully. "I remember."

Again Aaron smiled coldly. "Ah, but I have not come to open old wounds, Van Zandt. There is a current matter that needs attending." He pressed the sharp point of his dirk a bit harder against the wattle of

356

flesh.

"You have dealt most dishonorably with a friend of mine. I shall see it ends now, before real harm is done."

Again Van Zandt's eyes flickered with recognition and he hissed, "Dat Slut . . ."

"Lady Brien," Aaron corrected him coolly. "You will not press her to sell to you, nor will you make good your threats." Aaron gambled that he would soon draw out the nature of those threats from this miserly mass, and he was soon rewarded.

"Zoon every-one know her for da zlut she isss."

Aaron fought to restrain his hand from plunging the blade into the scurrilous heap. Cold determination set his face with predatory sharpness, turning his pleasant features into a stonelike work of malice.

"You propose to embarrass the lady? Most unchivalrous."

"You tink you scare me?" the fat man challenged. "Go tell your whore she pay for dis."

"My—" Aaron stopped. The anger rising hot inside him was more dangerous than any of Van Zandt's baiting. It would be so easy; it was so tempting to let his hand apply a fraction more pressure and so rid the world of this wretch's evil. But his own anger would thus be his enemy—at odds with all his hopes for the future. He must have a cool hand and clear mind.

"Do not underestimate her, Van Zandt. She did not send me here. She is a true lady—overproud and stubborn to a fault, but not a whore or a coward. You thought to extort Weston Trading from her?" Aaron smiled humorlessly. "Think again, Herr Swine. Methinks the air of all Boston would smell sweeter with you absent. You will sell this house and leave Boston for good."

"Vat makes you tink you scare me, Dur-ham?" Van

Zandt's challenge was more cautious as he studied well the measure of the man who held him captive in his own bed. "I own dis house—I vill not zell." He gurgled and growled like a trapped animal.

"I have friends, Van Zandt." Aaron's voice matched well his blade, cold and sharp. "They remember well, as do I, your activities during the war. They have placed at my disposal certain documents and would willingly give testimony about your wartime deceptions—testimony that would hang you in any of these thirteen colonies." His golden eyes were glowing brands. "If you are not gone on tomorrow's tide, I will lead the soldiers to your door myself. And I will enjoy your dance upon the air—as you hang."

Long-held rage and supressed memories flooded back to tighten Aaron's throat and shiver his taut muscles with tension. The burning powder's smoke once more burned his eyes and seared his lungs. His own blood from a gash in his face now mingled with that of colonial sons on his shirt, boots, and blade. And in the face of what transpired before his aching eyes, he felt a bond of kinship forged with those he had not long before called enemy. A fat, quavering mass stood before his captain on board the *Challenger,* a smuggler caught running the blockade under cover of a colonial warship. The man now wheedled and begged and bargained. This younger Van Zandt had been no less conniving or repulsive.

In the end, Van Zandt had won a stay, bought with treachery and blood. He'd agreed to furnish information on colonial movements, even other smugglers, for the right to ply his trade unhindered and free of competition. The captain, against his own fiber, struck the bargain—only to see it fulfilled admirably, almost joyfully, by Van Zandt.

As the war dragged on, Aaron witnessed the hideous

accuracy of Van Zandt's information and his disgust turned to loathing as the decks of good ships ran red with his treachery. Playing friend to the colonial cause, Van Zandt lined his pockets while betraying the rebels at every turn. And ironically, Van Zandt was proclaimed heroic by the colonials for his successful breach of the British blockade. They never suspected that his "luck" was provided by the British navy itself.

"Your treason will hang you, swine," Aaron spat, "if I do not finish you first. Which shall it be? A plantation in the Indies—or the gallows of Boston?" Aaron snarled. "The choice is far more than you deserve."

Van Zandt pushed his bulk laboriously about his lavishly furnished bed chamber. His hands snatched at small, costly items, gathering them to him as he grumbled and growled his hatred of the man who forced this flight. A small gray-faced serving woman moved similarly about the adjoining sitting room, hurriedly packing what she could into two large wooden barrels in the middle of the room. The scene was repeated in other worthy rooms of the spacious house, but much would be left behind, for there was little time to see to material goods.

"Hulda!" Van Zandt's gravelly voice rang out suddenly, and the little woman scurried to appear before her master.

"*Ja, mein herr?*" She dipped nervously before him, gauging his murderous mood and the safety of her proximity to him.

His porcine jowls were bloated with anger. "For-get vat you do. Go to da front and zee dese bas-tards load de wagon right." His loglike arm thrust toward the front of the house in a gesture of command, and the little woman dipped once more, grateful to exit his indiscriminate wrath.

Van Zandt watched her go and when she closed the outer door behind her he shuffled his mass to the side of the massive canopied bed and grunted and snorted as he moved the night stand from its place to reveal a small safe imbedded in the masonry wall. In a bare moment, the door was opened and his fleshy paws were digging into the contents; raking jewelry, stacks of gold coins, and bank notes into bags he took from inside the safe itself. Here was a part of his blood-tainted fortune which was always with him. And he would have need of it where he was going. Only money and the power it brings would see him comfortable in the lands of lawless men to which he was exiled.

As he worked, he checked the sun's progress along the afternoon sky with a tilt of his head toward the window, and then his work became feverish. He had much yet to do before his way was secure. The morning was wasted with solicitors and legal manipulations of property, leaving him less time than he needed to see to his household treasures. His mind worked apace with his grasping fingers, and his festering hatred roiled anew.

"Dur-ham, you bas-tard. I zee you pay for dis." Then as he heaved himself up from his work, an ominous gleam shone in his eyes. He moved to the window that faced the street side of the house. Two burly seamen bearing spars watched conspicuously from across the street as the wagon was loaded. Durham was as careful as he was clever, and Van Zandt knew that the documents he spoke of would be real. But Van Zandt now knew what mattered to his old adversary and would use it to see that he paid well.

"Dat bitch." His yellow smirk appeared. "Her und dat biz-ness she hoards . . . I leave dem both zomething to remember. Dey pay . . . both of dem." Hulda!" His voice rumbled through the house over and over until the woman appeared once more at his bedchamber door. Van Zandt noted with satisfaction how her hand trembled on the door latch and his decaying smile again appeared.

"Fetch Stacks and Mal-ory. I haf one last job for dem to do."

The next morning Van Zandt was in a cabin on the ship *Marguerite*, bound later in the day for the islands. The captain had orders to sail with the tide for Jamaica and an armed watch from the *Secret* guarded the ship until late afternoon when she sailed.

As Aaron watched the ship clearing the harbor, a chill overtook him. There has been great risk in what he had done. And something in Van Zandt's manner had made Aaron uneasy; he had surrendered too quickly and with less resistance than Aaron had anticipated. He had glumly accepted the exile with a simmering hatred in his face. Now he was gone and Aaron felt little relief at his departure. He sought out the chief magistrate of Boston and deposited with him a packet of documents that proved beyond doubt Van Zandt's role during the war and his treason. Warrants would be drawn if ever he set foot again on American soil.

And still Aaron felt uneasy. It was only his last meeting with Brien that cast such gloom on his thoughts, he chided himself, but his customary confidence and optimism failed him. Try as he might, he could think of no way to resolve the dilemma he found himself in.

Once more on board ship, Aaron puzzled over his continued distress. No longer able to rest or work, he paced the deck under the thoughtful eye of Hicks. Why had Van Zandt left so quietly? Did he plan to bribe his way back to Boston? No . . . the *Marguerite*'s captain was to be trusted; the man's dislike for Van Zandt rivaled Aaron's own.

What then? A plan for revenge? It would be weeks before they reached Jamaica and again as long before Van Zandt could mount an expedition. Revenge postponed must be long savored. Van Zandt's acceptance of exile must be accompanied by more immediate revenge.

The *Secret*? She would sail within two weeks for England—too soon to feel the pirated wrath of the Dutchman. She would lie safe in Bristol harbor by the time Van Zandt was underway.

And it weighed on his mind the day long—robbing him of concentration and the satisfaction he should have felt.

Just past six that evening, Aaron prevailed upon Hicks to pay a call on Jeannie Trowbridge and in so doing to carry a message to Dyso. It was just before sunset when the hulk appeared on the gangway once more.

Fearing a repeat of the previous night, Aaron had stayed on board to meet the lady's protector.

"My friend, something is not right." He folded his muscular arms across his chest, scowling thoughtfully. "Van Zandt departed on the tide as planned, but with less argument than is characteristic. I fear a plan is already set." His words surprised him, but he owned the product of his day's restlessness. But it was not the coward's way to strike directly at his target.

"I can only deduce that our lady, her property —or both—are in danger." He watched the big man carefully. "You must not leave her, even for the shortest time, until the plot be uncovered. Can you manage that?"

A quick, determined nod was the reply. Then before Aaron could continue, one huge hand knotted into a fist and was soon wrapped carefully, almost tenderly in the other hand.

Fascinated by the simple eloquence of the gesture, Aaron stared openly at him. Then he shook his head to clear it and once more focus his mind.

"I shall set watch at the warehouse—with some of my men. I'll send Hicks round to check with you every few hours. I think it best that Brien not know of our concern or our efforts. Will you need help?"

Dyso turned back from the door with a glimmer of what Aaron fancied as amusement in his eyes. Aaron felt the question foolish. And the paradoxical man was gone.

The warmth of the July night droned onward, making the vigil a battle between boredom and fatigue. From his perch atop a neighboring structure, Aaron could feel no rustle of air in the soundless heat. Sweat trickled down his neck and the occasional buzz of an insect near his ear increased his annoyance with each passing moment. Perhaps he'd read it wrong, he mused. This vigil might be for naught.

But then he saw again the bilious black eyes, cold and hateful, and shaking his head to clear it, he renewed his determined watch.

Toward dawn his determination was rewarded. A faint light glowed in the alleyway below, near the rear door of the warehouse. He rose stiffly to his knees and waved to a crouched figure on the warehouse roof, who repeated the signal to another in the chain.

They must have time to set the fire. Aaron's mind coldly calculated their steps as he climbed over the rooftops to join two dark figures near the warehouse gable. And a handful of shadows collected in the alley below. As arranged, they moved swiftly to cover the doors with a brace of loaded pistols, and some stationed themselves under the lower windows to cut off any escape attempt.

The gable window was well weathered and yielded easily to the pressure of Aaron's shoulder. His heart drummed steadily as their rope uncoiled into the dark void below. The oil barrels in this part of the warehouse would provide them cover while their eyes adjusted further to the darkness. The descent seemed to last forever, the rope eating into his hands as his eyes raked the darkness for signs of their detection.

Once at the bottom, he tugged the rope as a signal and silently moved away, unsheathing a foot-long dirk from his belt. Feeling for the wall he knew must be near, he touched the cool, rough brick and suddenly had his bearings. His own breathing drowned out the other sounds he strained to hear, and his muscles coiled in natural response.

When Hicks was at last beside him, he put one hand on the mate's shoulder to orient him. For a long moment they searched the silent darkness. The blackness gave way to dim outlines, then gray shapes about them. They began to move along the paths of memory on soft-booted feet. Past the barrels and bales, a bare expanse opened before them at the center of the main floor. Aaron flattened against a huge bale instinctively, then edged forward to spy out the area around the corner. Motioning to Hicks, he moved stealthily along the crates, eyes straining, toward the offices. Each passing moment meant a greater chance for Van Zandt's men to do real harm.

Suddenly, there it was! A muffled voice and a light ahead of them. Hicks crept quietly to the shelter of a stack of barrels across the way from Aaron. They watched. There were only two of them. Van Zandt hadn't cared to pay too handsomely for his revenge.

Small, bright tongues of flame licked at oil-soaked rags at the bottom of some cotton bales.

"It's caught," the shorter, scrawny figure rubbed his sweaty palms on his thighs.

"Aye," the other one growled. " 'At's good enough. Let's git now. Our part's done." In a hurry to see the job done, they turned to leave the growing circle of light. But they stopped short, eyes widening.

The cold silver-blue of Aaron's dirk hovered inches away from the short one's throat.

"No sudden moves, gents," Aaron said with icy calm.

"My captain is a man to be obeyed," Hicks said stepping out of the shadows, his own sword drawn and itching for mischief. He circled the buckle on the bigger man's belt with the tip of it. "Arms up high—and turn around!" He searched them for weapons and took in the strong smell of rum.

"Just knives, Captain. They're half drunk to boot."

The flames licked hungrily at the bales and showed an eagerness to spread. A quick glance told Aaron there was no more time to lose.

"Get the others," he ordered Hicks, reaching out one hand to take the junior officer's sword.

As Hicks moved off into the gloom, Aaron sneered, "Just like Van Zandt—sending drunken cowards to do his dirty work."

If the arsonists thought of attempting escape, they quickly decided against it. The fierceness of Aaron's glowing eyes told them that he would relish their punishment for so foolhardy an act. Had any of his social acquaintances seen his face just then, they would have been chilled by the horrible power and violence that changed his handsome features.

* * *

The news of the arson attempt and its timely discovery drew mixed reaction from Brien. She was at once shaking with rage and weak with relief. Silas unfolded the story as told to him by the constable investigating.

A pair of half-sobered sailors, rousted from their night's amusement for lack of funds to continue, had ventured by on the way to their ship's berth. Having spotted the fire, so near their dockage, they sounded the alarm. Quite by accident, the arsonists were trapped inside by the commotion and were unable to flee the building. Brought out sniveling and gasping, they confessed readily to a plot that, if carried out, would have seen all of the Weston properties burned, one by one.

Damage had been confined to one part of the warehouse and had luckily not reached the barrels of oil stacked precariously nearby. With the help of sailors and rousted tavern patrons, the flames had been extinguished in fortuitously short order.

Brien sniffed with indignation as Silas announced the fate of the malefactors and the one who employed their services—Van Zandt. The bloated jackal would be charged with arson if he could be found. A cursory search of his residence showed he had fled, taking little with him. The search would continue, but it was felt he was well away from Boston by now.

When Brien insisted on dressing and going down to the docks to see the damage herself, Silas tsked and tutted so that she abandoned the idea. The damage was light enough, he reasoned, and the shock of the news was enough for one day.

Two days later, in the wake of the fire, an offer came for the purchase of Weston Trading. A man named Harrison from New York made a firm offer of 14,000 sterling. Brien received the news with overwhelming relief and set about making plans to return home. Within another week she boarded the *Morning Star* bound for England, leaving the turnover of the property—and disturbing memories—behind.

Twenty-four

The passage home was long and miserable. The *Star* was not designed with passengers in mind and her square bottom rolled and pitched like an old bucket set adrift. Brien fell sick two days out of port and found her mornings just after rising spent hovered over the chamber pot. As the day wore one, her health improved and she was sure it would pass, this periodic seasickness. But the next morning she would be seized by violent spasms once more and would curse the miserable craft for her inability to keep food on her stomach. Even worse, her illness abated little when the sea was calm and the ship swayed little. Fortunately, Jeannie was at last gaining her sea legs and was hardly troubled at all with the malady. Thus the little maid spent the mornings comforting her mistress as best she could, ignoring her less than genteel language when the illness seized her.

The strange illness kept her from exercise on deck and the little cabin she shared with her maid quickly became stifling, adding keenly to her discomfort. But time was abundant and she had solitude to think. She recalled the sleek details of Aaron's ship—his brain-child. She at last realized why others showed such interest in the vessel and in his ideas about ships. If the *Star* was typical, small wonder the *Secret* roused such comment. Brien was piqued at her own inexperience and inattention in such matters, for again, it seemed her judgment where Aaron Durham was concerned was found lacking.

The insight disturbed her greatly and she thrust it angrily to the back of her mind.

It was over, this silly infatuation with that reckless, wilful rebel. Once more the sober, analytical side of her took charge. It was only natural, the attraction she felt for him, for he had been the one to make her a woman and that alone would be enough to engender special feelings for him. And there was the element of adventure, of being far from home, in strange surroundings—and not least the hint of the danger. All quite predictable she chided herself. And she had presumed to give advice on matters of the heart of Jeannie.

At least no one in London would know of how she'd made a fool of herself, throwing her heart after a wild, conceited rake . . . and nearly ruining the very business she had come to recoup. They would have had quite a laugh.

Something in her heart cringed at her thoughts. Conceited? ''Now be fair, milady.'' Aaron's visage rose to challenge her. Well, perhaps not conceited—but wild and reckless at the very least.

'' 'Tis senseless to go on like this,'' she moaned on her narrow bunk. ''I shall never see the man again . . . and good riddance! He's caused me naught but turmoil of mind and body since we first met. I'll not abide his torture further! Why is this stupid sow of a ship so slow!''

And so she raved for the rest of the voyage. By the end of the fourth week at sea her strange malady seemed to ease a bit and she again felt real hunger. She was convinced that the only real remedy was solid land and yearned to have her things about her in her dear Harcourt. But only as the ship entered London harbor did she really focus on the joy of coming home, remembering the peace and comfort of the snug, warm rooms; the hot water; and the soft down coverlets. And she wanted badly to see her father, who from all reports had made a remarkable recovery from his brush with death and was most anxious to see her triumphant return. Brien realized guiltily that she had thought all too seldom of him during the excitement of her American adventure.

When she saw the Earl of Southwold waiting on the dock, her heart surged with joy. He had brought a carriage to meet her personally; he had missed her in the way that only a father can. And the moistness in her eyes told of how she had missed him. She hurried down the gangway into his outstretched arms, and it was a full minute before either could speak.

"Oh, Father, it's so good to be home . . . to see you!" she murmured, locked securely in his overtight embrace.

Weston's face was red and filled with unspoken emotion. He had felt her absence more than he'd dreamed possible. "Ah, I have missed you, child. Much has happened these months—the rumors of war and all. I was afraid you would have difficulty securing passage."

She locked her arm through his as he led her to the waiting open carriage. "War? What war, Father?" Had she been gone so long?

"War with France." His brow knitted in surprise. "Have you heard none of it?"

"I have been at sea for over a month; I have heard nothing."

"There's been a revolt in France. They've toppled the king and now there are rumors that the new regime will wage war on England." He helped her up into the seat of the carriage. "But, more of that later. Tell me first of your journey—and this buyer that you found so agreeable."

Brien winced inwardly as she recounted what few facts she knew of the Mr. Harrison who now laid claim to her pet project in the new world. She ended with, ". . . and so I haven't met the gentleman. But the drafts were drawn and legalized on the bank of England. Fortunate we were that he had assets to draw upon here in London for so speedy a payment. I would not have liked traveling with so large a sum of coin." She sighed, giving in a bit to the fatigue of relief. "I admit that I despaired of finding a buyer at times. The one Silas had earlier negotiated with proved totally unsuitable —even underhanded. But, it's done now. My mission was a complete success."

Noting the brilliant flash of her eyes and the moist pinkness of her cheeks Weston mused, "I'd say so. And the colonies, how did you find them? Primitive and inhospitable?"

Brien's eyes flew wide. "Surely you cannot believe such!" She seemed so outraged that Weston laughed heartily.

"Hardly, for how could I have sent my only daughter into a land I believed peopled by savages living in squalor. It's good to have my own judgment confirmed by so critical an observer."

Brien blushed becomingly at the violence of her reaction and sought to explain. "It's simply that I've heard

371

such horrid things . . . from quite educated people. It amazes me what tripe some people carry about for ideas and put on display at every opportunity. Just before we sailed for the colonies, I met a man who claimed to have visited there, and he would have had me quaking with fear with his talk of the beastly clods who chose the new England over the old. Quite prejudiced, really.''

"You've disproved the notions, then. And you act now as if you quite enjoyed your stay." He searched her face for clues as to the source of this new passion he detected in her.

"Enjoyed? Oh, yes. Silas and his wife Helen have a lovely family and wonderful friends. Their fourth child was born shortly after I arrived." Her mind flew back to that sweet May night and her expression assumed a softness new to it by Weston's observation.

She started back to the present, embarrassed by the drift of her thoughts.

"Their home is as gracious as any I have visited here and their friends are thoughtful, gentle people who welcomed me warmly and made me feel quite at home."

"And what does it look like, this new England?" Weston took his daughter's hand between his own.

"Much like the south country here—many trees and streams. A bit wild out from the towns, but ever so beautiful—and so full of life." She stopped, aware of his scrutiny and chagrined at her display of eagerness. "I . . . I'm rambling on. . . .''

"Oh, no—I'm fascinated," Weston urged. "It's clear you've given this country a place in your heart."

His casual observation jolted her. She did feel very close to the people who were so good to her—Silas and Helen. But the country? Aye, the country. She had to own that a part of her held genuine affection for the place. And it struck her that her father had observed in her the same feeling she had named in Aaron! The new land had cast its spell on her as well! That earthy bitch of a land that seemed to come between them now took on a new persona. She and Aaron now had one more common bond.

Her thoughtful silence told Weston more about his daughter than she could have imagined. She had thrived, blossomed, during the rigors of the journey. She had returned refreshed—more womanly, more beautiful than when she left. Now what could there be in this new land to invigorate a young widow so?

"And the journey—how good a sailor are you?" He broke the reverie that had settled over them.

"The trip over was smooth and easy—delightful, in fact. The ship was on her maiden voyage and quite an innovation in travel if even half the claims about her be true. The return was far less pleasant." She smiled wanly. "I'm afraid I was ill much of the return voyage, but I'm certain it was that bucket on which we sailed. I shall make a real traveler, Father. There's a whole world to see—and I mean to see it all!"

Weston's humor flickered and recovered quickly. What did she mean? Why was she so paradoxical? Was he never to be sure of her?

The rest of the ride to Harcourt, Brien chatted about sights and people and the business of Weston Trading in the colonies. And Weston again found his own thoughts occupied with the images she traced in his mind with her words.

At dinner that evening, Brien was alone with her father for a long, relaxed talk. Between sips of fragrant wine and bites of fresh trout, she related to him the highlights of her adventure—carefully edited to exclude all references to Aaron Durham.

"Much has happened here these past few weeks as well," Weston informed her. "This business of the French—abominable. Lord knows how it may spread to affect the landless classes in England. Many of the nobles have fled to Spain and England with only as much as they had on their backs."

He eyed his daughter closely as he made the pronouncement. "Your own relations have settled here in London."

Brien was busy attacking a bowl of fresh peaches smothered in cream. Her appetite had already improved remarkably. "Truly?" she said absently.

Jerking her head up in puzzlement, she frowned quizzically at him. "We have no . . ." Her voice trailed off into a whisper as her entire person froze with dread. Her face drained instantly of color and she tossed her head nervously, trying to recoup. "Whatever can you mean? We have no French relations."

"Not we, you." Weston smiled, disturbed that she was so slow to catch his meaning—or that she caught it all too well and denied it still. "The marquis has escaped to London and is even now searching for a suitable residence for his family.

Brien's heart nearly leaped from her chest and raced to make up for lost beats. No! Not here! Not now!

Weston went on, trying to ignore the magnitude of her reaction. "They're most fortunate. It seems the marquis had the foresight to invest whatever he could smuggle out of the country in London banks and brokerages. A most clever maneuver. They seem well fixed, despite their dreadful expatriation."

Brien was silent and gripped the edge of the table hard, her hands white with the effort.

Weston felt her discomfort keenly now and concentrated wholely on his own sumptous dessert. "The marquis called on me not long after his arrival. I've promised him whatever aid we might render in this most difficult situation. I daresay, they'll have a time getting any landowner to part with a good English

374

house and land. Feeling runs quite high and the government is in turmoil."

"Of course," Brien murmured. "Quite decent of you."

Weston now regarded her closely. "Only for your sake, Brien, and the brief, but close, alliance of our houses."

Unable to bear more, Brien jumped up, her hand fluttering to her brow nervously. "I'm sorry, Father . . . the trip, the excitement of homecoming, and now this news . . . I've had more than a full day. I am really quite tired. I beg your leave, I must retire."

"Are you ill? You look so pale." Weston rose to go to her, but she motioned for him to be seated once more.

"I shall be fine. Just a night's rest and I'll be keen and fit on the morrow. Good night, Father."

Brien slept badly on her first night home and awakened with a sense of foreboding she could not dismiss. The illness of the voyage proved to be still with her, though in milder form, and served to dampen her spirits further.

"I have nothing to fear," she chided herself. "Why should Raoul's family influence me in the slightest? I have only met one of them, besides Raoul. Our acquaintance was brief—as was my marriage. I pressed no claims on his estate. They have no real connection to me now. And so it shall remain!"

But for all her reasoning and logic her innermost heart was not convinced. What if they insisted on seeing her—on being included socially? Could she publicly contain the contempt she felt for the lot of them? How could she even vouch for them in society—knowing them to be unprincipled and opportunists?

Again, sweet reason prevailed. Raoul was a rebel.

Perhaps they were different. His greed and lust were but perversions of finer qualities, ones that his family might possess. She thought of gentle Louis and his sallow charm. She softened. In the end she would be fair—give them a chance. To do less would be to follow the same arrogant path she decried in Raoul.

More than two weeks passed before the Westons received another message from the marquis. In that time, Brien had rested and regained her temper and strength. She determined to be polite but distant, were they to meet, but she would not be the one to issue an invitation to their household. She would make it clear that the past was past and that she lived her own life now. Each passing day had renewed her confidence in her ability to handle the situation.

The message, delivered at luncheon by a liveried servant, was a simple, well-phrased greeting expressing delight at her safe return and an interest in meeting her at last.

"A handsome sentiment," Weston observed when she handed him the note.

"Quite," Brien said tersely. Realizing how abrupt she seemed, she forced a convincing smile.

Weston arched one brow and pursed his lips thoughtfully. "Brien, I realize that their presence may recall painful memories for you, but that is all in the past now. I am sure they will make no demands on you. And they deserve a civil welcome. Are you not even curious about them?"

Brien was relieved to speak her mind at last. "Not in the least curious. I only wish them to leave me alone. *If* we chance to meet, I shall be as courteous as possible, but I will not make or accept overtures."

Meeting his gaze firmly she knew now was the time

for truth.

"Ours was a marriage of convenience—mutual convenience—that was all. And all claims were voided by his untimely death. It may seem cold, but that is as it shall be." Her voice had risen with each statement to a vehemence that surprised Weston.

"Of course, Brien. It shall be as you wish. We have no real obligation. We shall entertain them only as you see fit. I leave it to you."

Brien cut short her lunch and left her father pondering his mercurial offspring. He wondered if she were not further from a settled, happy life than ever.

Candlelight, bent and scattered by crystal prisms, flooded the hall. The light shimmered in the sea green taffeta of Brien's dress and cast a golden glow about her tawny curls and creamy skin. Her cheeks were moist and pink in the August heat, but her excitement dispelled all discomfort. This was a party for her—to welcome her home from her travel—and she would be at her best.

The Countess of Albermarle greeted them warmly as they entered the grand salon of the great house. Admiring looks and murmurs came from every direction and Brien was openly pleased by the attention. This was her evening. Her anticipation mingled with trepidation when she let herself think about it. Would they remember her? Accept her as before?

As she circled the room on her father's arm, she reconquered any recalcitrant hearts made fickle by her absence. She had grown more beautiful in the interval. Graciously she parried jests and answered inquiries about the colonies and her homecoming. She was so absorbed in greeting friends that she missed the pair of dark eyes fixed on her in raw appraisal.

Talking pleasantly with friends, her gaze was drawn to a tall, dark figure nearby. She started, surprised to find him openly staring at her. And more surprised still to see Raoul Trechaud, plus twenty-five years, bearing down on her. Something inside her went cold as she noted each similar feature and mannerism. And she struggled valiantly to retain a gracious façade.

"Ah, Brien." He broke into the conversation boldly. "You are truly as beautiful as my son boasted." He reached for her unoffered hand and brushed it with his lips—Raoul's large, sensuous lips.

"Thank you, sir," she managed. This was deucedly awkward, meeting one's father-in-law for the first time in front of a roomful of strangers.

"You must forgive me. Your appearance startled me at first." Seeing his and others' frowns she continued, more for the others' benefit than for his. "Your family resemblance is quite remarkable. Raoul never mentioned it."

"My son was not one to bide time with unimportant matters. How could his description have done justice to your beauty, my daughter?" He held her gloved hand still and kissed it again before relinquishing it to her.

Brien withdrew apace, taken aback by his familiarity. She realized that she knew not what to call him. Marquis? . . . Papa? Ha! Papa indeed! So many eyes scrutinized this encounter, few realizing they had never met.

"I am delighted to meet you at last, marquis. I only regret that it must be under such unfortunate circumstances." Brien plied her fan vigorously to distract from the duplicity of her words.

"And I you, Lady Brien. Though now, as I grow accustomed to England, I find that even these dire straights yield unexpected pleasures—such as meeting you." He tore his eyes from Brien long enough to extend his hand to Lord Weston. "Good to see you once more, Lord Weston."

Weston extended his hand with a geniality he little felt. "A pleasure sir. Would that we had met in brighter circumstances."

"Yes. But for fortune's whim our houses might have been joined forever in the person of *l'enfant. Quelle dommage.*" And he forced a dazzling smile. "But it was not to be."

Brien felt his eyes probing her, assessing her as one might a potential acquisition, and she was instantly furious. She must contain this indignation.

"The marquise, did she attend?" Brien asked, looking past him obviously to scour the room. "I have only just returned from a strenuous journey—or I would have invited her to tea."

"Non," the marquis responded pleasantly. "Her health suffers in this tribulation. She seldom ventures out now. Still, you must come to see us—for dinner, and soon."

They drifted toward a sofa, and he waved her to sit. His assuming manner goaded Brien's very worst impulses.

"There is another who longs to see you. Louis will be devastated that he missed you this eve."

"Louis is in London as well?" she asked. "How nice." Brien found his exaggeration irritating. A foreboding overhung all his words and Brien wished to be anywhere in the world except in his presence.

There was a magnetism about the man, an animalism she had know full-force in Raoul. His presence overwhelmed and engulfed those about him—even her. It was not a pleasant surrender—as with Aaron Durham—but one that whispered sinister warnings to her every nerve to be on guard!

Brien was relieved to be seated several chairs away from him during the dinner and arranged with her father to leave earlier than originally planned. The gathering lost its sparkle as they departed.

At home Brien fell into a weary, benumbed slumber, punctuated by savage encounters with Raoul that melted into delicious moments with Aaron's arms about her, keeping her safe—loving her.

She awakened tired and listless, unable to shake off the somber spell Raoul's powerful father seemed to have cast on her.

Jeannie noted her distraction and asked what was wrong as she prepared Brien for bed the next evening.

"I simply dislike the man. I can say it no plainer. He talks and acts as though he has some particular claim on me. Jeannie, my marriage was neither long nor happy. I want nothing to do with any of Raoul's family."

"You . . . you weren't in love with monsieur?" The little maid seemed genuinely surprised.

"No, I was not," Brien answered tersely, taking the pins Jeannie handed her and putting them into a porcelain box on the vanity.

"I did not want to marry . . . him or anyone. In the end, the marriage was forced on me." Jeannie's wide eyes told Brien how well she had kept the secrets she bore. Jeannie had also believed their marriage to have been a great love match.

"I have few enough secrets from you. You might as well have that one too. Now you can see why I fear and distrust his father so. They are cut from the same cloth, both strong and handsome—and greedy and cunning. They take what they want whatever the price to others. They stop at nothing." Seeing Jeannie's eyes widen further, she stopped.

"I mustn't burden you with idle talk. Things will work out for the best." She patted the girl's hand as it lay on her shoulder. "As long as I have you and my

Dyso, what harm could befall?" She smiled with a bravery she little felt.

With the holiday season ahead, Brien engaged M. Lamont to create new winter clothing and festive holiday gowns. She enjoyed the caprices of September's weather enough to shop in the merchant district herself and found that the brisk trade and bustle and the exotic smells of the shops and stall enlivened her spirits. She found her thoughts turning once more to travel, while easily dismissing its less agreeable aspects.

As Brien, escorted by Dyso and Jeannie, crossed the boulevard toward the fashionable shops of the district, she noted a vaguely familiar figure alighting from a cab just ahead of her. Frowning with thought, she tried to recall the identity of the tall, thin-shouldered man before they were upon him and she might be caught unprepared if he should greet her. The man turned and Brien's heart fell into her stomach.

With a broad smile, Louis Trechaud doffed his elegant hat and greeted her. "Lady Brien! I knew it must be you! I had the driver stop immediately. I simply had to see you."

"Louis." She forced a smile. "How nice to see you again." She fervently hoped her manner seemed gracious despite her feelings.

"Mon père . . . my father told me of your return. I was sad to have missed you at the dinner party of *la comtesse.* I have only just arrived in London and I was most anxious to see you once more. And you," he rambled on, "grow more beautiful with the passing minutes." He took her hands in his and kissed them lightly. His eyes told of his genuine admiration.

"As always, Louis, you flatter me. Only now your English is so improved that I can understand you." She smiled, relaxing as she recalled the pleasant hours they had spent together at Dunstan before her betrothal. Gentle, pale Louis—so different from the passionate and cunning Raoul.

"It is good to see you," she said, taking the offer of his arm. She missed the visual violence that was exchanged between Louis and Dyso. "I have only just returned from America—a most fascinating experience. I confess to you, I went there on a business matter, but I enjoyed it as an adventure far above any profit gained. And you, you have been traveling too?"

"*C'est vrai,*" Louis said wanly, his face suddenly tired as he gazed longingly at her. "But my adventures pale beside yours, dear Brien."

"You are too kind, Louis." But Brien felt inexplicably uncomfortable once more.

"I have much to tell you," Louis continued. "Will you come to dinner soon? You and your father? You must permit us to repay in some small way the kindness of your house."

"Kindness?"

"But of course. Your father has found a small estate that will be quite suitable for our new home. It is not far from Dunstan Hall, I believe."

She stiffened. "How good of him. He had neglected to tell me." A smothering feeling overtook her, but Louis seemed to notice no outward signs of her distress. Mercifully, they were now at the door of M. Lamont's salon and Brien stopped, withdrawing her hand from Louis' arm.

"This is my destination. It was good to see you Louis." He caressed her hand lightly, bowing perfectly in the French manner.

"Until later, *ma chère* Brien."

As Brien turned back to the shop door she glimpsed Dyso's face and the simmering hatred and violence she saw there shook her whole being. Never in all the time he served her had she seen any indication of the ruthless potential she read there now. A chill caused her to shiver visibly. She put one hand on Dyso's arm instinctively.

As quickly as it had come, the violence vanished and Brien permitted herself to breathe once more. The whole encounter had taken but seconds, but she knew it had changed things for her. Dyso hated Louis—and more. Brien dared not even ponder why.

Inside the shop, Brien turned the encounter with Louis over and over in her mind as the little Frenchman flurried and fussed about in the fitting room, measuring and gossiping. She did not notice the meaningful interplay of glances between M. Lamont and his assistant, Chloe. Their easy chatter which slipped into and out of French and English was simple to follow with only half an ear while she pursued her own thoughts.

Louis' look had been one of pallid envy when she'd talked about her travel. Brien was stung by it now as she reflected on him and her feelings toward him. She had seen him as a quiet, honorable soul, simply outshined by his more dashing younger brother, Raoul. But she now had more experience with men and with the world and could put other names to his nature, names that pained her with their honesty—and appropriateness. He was a tired, worldy spirit who needed the strength of another to give his life direction and meaning. And she better understood how, being of a more timorous nature, life with men like Raoul and his father could have made him so weak. Yes, weak. They grew stronger by usurping the spirit and life from those around them. And that was Louis, explained.

M. Lamont's voice called her back to the present, as he straightened away from the hem of the rich blue wool skirt she wore. "I am glad your journey was pleasant and profitable. You have returned more beautiful than ever, madame . . . so . . ." he searched diligently for the correct word, ". . . Madonnalike."

The nuance of his emphasis struck Brien as odd, but she pushed it back to the recess of her mind.

"*La cuisine,* it must be good in these Americas." He watched her out of the corner of his eye as he fell to straightening a partly finished bodice on a form replicating Brien's ripe curves.

"Far more civilized than most English are willing to believe," Brien responded, puzzled at this twist of conversation. What was it she was missing? She had the feeling of being outside the real meaning of his words, without a clue as to the drift of his thoughts. Ah, then, he had the obscurity of the French. Who could ever tell what they were truly thinking?

"You would not find the cuisine or the society as elegant as in London"—she sought to direct her wandering thoughts—"but they are charming all the same."

"Will you return there soon?" M. Lamont carefully avoided her gaze while Chloe helped her down from her carpeted pedestal to the privacy of the screen where she removed the skirt.

"No, I think not," Brien answered, her mind drifting back lazily to a sweet May night that still pulsed in her veins. "There are too many places to see in the world. And I'm barely recovered from the last wretched voyage."

"It may yet be a few months before she recovers," thought M. Lamont, impishly. And he grinned surreptitiously. He wondered if she knew and shook his head at the thought. No, she had not stiffened or blanched at any of his insinuations. Again, the dressmaker was the first to know, he smiled triumphantly.

When Brien was clothed once more in an azure blue silk wrapper, she emerged from behind the screen and

384

took M. Lamont's extended hand. He placed her delicately on the settee and turned to his assistant. "Have Joan bring in tea for Lady Brien and myself." He gave her a meaningful look and she respectfully curtsied and withdrew, closing the elegant paneled door softly behind her.

Again, Brien found a strangeness in his manner, a distance he had long since ceased to maintain with her. They had seen many changes together, and Brien had come to count him among those in the world who knew her best. But now something hung on the air between them, heavy and disturbing. Unsure how to broach the subject, or if it needed to be raised at all, she kept an uneasy silence and toyed with the delicate Belgian lace that graced the front of her light wrapper.

M. Lamont busied himself with the soft blue woolen skirt she had just removed and settled it over the form holding the bodice. He fussed with the waist and front a bit, drawing Brien's troubled gaze as he chalked and reset lines to be redone.

"Will you make changes in it then? I thought it settled fine about the waist," she ventured, relieved to be able to comment at last on something to this old and valued friend.

She did not see the mischievous twinkle in his eyes as he worked. "Fine the fit is now, but soon it will grow tight. I think it must be altered now or you will waste a season before you can wear it."

The nuances took shape in her mind and she laughed aloud with relief, a pleasant throaty sound that made even the impervious Lamont wish to hear more.

"I see. You believe I have returned to my old habits. My waistline worries you, does it? I promise you, I shall keep it under control, even if I have to fast to see to it. Leave that waist just as is." Her lovely eyes were sparkling pools of exceptional clarity and her cheeks were blushed with moist pinkness.

Turning to her, M. Lamont caught his breath at the sight. She was indeed ravishing. He wondered what man had so captured her well-hidden heart as to see her into this state. A surge of unaccustomed protectiveness passed through him. She would know soon enough without his help. He would not be the one to bring her sorrow.

"I doubt your will not in the least, Lady Brien. But there are temptations in this life that no mortal may resist. We will follow their course no matter where they lead us." And then he smiled endearingly.

Brien sighed pleasantly at her friend's musings. There was a surprise in every man, she decided. And a philosopher in M. Lamont.

Just then, Joan arrived with the tea and Brien settled back to enjoy the delicate flavors of her cup while M. Lamont sketched a new gown for her.

Twenty-five

Lord Weston accompanied Brien to the home of the marquis in Pemberly Place when the invitation came. The house was sumptuously appointed with carved and gilded furnishings and sparkling crystal and lush Persian carpets.

The marquis and marquise greeted them in the drawing room. The marquise was a pale, slender woman clothed conservatively in a violet gown trimmed at the neck with a voile ruff. Her features were delicate, patrician, and her dark hair and large dark eyes spoke of a great beauty, poorly aged, but still genteel. Her English was heavily accented and Brien mused that she must expend great effort to attempt it at all.

"Ma chèrie." She drew Brien to the sofa with her. "I can see how Raoul was so drawn to you. You have . . . *la printemps* in you." She smiled genuinely but her hands were icy as she held Brien's.

"And now I see from whom Louis has his gift of flattery," Brien countered, feeling slightly discomforted at their close scrutiny.

The marquis laughed heartily. "But certainly not from Arianne."

Brien cast a puzzled look at the marquis and back to the marquise who explained.

"Louis is not my son, but my stepson. Raoul was my only child." Brief pain in her face clutched at Brien's heart. This woman's only child and pride was the wilful, arrogant, and callous rogue she had married. Brien could barely stand the irony.

"I did not know. Raoul seldom spoke of family matters," Brien explained.

"How like him." The marquise brushed it off. "But now . . . you. How is it you live now?"

Through the awkward construction Brien glimpsed her meaning and nodded. "I live with my father now; see to his house and do charity work as time permits."

"Mostly," Louis interrupted, "she evades suitors and claims loyal hearts among the men of London."

"Louis!" Brien was embarrassed.

"Ah, my daughter—you cannot deny for modesty's sake what is plain to all." The marquis laughed arrogantly. "You are a most beautiful and eligible young woman. The men of London must certainly appreciate both assets."

Blushing becomingly at the boldness of the acclaim, Brien seized the chance to set straight their thinking.

"As to my beauty, the beholder must judge; as one thinks me, so I am. But eligible, I am not. I shall never marry again." She met the penetrating gaze of the marquis head on. His eyes widened slightly at her pronouncement, but he maintained an amused façade.

"So firm a stand for one so young," he remarked, turning his head to Lord Weston.

Feeling the strong undercurrent, Weston carefully measured his words. "Those were my own sentiments, sir. But as you know my daughter better, you will find a clever and wizened head on those lovely shoulders."

"But surely—" the marquis began.

"Yes," Weston interrupted. "I, too, have tried to dislodge this idea from her mind. To grow old, companionless—it is a bitter thing. But in the end she will decide this for herself. It seems a natural reluctance in view of her marriage to your son."

Brien was thunderstruck by her father's casual way of summarizing her feelings. And she smiled gratefully, lovingly at Weston. His carefully chosen words all were true, but had a double meaning. How clever of him to wield so double-edged a truth in her behalf.

"Certainement," the marquise, Arianne, was quick to agree. "There is much time and in the end Brien decides this, yes?" She patted Brien's hand delicately.

A servant appeared at the door to announce dinner and they moved to the dining room at the marquise's request. The remainder of the evening was far less tedious than Brien had feared. She felt free now; they knew her plans. She, with her wonderful father's help, had declared her independence and now could deal openly with their innuendos and blatant attempts to ingratiate themselves.

As they left, Louis asked if she would attend the Opera Gala a fortnight away. In an expansive mood, Brien agreed to have Louis accompany them to the dance—and promised to introduce him widely.

In the carriage, Brien was the first to comment on their evening.

"Thank you, Father, for your words on my behalf."

Weston looked out the window of the carriage to avoid her eyes. "I spoke only the truth. It is your right to decide; I shall never coerce you again in the matter of marriage. That does not mean I approve your charted course. But you shall have the choice."

She sought his hand on the seat between them and squeezed it affectionately. This seemed a time for frankness and she continued.

"It seems clear they intend a match between Louis and me."

He turned to regard her closely in the dim lantern light. "How do you feel about Louis?"

"I have stated my feelings about marriage numerous times. Louis is a pleasant, agreeable man, but I shall not marry again." She could not bring herself to chronicle the defects of the spiritless Louis to her father. And she dared not even think of the real reason she found him so lacking. There was one in her heart beside whom all other men were small and insignificant. That man had made her a woman, then had challenged her and given her back her heart when it had been tortured from her. As she thought of Louis now—poor Louis, as she had come to think of him—Aaron Durham loomed up to snatch away her approval and affection. And strangely, she did not mind. He was so far away she felt it safe to dream a little of him. The sweetness of the dreams compensated for the pain of their unreality.

A fortnight later, on the eve of the Opera Gala, Lawrence Weston was summoned to Bristol by an urgent communiqué from his solicitors. Two ships of the Weston fleet were lost at sea; their valuable cargoes would mean a heavy loss to Weston Trading. Nervous investors and creditors now clamored for payment. Weston's calm, reassuring manner were needed to help restore order to the situation. He left Brien with strict instructions to carry on as though nothing were amiss. She must attend the Opera Gala with Louis as planned —for Weston Trading, if for nothing else. Her most urgent pleas could not move him to relent and allow her to accompany him. Brien was angry at first, but saw the logic in the end and agreed to attend the ball.

As she dressed the next evening Jeannie took great pains with her coif and remarked incessantly how grand she would look. And Brien felt a guilty twinge of excitement at the thought of her entrance at the ball.

When Louis arrived with the carriage, Brien floated down the great staircase to greet him, her wine and pink gown casting a rosy glow over her perfect skin. Her eyes sparkled as brilliantly as the diamonds that graced her creamy throat. Louis was speechless and Brien knew not whether to feel guilty or to enjoy it. In this game she felt she had unfair advantage.

To Brien's imagination, the lights were brighter and the mood gayer than ever before. The talk of certain war with France had heightened the pleasures of the here and now. There was an abounding feeling that "now" was all that could be grasped, and with the feeling came a freedom to take pleasures as they came. This was the last fling before the rigors of war settled over London. The gowns were more daring, the music louder, and the champagne flowed freer—or so it seemed.

Into this heady estate Brien entered as a conquering queen—beauty and privilege embodied for all of London society to marvel at. A delicious thrill coursed through her as they were announced and a murmur rose up about them. This was to be her night.

When she could be pried from Louis' arms Charles Medford or Reydon Harwick were there to claim her favors and her dances. Brien was only dimly aware of the arrival of the marquis and marquise de Saunier. As expatriates of the revolutionary muddle across the channel, they were welcomed roundly by their fellow aristocrats.

The revelry continued and grew merrier at a frantic

pace. The crowd was noisy and well wined. Brien herself was in a recklessly joyful mood—delighting in the old and new faces that were now so much a part of her life. Louis now routinely claimed her dances, ignoring the stares of the other swains.

Suddenly the dance floor was clearing as she and Louis swept gracefully about—a charming spectacle. Aware now of the cause, Brien laughed openly with Louis and they redoubled their efforts so as to be worthy of the attention. The pleasant buzzing in her head from the punch and champagne blotted out all but the music and the easy movement of the dance.

She could not see the orchestra or the marquis as he mounted the small stage. The volume of the music lowered, but the strains continued—as did their dancing. Unaware of the shock wave of murmuring moving toward them, they continued to laugh and dance.

Suddenly, they were swept up in a rush of well-wishers—simply overly enthusiastic patrons of the art of the dance, Brien thought. She giddily accepted their congratulations and hugged Louis warmly to the wild display of approval of the half-drunken revelers besieging them.

But then it seemed the congratulations went on too long and Brien caught the word "engaged" being tossed about. She shook her head good-naturedly, but the buzzing continued. She was unable to stop smiling at the jest that now sank into her befuddled mind. Did they think her engaged? To whom? She laughed almost hysterically at the thought.

Then she and Louis were thrust along at the head of the crowd toward the banquet room. A glass of champagne was thrust into her hand and Louis was again beside her. And someone proposed a toast to something. As she strained to hear, Louis said loudly into her ear, "They're all drunk! or mad! They loved our dancing so, we should go on the stage. We'd soon be rich!''

Brien laughed. ''But I'm already rich!''

The crowd roared approval at her jest and as she turned slightly she caught sight of the marquis, who lifted his glass and drained it, beaming triumphantly.

The sight of his face brought Brien around quickly and she began to sober. She was not used to such drinking and now realized that something had just happened, something she knew nothing of. And whatever it was it made the marquis appear—as a cat gorged on fishtails—full and satisfied. His satisfaction dealt with her, she realized with a shudder . . . and she turned to Louis beside her. Her and Louis! She looked quickly about her, befuddled by the reddened faces pressing her, offering congratulations, and ribald advice.

An unreasoning dread seized her. Grabbing Louis' arm, she had to yell to make herself heard above the noise.

''What's happened, Louis? What do they mean?''

Louis' wine-reddened face laughed back at her. ''I think we're all drunk, Brien.''

''Louis,'' she squeezed his arm, ''take me home—now!''

She pulled his arm and struggled through the crowd toward the great hall. The voices became taunts to her ears—''Eager to be off!''—''He's eager to be on!''—and uproarious laughter.

Drunken maniacs! If Louis would not take her home, she would go alone! But suddenly Louis was there, more sober and rebuffing the hangers-on as he summoned the carriage.

Once outside in the cool night air, they both sobered quickly. Brien, frantic to understand what had just transpired, was fearful that she already knew. Shaking with tension and fear, she grasped Louis' arm once they were safely inside the carriage.

"What has happened, Louis? What did they mean?" Her eyes were wide and her voice agonized. Her head pounded with the effects of unaccustomed strong drink.

"Brien, my lovely," Louis said thickly, "I believe we are engaged."

Brien felt as though icy water poured over her. "Engaged," she breathed. The full impact and nuances of events could not arrange themselves in her muddled mind. A wave of nausea struck her and she clenched her fists, willing it away.

"How could they think such, Louis?" And she realized how just as Louis said it.

"Because my father announced it this evening."

"He what?" She was now at fever pitch. "How dare he! Are you sure?" Louis nodded tiredly and Brien realized he knew . . . he had known all along!

The wine, the dancing, the loud comments at just the right time to prevent her from hearing what was said. And she had appeared the blushing, eager bride-to-be. She recalled the ribald comments of their fellow revelers as they left the ballroom.

"Louis, this cannot be!" Her eyes flashed and anger magnified the trembling of her body that panic had begun. "And you—you were a party to it! You knew it all along, didn't you?" When he did not respond, she screamed it. "Didn't you!"

"Yes," he blurted out. "I knew." His hand came up to cover his face and he drew a long, shuddering breath in the acrid silence that followed.

When Louis next looked up, he was jolted at the transformation in her lovely eyes; they now blazed at him with scorn. Her jaw was set with raw contempt.

"I trusted you . . . told myself you were different from Raoul."

"Brien," he pleaded, "I had to do it. The marquis

will have us married; it is inevitable.''

"Is it? We shall see. Engagements may be broken. Rest assured this one shall be, first thing tomorrow.''

"Brien, you do not understand. The marquis is a powerful man—and ruthless. He gets whatever he wants. And he wants this marriage. We have no choice.''

"*You* have no choice. But he does not own me and never will. Tomorrow all London will know of the loathsome tactics he employs to acquire good English land and wealth.'' She glared at Louis who was pressed miserably back against the seat. She felt only contempt for this worm of a man who would let himself be used to so trap a woman.

"You disgust me,'' she spat as a wave of giddiness and nausea flowed over her, pushing her further into despair.

She spoke not another word until she alighted from the carriage in front of Harcourt. Her voice was low, but distinct, as she ordered the driver, "Dispose of this baggage as you will.''

Once inside, Brien grasped the candelabrum that had been left for her on the center hall table and made her way upstairs. Having emptied the contents of her stomach into the chamber pot, she fell across the bed into a troubled sleep that saw her rise as fatigued as when she had put her head to pillow. At the morning's early light that peculiar malady, which now seemed to her a legacy of the colonies, gripped her firmly once again—just as she had thought herself rid of it. It only added to her misery.

Brien rose late that morning, taking tea in her rooms and steadying her capricious stomach with a plate of scones and marmalade. Jeannie's concern was plain as she began Brien's toilette, but Brien was too absorbed to mind her knitted brows and the lines of concern forming about her mouth. As the little maid put the finishing touches on her coiffure, Brien rose to pour a cup of tea and nursed it thoughtfully, giving the girl a subtle message that she required solitude. Alone for a while, she sought a clear direction out of the muddle in which she found herself.

Brien stared out the window into the garden below; it was changing colors at the cooler kiss of autumn. Jeannie burst in at a run, quite beside herself and red-faced.

"The marquis—" she heaved breathlessly. "He's down in the parlor with another man." She gripped her side and leaned for support upon the vanity. "We tried not to let him in, telling him you were not receiving, but he shoved past Phillips and demanded to see you immediately! If only Dyso were here," she moaned. "He took two of the horses to the smithy this morn."

"No," Brien said, recovering her voice from the shock. "It is well that Dyso is not about." She shuddered to recall the violence he harbored toward Louis and most likely the marquis as well. "I shall have to deal with this myself. What harm can he do me in my own house?" But a seed of dread had sprouted inside her and grew too quickly to full flower. "I shall tell him his shallow plot has failed and there will be no further contact between us. We will make it well known that he is a blackguard—not to be trusted."

Jeannie's face was pale as she struggled to understand. "What is it he's done, ma'am?"

Brien could not bear to look at her, fearing the anxiety in the girl's face might be contagious. Her head pounded and her stomach churned again as it had on the high seas. Without answering she breathed deeply and smoothed her skirts with her hands. Swallowing hard and straightening visibly, she proceeded to the parlor where her adversary waited.

The marquis was accompanied by a man Brien had never seen before, and as Brien entered both men bowed elegantly, a sardonic smile twisting the marquis' face into an evil parody of handsomeness.

"My daughter," he greeted her, "how lovely you—"

"How dare you push past my servants into this house." Brien's strategy would be straight to the point and have them out as quickly as possible. She noted with dismay that the other man had drawn the parlor doors together to shield them from the prying ears of the servants. The act unnerved her.

"I must ask you to leave immediately." The anger in her churning stomach began to spread welcome heat into her icy limbs and her lovely features hardened with resolve.

"My dear—" the marquis began with ill-disguised irritation.

"I am not now, nor shall I ever be anything more to you than Lady Brien Trechaud . . . certainly not your 'dear.' Your visit here this morning is pure effrontery! Before you leave I have only this to say to you. I would never consent to marry that sniveling wretch you call a son. Your deviousness surpasses Raoul's. Clever of you to maneuver the announcement of my engagement so that I was the last to know." The sparks in her eyes had been fanned to full flame by indignation.

"Non, ma chèrie." The marquis spoke through clenched teeth as his eyes narrowed menacingly. "I shall not leave until you have heard me out." It was clear he had not expected such resistance, but his stance and hardening gaze revealed his determination to have the best of the battle.

"You have nothing to say to me—except an apology. To spit upon my father's hospitality and honor as soon as he is called away . . . and to presume and plot

397

against me, who was once married to your son—''

"And will be again!" He folded his arms across his chest and the gesture made him seem to grow in stature before her eyes. "You will, despite your feeble protestations, marry Louis and once again ally our great and powerful houses."

He ordered her to obey! Standing in her own parlor, threatening and ordering her! Face ablaze, she ran toward the bellpull near the fireplace.

Before she could reach it, the marquis lunged for her and held her in an ironlike grasp, glaring down into her face. The fierceness of his black, fathomless eyes ate into Brien's determination and she struggled to free her captive arms to no avail.

He was ready to harm her physically if necessary to have his way. The realization broke through her resistance and cold fear constricted her chest, slowing her struggles.

He dragged her over to the sofa and thrust her down upon it, his face contorting into a snarl. "You little bitch . . . you think you have only to snap your fingers and we will be gone." He loomed over her ominously, his chest heaving from the exertion. "You will acknowledge the engagement and will marry Louis or all London will laugh at your pretentions as you go to your hanging . . . for murder." His black eyes scorched the words into her dry wits.

"Murder," she murmured in disbelief. "Preposterous . . ." Her eyes widened at the growing realization of the desperate and ruthless course he pursued. He would have the marriage with or without her consent, and now there was no one for her to turn to. She was alone.

"Murder?" she murmured again, bewildered by his unexpected turn of thought.

"Yes, murder. You killed my son, Raoul." The malevolence of his face was nearly gleeful. He held her now by force of will, as powerful as any physical grasp.

She was stunned. "Raoul? This is insane. No one would believe that. Raoul died in the fire. Everyone saw—"

"I have a witness who claims otherwise." He stepped back cautiously and cast a glance over his shoulder at the other figure who had casually draped his frame over one of the graceful stuffed chairs. The man rose and loomed large in front of her. Physically, he was rather nondescript, of foppish bent and not as young as she had at first supposed. Brien's benumbed mind raced to recall him, but found no memory to draw forth. How could this stranger know anything about her and Raoul?

"I've never seen this man before—"

"Of course, you may not remember me . . . as one of the myriad guests at your magnificent wedding," the stranger spoke quietly. His accent was not French, but rather a flat, lower-London English; and his pallid complexion and watery blue eyes made him appear as unhealthy as his speech was common.

"I was your husband's companion during your illness after your marriage. He confided to me the nature of your particular . . . ah . . . malady . . . and his proposed cure."

The man's voice irritated her, teasing out a wisp of recollection that she struggled to bring to full awareness. It was him! She was devastated at the suddenness and sureness of the recognition. This was the man Raoul had conspired with that night at Weston Place— the night she had first learned the truth about her intended. This was the man to whom Raoul had drunkenly reviled her and revealed his loathsome opportunism. And he had been at Weston Place all the time she was imprisoned there—Raoul's companion and accomplice. The thought made her shiver involuntarily.

"This is outrageous! If there was any murder attempt, it was on my life, not Raoul's!" Only as the words left her lips did she finally realize the truth of them and how she had denied it to herself.

"Not so, milady," the stranger intoned saccharinely. "Before his death your husband confided to me that you had taken a lover before your marriage. He said you only married him to provide a name for the child you bore. As soon as the child was born, you intended to leave him—a plan he resisted. Finding no other solution to your passions, you schemed to lose him in a fire."

"Lies!" she shouted, fear growing in her beyond her capacity to deal with it. Her voice sounded small and desperate in her own ears.

"You twist it cleverly but it is still a lie! I wanted an annulment, it is true. Raoul refused and held me at Weston Place against my will. There was no child. . . . I barely escaped with my life!" Her reason faltered under the onslaught of fears and memories that pressed her. She shook her tawny head as if to clear it. "And who would believe this nameless cur?"

The marquis' lip curled into an ugly sneer. "This 'cur' is my nephew Cornelius Pitt, Raoul's cousin. His parentage is English and his story would be heard with due consideration before an English magistrate. If you were held prisoner, how is it you escaped and my son is dead? Could it be your lover helped you escape and set fire to the house to do away with my son?"

"N-n-no!" she stammered, her mind reeling with the plausibility of his fabrication. She pointed to the accusing Pitt. "You were there, you must know what happened! Raoul must have set the fire himself!"

The man smirked. "Believe what you will. It does not alter what others will say when I tell of how Raoul pleaded with you to stay and not to use him so callously.''

''The spite was his, the pleading mine! 'Twas he who plotted to kill me—to be heir to Weston Trading and the wealth of Southwold. No doubt you plotted with him.'' Brien noted, even in her distraction that he had not denied her charge. Raoul had planned to do away with her! Steadied by the flow of her own logic once more, Brien grasped desperately for her own defense.

''Raoul's blood was too hot for you.'' The marquis glowered. ''He demanded his own special revenge and in his foolishness, he was consumed himself. We all lost in the bargain. Rest assured, I shall not fall prey to the same weakness, in spite of your abundant charms.'' The coldness with which he spoke of his son was eerie. ''But this time you cannot withdraw, except to a far worse fate. You will marry Louis and live with him or you will pay dearly for it.'' He paused and straightened, running his lean, muscular hands down the front of his waistcoat as if savoring this next proclamation.

''No doubt it would be easy to prove the existence of this lover and to induce him to come forward on the side of justice. You haven't a choice.''

Aaron! Did they know of Aaron?

''There was no lover,'' she declared, her face flaming suddenly.

''There may have been many lovers!'' the marquis sneered. ''To boast of bedding you would only sweeten the jingle of silver in a freeman's pocket.''

''You couldn't . . .'' Brien breathed, the true terror of her predicament seeping through to her. There were many who might be willing to believe that the cool, aloof widow had spurned the favors of honorable men while satisfying her hot desires in secret—especially those who had tasted that coolness themselves.

Watching in her face the softening of her will, the marquis pressed on. ''You said it yourself, *chérie* . . . I am more cunning than Raoul. I would not allow passion or pride to interfere with my plans as did he. You will remain the beloved intended of my last son . . . and you will act the part in every way." The marquis moved closer and put one hand on her bare shoulder. "And you shall do as I say after the wedding as well." His hand slid possessively downward toward her breast and lingered there as his eyes gleamed with a twisted desire—whether for her wealth or for her she dared not think.

Stunned and horrified, Brien sat, wordless, as they withdrew to the door.

"You will issue a statement confirming your intention to marry Louis and to hold the ceremony within the month. I have taken the liberty of sending a letter to your father informing him of your betrothal and assuring him of your delight in the match. You will in all things be the joyous and eager bride." He paused before the door, satisfaction sitting smugly on his features. "I am most eager to have you as my . . . daughter once more."

Brien was still wordless as they left the parlor and entered the center hall. Every ounce of will and fortitude was drained from her. Mutely she listened to their retreating footsteps and their parting niceties to the manservant. How cool and merciless he seemed.

Brien did not hear Jeannie creep through the door or the girl's words of concern at her mistress' paleness and trembling. Panic seized her and she trembled violently as she began to mumble.

"They will force me . . ." she murmured brokenly. "They will force me to marry that gutless excuse of a man . . . they will force me. . . ."

Jeannie was waiting in the stable when Dyso returned that afternoon.

"Thank God you are here," she breathed, touching his arm hesitantly so that he would look at her. "Milady is in trouble, terrible trouble. The marquis was here, and he will force Lady Brien to marry his son Louis." Seeing the darkness welling up inside him she hurried on. "We must find a way to help her. Perhaps you could go to her father in Bristol." She felt foolish as she gazed up into his brooding face and remembered.

"No," she thought aloud. "How could you tell him? A letter?" She looked up at him and he brought two massive fists together with bruising force. Another movement and Jeannie read all too well what he planned.

"No! You cannot harm the marquis. He has something on milady that he's threatened her with . . . and another man came as well. If you try to harm him, they will blame milady. Please, Dyso," she pleaded, "we must find another way."

Smoldering belligerence filled the big man as he turned to lead the horses back to their stalls. Jeannie now feared what he might do. It had been a mistake to tell him.

"Dyso," she pleaded, "you must do nothing. We will send for Lord Weston. He may be able to do something to find a way out for milady." She caught up with him and clutched at his sleeve, hindering him little. "Promise you will do him no harm . . . the marquis." She shook his arm fearfully. "Promise!"

He turned to stare down at her unblinkingly. A dark brooding magnified his fearsome and tortured features. There was no agreement to be found in his frightening visage. He turned away from her and wrenched his arm free of her grasp.

Watching him lumber away toward his quarters, she called after him, "Dyso, wait!" But he neither looked back nor slowed his determined pace.

The following day Brien called Jeannie to her in the study. "I cannot stay here in London. Any distance I can put between myself and that jackal will ease my mind and may help me think of a way out of this. Have Dyso see to the carriage and then come help me pack a few things."

Jeannie's stricken look jolted Brien.

"What is it? What has happened?"

"I . . . I told Dyso about the marquis and what he would force you to. He was in a rage. I tried to calm him but he wouldn't listen. This morn when cook went to call him for breakfast he was gone. He didn't take anything with him—just left." She looked timidly at Brien as if fearing retribution for her actions. "I fear he might do the marquis harm; he was so angry." The girl looked about to cry and Brien put a gentle arm around her.

"It was not your fault . . . he had to learn sometime. If he has gone to the marquis there is naught we can do about it, but get us from London as quickly as possible. Go now, ready my trunk and send Phillips to me."

Alone once more, Brien was filled with mixed emotions. She hated the marquis with all that was in her and part of her wished to see him punished or destroyed. But her Dyso—he would be hunted and tracked and disposed of like an animal if he made good the threats of violence that his look at Louis had promised.

And what of her departure? Would the marquis read it as treachery and make good his threats?

Phillips arrived. "Yes ma'am?"

"I shall draft a short letter and as soon as I have gone you will see it safely to the office of the *Times* yourself. If anyone, especially the marquis calls you must tell them I have gone to our country house at Dunstan to prepare for my wedding. Is that clear?"

"Perfectly, milady."

"Phillips, I'll need a carriage and tell Mrs. Herriot I'll need a hamper for the journey. I'll take only Jeannie with me; I can make do with the house staff there. I wish to leave before noon."

A polite nod and he was off to do her bidding, concern lining his usually aloof features.

Brien settled herself at her father's massive mahogany desk and took quill in hand to write a confirmation of her engagement and forthcoming marriage. Perhaps with this concession she could gain time. She would set the date three months hence.

Twenty-six

In the growing darkness, mud spattered up from the horse's hooves. The streets at the outskirts of Bristol were rutted and hard to navigate. But the rider bent well to his animal's labor and pushed on relentlessly.

Picking his way through ill-remembered streets, he made his way to the waterfront where, looming dark and silent, warehouses nestled against the docks. Looking up from entrance to entrance as he rode by, the man compared each sign to one etched in his memory. At last he drew his exhausted animal to a halt in front of a huge brick structure bearing the name he sought. As dark and quiet as the others, the warehouse gave forth no signs of life, not even from the small windows high above the street.

The searcher let fall several resounding bangs on the door with his huge fist. The silence of the street and the faint echo of his action in the damp night were the only reply. The large man heaved a sigh of fatigue and leaned his massive shoulder against the door frame. After a long moment, he turned to survey the animal who had spent its very wind to bring him thus far.

He ran one hand tenderly down the horse's neck and felt a responding flicker of appreciation. Before deciding on a further course, he would see to the weary beast's needs.

It was well into the night before Aaron Durham settled the tasks before him and thought of sleep. The *Secret* lay berthed in Bristol's harbor, haivng just unloaded a cargo from Virginia in the colonies. The day had been hectic and not half so rewarding as Aaron had anticipated. The moneys were good. The raw materials from the colonies were sorely needed in Britain now— with war again—and profits were handily turned by even the poorest of traders. But the excitement, the feeling of completion he wanted would not come.

He was restless still and felt a gnawing inside. He had been sure that the successful completion of the voyage would send his spirits soaring and return to him that contentment he had always found as master of his own fate. Now the time had come and he only felt the same vague dissatisfaction that had plagued him for months.

As he unbuttoned his shirt to prepare for rest he mused on the source of his discontent. She had been no further from his mind than this; he could with only a moment's thought feel her in his arms and smell the faint scent of roses in her hair once more. How could the absence of one woman take away all the joy and meaning of his life? It was a mystery to him, one that left him humbled for the first time in his life.

Sleep came slowly these nights, if at all. Toward the early morning hours he would often rise and go topside to pace or steer. Now, in port, there was even less to do and the longing and impatience increased unbearably.

The ship itself was alive with Brien. Aaron had sold the *Secret* in New York for a handsome sum but when the time came to give her up he could not. Too much of the Lady lived and breathed in the vessel itself. He could no more part with the ship that bore her spirit than he could rid himself of the longing for her.

He was past loathing himself for the weakness that admitted a need for her. Somehow he felt they were meant to be together—to need and love each other as halves of some better whole. But with her willfulness and pride there was little chance of happiness with her now. She feared, as he once had, that to be free and in control was to be strong. And in so thinking she became slave to the most rigorous of masters—an ideal, an unattainable thing.

In the dark of his cabin his own thoughts jarred him. That was it, the hard-won wisdom he had wrestled in his soul to gain. They were so similar, so kindred. What he saw in her was a mirror of his own independence and arrogant defiance of convention and tradition. She had said it so well on board ship; she clung to her freedom against its major foe—marriage; and he clung to his freedom against tradition and succession to title. The thought nagged him that his own struggle might seem as hurtful and futile as hers. He shook away the thought as if it were poison, but he could not dismiss its bitter aftertaste. Where was the difference? His victory was far easier than hers would be. But where was the right of it?

Throwing himself on his bunk, he tried to turn his thoughts from those unsettling ones and partly succeeded. He smiled wryly at the ironic twist of his hitherto cavalier life. He mused uncomfortably on the comely maids who had set their caps for him and had met with utter disappointment. He had never stopped to ponder the carnage of pride he had left in his wake until now and the taste of awareness was sour in his mouth. He had at last found one to set his body and soul so aquiver with excitement it seemed no longer in his control. She haunted his dreams and his blood, making him think the unthinkable and desire that which he had decried as fit for weaker men alone. Now that which he berated as commonplace and dull became the burning focus of all his desires: he wanted her for his wife, to live his life and realize his dreams with her at his side—loving him and sharing her life with him. Ah, God the ache was unbearable! And the long night stretched out in leisurely fashion before him.

Just before dawn, Aaron was awakened by a loud scuffling and muffled cries on deck above him. Reacting instinctively, he bounded out of the bunk and reached for his sword. In three steps he was at the door, its blade now revealed and the sleep jarred from his eyes and mind. In a few strides he had gained the steps and then the hatch. The shouts and cries were louder now and more numerous in the gray mist of early dawn.

Swinging up through the hatch Aaron saw a small knotted jumble of writhing arms and legs and thrashing bodies locked in combat on the main deck near the gangway. Two bleary-eyed seamen with weapons drawn looked on in confusion as two of their mates struggled for their very lives against a raging typhoon of a man, whose size and agility were more than a contest for them both.

"Don't just stand there," he snarled at the wary noncombatants. "Help them out!"

Aaron struggled to make sense of the melee and saw with growing alarm that the two late-comers were of little help and were soon dispatched to other parts of the deck. Venturing closer in the dim light, Aaron froze.

The form was recognizable and he called the intruder by name. "Dyso?"

A noticeable pause in the big man's activity gave the defenders just the chance they needed to land well placed and devastating blows. The big man lay still at last on the deck and the seamen, dazed and exhausted pulled themselves away to rest near the rail.

Aaron knelt by the silent figure in thought. It was indeed Dyso. His thoughts raced to suggest why he might have come so far and why to him. The only answer would be trouble for Brien—and now for him as well.

Aaron had the crewmen bind him tightly and carry him downstairs to the captain's cabin. Rousting the cook, Aaron ordered coffee and some food prepared. Then he settled down to await the revival of the hulk, his saber across his knees.

First an hour dragged by, then two. Dyso's slumber was more a testament to his fatigue than to the strength of Aaron's crew. The hot, strong coffee warmed Aaron and prepared him for the ordeal he feared would come when the hulk awakened.

A low growl proceeded from the form on the bunk, and Aaron started to his feet, handling the sword nervously. He stepped to the door and called into the corridor for Hicks, who had just awakened. Hicks appeared in a flash at the cabin door and was amazed at the now-thrashing figure on the bunk. Aaron thrust the sword into the mate's hand and ordered, "Hold this and use it if you must. He's strong as a team of oxen."

Aaron approached the bunk warily, eying the straining ropes and bulging muscles.

"Dyso," he called. "Dyso, this is Captain Durham. Do you hear me? If so, calm yourself."

The struggling slowed at first, then stopped. Aaron paused, cast a worried look to Hicks, then stood by the bunk.

"If I untie you, do I have your pledge there will be no more violence?"

Aaron thought he perceived a quick movement of agreement and looked to Hicks for confirmation. A shrug from Hicks and Aaron was left to make the decision on his own.

"I'll cut you loose, but I'll have no more violence." He took a dagger from the desk and deftly sliced through the bonds, jumping backward at the first movement of the man.

As they held their breath, the hulk sat up slowly and rubbed his eyes wearily. With slow, methodical movements, he swung his legs over the side of the bunk and heaved a sigh. His face seemed lined with fatigue and dull pain.

Aaron relaxed visibly and moved slowly to the desk to pour the man a cup of coffee. Offering it to him cautiously, Aaron was shaken when Dyso looked up and met his gaze. The big man's eyes were haunted, like those of a hunted, trapped animal pleading for kindness. The look and the rumpled and mud-stained clothing told of his haste and the urgency of his mission.

"Why have you come, my friend?" Aaron said easing into a chair near him. "Are you in trouble?"

Dyso shook his head and with his free hand traced a curved line.

"Brien . . . she is in trouble?" Getting an affirmative nod, Aaron continued. "Did she send you?" Again negative. "You came to get me to help her?" Affirmative. "What has happened—what danger is she in?"

Dyso's face showed more animation than Aaron had ever seen there before. This newest danger must be dire, indeed. The big man cast his eyes about him and settled on a thin brass rod attached to a candle snuffer.

In a twinkling, he bent it about the third finger of his left hand and held it up for Aaron to see.

Caught up in the symbolism of the bending, Aaron missed the tangible point. "Someone bends her? Forces her? To what?"

Dyso shook his head in frustration and pointed, grunting to the twisted ring of brass on his hand. It was a moment before the meaning broke through to him.

"She's getting married?"

The hulk grimaced as if it pained him to admit it.

"Well, whatever your or my feelings, it is no business of ours. She will do what she wants. She's made that plain enough." But the thought stuck, wedged uncomfortably beside the knowledge that she would never agree to a marriage now. He knew she cared for him above other men, but even that was not enough to cause her to surrender her precious freedom.

Dyso now grabbed Aaron's arm and squeezed it mightily drawing protest from him. Then the big man pulled the twisted brass from his hand and pantomimed the forcing of the metal onto his finger. Drawing only puzzlement, he repeated the action.

Frantic to communicate, he grabbed Aaron's hand in a viselike grip and forced the metal onto Aaron's finger, even as the Captain protested.

Hicks was the first to glimpse the truth behind this grotesque mimicry. He straightened and proposed, "She's being forced to marry—is that it?"

Responding with a relieved nod, the big man turned to Aaron with something akin to pleading in his face. Several quick hand motions explained what Aaron had already guessed; Dyso wanted his help for their lady once more. He could find no resistance in him. Brien needed him—now. He would go.

* * *

Dunstan's sober and stately comfort relieved Brien little upon her arrival. Be setting the wedding date three months hence, she had won a stay of time in which to think and to plan. It was small comfort to her to know the identity of her false accuser, the man, Cornelius Pitt. So there was one who knew the whole truth of her marriage; the knowledge sent chills through her. He knew well what punishment Raoul had exacted and knew well Raoul's plan. Raoul had planned to do away with her; the Marquis had said as much. Then how had Raoul been trapped in the fire? An accident? Would she ever know?

Raoul—the very name impaled her. She had fought to erase nearly every memory of him but now they came rushing back upon her with a vengeance. He had never cared for her—not even in the depths of his passion. He professed to hold her there until she bore proof of his seed, all the while planning her murder. No woman could have ever shared a life with him; his cunning and avarice would have prevented it. He would have taken and taken until her very life was drained from her by child-bearing and pain. Then she would have been cast aside as were the others he spoke of so callously. Raoul, aged and well-practiced, would have become the marquis, the basest and worst in man perfected and magnified in one man. She shuddered anew. The full power of that evil intent was now turned on her and her heart sank at the thought. There seemed no way out.

But what of her father? Would he stand by her in this? Her troubled thoughts returned again and again to the day he had returned from Weston Place and his confrontation with Raoul. If he heard the story of the marquis would he not have some cause for suspicion? Would he believe her? Despite their recent closeness, Brien remembered all too vividly the anger at betrayal on his face as he sentenced her to be married to protect the family honor. How could she ask him to understand—to defend her—without telling him the whole truth? Soon the marquis' message would reach him in Bristol. Surely he would not be so easily led in to thinking she could change her mind so capriciously. He must realize this did not transpire with her consent!

She brightened at the thought. After dinner at the home of the marquis, in the carriage, she had made plain her thoughts about Louis and any prospect of marriage with him. He must remember that!

She flew to the study and penned a message to her father asking that he return to Dunstan immediately on a matter of the gravest importance. She smiled wanly as she perused the final letter and then sealed it with his own stamp. He must suspect the cause when this message arrived so close on the heels of that from the marquis. He would hurry to her side. Her confidence mounted as she called the butler, Davidson, to her.

"This message must reach my father as quickly as possible in Bristol. It is critical. Have Harold take a good mount and ride hard." She drew a few gold sovereigns from the desk drawer and placed them in his hand alongside the letter. "He will need food and a fresh mount. Give him these and bid him hurry."

Davidson's face reflected concern behind his carefully cultivated indifference, but with his customary good manners, he asked no questions. With a brief bow, he was gone.

Brien had slept poorly in the two nights since arriving at Dunstan. Her dreams were tortured snatches of her time with Raoul that somehow melted into nightmares of the marquis and Louis and laughing faces and hands clutching at her. She ran—to be stopped by a body of foul black water. Hearing the onslaught behind her, she waded in to be swallowed alive. Drowning, she awakened, shaking uncontrollably and with her night-gown drenched and cold against her. She sat in mute horror, great tears rolling down her blazing cheeks. Jeannie found her thus and comforted her as best she could.

The days were little more pleasant. Brien found her-self easily tired and was unexpectedly cross with ser-vants, even Jeannie. She seemed little like herself, and was unable to string two coherent thoughts together. She laid it all at the feet of the marquis, for he was the source of all her difficulty.

A cold autumn rain had begun over the countryside and drove the fading color from the garden. From the library window Brien watched the closing darkness out-side and mused that the rain seemed to wash the last hope from her heart as well.

This restlessness born of waiting was hard to endure. Now a full week had passed quietly at Dunstan and all real terror seemed suspended in this safe haven. She paced and read and slept and paced again. Her mes-sage had had time to reach Bristol by now, and Lord Weston would soon start for their home, she was sure. Still, she could not be certain of his response once he ar-rived and learned of her predicament. All her thoughts ran into dizzy spirals that always returned to the start-ing point of despair.

She dressed for dinner each night to occupy time and to appease the staff. Even under stress one had obliga-tions. The more she conformed to normal customs, the more bearable the waiting seemed.

Tonight she insisted that Jeannie keep her company at dinner, even though the little maid insisted that she would be more comfortable in the servants' hall. They spoke little, Brien ignoring the injured sensibilities of

Davidson and the other staff as they served her guest of the evening.

As they took coffee in the parlor a commotion arose in the hallway; a door banged, feet shuffled, and voices sounded. Brien bounded up abruptly, hope in her face, and cast a relieved glance at her maid. It must be her father!

Before the cool breath of reason could be felt, she was at the door and sweeping into the hall.

"Father," she stopped short, letting the other words die in her throat. Recovering quickly, she drew a breath to steady herself.

"Brien, my daughter, so kind of you to greet your new relations so warmly." The marquis bowed low before her in a mockery of deference. When he rose, the gleam in his eyes told of the mischief he brought on this gloomy night.

"Whatever brings you here, sir, uninvited and unannounced? You might have given fair warning of your intent. We could have prepared dinner for you and your companions." Her eyes drank in the two figures that had accompanied the jackal in this assault on her privacy. Louis affected a wan smile, and a strange, coarse-looking man in ill-fitting clothes doffed his hat awkwardly, staring openly at her. The sense of it seeped through to her. This unpleasant combination abroad on such a nasty night—it boded ill. She could retain her bearing only by observing what few pleasantries she could until she found their intent.

Davidson stood by, eying the group uncomfortably and Brien turned to him with a wealth of meaning in her eyes.

"Davidson, we shall be in the drawing room. Please bring in coffee and brandy for these gentlemen. And see to their cloaks."

Before he could protest Brien whirled away and led

416

the way to the great room. Mind racing and stomach churning, she searched for ways to summon help without being detected.

"Jeannie," she turned to the little maid, "please go now and make my rooms ready for the night." The intensity of her gaze warned the girl, and she nodded briefly and turned to obey.

Before the girl was three steps, the marquis' henchman, for that was all he could be called, blocked her way. She turned back to Brien, her eyes wide with alarm.

"What is the meaning of this?" Brien demanded of the marquis.

"She will not need to prepare your rooms for the night," he uttered. "She will stay with us here for the present."

"You give orders to my servants, here in my own house!" Brien's rising voice was a fair counterfeit of anger, when in reality it was fear she felt most.

"Soon to be the shared inheritance of your husband."

"Not for some time," Brien insisted.

"On the contrary, my daughter," the marquis intoned menacingly. "You thought to delay the time of the wedding to find a way to prevent it. Clever of you to set the date three months hence. But it is to no avail. Your wedding, *chèrie*, was never meant to wait upon the bans. No matter when you set the time, the result would have been the same."

Brien was stunned! He had planned this all along. Her mind raced in fruitless circles. If only she had not hesitated in sending for her father. She knew with certainty that he would have defended her against this mongrel. She lifted her chin proudly in spite of the coldness of her blood.

"I make no pretense of delight in this charade. You

417

know me little to think I would submit so easily.''

"That is as I knew it would be.'' The marquis sauntered casually about the large room, touching the elegant furnishings appraisingly. "So we have come this night to see your properly wedded before some foolish action might mar your chance for marital bliss.''

"See me wed . . . this night?'' Brien again reeled.

A taunting concern bent the marquis' full mouth to a cruel smile. "Beautiful as you are, even a simple dinner frock will suffice as a bridal gown.'' His heavy brows knit in concentration as his black eyes bored into her own.

"You will come with us, daughter, to the church shortly—to marry Louis this eve. My man has gone ahead to alert the priest. He will have made ready by the time we arrive.''

"I will not go . . . you cannot force me. The marriage will not stand if I am forced.'' The spark of defiance was hard to find amongst the shambles of her will.

A sharp, irritated sigh and a curt nod from the marquis and the large man grabbed Jeannie and cruelly held her and twisted her arm until she cried out.

Horrified, Brien shouted, "Stop it!'' Her eyes blazed with anger and full hatred now unleashed. "You whoreson. You stop at nothing to have your way.''

"I accept your compliment readily. I shall soon have you as daughter and the promise of the Weston fortune besides. To insure your cooperation, Eads here will stay with your maid until we return. If you fail to cooperate in any way, I promise she will suffer in most eloquent ways.''

Brien felt numb. She was bested. She would hazard her own safety and her own fortune, but she would not barter the very life of those who served her faithfully.

Through the pain she suffered at the big man's brutality, Jeannie managed to utter, "No, milady, don't—" But a further tightening of her arm cut off the flow of words and brought tears to her pale cheeks.

Brien moved instinctively toward her and stopped, powerless to stop this hideous cruelty. After a brief silence, she straightened and turned to her tormentor.

"I shall go with you and I shall marry Louis." Her eyes were now cold and devoid of all but contempt. "If aught befalls this girl or any other of my household, I'll not be married long—whatever the price."

Satisfaction settled over the marquis, the smugness she had seen the night of the ball and of her engagement. He had won and how he reveled in it. She would soon be Madame Trechaud in earnest once more. Numbness settled over her as the marquis directed Louis to see to his bride, a small blessing, for she barely felt his hand on her arm. Louis meekly led her to the hall where a confused and concerned Davidson helped her on with her cloak.

The passing of time was illusory—a moment, an hour, an age. Then the carriage slowed its rocking motion and stopped. Louis and the Marquis were soon out and Brien—now a spectator of her fate, imprisoned in her own flesh—was moving through the carriage door into the arms of her waiting captor. The details of the courtyard of St. Anne's became clear in the dank night air that was only feebly parted by the lantern light.

Brien raised her head briefly with a hopeful expression but no friendly face greeted them at the door. A gaunt, dour-faced man in cleric's garb admitted them to the rectory. She roused long enough to ask through her disappointment, "Where is Vicar Harold?"

The narrowed, disapproving eyes of the new priest turned on her as he answered. "The Vicar Stonegate was transferred nearly two months ago to a parish in Cornwall."

Her last small flicker of hope was effectively doused. Louis removed her cloak and lead her to a seat by the fire, his eyes weary and apologetic. The sneering Cornelius Pitt, already indulging in the liquid refreshment provided, raised a mocking glass to her.

The marquis drew the vicar aside and was soon in deep conversation with him. The cleric cast doubtful, then disapproving glances toward Brien and nodded gravely as the marquis talked. The metallic clink of silver was barely audible as the men parted.

"After you've warmed youselves with a glass of sherry, we'll begin," the priest announced, gesturing to a small bare wooden table near the fireplace on which sat a bottle of sherry and several glasses. Then he left to light the chancel where the unhappy event would take place.

Brien shivered with dread as she took the glass offered to her and sipped the contents. The warm sweetness of the liquid was a small, distinct comfort. Now she little cared what anyone did or said. It would soon be over.

A small knot of servants sat huddled by the fireplace in the great kitchen warming themselves and wondering at the events that took place in the same house. For no reason he could name, Davidson glanced nervously at the others and then at the window. They spoke seldom and always in low tones as if afraid of giving offense by pondering or discussing their mistress' fate.

The sound was faint enough at first but Davidson's ears, sensitive from years of close attendance upon subtleties of sound and gesture, detected it. Rising, he moved carefully toward the window, listening keenly after each step. There was no mistaking it. He grabbed the globed candlestick from the long table in the center of the kitchen and jerked open the door that led to the side yard. Dashing out in his shirtsleeves, he shielded the flickering flame from the light drizzle with his hand and scanned the drive before him for the source of the noise. Soon he was pressed back by three riders, and he wheeled to make out who they might be. They dismounted hurriedly and were drawn to the source of the light. He could see they were big men, equipped for the foul weather and a hard ride.

"Dyso!" Davidson's eyes were wide with relief. He had never been at ease with the scarred giant, but the strange hulk's loyalty to Lady Brien could not be questioned. "Come in out of the weather," he beckoned, leading them inside.

The door now closed against the worsening elements, the three riders peeled off their dripping outer cloaks and hats near the portal as the other servants stood gawking at the trio.

"Permit me." One man stepped forward, still occupied with shaking water from his clothing and smoothing back his copper hair. "I am Aaron Durham of Bristol, Captain of the *Lady's Secret* and a friend of Lady Brien's." He gestured to Dyso after seeing the mistrustful frown on the butler's face. "Dyso came to fetch me all the way from port, and we have kept a grueling pace to be here in time. We must see Lady Brien at once."

Davidson eyed the man sternly and decided that he might be trusted with this much. "Milady is not here at the present."

When he failed to continue, Aaron grew short-tempered with his reluctance to speak further and snapped, "Then where is she? We haven't ridden day and night in this hellish weather to play at guessing games." His golden eyes danced with his ire.

The butler's spine straightened in defiance and the other three servants drew back, fully expecting the worst. But before Davidson could summon an indignant response, Aaron thought better of his threatening stance and rubbed his eyes with his hand.

"What I am trying to say is we've come to the lady's aid. I know she is being forced to marry against her will, and we would lend ourselves to her cause." Remembering, he continued, "Dyso will affirm my words." As the hulk nodded tersely, resting his shoulder against the fireplace, Aaron indicated the third figure. "This is Mr. Robert Hicks, my first mate and a close friend of Jeannie Trowbridge." Then it struck him. "She could verify our identity and confirm our story. Where is she?"

"I . . . I can't say, sir. I haven't seen her for a time." Davidson, indeed the entire staff, had known Lady Brien was sorely troubled on some account, for her hurried arrival and morose mood were unlike her normal even disposition. But the cause they were left to ponder on their own, for even Jeannie kept the secret well and none dared question her closely. It could do no harm to reveal what he knew, Dyso's presence confirmed to some extent their story.

"I am not sure of Jeannie's whereabouts, but milady was escorted from the house scarcely half an hour ago by the Marquis de Saunier and his son, Louis." As he said it he realized what must have transpired under his very nose. He knew from her mood and distraction that she did not accompany them willingly. "I cannot be sure where they were bound, but I am sure that Lady Brien was much distressed. Wait! There were three arrived, but only the marquis and the son left with milady. The other must still be here!"

Galvanized into action by the man's words, Aaron jumped forward anxiously. "Where were they?"

"In the drawing room—I'll show you the way." But even in his excitement the habits of a lifetime prevailed and Davidson grabbed his coat and donned it as he led them out of the kitchen and through the narrow hallway toward the drawing room. Aaron stole a look at Hicks, and they drew their swords, each knowing the other's mind.

Davidson paused outside the massive doors to the room and pressed his hand to his lips in a plea for silence as he listened. Then he drew them away from the door and whispered, "He's still there, I'm sure of it." He swallowed hard. "And I think Jeannie is with him."

Hicks's face reddened immediately. "He's holding her there; I'll set her free."

Aaron's hand on his arm constrained him as he turned to Davidson. "Can you get him to open the door? It may be locked and to try it would arouse suspicion."

With a nod Davidson disappeared silently and in a twinkling reappeared with a tray bearing brandy glasses and a decanter. He went straight to the door and cocked his head to them, leaving them to intuit his plan and position themselves before he knocked.

The gruff voice of the man called Eads objected to the interruption in sharp and unmistakable terms. But Davidson, in perfect, natural tones announced his purpose, stating that milady had instructed him to see to their comfort.

A breathless moment later, the key scraped in the lock and the door was swinging open. Aaron and his companions moved upon the retreating wood and the man behind it with stunning speed and effect. Eads was thrown back momentarily and snarled a curse that he had allowed himself to be caught off guard by so light a ruse. Hicks rushed Eads in a fury, having caught sight of Jeannie with bodice torn and hair disheveled. He cast aside his blade and made for the malefactor with bare hands and a savage growl. Aaron pulled Dyso's arm to restrain him and together they watched the mismatched struggle, allowing Hicks his retribution.

Twisting and pounding, each combatant sought the advantage, but the contest was weighted unfairly in the brute's favor and soon Hicks was on the floor, scuffling to escape the man's choking hands. Just as Eads saw his first victory in hand he was lifted bodily from his position astride Hicks and thrown with tremendous force against the wall nearby. Soon furniture flew and crashed and skittered under the mammoth weights and blows of the more evenly matched contenders. Eads sought a quicker end to the battle and grabbed a fireplace iron, swinging it viciously at Dyso, who ducked and weaved almost gracefully. Still, there was danger in being unarmed so Aaron stepped into the fray offering his sword as diversion. Pressed back now on two sides, Eads saw the seriousness of his plight and again began to curse vilely as his worried frown flickered from giant to gentleman. He struck out again and again, invariably finding the space he sought with his weapon vacated before its arrival.

Tiring quickly the man's arm drooped with the lethal iron, and he swung more slowly, slowly enough for a great leg and foot to find an opening mid-swing and to knock the iron to the floor. Dyso charged in before Aaron had a chance to offer him surrender, and soon they were writhing on the floor, locked in a horrible grip. Dyso's hands found the man's throat, and he showed the same mercy as the brute had to Hicks. Seeing the man go limp under the giant's crushing grasp, Aaron called to his comrade to stop. But through the rushing of blood in his ears, Dyso heard nothing, so Aaron mobilized the still dazed Hicks to help him drag Dyso away before he killed the man.

They stood, panting heavily from their effort and staring down at the vanquished one, each for his own separate reason. Hearing Jeannie's muffled weeping,

Hicks and Aaron turned to her, and the first mate gathered her into his stout arms protectively.

"It's all right, love," he murmured. "Are you hurt?" His voice was full of emotion as he held her trembling frame to him.

"No . . . not really. He tried . . ." She hid her face in Hicks's coat and could say no more until after Aaron had bound her captor with a cord from the draperies and had returned to them. He knelt on one knee before her.

"Can you tell me where they've taken Brien?" he questioned her gently, but urgently.

She lifted her tear-streaked face to him as if only now remembering the jeopardy of her mistress. "To the abbey . . . they're to be married this very night. She refused at first . . . but they hurt me to force her . . . and she went—to save me." She could not continue, her sorrowful face now a mute but eloquent plea for her lady.

"Hicks," Aaron ordered unnecessarily, "stay here with Jeannie and see this villain well guarded. I cannot say when we'll return; you'll have to manage—even with the redcoats." A nod was the mate's only reply.

Aaron motioned to Dyso and they both headed toward the door. "Do you know the way to the abbey?" At the man's nod, Aaron responded, "Then we've not a minute to lose."

Two horsemen rode hard in the worsening weather and darkness. The road disappeared just in front of the horses' hooves and the cold damp air clung to the riders and tortured their lungs. Every fiber, every sinew of Aaron's body ached from want of rest. They had ridden hard for two days, and nearly all of the previous night. Nearing their destination, they had stopped only a short while to find food and fresh mounts.

But the muffled splashing and straining of the animals and his own rapid heart pounding in his ears were enough to keep him awake and spur him on. He must reach her in time. He had no plan, knew not in what manner he would find her. But he must endure this to succeed. And he ground his teeth to ward off the aches in his cramped legs and arms.

The road seemed to wind and careen crazily in the close darkness. But for the muffled sound of the horse beside him, he might have been alone. Fatigue and pain spawned anger at the cause of this mad journey—anger at Brien and the pride and stubbornness that drew her into trouble and beckoned him to her rescue.

How dare the wench be so arbitrary and headstrong when she was unable to defend herself? If she would grow up, stop chasing some damnable ideal. . . .

"She puts other to great trouble to see her whimsy satisfied!" he growled to himself. "Well, no more! I'll not rescue her again! By God in heaven—never again! I'll see it finished this time!"

Light from the rectory windows glowed a dull yellow as they reined up outside the churchyard. Through the open gate in the stone wall, Aaron glimpsed the empty carriage and a quick perusal of the area told him no watch was posted. Aaron smiled, straightening and stretching his shoulders and legs. The marquis was oversure of himself. A careful villain, like a careful general, prepares for all possibilities. This new evidence increased his confidence. He would succeed.

Swinging down from his horse near the carriage, he tied the animal to the rear of it and motioned Dyso to do the same. They would need a conveyance for Brien and the carriage must do. He surveyed the outline of the building as it disappeared into the mist and gloom.

Then he turned to Dyso.

"Do you know this place well?"

A nod.

"Can I reach the chapel through here?" He gestured to the door near them.

Another nod.

"We must take separate routes. I'll go this way. Can you find another?"

Affirmed.

"Then show yourself when you hear my voice. We must strike quickly, they may outnumber us."

The big man turned to go, but Aaron caught his arm. As the fierce features turned to him, Aaron suppressed a shudder. There was cold violence in the hulk's battered visage. That worried Aaron most of all.

"We will use force only if it is needed to see Brien free. More than that would set the law upon us."

Dyso's face showed no trace of agreement, and he turned to go.

Aaron pulled him back by the arm once more.

"No violence!" he insisted. "Your lady will not be helped by would-be rescuers rotting in prison or hanged. Swear to me."

Still no response.

"Swear it!" Aaron demanded.

A long moment dragged by before a barely perceptible nod signified the big man's pledge of cooperation.

Aaron relaxed. "Good."

Then Aaron was alone at the rectory door, listening, straining to hear if anyone were inside. Silence rewarded his effort and he lifted the latch quietly. As he entered, his scabbard scraped the doorway and he quickly shut the portal behind him to listen for signs of his detection. He was in a hallway that opened into a plainly furnished room, a parlor. One short glance about and he moved toward the only other door to the room on soft-booted feet.

Momentarily he wondered if they had come to the right place. But, shaking his head to clear it, he quelled his doubts. She would be here—and well-nigh married by now while he dawdled.

He opened the door and peered into the semi-darkness beyond—a hallway. He entered and followed it without reservation. His steps were quick and soft and he felt the wooden floor give way to slabs of stone beneath his feet as he guided himself along the stone walls with his hands. The air was damper now, unheated and inhospitable.

Then he heard the voice. A high-pitched male voice droned on in an ecclesiastical manner. The sanctuary. It was near now. He drew his sword and approached the source of the sound, nearly deafened by the wild beating of his own heart. Was she already another's bride?

Brien had quite unconsciously called on feminine wiles to delay the inevitable. She'd had chills and been comforted with a second glass of sherry and a blanket for her lap. Then she'd become overheated and swooned, and they'd allowed her to lie down for a few moments on the threadbare sofa.

The vicar had clearly shown annoyance at her frailties. And the marquis' nostrils flared and his teeth were on edge. Brien strained his pretense at concern to the limit. In the end, a half-hour's respite was all her malaise could bring.

To any normal human, the circumstances of this hurried match would have seemed strange, and Brien's difficulties would have been interpreted rightly as reluctance. But the Vicar was a poor country cleric, with real silver in his pocket for the first time in a long while.

He would ignore the nuances and proceed to unite the fornicating twosome. After all, women who are with child are frequently sick.

In the end, they had wrapped her in her cloak, and she had straightened with one last shred of dignity. She approached this as does a prisoner the gallows, terrified and yet relieved that it would soon be over.

". . . into this holy estate God draws man and woman to live honorably together all their lives. To comfort and attend one another, to provide for the proper rearing of children and to make a stable base for society to rest upon. It is for this reason we have gathered here. Let us proceed."

And proceed he did, with a stern sermon on the lusts of the flesh and the weakness of womankind and the duty of man to strengthen and constrain this weaker vessel. Brien drifted in and out of awareness, snatching enough of the vicar's lesson to chafe uncomfortably under his hostile gaze. It was clear he thought her a soiled vessel and felt sure he'd set to rights the unholy situation. The irony was almost too much to bear silently.

Brien trembled now with weakness. Her face was ashen as the gray stone walls of the chapel itself. Her mind wandered to the time she had stood here with another groom, also trembling—being swallowed up. It was happening again. Perhaps she deserved this misery for presuming to that which is never a woman's fate— freedom.

"Do you, Louis Armand Phillipe Trechaud, take this woman to wife, to love, honor, and protect her as long as you both shall live?"

"Of course he would!" A clear, deep voice rang out. "Were he a man to take a woman at all!"

The shock registered through the whole party as a figure with drawn sword appeared as by magic inside the sacristy door.

429

In a single, fluid movement Aaron Durham placed himself beside the stunned Vicar, sword tip randy about the throat of Louis Trechaud.

"Who are you?" the vicar demanded.

"How dare you!" the marquis blurted out angrily, starting forward.

"No, no," Aaron warned him back, brandishing the tip of his blade in Louis' face. "Make no sudden moves, gentleman, or this farce of a wedding will become an earnest funeral."

"How dare you desecrate the House of God—" the vicar fumed, clutching his service book tightly. He now heartily regretted his participation in this rite.

"How dare you desecrate your holy office by this farce! This wedding is not one of consent—it could not be." Aaron's gaze swept the small gathering, noting the sword that hung by the marquis' side. The other seemed unarmed, but the odds were three to one. Where in the bloody hell was Dyso?

"Forced or not," the vicar nervously defended himself, "the woman is with child and must be put to rights."

Aaron glanced briefly at Brien who was wide-eyed and seemingly numb. She would lend little aid or encouragement to his next pronouncement.

"Aye, she's with child; but the fault is mine, not this lily-handed bastard's." He spat out the words contemptuously.

The marquis edged toward them, stopping as Aaron perceived the motion and swung a murderous gaze in his direction.

"Unless you would lose this excuse of a son, you dare not move again. Draw your blade and toss it behind you."

The marquis moved slowly to comply and while Aaron's attention was focused on his movements the accusing Cornelius Pitt slid his feet silently closer to Louis and out of Aaron's line of sight.

Then he made his move, lunging forward to be suddenly stopped in midair by an explosion of human flesh from the nearby pulpit. The two bodies hit the slate floor with bone-cracking force, and after a moment of thudding fists and grappling flesh, the ambitious Pitt lay unconscious under the crushing weight of his assailant.

The marquis had seized the diversion to grasp the handle of his sword and in an instant had it free of its sheath. Aaron thrust the stunned Louis aside savagely, and with a single vicious stroke of his blade sent the other weapon flying into the front pews some distance away.

Now pressing the cold eager point of his blade under the chin of the shocked marquis, Aaron sneered, "That was foolish of you, marquis. Your soft life no doubt has slowed your reflexes. Now you will obey my orders or my large friend here will gladly take you outside and teach you proper respect. I presume you have met him." Aaron's burning eyes belied the light, mocking tone of his words.

The marquis shot a hard stare at the tightly reined giant who now murdered him mentally. His snort of recognition contained an acknowledgment of a private irony.

Brien discovered her voice as she too gazed at the hulk. "Dyso?" She was sleeping and yet walking and talking. Benumbed and still in shock, she said no more. Her blankness shook Aaron to the very core. What was the matter with her? Why did she not acknowledge him . . . or say something?

Shoving that concern to the back of his mind so he might better concentrate on the events of the present, he tossed his head ordering the marquis to stand over beside the ashen vicar. "Over here, where you can witness well the wedding that will take place."

Teetering ignominiously on tiptoes as he was held aloft by the point of Aaron's blade, he moved slowly, reddening with the blazing hatred boiling inside him. Louis made way for his bested leader and retreated to the side of the still unconscious Pitt.

Glancing backward now as he assumed Louis' former place beside Brien, he noted Dyso towering over both spiritless figures, clearly in charge. "Now, Vicar, you may proceed." He gathered Brien into his free arm and held her possessively against his side. She made no sound, but Aaron felt her melt against him, trembling.

"I cannot," the vicar protested feebly, wincing at the potential attack he feared would come.

Aaron shot a glance at the smoldering nobleman that teetered on the tip of his blade.

"As I see it," Aaron said calmly but with a distinct threat, "you have no choice. The sword and the woman are mine. Unless you intend to carry this miserable bastard's blood on your head, you will marry us— and now!" His voice had a growl about it at the finish that lent credence to the threat.

"I . . . I . . ." The vicar was befuddled.

"Just begin where you left off. That will do nicely." The exaggerated civility of his words gave evidence of the tension that slowly ebbed from his muscles. He was in control, his task nearly accomplished.

"The marriage will never stand," the marquis ground out from between clenched teeth.

"Enough from you, swine," Aaron snapped, jabbing the point harder against the enraged nobleman's throat. "The lady *is* willing."

The vicar, wide-eyed and trembling turned to Brien, who met his question with equally wide eyes.

"Do you consent?"

Aaron held his breath.

"I . . ."—she looked from Aaron to the marquis and back to Aaron—"consent."

"Now on with it," Aaron breathed again.

Relenting at last the Vicar opened his service book and resumed in halting voice.

"Do you—I don't have your name."

"Aaron Nathaniel Thomas Durham."

"Do you, Aaron Nathaniel Thomas Durham, take this woman to wife; to love, honor, and protect her as long as you both shall live? Then answer 'I do.' " The Vicar relaxed visibly as if the full name struck a chord of remembrance.

He turned to Brien. "Do you, Brien Carolyn Weston Trechaud, take this man for your wedded husband; to love, honor, and obey him as long as you both shall live? Then answer 'I do.' "

A breathless moment passed before her voice was heard. "I do."

"Then by the power and authority of my office as a priest of the great Church of England and in the name of her head, our most sovereign and gracious King, I do pronounce you man and wife. Whom God has joined together let no man set asunder." He closed the service book and looked at Aaron expectantly.

Aaron's smile was sardonic. "Well done, parson. You have executed your office properly. Now let us see to the papers." He nodded toward the sacristy door that lead back to the rectory.

The vicar led the strange procession and Dyso followed, carrying one limp form and prodding another impatiently. The marquis walked reluctantly in front of Aaron's sword and Aaron drew his bride along with him, half carrying her, for she seemed weak and nearly incapable of supporting herself on her own limbs.

"Think carefully," the marquis taunted as they

moved through the dim hallway. "You will not get away with this outrage. The marriage is not legal. You will be hunted and tried and hanged as a kidnapper."

"It is as legal as any you would have forced her to," Aaron countered. "She gave her consent. And now there is no more you can do to her."

They emerged into the rectory where Dyso had dumped the hapless blackmailer on the floor and thrust Louis down beside him.

"Have you a rope, Vicar?"

"No." Then a menacing look from Aaron brought a softer reply. "Not in the rectory." It was increasingly difficult to tell which side he should aid in this strange drama.

"The stable, then. Dyso, see if you can find rope to bind these bastards."

While the big man left to search for rope, the Vicar removed his surplice and, at Aaron's none-too-gentle prodding, drew another marriage contract. He placed his official seal on the document before presenting it to Aaron. After scrutinizing the document and finding the contents satisfactory, Aaron affixed his name and took the quill to Brien, who sat staring numbly out in front of her. He smiled down into her dazed, sweet face and felt a tremendous surge of fierce protectiveness toward her.

"You have only to sign your name, Brien," he said softly.

She frowned briefly, then bent her head and signed her name with an unmistakable flourish.

" 'Tis done," Aaron said tersely, handing the document to the vicar for recording in the huge record book that lay open nearby.

The marquis' lip curled into an ugly smile. "We'll come after you, you know. And we'll find you. A kidnapper, that's what you are. Or a fortune hunter. What is your price, rogue?''

"There will be no ransom,'' Aaron said quietly. "I want nothing from Brien and will take nothing from her. You must learn not to judge others by your own contemptible standard.''

Dyso arrived with the rope and secured the three abductors on the floor, well away from each other.

Aaron's customary courtesy returned when they were securely bound, and he bade the Vicar sit comfortably in the straight chair beside the fire, binding him closely, but not uncomfortably.

During it all, Brien had sat across the room, withdrawn, seeming insensible to what transpired about her. Her distraction was of increasing concern to Aaron, who longed to hold her and love her back to her senses.

He sheathed his blade and gathered her into his arms, lifting her as easily as a child and holding her against his strong chest.

"We must go, Brien.''

At the sound of his voice and with the warmth of his arms cradling her, something in her snapped and she came to life once more.

"Aaron . . . what are you doing here? How did you find me?'' She looked about, alarmed at the sight of the bound figures on the floor. Her gaze struck the marquis and fled on to Dyso who stood near them, awaiting Aaron's word.

"Dyso! My Dyso!'' She reached out to squeeze his arm as they moved to the door.

The recognition and gratitude in her face were not missed by the pallorous Vicar.

Outside, Aaron helped Brien into the carriage while Dyso climbed without bidding into the driver's seat. The rain had begun, Aaron noted gratefully. By the time the marquis was found and freed, the carriage tracks would be only one more rut in a muddy road. It gave him time to think and they could travel slowly. Aaron climbed upon the front wheel and touched Dyso's shoulder.

"We've done well, my friend. Do you know the road to Kennesley? There's an inn there where we can stop and rest. It will be several hours; can you manage while I see to Brien?"

Dyso nodded and pulled the oilskin over his head. Aaron felt a twinge of conscience as he climbed down into the dry comfort of the luxurious coach. But one breath of the sweat scent of Brien and the regret vanished. The coach lurched as they started, and in the dim light of the lantern, Aaron saw Brien's lovely eyes turned on him.

"Is it really you?" she breathed, fearing to question his presence lest the wonderful apparition vaporize before her.

"Aye, Aaron Durham, at your service, milady."

"Oh, Aaron, I . . . I thought I'd never see you again." She reached out impulsively to touch his face. Before she could think better of it and withdraw, he had gathered her into his arms and was pressing her against his warm, hard chest. Abandoning herself to the pleasure of his strength about her, she nuzzled against him.

For a long moment she luxuriated in his presence. Then the night's events flashed with awful clarity in her mind and she jerked up to look at him.

"How did you find me? Did Dyso bring you?"

"Of course," Aaron smiled cautiously, now wondering how much of the events she truly remembered. "Where else would he go with you in trouble?"

"I had hoped he would bring my father . . ." she began, but seeing his consternation quickly modified her statement. "But I am glad it was you he found. Jeannie! That man has her! We must—"

Aaron put his hand to her lips and gently stopped the flow of words. "No cause for alarm. She is this minute safely in the arms of Robert Hicks, no doubt sampling the delight of prenuptial bliss."

"But how—"

"We went first to your home, Dunstan, and learned what had happened. After seeing Jeannie safe, Dyso and I came straight on to St. Anne's. God, you had me worried. I could see you already married and in the slavering jaws of that degenerate." He thrust her from him at arm's length to inspect her anxiously. "You're not harmed?"

"No, I'm safe, and I have you to thank for that." Her trusting and openly adoring gaze gave Aaron a pang of conscience. It was clear to him now that she little remembered what transpired between them in the sanctuary a short while before. But that could wait.

He grinned wickedly at her. "I'll collect that debt of gratitude later, of that you can be sure."

She seemed to only half-hear his suggestive remark, her mind now drifting back to something fearsome in the recent past. She raised her once more haunted eyes to his.

"I had no choice, Aaron. The marquis announced our engagement in public without my knowledge. Then when I insisted on issuing a denial he threatened me." She trembled again at the memory of his lurid anger.

Aaron's quiet rage returned at the terror in her voice. Now he wished he had punished the blackguard fully.

"He produced a witness—that other man, Pitt—to swear I had started the blaze that killed Raoul. He swore I would be hanged for a murderess if I did not marry Louis. It was all lies, Aaron. But Father was called to Bristol and I had no one to turn to." Her eyes glistened in the dim light.

"I only wanted an annulment. He refused . . ." Her voice was small and she was far away from him now, back in time at Weston Place—with him. "He locked me up, he—"

Her voice broke as he grasped her to him and she sobbed quietly in the safety of his arms. The tensions of the last week flowed out of her with the cleansing tears. She cared for nothing but the feeling of him near her and his warmth that infused her with long-sought peace.

In the semidark of the carriage there seemed no other world. The strain and fatigue she felt was settled by the peace between them and in moments she was asleep in his arms.

Twenty-seven

The halting of the carriage brought Aaron bolt upright and wide awake. He lifted the curtain at the window and peered into the gray predawn light.

The door was jerked open before he could shift positions or move the tender burden of Brien's sleepy head from his shoulder. Dyso squinted into the now darkened carriage and beckoned to Aaron.

Lifting Brien from him and lowering her to the seat, he swung down from the carriage, ignoring the steps, to stand and survey their location. He recognized the courtyard in the ever-increasing light. A tired smile appeared at the corners of his generous mouth. "So, we're here. Stay by your lady while I waken the innkeeper. We'll need food and rest before going on."

The innkeeper complained loudly at being roused from a warm bed in the earliest of morning light, but seeing Aaron and feeling the weight of plenteous silver in his hand, calmed his outrage and set about readying his finest rooms.

The innkeeper had known Aaron Durham of old and

smirked secretly when told a lady accompanied them. One look at Aaron's odd companion, waiting beside the luxurious carriage, told him this was not an ordinary visit—but something important was transpiring under his very roof. All of the possible explanations for so secretive and hurried an arrival with a beautiful lady and a battle-scarred giant were intriguing. As of old, he would be the soul of discretion.

When Aaron carried the sleeping beauty in from the carriage, the innkeeper raised eyebrows in silent tribute. This was special indeed. But then the captain had always had exceptional luck with the ladies—and beautiful ones at that.

A blazing fire soon dispelled the chill and gloom of the best room in the house. The bed had been hurriedly made with fresh linen and fresh water and towels were made available for their convenience.

Aaron placed his sleeping bride on the canopied bed and arched his aching back, rubbing his corded neck with one bronzed hand. The fleeting moments he had drifted into unconsciousness were not enough to renew his energy. He needed the comforts of both food and rest.

As he contemplated which to pursue he gazed at Brien who stirred slightly in the comforting warmth of her cloak. A wisp of her tawny hair trailed across her smooth, dream-blushed cheek. Her eyelashes were a dark, thick fringe against her fair skin and her lips were parted alluringly. He imagined them moist and luscious against his own. In repose she possessed a sweetness and innocence like that of a child at slumber. No guile, no wilfulness. He longed to capture that fleeting spirit in his arms and hold her close to his heart forever.

An ache in his chest warned him that it could not be so. She was indeed his bride, but would she ever be his wife? His better sense whispered that he should brace

440

for a tempest when she discovered what course he had taken to set her free. He steadfastly turned his mind from the nagging thought that he might have rescued her without marrying her. It had to be that way, he thought. And with a reckless confidence he admitted this was just what he wanted.

Under his warming gaze, Brien roused and her eyelids fluttered open. The caressing softness of the down bed below her and the canopy above her puzzled her, and she frowned. But these pleasant sensations were no illusion.

She raised her head to look about. A postered bed, a small, comfortable room and . . . Aaron standing close by, hands on hips and a jaunty, smug smile about his handsome mouth. His eyes roamed her openly, devouring the newly awakened earthiness of her, stroking her. The gratefulness she had felt in the carriage last night now vanished like a vapor in the face of this effrontery.

She sat up quickly, her cloak sliding from her shoulders. She was relieved to find her clothing still intact and blushed guiltily at the thoughts that prompted her inspection.

Aaron's casual, sensual pose and air of amusement at her vexation goaded her self-assurance. She shook her head to clear it and recalled in a horrible rush the events of the previous night that had brought them together once more. And she blushed again at the thought of being rescued by *him*. Aaron's grin was now wolfish and told her plainly he was enjoying her confusion. Well, why didn't he say something?

"What are you staring at?" she bristled.

"Ah, you waken in such sweet humor, milady. If only you were feast to the ears as you are to the eyes." His mocking tone barely covered the feeling she had aroused in him.

She slid from the bed and put one hand to her forehead. What had happened to her? Why could she not remember? It all seemed too jumbled!

"Where are we?" she said, thinking it might help to begin with the basics.

"The inn at Kennesley." He shrugged. "Doubt anyone will look for us here. Once they learn who I am, they will undoubtedly search the roads between Dunstan and Bristol." He strolled to the fireplace and set one heavy boot on the hearth as he leaned an elbow on the mantelpiece.

"We'll be safe here for a time . . . long enough to rest."

Brien's mind gradually sorted out the events that had led them here. Aaron had come to the church for her—rescued her from her "wedding." But there were so many pieces missing. She closed her eyes and tried hard to recall.

"How long will you stay?" she asked absently, her mind really elsewhere. It never occurred to her that he had other plans. Now that he had rescued her, his continued presence would be more irritating and embarrassing with each passing moment. Surely he would have the gentlemanly decency to withdraw gracefully . . . unless—the thought impaled her—he might demand a reward for his services!

"We can stay as long as we like," Aaron replied with special emphasis on the "we."

"We?" Brien's heart stopped and dropped to where her churning stomach lay. "If they find us here you'll be arrested! The marquis has friends in high places and there is no way to tell how my father will react—at least until I have a chance to explain it all to him." She rubbed her hands together nervously and slid off the bed to pace. Dolt! How could he not see the danger his continued presence brought on them both? Oh, must men ever be at proving their bravado?

A throaty chuckle caught Brien by surprise, and she looked at Aaron only to find that same reckless amusement that she found so irritating yet so endearing.

"You find strange amusement in our predicament. Do you know what will happen if we are found together like this?"

"Your father will welcome me into the family?" Aaron grinned wickedly.

"What?" Brien exclaimed. "Don't pretend you've gone mad—'tis no defense!"

"But is it madness that husband and wife share bed and board? I always thought it the custom." He folded his muscular arms across his broad chest and watched as his words found their mark. The subject had been raised with greater ease than he had expected. Now as to its reception . . .

"Man and wife?" she puzzled. And then swept it aside. "Don't be . . ." But the little flame flickering at the back of his eyes convinced her this was more than another taunt.

"We're not . . ." She could not even say it.

"Married? Oh, duly and legally so." He moved to the chair where he had tossed his coat and produced a document neatly tied with scarlet ribbon. He held it up to her gaze and placed it on the table before her.

Dumfounded, she stared unbelievingly at him, then tore into the ribbon that bound the fearsome parchment.

As she read it, the color drained from her face. Her own signature!

She stared first at the parchment and then at the grinning rake who had cosigned.

"You're serious! You're bloody well serious!"

"Never more so," he said firmly.

"We're married!" she exclaimed, as though the full

443

idea had only now burst upon her mind.

"Most definitely—in the eyes of the Church of England and by the authority of the good King George himself." He bowed slightly in mocking deference. He could not tell whether she was taking the news well or not. He hadn't exactly expected her to fall into his arms gratefully, but she seemed so deeply shocked. Oh, well, it might take several days for her to come around to the idea, but come around she would.

"This is outrageous! Married without my own knowledge or consent!"

"Not so. You consented. And *we* have the word of a priest of the church on that. You signed that document of your own will and in your own hand." Now that the dreaded moment was here and nearly past, the fatigue of two sleepless nights came crashing down on him, and he was rapidly losing all humor in this verbal duel.

"So," Brien spat heatedly at him like a cornered vixen, "I have been rescued from the marquis' trap only to be snared in yours! I have traded bondage for bondage—without even knowing it!"

Aaron stretched tiredly, feeling a graininess to his eyes and a heaviness to their lids. "For my part, lady, I have ridden solidly for two days and endured hazard of life and limb to see you free of trouble."

"Only to trick me into marriage yourself!" Brien sputtered, feeling a creeping guilt at the realization of the heroic effort that had kept her from a second marriage into the marked Trechaud lineage.

Aaron stared squarely into her face.

"Such a prize you are, milady." His tone was biting. "So gentle and loving—a treasure to hold close to a man's heart on his wedding night." The mockery savaged her pride.

"Well then"—her eyes narrowed—"why did you marry me if I am such a troublesome bore?"

Aaron smirked at his sudden rememberance of the vicar's words. "Someone had to marry you."

"Someone . . . what? Too much salt air has rotted your brain, Aaron Durham. I don't need marriage to you or any other prancing posturing swain! Dear God deliver me from this world of pompous, arrogant males!" She clenched her fists and pressed them to her eyes to steady and control her responses.

"Someone had to make an honest woman of you and own up to the child you carry . . . unless there is another I should defer to in truth." The thought turned his stomach over, but he shook free of it. Could she . . . would she . . . have taken another to her? He smiled, remembering her icy reserve. Not likely.

Her eyes were wide and shocked. "What in heaven's name are you prattling on about?" she demanded. A vague rumble of memory stirred within her but she struck it down in her hurry to do battle with this one who dared so much with her.

"The vicar was quite unmistakable as to why he participated in so hurried a match. He said you were with child. Are you?"

As soon as he spoke, he wished to choke those and all such words from this own throat. The words went through Brien like a rush of flame, reddening her face and bosom and setting sparks from her eyes.

How dare he! She was stunned temporarily—on the verge of raging at him and yet torn another way, to laugh at him, at this irony. So on the outside she seemed ready to explode, but as the moments passed a change came over her countenance, an incensed, determined look that made Aaron less certain of his course with his bride.

Then she recovered her voice. "Your conceit is monumental! You must think your seed quite potent to believe I could bear your child after only one night of your intense affections." Her face flamed at the realization of the topic she had launched forth upon, but she would not retreat. "And now I am to be sacrificed to your own grand ideas of your manhood! Did it never occur to you that the marquis lied to the gullible vicar?" She turned away from him in disgust. "Save me from all such vain manhood!" The marquis had been degraded enough to set forth such a lie, but what of Aaron, who by all appearances believed it? She knew not which she loathed more at the moment.

Aaron watched her rant and fume and noted well that she had not truly denied the accusation at all. Was that a slip on her part, or had she just felt it beneath her to deny it? He would find no answers in endless quarreling. This could go on for hours. Aaron yawned broadly—from fatigue, but also for effect.

"I shall not discuss this with you when you are not rational." He sat down heavily on the edge of the bed and began to unbutton his shirt.

"I . . . not rational?" she screeched. "I have been abducted twice this very night, accused of harlotry and pronounced with child, forced to marry at swordpoint. . . ." She stopped inexplicably and threw her arms wide in exasperation. How could he! "This very moment half of Britain may be combing the countryside—searching for us!"

He worked on removing his tall, black boots, little interested in her tirade.

"It would be enough to try the patience of Saint Francis himself!" Her eyes widened in disbelief as she realized that none of what she'd said had any impact upon him. "How dare you act as though you have no cares in the world and lie down to sleep!"

Bare-chested, bootless, and barelegged now, Aaron threw her cloak over a nearby chair and pulled back bedclothes. Slipping under the down coverlet, he groaned magnificently.

"Don't you dare fall asleep, Aaron Durham," she threatened.

He raised on one elbow and quipped, "Wife, just getting married to you was so strenuous, I am too tired to do anything else." Then, patting the bed beside him he smiled lazily. "Some rest might even improve your disposition."

"Not on your life!" she declared.

"Suit yourself," he muttered sleepily as he turned his back to her.

Exasperated, she whirled about, and her eyes falling on the document that bound her to him, she grabbed it up to examine once more. Her own hand. How could she have done it? Consented to marry this . . . Or was this some trick? Oh, why couldn't she remember?

Perhaps if she tried a softer tack. She stole over to the bed and stood looking down at Aaron, noticing how his copper hair waved slightly in the dampness and glowed richly in the candlelight. The determined glint in her eyes became a wayward gleam as she took in the relaxed splendor of his big frame and the corded, sun-browned muscles of his arms. She knew his skin would taste salty and firm under exploring lips. His eyes were shadowed from sleeplessness—caused by concern for her. His high cheekbones were blushed with a bronzed vitality that even in sleep commanded awe—affection. He seemed less fierce now, of more human dimensions and more likely to attend to a woman's plea. Something in her felt an unwelcome ambivalence toward taking up the argument again, but she angrily pushed the feeling aside, irritated by her own traitorous impulses.

"Aaron," she said softly, twiningly. "I am sorry, I was rash. Come, let us discuss this calmly."

There was no response, not even a flicker of consciousness.

"Aaron . . ." Her tone was even more honeyed, cloying even to her own ears. She reached out to touch his broad shoulder where the covers exposed it. It was as she feared, warm and smooth and hard. She jerked her hand back as if shocked.

"Aaron," she insisted, somewhat louder. And still there was no response. She bent close to his face. His breathing was slow and shallow. He was asleep!

What a turn! Abducted, married at swordpoint, and closeted with a notorious rake for a husband—who promptly falls asleep on their wedding night. The irony of it struck her and she laughed. First, a smile, then a chuckle, then a clear sparkling laughter that purged all the hostility she held toward this madman who claimed to be her husband.

Weakened with laughter and holding her side from its pain, she turned it all over in her mind. What other man would travel two days and nights, fight for a lady's freedom, marry her in the jaws of great personal jeopardy, carry her off to a secluded inn—then fall fast asleep without even touching her? She was calm once more. Only a man like Aaron Durham. And suddenly she was very glad he was asleep.

The dull ache in her neck and the heaviness of her limbs grew more persistent. She was too tired for clear reasoning. The practical captain took his ease. Why not a truce, then? A chance to repair to the rear and regroup.

But in her innermost thoughts Brien was aware of her increasing reluctance to do battle at all. She ignored the feeling and the fact that it grew with each moment she spent in the same room with him.

Snuffing out the candles on the table, she grasped her cloak from the chair and drew it around her. She sat down in the big, comfortable chair nearest the fire and was instantly asleep.

.

The fire in the fireplace had long since died and a chill had again invaded the room. A thin, gray light intruded from a single window, scant evidence of the long progress of the day. The door opened quickly under the shoulder of a man. Dyso swayed into the room under a huge armload of wood that he soon deposited noisily in the woodbox by the grate.

The noise caused Brien to start awake and inhale deeply of the cool air. Seeing Dyso, she settled back into the small comfort of her resting place, relieved.

"Dyso, you frightened me. I thought—" She stopped, wondering if he listened, for he gave little evidence of it as he bent over the grate, laying a new fire.

Stiffness in her neck and shoulders sent shivers of pain down her arms and into her back as she moved and stretched. She paid a dear price for her stubbornness. She might have shared a warm, soft— She glanced quickly toward the now empty bed. Sometimes she gravely doubted her own mental competence.

Her last thoughts of the previous night came parading back. And here was her answer, lighting a fire for her comfort. She drew her cloak closely about her and knelt beside Dyso in front of the fireplace.

"Dyso," she placed one hand on his arm to halt his work. "I must thank you once again for saving me."

His hand came up to protest as he turned to her, and he shook his head. A tired peacefulness filled his face, and he reached for her slender hand, holding it gently in his great paw. Brien was as mystified as ever at this man's devotion to her.

"You have only to ask and it will be yours."

He smiled and Brien fancied a bit of color hinting at embarrassment in his cheeks.

"Why did you bring the captain, Dyso? Why not my father?" The question was rhetorical, as she did not expect any answer. To her surprise, Dyso dropped her hand and gestured to the door. Then his burly arms crossed almost daintily over his chest in a hugging, cradling motion. Then his hands swept toward her. Seeing her puzzlement, he repeated the sequence.

Having suspected the meaning the first time, Brien was stunned at the sureness she felt upon the repetition. He brought Aaron because he knew Aaron cared for her. Dyso knew. Probably everyone in Boston knew. And she alone, wilful and independent, prideful to a fault, had searched for deeper motives with a shabby list of paltry accusations and complaints.

"I must know, my friend. Are we truly married?"

He smiled a second time, a remarkably tender expression, and he nodded.

"You were there? You saw?"

Again he nodded, the enigmatic smile lighting his battered features.

"Thank you, my Dyso," Brien murmured softly, squeezing his massive arm with gratitude.

She stood up, reeling at the impact of his confirmation. She did not hear Dyso slip out.

Married! And to Aaron Durham! What now of the marquis' threat? What would he do? Count the experience a loss and seek easier game? Seek vengeance? And what of this marriage?

As she mulled over these problems, the door swung open a second time. She twirled on the spot and beheld her husband carrying a large tray laden with food and drink. He caught the door with his foot and slammed it behind him.

"Your first day of married life," he taunted good-naturedly, "and you sleep well into the afternoon! I tell you, wife, it bodes ill." Placing the tray on the table, he

450

drew up the two chairs and motioned for her to be seated. His good humor was like salt on an open sore.

Seated now, himself, he put his hands on his thighs and gazed at her. "Well?" Seeing her hesitate, he shrugged. "Suit yourself. 'Twill be a long wait for supper."

He looked up from biting a warm piece of fresh bread. His eyes glowed with an animal-like satisfaction that rattled her thoroughly. How dare he be so bright and handsome this morning!

"Forgive my impertinence, Brien, but you don't look well. Was the chair not comfortable?"

She longed to slap the smirk from his face and was surprised by the heat and embarrassment of her own reaction. Neither would he let it lie.

"Ah," he closed his eyes as if savoring the sensations still, "it is a marvelous bed. I have not slept so well in months."

Piqued at the reference to her appearance, she let one hand fly to her mussed hair and then down over her bodice to her rumpled skirt. She straightened the skirt of her dress about her waistline quite haughtily as she returned his penetrating gaze.

He must have awakened much earlier. He was washed and shaved, as handsome and bright as she had ever seen him. The swine. His broad shoulders flexed as he reached across the table for the tea and against her will Brien's eyes were drawn to that easy, graceful movement. She swallowed hard and shook her head in annoyance. How dare he make sport of her appearance after all she had been through!

He poured a cup of the fragrant tea and sipped it noisily. The delicious odors of the tea and food beckoned to her and she relented under the ravages of outraged hunger, removing her cloak and taking the chair opposite him. 'Twas not total surrender to feed one's

451

natural hunger.

Aaron looked up from his diminishing plate with mischief dancing at the back of his marvelous golden eyes. "Talkative you are of a morn. I never noticed it before." He cocked his head and eyed her appreciatively. "But then we never spent much time in conversation of a morn."

She smiled at him most hatefully and defiantly filled her plate and quaffed a full cup of tea before looking at him again. She was positively ravenous. When she at last looked up, it was just as she feared. He was staring at her, amused, expectant . . . as if he awaited . . . something.

"I wish you would stop gawking at me," she complained, though it pained her to admit he could bother her at all.

"She talks!" he exclaimed, his eyes wide in feigned astonishment.

Through severely narrowed eyes she shot daggers at him. "At least allow me to take nourishment in peace."

With a flourish of deference, he took his cup and stood near the fireplace sipping from it.

Once or twice she glimpsed him from the corner of her eye. But he looked elsewhere, his large, graceful frame draped casually over the mantel. She felt a now familiar twinge of guilt and another fluttery feeling that disturbed her far more, though she refused to name it. Shrew, that's what she was . . . an ungrateful shrew! And a properly miserable one at that.

Now she faced the most disagreeable task of her life. She knew it would be far better to set him away from her at the start—before she again found herself surrendering to the delicious feelings he constantly aroused in her. Best to have it out now, even if she did come out of it looking shrewish and ungrateful. Now . . . do it now, she prodded herself in the silence that had settled between them. Unwittingly she set in motion the very words and acts that would prove the undoing of her plan.

Finishing her last mouthful of the tasty breakfast—or lunch—she turned to him, wiping her hand daintily on the provided napkin.

"Aaron, I want you to know how grateful I am for all the trouble you've gone to in seeing me free and safe." She dared not look directly into his face and found herself staring at his tall, black boots instead.

Something in the tone of her voice and the innocuous, patronizing words alerted him to what was to follow. He reminded himself to keep his temper in check and to meet her every denial with unabashed good humor. That would buy him time to let their proximity and the diligent urgings of nature put forth the most eloquent argument on his behalf.

His very battle plan Brien intuitively guessed and sought to thwart it at the start.

"Aaron, I feel now is the time to set things right between us." She glanced up and then away. His wary look warned her, but she continued all the same.

"Right?"

"Yes, about this marriage . . ." She read a change taking place in his face with another furtive glance.

"Things are right, Brien." His voice was low and calm, much too calm. He suddenly seemed larger and more powerful that Brien had realized and with each passing minute she was more reluctant to run the course she had set for herself. Only the last clutching of an old dream upon her heart and a buffeted and bruised pride held her to it.

"We are legally—and morally—married. That is how it shall stay." Aaron had lost the battle for control of his temper the minute she presumed to dictate to him as though he were a troublesome servant. Perhaps the wench needed a firmer hand than he had been willing to employ. Thus his pride was needled into a real display.

Brien's milder feelings and better judgment bludgeoned into submission, she launched forth again. She would make him see. "And who gave you the right to decide my fate, milord? To declare yourself my lord and master? I will not be married—not to anyone!" Her heart was pounding and she was aware of dryness in her throat and a wetness in her palms. Her face was scarlet with indignation.

His calm was almost deadly and his eyes hardened visibly. She was pushing him past his limit, leaving no room for retreat or negotiation.

"You ungrateful, pig-headed . . ." he snarled. "I took that right when I rescued you!" He looked her up and down with tightly reined anger. "You may have it back—gladly will I relinquish it—when you can defend it yourself!"

"It seems the only one I need defend myself against is you!" she snapped.

She heard his jaw snap shut sharply and in a flash his big, muscular hands closed on her shoulders and dragged her struggling to him.

"No, Aaron . . ."

But his mouth on hers stopped her protest. His corded arms crushed her to him, easily overcoming her resistance. She moaned and pushed with all her might against his chest, winning only an increase in heat for her effort. His big hard body engulfed her, bending her backward with the force of his deliberately ungentle kisses. It seemed he meant to brand them upon her very heart.

Her mind exploded with outrage and she renewed the struggle to be free, only faintly aware of the warming of her body that melted the last stronghold of her will against him. Heat is heat and translated by the wilful and hungry heart is sometimes made into the heady stuff of full-blown passion.

Somewhere in the press of hot, demanding lips and marauding hands that set fire to her skin even through her clothes, Brien's arms twined up and about his neck and her fingers locked themselves into his heavy copper hair. She felt him relax as she responded lustfully to his thrusting tongue and pressed her eager body full against him. His hands drifted downward over her seductively rounded buttocks, each stroke laying permanent claim to the territory it covered. She longed to have him possess it fully.

Her very bones seemed to have weakened, turned fluid with desire, and she clung to him, her heart rising and sinking with each hot breath he panted into her. Just as she feared, her passion for him consumed her totally, blocking all thought but the rightness of it and all need but the need to have him, be with him at all costs. In this long, stunning union all past and future pleasure met.

A loud knock at the door brought them jolting back to the present and Brien pushed away from him, her eyes locked to his gaze, absorbed in the wild torrent of feeling that had fought heroically for expression and had won.

Aaron felt a white-hot shaft of pain course through him at the sight of her—shining eyes, full heaving breasts and bee-stung mouth. It would be so easy to ignore the knock . . . to seize the opportunity to make their union more binding still.

The knock came again, harsh and insistent, and Aaron called out, "Well, what is it?" His voice had an easily recognizable huskiness to it.

". . . the carriage . . . ," came the reply.

Damn the carriage, he thought bitterly. But the pragmatism of his nature rescued his faltering judgment again. They needed to move on. He had finally decided their destination and knew they would not be truly safe from detection until off the roads and out of public houses. There would be time for this later. The wait would be easier with pure victory in sight.

Brien's eyes were wide with questions. The exchange between them left her heart and mind reeling and wanting, needing more. But she secretly blessed the owner of the voice on the other side of the door. So much had happened—and she was so confused. She knew something fundamental between them had just been altered but she was reluctant to explore it all just now.

"Where are we going?" she managed, realizing with chagrin that she had not allowed the possibility that he might be leaving alone.

Suddenly he was in motion, and she was lifted joyously up and then slung over his shoulder like a sack, an uncommonly precious sack with its rear pointing degradingly skyward. He laughed exultantly—a booming, free noise that reverberated through her as well.

Brien shrieked and pounded his back with white, ineffectual fists, squirming uncomfortably as she pleaded to be released. Her earnest pleas became urgent demands as they descended the stairs to the common room of the inn and the chuckles of the tavern's patrons greeted her.

Striding easily with his delicate burden well balanced, he nodded gallantly to the slack-jawed innkeeper and the fellow patrons and exited to a chorus of ribald advice about how to keep a woman in her place—bed.

Aaron dropped her gently on the seat of the carriage and closed the door quickly on her as she screeched her ire in most unladylike language. Then quickly he sprang up to the driver's seat beside an amused Dyso and took the reins himself.

As they rolled and rocked along the rutted road, Aaron chided himself for giving in to his cavalier impulse. God and the devil, she was angry! But in the long ride ahead she would have time to cool her anger and conquer that stiff-necked pride of hers. If she could overcome this, he reasoned with a coolness that surprised him, then it was only a small step to the sweet surrender of her love and the promise of herself as wife. It wasn't bad for a spur-of-the-moment test.

Twenty-eight

Aaron would have been far less optimistic if he could have seen the state of his bride at that moment. Her face was hot with murderous rage and she panted fury and flung the cushions from the seats about mercilessly. When that no longer satisfied her anger, she beat on the seat with whitened fists and kicked the opposing seat hard with her slippered foot. At last the angry energy drained away from her and she settled back tiredly into the comfort of the plush seat. She was achingly aware that the great expenditure of energy netted her nothing.

How dare he? Treating her like a common doxy in front of a tavern full of lowlifes. And only minutes before she had been on the verge of melting into his arms, heeding his demand for her to respect the vows spoken between them. Demanding she play the loving wife while he decried with roguish nonchalance his role as caring husband—typical man, she spat. Let him think he might lose a round honestly and he resorts to brute force—sheer muscle power.

As her thoughts twined satisfyingly around the last

charge she dropped her guard for a moment. But a moment was all that was needed and a torrent of feeling flooded back over her, reminding her vividly of the minutes before their ignominious departure when she was in Aaron's arms.

Closing her eyes against the sensations only served to enchance her concentration on them. And again he filled her vision, her arms, her heart. She let her head drop back against the seat as that same peculiar weakness overcame her. She found it hard to swallow. This was like being on a runaway horse that raced and careened and plunged, taking her breath and defying her to let go.

She smiled weakly. There was nothing strange and mysterious here. He simply took possession of her—ownership—whenever he took her in his arms. She responded the way a fine mare responds only to her master's touch. She took in breath sharply at the comparison. Is that what you want, she sneered—to be owned and tamed by a clever-handed rake? Just another conquest for his stable?

But in all fairness, she could not press that argument hard against him. He had demanded little of her, had only dared to claim a part of her she was determined not to yield. He had only married her to see her safe.

No! The thought pierced her. Only safe? Then she remembered their words of the previous night. He had married her because he thought he saved her from disgrace! O-o-oh, she moaned. He was more than willing to believe the worst of her, or was it that he was eager to believe the most of himself? She burned with the thought and the irony it held for her. She, who was undoubtedly barren, was forced into marriage because of a child she supposedly bore. Before, when she had been close to choosing a new life with Aaron in a new land, her infertility had risen before her like a deformed minion of Raoul's hatred. And now there was no helping it, it would be faced and in the open before long.

Tears sprang to her eyes at the pity she knew Aaron would hold for her. Why had nature seen fit to give her a body bound to entice men's attentions, while withholding the real substance of womanhood from her? She closed her eyes once more and tried to rest but the thoughts nagged at her, robbing her of even that small comfort.

Opening her eyes again and trying to clear her mind of these disturbing preoccupations, she absently touched her waist and stroked the front of her gown above her stomach and belly. Her eyes were drawn to the movement, the idleness of it redirecting her attention and bending it to more useful purpose.

More intently now, her fingertips caressed her waist as a thought, then a wave of tumult, bore down upon her. Her memory flew and tripped and stumbled over first one fragment and then another as her heart began to hammer in her chest. Snatches of comments and events crowded together clamoring for recognition in her mind, forcing her to contend with that which she had long ignored.

Oh, why could she not swoon like a proper lady and staunch this flow of wild ideas? But her interest, piqued, was drawn like metal to a lodestone as each successive piece fell cozily into place, making the puzzle take awesome shape in her mind.

M. Lamont and his insinuating comments on her waistline; her illness during the voyage when Jeannie had felt perfectly fine; her strange lingering malady that sent her numerous mornings to the chamber pot, heaving—and her recent ravenous appetite! It was just as Helen had said it was with her! And her inability to control her erratic emotions of late! It all fit so neatly that chagrin colored Brien to the very roots of her hair.

How ignorant could a woman be of her own state? Even the effete Lamont could guess from the subtle changes in her waistline and the new permanent pinkness of her cheeks. But then, Lamont often seemed to know women better than they knew themselves.

Think! she commanded herself. What are the other signs? She must be absolutely sure. She had lost track of her monthly courses; they seemed irrelevant. She took them as they came, never dreaming that the cessation of so natural a function could go so unnoticed—even by her little maid. Think! When was the last? As she scoured her memory, it seemed the last was just after she'd arrived in Boston. . . .

Boston! There was but one time that this thing could have happened to her. One time! That night in her room in the Hastings house. And her own words rushed back to taunt her, "one night in his arms and a bastard babe to remind her forever of a moment's weakness." Yet she had swept away all caution and resolution the instant his hands closed on her shoulders and he drew her to him. It didn't matter, she had convinced herself—she was barren.

Bubbles of laughter grew in her stomach and exploded upward, trembling and tickling her as they forced open her mouth to pour forth in giggles and gulps. It was the cleansing laughter of irony and she abandoned herself to it gratefully.

She had been so sure she was never to have children, and yet, one night in his bed—or with him in hers—had brought her to this. She bore Aaron Durham's child. She now recalled her words to him that very morning and reddened anew with the irony. She had thrown his conceit in his teeth for even suggesting what she now knew as fact. She flushed deeply even in her solitude. Conceit or not, he had gotten her with child in one wild, sweet night that had tempted and taunted her every night since.

Weak with laughter, she collapsed back against the seat once more, feeling the hot crimson of her face with the back of her hand. She smiled tenderly as a wave of fresh, new feeling washed over her, a consuming adoration for the man she loved and now had married, however strangely. And there was more; there was a babe growing inside her, her babe, his babe.

She sobered slowly as the ramifications of her state arrayed themselves in her mind. What now? She was a woman with child and married rightly to the father. Thus far, quite good. The babe was no bastard. But she could not tell him of the child.

No! He had married her because he felt responsible for her state, had he not? And just last night she had denied it hotly. How could she face him now with the reverse of her story and not seem a devious little chit or worse, a witless and capricious child? She might bear any of society's jibes for the sake of the babe. But what of him? How could she face him?

How had the marquis known of the babe—even when she had not? Her heart skipped several beats and then thumped wildly. But her reason was now her rescue. The marquis was deucedly clever; what better way to convince a country cleric to waive the bans and marry an unlucky couple at once and in such secrecy? Whatever the blackguard's knowledge or intent, it mattered little now. Only the high irony of it remained. She wagged her head, smiling sheepishly.

Again her thoughts turned to Aaron and his possible reactions to her state. He had made it clear he would insist the marriage stand, and she would have less grounds to object now that an innocent child was involved. In fact, there was more weight to his argument with the passing seconds. Her freedom was now forfeit forever—at least in the life she had planned; there remained only the issue of her pride. This too might bear a well-planned surrender. She smiled knowingly at her lusty memories.

What of the man himself? Brien freely admitted that her fascination with him possessed her totally, involving every aspect of her—mind, body and soul. She had often chronicled his assets and now realized that not least on that list was the strength that allowed him to take what he wanted. That power lay coiled in his sleeping body, stretched with his sensual stride; and rang out in his calm, commanding voice as it boomed over the quarterdeck of his ship. She admired that power—was excited by it. And yet, she well knew that he had never used that power against her. At every turn she had provoked him and he had only shown restraint on her behalf. Only now, with much at stake, did he exert his will, and not without at least some cooperation on her part, for she had signed the marriage document in her own hand of her own volition, albeit without her real agreement. Some part of her had wanted to yield to him or she would never have signed.

This was no deep mystery. She loved the man, there was no room for doubt. Now there was no reason to withhold the fruits of that love from him or herself any longer. The newly wakened womanly part of her drew another scene before her mind's eye . . . Aaron as a father. Could she deny him the right to claim and love his own child? Could she deny the babe a father such as she knew he would be?

What a muddle this was! It was beyond her how it would all work out. And for once in her prideful, well-planned life she refused to chart a course or plan a strategy to see her through the confusion. Hard-won wisdom whispered rightly that this was one solution she could not seek alone.

A slight shift in the coach's direction pitched her

slightly to one side and she heard a muffled shout from the voice that it had taken her a moment to remember for a lifetime. She smiled, reassured by his presence. All would work itself out in the end.

And in the long ride, the hypnotic sway of the coach lulled her into a much-needed sleep.

Aaron jerked open the coach door and gazed fondly at his sleeping bride. Dearest God, what a beautiful woman! Instantly, he scowled at his own thoughts. Beautiful sleeping, and pure trouble awake. He climbed into the carriage and lifted her into his arms, reveling in the cozy way she curled up against him. He ascended the marble steps before him easily and slack-jawed servants in full livery stared as he carried her through the massive brass-bound doors and started up the sweeping staircase with her.

"Master Aaron," the ranking manservant bowed awkwardly as he passed.

"The master suite," Aaron threw over his shoulder, "is *he* here?"

"No, sir. Cambridge, sir," the butler answered.

"Good!" Aaron called from the landing. He felt his heart pounding as he gained the top of the stairs, whether from the exertion or the proximity of his voluptuous burden he knew not—and little cared. He felt alive and pulsing with strength.

His voice had completely roused Brien who had thrown her arms about his neck as if afraid he would drop her. She felt the pounding of his heart and the heat of his body through both of their clothes and it stirred a quivery excitement in her fluttering stomach. She stared at his square jaw and the rakish scar that seemed to better his nearly perfect features. And soon she was staring hungrily at his lips, mentally measuring their nearness to her own.

A heavy blow from his boot opened the door to a

sumptuously furnished chamber, dominated by a massive, canopied bed and large, brocade-covered windows. Plopping her unceremoniously on the big bed, he began throwing back the heavy draperies to admit light to the palatial chamber.

Brien blinked and shook her head in disbelief, struggling for her voice. "Where are we?" Her voice sounded small and timid to her own ears.

"Coleraine," came Aaron's booming reply.

"What's that?" She stared about her at the lavish furnishings that put Dunstan to shame.

"Home of the Count of Wiltshire." He whipped off his damp coat and cast it carelessly on the lounge nearby.

"What? Who?" She again shook her head to clear it. Saints! The man was truly daft! Invading the home of a strange nobleman with a kidnapped bride!

"Peters!" he bellowed with enough force to shake the room itself, "Peters!"

The tall, gray man appeared at the door, obviously shaken, but with his customary elegant manner intact. "Master Aaron?" he sniffed.

"The lady—Nay, my bride will need a warm bath, Peters." He turned to survey the rumpled, red-faced form upon the bed behind him. His eyes twinkled roguishly. "And some clothing . . . surely one of the Count's . . . ah . . . friends has left something suitable. Send up one of the maids to assist her. And see to some dinner, we're famished." As the tight-lipped butler turned to go, Aaron called him back. "And Peters, the man Dyso, who accompanied us . . . see him to a fine guest room and offer him your best food and drink aplenty. He has this day served more than faithfully."

"Of course, sir," Peters said dourly, eying Brien dubiously and bowing stiffly as he departed.

Her thoughts returning to order, Brien had caught

465

the servant's term of respect, "Master" Aaron. He knew this place well and was known here as one of noble birth. Aaron turned to her just then, determination in his eyes and amusement about his mouth.

"Just where in the sweet creation are we?" Brien demanded, rising to her knees and tucking her feet beneath her. Her shoulders squared and she brought to bear every shred of dignity she could muster. How had she ever been so foolish, or desperate, as to involve a madman in her life? She was confused and more than a bit annoyed at his treatment and worse, his smugness. Before she could hurl further imprecations, the revelation of her coach ride descended upon her with a vengeance, harrying her befuddled thinking even further. This was not an auspicious start to an explanation or a solution to her evermore complex difficulties.

"My father's house, Coleraine." He smirked slightly at her widening eyes and flung one arm about her grandly. "Don't worry, love, he is not at home. And no one would think of looking for us here."

"No one will—" She caught herself. Her pride was again boiling over, scalding her common sense. "And I suppose you expect my undying gratitude for finding me a safe prison!" Her eyes flashed and her arms crossed over her chest, pushing her breasts a smidgen higher above her dress. She had unwittingly committed a foul in the game of chase and would suffer the consequences.

As his eyes sauntered over her with outrageous leisure, noting every inviting roundness and the delicate huing of her skin in the lowering light, they darkened to a smoky brown, and his bronzed cheekbones showed a surge of red beneath them.

Brien blushed scarlet as she read his thoughts plainly. Not now, she thought, not with so much unsettled.

She moved backward on the bed and whirled to slip off the other side of the mattress, putting the large bed between them. "You're mad. What must the servants think?"

"Let them think 'Master Aaron' has brought home a bride at last and intends to enjoy his honeymoon to the full." Aaron grinned at her wolfishly, feeling his excitement grow with her every moment. He would have her and soon, and he was anxious to end this sparring.

Brien swallowed hard. This would be difficult, forestalling the inevitable. Even she admitted it was only a matter of moments before his will would be exercised, and she was increasingly reluctant to attempt to thwart it.

But perhaps there was a way. . . .

"Before you take one step toward me, I would know one thing of you," she insisted, eying him warily.

Aaron stopped and straightened, suspicion plain in his narrowed eyes. So far his bold tactic had carried the day. Her coach ride had cooled her anger, even if it had not curbed her tongue. That was what was needed here, a firm hand, never allowing her to think he was not in complete control. They made progress with every exchange. That thought bolstered his spirits and he asked, putting his hands on his hips and leaning back on one leg, "What, then?"

"Why did you marry me?" She delivered the question with the exact timing and inflection necessary to remove all hints as to her state of mind—or what answer would suit her best.

He felt his heart sink suddenly. This might prove more difficult than he had anticipated. She did not seem angry. What was her motive? Ye gods! Why must women ever torture men for the why of things? He pursed his lips and studied her. Now was the time for truth.

"I married you because I wanted to." Proud of his declaration, he stuck his thumbs into his belt and braced for her angry assault.

When she spoke, her voice was low and controlled, but he could feel, rather than hear the emotion, roiling underneath. It added little to his confidence about his present course.

"Without any thought of my preference or consent? Just because you wanted to?"

"As I remember, there was little time to debate the finer points. As I recall, my arm and my blade were all that kept you from becoming Madame Trechaud in earnest once more." His head cocked to one side, he studied her openly. "And there was the business of the babe. It seemed easier if I claimed it and had us married legally before taking you with me." He felt a twinge of guilt at presenting it to her thus, when in fact he had not thought of these reasons until much later. At the time he had only thought of her and how he wanted her.

"Gallant of you," she steamed, "to remind me of my indebtedness. But it seems you have taken your reward prematurely. We may yet be found and you punished for what you have done."

"True, Brien, the sweet reward of marriage has yet eluded me. But soon I'll see the bargain's worth." His eyes again darkened and a peculiar gleam lit their centers, making Brien feel jittery all over.

"Knowing how I so hate and despise marriage, how could you force this on me?" She again tried to thwart his lustful intent, now at a complete loss as to how to bring forth the topic uppermost in her mind.

He sighed impatiently, running one large hand through his thick mane. He knew now she played for time and wondered at her game. For his part, he was less willing each second to bicker and niggle. There was fairer sport to be had this night. Underneath his passion came a growing irritation with her idealistic notions and selfish disregard of others' feelings . . . his feelings.

"You speak as if I dishonored you . . . raped or beat you! In fact, Lady," his voice rose with each word, giving vent to more wrath than he realized he contained, "I only put to rights what already existed between us. We are . . . have been . . . joined in all but name since that first night we met." Even he was shocked by the inherent prudery of his statement, but he forged on, daring more. "I do not count, Brien, that you were ever married otherwise." How came these words from his mouth without first entering his head? Still, he owned the sentiment, if not the exact wording.

Brien's jaw dropped sharply. Her mind staggered, her wits scattered. "I know not what a true marriage is, but I am sure a few stolen nights of pleasure do not qualify!" The real insult of his words now seeped through to her and she flamed anew with their sting. "You speak as if I were some trollop . . . playing a whore and giving myself to that cur willingly! That marriage was forced on me, you lout! And now you have done the same. You are no better than he!" She hurled the words from habit and gave no thought as to their reception.

The ungrateful vixen! He had tried to be truthful and she had twisted his words and thrown them back in his face. Real anger now rushed through him, setting his heart to pounding.

"All right!" he roared. His time had come. "I married you because I wanted you! God knows why! There has been little enough of love or tenderness you have shown me." He spoke to wound as he had been wounded. "You prance about chasing some damnable ideal . . . like a child, using and discarding people as playthings. I doubt you even know the meaning of the word love!'' His face was fierce and bigger in anger. ''You needn't fear, I won't force myself on you. We're married, by my own deed, and I accept the blame for that. But it is clear to me now that you would never make a real wife, loving and caring for a man and sharing his life.'' The words came from anger and flayed her savagely. She stood, speechless and drained of color, her eyes wide and horrified at his words and the hurt that spawned them.

He closed his eyes to gain his bearings and calm himself. But when he opened them, Brien had turned away from him, her shoulders straight and her bearing erect. He imagined her rage building and knew he must leave before he lost control completely.

''The marriage''—he spoke with bitter calm—''annul it or not. I'll soon learn to care little enough whatever you choose to do.'' The lie caught in his throat but he swallowed hard and went on. ''You may keep my name and its protection; I'll have no need of it for another. But at least be discreet as you take your pleasures. My name means much to me. I have not given it lightly and I would not see it shamed.'' His voice was curiously husky at the end. The next sound Brien heard was the slamming of the door as her husband left her.

Twenty-nine

Brien lay on the huge bed weeping softly, miserably, as a soft rap came upon the door. She dragged herself up to answer it—knowing it could not be Aaron, yet hoping it would be.

Peters straightened visibly at the sight of her reddened and swollen eyes. "The carriage is ready for you ma'am." He tried to avoid looking directly at her to save her embarrassment.

Brien leaned heavily on the door as she sniffed and wiped her nose on the back of her hand. Just now she very much felt like the child Aaron had accused her of being. "What carriage, Peters? Is it—"

"Yes, ma'am," he said politely, still staring past her. "Your carriage back to London, Ma'am."

Brien bristled and her face reddened further. "Well, you can tell Captain Durham I won't go until I've had a chance to rest. . . . I shan't budge, I tell you!"

Peters winced visibly and glanced at her. "Master Aaron is not here, Ma'am. He left on horseback more than an hour ago. He gave orders to see to your comfort and to ready the carriage, Ma'am.''

"Where did he go?" Brien was aghast.

"I don't know, Ma'am."

"When will he return?"

"I have no way of knowing ma'am."

"Dash it all, Peters! What do you know?" she demanded angrily.

"Very little, Ma'am'" the tall servant said with a sniff of indignation.

Brien glanced about the room and snatched her cloak from the lounge. Then she shoved past the long-suffering manservant and headed for the staircase. Here was the true beast, at last, she thought bitterly. Packing her off like unwelcome baggage! Just when she needed him most!

She led Peters down the stairs to the great hall where Dyso waited, his face lined with concern at the sight of her distraught mien. As the butler helped her on with her cloak, she could make out the outline of the carriage in the glow of the lantern light outside.

In the back of her mind a kaleidoscope of thoughts raced in crazy circles. She had wanted her freedom— now she had it! And Aaron had thrown in an honorable name for good measure. He'd surrendered even his child to her before he knew of its existence.

What was it he had said? ". . . I'll have no need of my name for another!" If she accepted his name, to name her child, she would deprive him of the chance to marry again. Good! She didn't want him to ever marry again! Not while . . . Dolt! Idiot!

With each step her anger had mounted until at last she paused, furious, before the carriage steps. She turned, exploding on an astonished Dyso and a most confused Peters.

"Who does he think he is?" she raved. "It would serve him right if I stayed. He'd get his reward! Packing me off . . . I'll go when I'm good and ready! Not before!''

She lifted her skirts and stomped back into the great hall.

"Peters," she ordered as the bewildered man took her cloak once more, "I'll have that bath right away and see to some suitable night clothes." Before he could be away to do her bidding, she had further instructions. "Then lay a cold supper and ice your best champagne. And heat water for Captain Durham's bath and prepare him some fresh clothing as soon as he arrives—however late that might be."

Peters nodded somewhat dumbly at this changeable but authoritative young woman who now expected the household to snap to at her command. Master Aaron *had* referred to her as his "bride" and *had* given orders to see to her comfort. Far be it from him to pass judgment on the quirks of the nobility. Still . . . perhaps something should be done. . . .

After an assurance to Dyso, Brien hurried back upstairs to the master suite and began to take the pins from her tawny, disheveled hair.

"It would serve him right if I stayed married to him," she said aloud as she began to brush the snarls out of her hair in front of a vanity mirror. In fact, the thought appealed to her more with each passing minute. Twice she had thought him lost to her and twice she had mourned and moped about as if half dead. There was no living with him—or without him, it seemed.

And in the fray, she had nearly forgotten the babe. What would Aaron say to that? Would he laugh and taunt her mercilessly; or would he grow soft and loving, as she had seen him before, and draw her into his arms and further . . . into his love? Her brow knit in consternation at her own wilful and irascible nature. Why was it so hard for her to admit that she wanted this man, this marriage, this babe? What more could she have hoped to glean from life? She groaned inwardly and then aloud at her own shallowness. Perhaps Aaron was right, she was a child, chasing sprites and visions and ideals. She had held fast to the idea of freedom, never realizing it could be itself a fearsome trap, binding her hand and foot, beguiling her away from the true joy and meaning of love and life. And the thought haunted her that it might even now be too late.

Later, she soaked in the warm water of the copper bath, breathing in the sweet scent of the oil, and she thought of Aaron. What could compare with the feeling of his big, hard body next to hers in the morning, every morning. To awaken to his gentle touch and adoring eyes. To lie down each night to his hot, intoxicating kisses and marauding hands. She felt her whole body flush violently at the thought. What was it Raoul had said? A warm, passionate wife was a treasure to be cherished? She smiled secretively. She planned to be the most cherished woman in Britain by morning.

Freshly bathed and robed now in a shell pink silk dressing gown which was trimmed in flounces of lace at the hem and sleeves, Brien sat down to wait for her husband. One thought after another pricked her, and she jumped when the door opened to admit the servants to take away her bath.

What if he didn't come? What if he had ridden to Bristol to set sail again? What if—But she stopped herself firmly. No good would come from such foolish, dark broodings and imaginings. He was tired, would need food and rest. He would think her gone and would soon return to take his ease.

In the end she ate dinner alone in her chamber. She

had little desire for food, but realized when she saw the sumptuous fare that she had hardly eaten in two days. The excellent wine seemed to ease the tension that grew in every muscle of her body.

She paced the room and ran her fingers over the heavy brocades at the windows. His home, he had brought her to his home. She looked about her with new eyes. He had grown up here among these rooms and with these people. And he'd now brought her and, unknown to him, his child back to these walls for safety. She wondered about his boyhood and the warring passions that sent him from here into an uncertain world at a tender age. Would he remember it when his sons and daughters chafed at his most reasonable rule?

Would Aaron regret the marriage when he returned and found that she was with child? What if he questioned his part in the babe's making? She paled at the thought. It would be the real test of their love, and the beginning or end of their life together.

It was near ten o'clock when the maidservant built up the fire for the night and bade her sleep well. She sat sleepily nestled in a large velvet-covered chair near the fire. Her eyes drooped and closed now and then as she gazed at the flames that lighted and warmed the great chamber. She was on the verge of succumbing to doubt and fatigue when she heard low, muffled voices coming closer to the room. Her heart stopped, lurched, then beat wildly.

The massive mahogany door opened swiftly and Aaron loomed large in the opening as he paused to survey the chamber with obvious disbelief. His eyes widened as they fixed on Brien, curled like a tame kitten in the big chair by the fire.

She gazed at him unsteadily. His clothing was spattered with mud and he looked tired, as though he returned from a grueling ride.

For one awkward moment, Brien was embarrassed. Do what any wife would do—whatever that is, she thought desperately. She uncurled her legs and rose to pull the bell for Aaron's bath, then turned to him. Her hands shook and she clasped them together, hoping he would not notice.

He had closed the door behind him and now turned to inspect the array of dishes on the table. He lifted a few and sniffed the contents. Brien thought she detected a slight smile on his handsome mouth.

"I thought you might be hungry when you returned," she volunteered casually as she pulled out a chair for him. Why did she feel so girlish, giddy under his warm scrutiny. She tossed her head defiantly, but inwardly, she admitted ignorance in the arts of seduction.

Brien needn't have worried. This sight of her, warm and contented and so obviously waiting for him, was enough to fire his blood. His disbelief turned quickly to amused anticipation as he noted the effort she had expended to see to his comfort.

As he tasted the roast ham and sipped a glass of the fine claret, Brien studied him from the corner of her eye. The firelight made his copper hair dance with streaks of fire and a slight movement of his jaw as he ate sent a wave of hunger through her stomach and below. She shook her head to clear it of these sensations; there was much to settle before there was time for that.

"Where did you go?" she asked nonchalantly.

"Errands."

Annoyed suddenly by his casual acceptance of her monumental change of heart, she probed further, not caring that her irritation showed. "They must have been important indeed to take you away for so long."

"Yes." He smiled into his goblet. How dearly he longed to test this new attitude of hers. But he recalled her changeable nature and wondered if he should question this turn of fortune at all.

Enough, she thought guiltily, where he goes is his business. If he has not the courtesy to share it with me, I shall not pry like some jealous paramour. She'd not press her luck, too much hung in the balance. Her hand moved without her bidding to her stomach and she stroked it absently. The gesture was not unnoticed and in it Aaron read yet another question to be settled . . . later . . . much later.

The door opened to admit two husky menservants bearing a large copper tub, half filled with water. They moved silently, nodding to Aaron in deference as Brien directed them to place it near the fire. Then they left to fetch the hot water to finish filling it.

When Brien raised her eyes toward Aaron, the surprise on his face made her uneasy. Perhaps she had presumed too much, acted too wifely for his tastes. How did a wife treat her husband . . . see to his comfort?

"I thought you might like a bath after such a long day," she said matter-of-factly, feeling anything but matter-of-fact inside.

Smiling annoyingly, he rose and sighed, stretching sensually, setting Brien's limbs atremble as he began to peel off his coat.

"Ah," he half-moaned, "a hot bath would feel good just now." His own spirits soared at this further evidence of her change of heart.

When the servants had filled the bath and withdrawn, Brien felt a mild panic rising inside her and she picked up her gown and climbed up onto the bed while he stripped off the rest of his clothing. He seemed quite natural about it, as if he always enjoyed an audience at his bathing. Brien stole furtive glances at him from behind partly closed eyes. She was far from admitting that the sight of him naked shocked her, but it did. And it fascinated her as well. She saw the wide, tanned shoulders and muscular back that tapered to a much smaller waist and lighter-skinned buttocks, round and tight, below. His legs were long and tapered, well muscled, but smooth. She clamped her eyes shut as he turned around and thus missed his amusement at her display of modesty. Instinctively he knew that even though they had been together before, had loved and explored each other freely, this night was different. . . . This was the beginning of a life together, and an unprecedented sharing of intimacies. He smiled knowingly and gently at her nervousness.

She heard him moan with sheer pleasure at the warmth of the water as he sank into it. When she thought it safe, she ventured to open her eyes and look at him. His head rested on the edge of the large tub and his dark-fringed eyes were closed. But he spoke as though he knew she watched him.

"This is marvelous, Brien. Kind of you to think of it for me. Only one thing would improve it."

She held her breath. "What is that, Aaron?"

He smiled triumphantly at the soft sound of his name on her lips. "Someone to scrub my back and rub my aching shoulders."

Stifling an urge to run, she rolled her eyes in exasperation, slipping from the bed to venture near the tub. "I could call a servant," she eyed him warily.

"Or you could do it yourself," he counteroffered, handing her the dripping sponge.

Sighing with resignation she now realized this was a part of the penance he would exact for her earlier obstinance. She nearly hissed at him again, but a glint of firelight off his wet, bronzed shoulder stopped her. She swallowed hard and pushed up her sleeves resolutely to kneel behind him with sponge in hand. Timidly at first, she put soap to his well-hardened back and rubbed it. The light continued to dazzle her as it cast over him a golden, savage glow. Each time her fingertips touched his skin she felt an exchange. Daring more, she discarded the sponge and gently massaged his shoulders with her strong, supple fingers.

The excitement grew between them with each successive stroke. Almost independently of her will, she was rinsing her hands of soap and drying them. Then she retrieved the linen toweling from the stand and held them out for him.

The gold of his eyes met the softening gray of hers and widened at the light growing in them. Her hair was tumbled carelessly about her face and shoulders and the color of the dressing gown brought a flash of pink across the flawless skin of her breast.

Warming quickly now to the sight of her, he stood up to dry and Brien surprised them both as she openly, hungrily drank in the details of his magnificent body and manhood.

Wrapped in the toweling, Aaron approached her, feeling his heart pound as though any second it would spring free of his chest. She slipped easily into his strong arms and lifted her face to his. The tenderness in her look and the light in her eyes shot through him like a thunderbolt; she was his now. He closed his eyes, murmuring a wordless prayer of thanks for the joy he was discovering at last with his Lady. He buried his face in the fragrant mass of her hair and breathed deeply of its sweetness. The gentleness and softness of her overwhelmed him and he held her in this tender embrace for what seemed a long time. There was no hesitation in him, only a desire to savor each touch, each stroke, each sensation of this time with her.

Her hand came up to touch his face and her fingers

threaded themselves through his thick hair. The gentle pressure of his chest against her breasts infused a pleasant, tingling warmth through her that reached down into her loins . . . she wanted to press closer to his hard body—closer.

He scooped her up into his arms and carried her to the bed. Placing her gently on the soft mattress, he sat beside her and undid the ribbons that held the frothy dressing gown together in front, his hands trembling with eagerness. Beneath the garment was only her silken skin and her full breasts with their rosy, erect nipples. He breathed in sharply at the sight and she reached for his hand and pressed it to her breast as her eyes sought his. There was no more guard at the door of her heart and in her eyes Aaron read the depth of her true feeling for him. Shedding his towel and lying beside her, he pressed his lips softly against the curve of her neck as he murmured, "Stay with me, Brien."

"I will."

His face came up to hers and his lips now tantalized hers as his big hand dallied over her taut nipples. She squirmed deliciously against him, mindlessly heeding the natural impulses of her lithe, young body. His hands drifted downward over her smooth belly and found the provocative roundness of her undulating hips. He groaned with satisfaction as she rubbed against him and urged him on top of her. He moved gently, tenderly at first, as if afraid of hurting her, but gradually the speed and power of his strokes increased with the urgency of their need for each other. Her legs came up to stroke his with her feet, exploring the new crispness of the dark hair on them. Then in a wave of pleasure, she wrapped him with her legs as though she claimed him and wanted to absorb him into the very depths of her—making him a part of her forever.

He took her to the edge and leisurely she tumbled

over in spasms of pure delight, drawing him after her.

Later she lay nestled against him, marveling at how different it had been each time they had made love. She wondered if it were possible that it would always be like this between them, always discovering and pleasing each other. And she drifted pleasantly until Aaron's voice rumbled in her ear.

"Do you want to know what I did this eve?"

"Um-hum," she murmured, not really curious any longer.

He slipped from the bed and found his coat. Soon he was back beside her, propped up on a pillow and watching her intently. She had a smugly contented smile at the corner of her reddened lips and her hair poured over the pillows about her in a torrent of sun-streaked softness. When her eyes fluttered open they were glazed with satisfaction and she smiled lazily, yielding her hand to him when he reached for it. With a slight frown she watched as he slipped something on her finger and slowly the impact of it registered on her mind. It was a beautifully worked wide band of gold, set with a single cut diamond of no small value. It fit perfectly, sparkling even in the dim light.

She shook her head to clear it and blinked several times as her eyes misted. She looked first at him, then at her hand and back to him again.

"But . . . but . . ." she stammered, "why did you buy a ring when you had sent me back to London?"

"I didn't buy it, I just retrieved it from a banker friend of mine who held it for me. I meant to send it to you in London," he said softly, searching her face. "It wouldn't be right for the wife of a wealthy man to wear no ring in public. I would that my wife wear my ring, the ring that has been held for her since my mother's death."

"Oh, Aaron.' Her voice was breathy. "It is beautiful.'' She held it up to admire even as her husband admired her.

''Why did you stay, Brien?''

That dreaded question held less terror for her now and no flippant reply or excuse would do. She sat up, pulling the soft sheet against her and looked into Aaron's handsome face and promise-filled golden eyes.

''It takes no cleverness to see it, Aaron. I love you. What other reason could there be?'' With that, the perfect truth, she surrendered and conquered in the same instant.

Aaron grasped his wife to him and kissed her hard upon the mouth, feeling with exhilaration that she responded along the entire length of him by pressing closer and shivering slightly as he poured his heat into her again. He muttered against her lips, ''You know what this means.'' He was hoarse and sounded faintly ominous. ''I'll never let you go now.''

Brien pulled her face away from his, grinning impishly, but he held her body clasped fast against his, his legs pinioning her. Her eyes twinkled and she wiggled purposefully against his hardened touch, rousing him.

''Why did you marry me, Aaron?'' She smiled mischievously, knowing that his stern expression would soon give way to the warmer feelings she was stirring inside him.

He frowned with a gruffness he little felt. ''Because I wanted to . . .'' He thought better of it and smiled dazzlingly into her melting gaze. ''And because I love you. I want to live with you, touch you freely and openly. I want you to look at me with the love you bear me in your face, the way you look at me now. We were meant for each other, Brien. Together we make something better than even the sum of us. I have never been more sure of anything in my life . . . and never more happy than now with you in my arms. I love you, my

Lady.''

Brien smiled sleepily as she snuggled against him, pressing her lips against the hardened skin over his collarbone. ''I thought so.''

Their passion soared and spiraled again before they found rest, wrapped in each other's bodies as if reluctant to part even in repose.

Thirty

It was morning by the light filtering in around the heavy brocades at the windows. A servant had been in earlier to rebuild the fire and had, upon a meaningful scowl from his master's son, withdrawn discreetly and warned the other servants that they must not be disturbed. That had been nearly an hour before and Aaron was content to lie beside his beautiful, sleeping bride—lost in her passion and her beauty.

Now he heard it first, a murmuring that sounded like voices, men's voices, and the muffled sounds of movement grew louder. He slipped gingerly from the bed and hurriedly donned his breeches. As the voices grew louder and more insistent, so the beat of his heart kept pace, louder and faster. Only a few seconds passed before the veil of sleep was swept from his mind and the unwelcome intrusion made sense. The voices were loud and angry now—just outside their chamber door.

Aaron glanced quickly at his beloved, now tossing wakefully on the postered bed. They had been found. He had hoped to avoid violence but now found himself reaching for his blade and drawing the keen edge from its lodgings.

Damn it! Why did he not keep a brace of pistols instead of this relic? It was next to useless against a firearm and brought a man too close to his adversary in group fighting. Still, it was all he had.

Brien sat up sleepily, rubbing her eyes. The noise and banging against the door confused her and her eyes sought Aaron. He stood facing the door, sword drawn and muscles coiled. The banging nearly drowned out the voice of a man ordering, "Open up in the name of the crown!" Aaron neither moved nor acknowledged the command.

Brien now crouched back in the bed, fully awake, her heart pounding with fear as she drew the soft sheet about her naked body.

"What do they want? Who are they? Oh, love, be careful!" Her words ended in a wail that caused Aaron to glance over his shoulder at her. His face was grim, lined with determination, and she suddenly knew what was happening.

The mahogany doors finally gave way with a groan and then a cracking and splintering as the wood was rent asunder by their collective force. Scarlet-clad figures poured into the breach with muskets and swords eager for mischief.

A cry strangled in Brien's throat as she saw Aaron take on two with drawn swords and heard the muffled order to " 'Old yer fire! There's but one an' 'e's to save fer 'angin'."

The clanging of their blades drove Brien into a frenzy and she rose to her knees clutching the sheet to her, her eyes wild and her words and muffled cries incoherent.

Aaron backed further into the room wielding his blade deftly and with great force, again and again causing the attackers to relent and allow ground. But in an unguarded moment, one soldier separated from the other and Aaron now fought savagely on two sides, knocking one swordsman's blade from his hand and turning on the other with a snarl. But he was too late, as another soldier was now close behind and swung at his head with the butt end of a musket. A cry from Brien warned him and he swayed, but not quickly enough to avoid a healthy blow to the head that sent him sprawling into solemn blackness on the floor.

The soldiers now stood panting from their exertion and seemed relieved to sheath unbloodied blades.

Brien was paralyzed with fear and horror. Aaron, her love, lay in a heap on the floor, mangled by these cutthroats in soldiers' garb. She could only stare at him, mute, shaking her head.

In the doorway, the remaining soldiers moved aside to admit a tall, richly-clad figure, dark of face and disposition. The Marquis de Saunier surveyed the room and Brien's half-revealed form haughtily, an evil smile breaking over his cruel lips. Brien's numbness abated now as the bile rose in her throat at the sight of him.

"We're obviously too late, Lord Weston." He stepped farther into the room to admit another well-dressed form. And Lawrence Weston's face drained of color at the sight of his daughter, obviously naked and with her hair tossed wildly about. She had the look of an abused animal, stunned, ravaged.

"Be assured, sir," the onerous voice droned on, "this loathsome cur will be properly punished for what he has done."

The callow-faced officer in charge roused his leering men with the order to remove the prisoner and put chains on him before he came to his senses. In what seemed a twinkling he was being hauled up and out of out of the lady's sight.

"No!" Brien cried, having only now realized what they planned to do. "No! You can't!" She would have run to him but was suddenly aware of several pairs of eyes perusing her. She tugged violently at the sheet that covered her and wrapped it about her tucking it under her arms. Weston was now beside the bed, offering her the shelter of his arms and murmuring words of comfort.

"Stop them!" Brien wailed as they jerked the form of her husband to his feet. His head rolled to the side in his senseless state, and Brien was filled with enraged panic. She moved across the bed quickly and pulled frantically at her father's coat. "Stop them! He's done nothing wrong! Make them stop!"

Weston grasped her tightly to him, trying to restrain his meagerly clad daughter from rushing at her tormentor-abductor. Seeing her dressing gown nearby on the bed, he struggled to reach it and wrapped it about her.

"Brien, daughter, you're hysterical. You'll be all right. We have you now and that beast will be properly punished. You're safe now, hush now."

"No!" she wailed, "Don't hurt him!" She began to struggle against Weston's hard grip.

"You're upset, Brien you can't know what you're saying. Hush, now." He threw a withering glance at the officer who, with some of his men, still lingered in the room, their faces ripe with speculation about this wriggling female who was frenzied over the treatment of her abductor.

She pounded at Weston's chest with her fists. "No, father, you must make them stop!" she screamed.

The marquis barked an enraged order at the officer to divert the soldiers' attention. "Remove that swine from this house immediately, sir. Can you not see what effect his presence has on the poor deranged girl?" He took hold of the arm of a nearby soldier and gave him a shove toward the door.

"All right, you louts! Get the rogue out of here, out of the house," the officer barked, irritated at the marquis' high-handed treatment.

Aaron was well into the hallway when Brien could gather her scattered wits and find her tongue once more. She moaned as she struggled against her father's embrace. "You can't let them hurt him! He only tried to save me." She glanced wildly about her and sucked in her breath sharply as her eyes came to rest on the face of the marquis. His eyes glittered triumphantly. "No-o-o-o!" she moaned and collapsed against her father momentarily, feeling all of her strength flee. What was the matter with her?

A sudden loud shouting and confusion assaulted their ears from the staircase and the great hall. In an instant the marquis and the two remaining soldiers were through the door and bounding for the stairs and the source of the noise. The shouting grew louder and more frantic, and distracted Weston from his restraint of his daughter. She seized the chance to thrust hard against him and free herself from his embrace. In a flash, her feet were on the floor and she was running into the hallway and along the balustrade with Weston at her heels. Her movement had left the sheet behind, and she pushed her arms through the sleeves of the thin gown and clasped it together in front with both hands.

The fracas was just over as Brien reached the top of the grand staircase and she froze at the sight below her on the steps and the floor of the hall. Aaron's manacled form lay sprawled where it had been dropped near the front doors, and two soldiers lay crumpled on the floor near him like twisted, inert toys. At the foot of the stairs lay Dyso, an ugly red gash oozing ominously from his bald pate. The marquis, standing near the bottom of the stairs, gripped the railing tightly as he leaned against it. His face was murderous as he glared at the silent form of his attacker. A red-stained dagger a bit farther up on the steps completed the picture. Dyso had attempted Aaron's rescue and when the marquis appeared he had turned his fury upon his former master and had met with violence himself.

"His accomplice, no doubt," the marquis spat, unaware of the presence of the lady on the steps behind him. "You have witnessed his attempt on my life. I know this man; he was once my servant and bears me great malice. I once had his tongue for his impertinence—now I shall have his head! Take him away with the other one."

Rage boiled up inside Brien now, empowering, enabling anger, her face hot and scarlet. When the officer made no move to obey the Marquis' order, the nobleman's gaze followed the line of the officer's to where Brien stood above him on the steps.

Sensing that she was once more in control, the marquis realized the need for haste and wheeled on the hapless officer to growl at him once more. "Did you hear? Get those filthy whoresons out of this house!"

But Brien had again broken from her father's grasp and flew down the steps even as the Lieutenant turned to his men to bark the order, "Move them out!"

As her fingers closed around the dagger, Brien felt a surge of strength and purpose course through her. Weston started to her again, but stopped, his eyes wide with astonishment as she brandished the bloodied blade about her and backed away. In another instant she was on the step above the Marquis pressing the point of the cold steel blade against the back of his neck. "Lieutenant!" she snapped, "bring them back here this moment—unless you relish the sight of French blood!"

The slack-jawed officer barked another order to halt his men and stared at the lady whose eyes blazed defiantly at them all. He fingered his own blade nervously. This was the woman they were to have rescued, and it seemed she had quite another idea about their actions. What was this twisted maze he had allowed himself and his men to become embroiled in?

It was a mighty gamble, Brien realized, to make use of their surprise and unwillingness to harm a woman. But wrapped in a precariously concealing gown, she could do little if they decided to move upon her.

"Brien!" Her father was outraged at her behavior. "You've lost your senses, girl! My God! What has that madman done to you?" He fell back against the stair railing for support.

"It was not Aaron Durham who wronged me, Father." She spit out the words. "But this son of Satan— he's the one!" She shoved the sharp point a bit harder against the strained reddened flesh of the marquis' neck. "And Dyso only meant to protect me from another attack by this rogue. Whatever he did, he did to protect me and I'll not see him abused for it!"

"She's hardly sensible . . . Lord Weston, I implore you . . ." the marquis began nervously.

"Shut up!" Brien snapped and then turned again to the officer. "Remove those cursed manacles from him immediately!" she order the lieutenant, who cast a doubtful look about him and then waved one hand to a soldier who stood near Aaron. The man dropped to one knee and produced a key to unlock the leg irons from the prisoner's feet and the chains on his hands.

Aaron struggled to his elbow, his head tossing and shaking as he struggled to regain his sensibilities. Brien was relieved at the sight; he would be himself again and would help to untangle this mess.

"Brien—" her father pleaded.

"Listen to me, Father, and listen well. That man is not my abductor." With her free hand she pointed to

490

where Aaron had drawn himself into a sitting position. "He is my husband!"

"But the marquis was there when he forced you to his will. You are not legally bound, child. The marriage was not of consent."

Her eyes filled with sparks as she turned slightly to answer him. "Did the marquis not tell you how we came to be in the abbey in the first place?"

"The abbey"—Weston frowned—"but I was told—"

"Did he omit how he and his miserable whelp had taken me from Dunstan by force and nearly had me married to that cur? Aaron Durham rescued me from this degenerate's hold. I married him willingly!" She nearly shouted.

She caught sight of Aaron, now alert and sitting with one arm slung casually across an upraised knee as though he had not a care in the world. His mouth bore an amused twist at the sight of her. Brien leveled her gaze to his and announced boldly, "And I consummated those vows most willingly."

A guffaw from one of the soldiers expressed their lurid delight at this unusual turn of events. A high-born lady, half-naked, proudly announcing her liaison with the man accused of kidnapping her! A bolt of lightning could not have induced them to abandon this fascinating muddle.

Weston gasped in indignation at the statement and the response it drew. "Brien, you can't mean this!"

More leers and guffaws drew scarlet coloring to Brien's cheeks. Now that the worst of the danger was past she was again aware of her exposed state and wished fervently to end this bizarre tribunal.

"Lieutenant," she said, summoning every shred of dignity left to her and straightening her shoulders, "please see that this scurrilous heap is escorted from the premises at once.'' She raised one shapely leg and planted her foot squarely on the marquis' posterior, giving a mighty kick that sent him sprawling and stumbling down the few remaining steps. ''And then take your men and be gone. We have no further need of you here.''

As the soldier withdrew, taking the burning marquis in hand, Brien flew to Dyso's motionless form and knelt to press one hand against his temple. Feeling the throbbing of his blood, she sighed with relief. ''You will be all right, my friend. Again you have saved me. You have my gratitude for a lifetime.'' She stood and beckoned to Peters, who stood huddled in the doorway nearby, ashen-faced. ''Peters, see that he's carried to his bed and then send for a physician to tend him. I think his wound may not be as serious as it first appeared. Let us hope it so.''

Aaron stared at his bride with lusty appreciation. She was queenly—even naked and wrapped in a robe! And he had proposed to protect her? He smiled at the chivalry. She was more than a match for any man—even him.

At Peters' shout, two servants appeared at the door and soon lifted Dyso and carried him up the great stairs toward his own room. Weston, slumped into a sitting position on the step, bewilderedly surveyed the brigand his daughter had so passionately defended. He was standing now and Weston could see he was a formidable man, tall and broad shouldered, and uncommonly handsome. The look in the man's striking eyes as they turned on his daughter shook Weston to the core. He turned to protest to Brien the man's effrontery, but was further shamed by the same heat now glowing in her face.

Since the soldiers and servants had withdrawn, they were alone. The lovers ran to each other's arms, and

Weston watched as his daughter abandoned herself in the most indecent display of kissing he had ever witnessed—or even imagined.

Drawing himself up in indignation he stomped down the stairs and started past them uttering self-abusive epithets. Just after he passed, Brien pulled away from Aaron abruptly and ran after her father, catching his sleeve in a vain attempt to halt him. Aaron followed closely to render whatever help he could in making an explanation. He knew whatever he said would be weighed against Weston's memory of his daughter naked in Aaron's bed. This was no way to endear himself to his powerful new father-in-law.

"Father, you must let me explain!" Brien begged fervently, clutching his tense, hardened arm and pulling on it. "Please hear me out—us out."

Weston stopped to stare at her with a look uncomfortably akin to contempt. "There is naught to explain, child." He looked from her to Aaron and back. "It is clear you had no need of rescuing. You have succeeded in making a mockery of me more than once on this very point. I'll not stand by and watch you pant and flaunt yourself about some rutting ne'er-do-well."

Brien was cut deeply by the hurt and shame in his face. "Father, please stay and give me a chance to explain. I needed your rescue more than you can know. You can't think me a disgrace to you or to my honor when you know the truth."

A long, silent moment passed in which the father searched his heart and the eager, anxious face of his daughter. And once again the man heeded the plea of his woman-child. He closed his eyes mustering every scrap of his tattered patience.

"I shall stay until noon," he sighed, unable to deny her a hearing, ". . . but only if you make yourself presentable."

Her skin flamed at the reference. Dearest Heaven! He must think her quite mad to be prancing about clad only in a thin wrapper—and wielding a blade, yet! Her voice was full of perfect contrition. "Yes, Papa," she demurred. It was a term she had not used for him since she was a small girl. It caught him by surprise and mellowed whatever part of him might have hardened against her.

Aaron's voice boomed out over the hall, "Peters!"

The stately man appeared as by magic at the head of the staircase, slightly rumpled and quite harried-looking. He managed a restrained bow as he answered the summons. "Yes, sir? Is everything all right, sir? I could not stop them, sir, try as I might."

"All is fine, Peters," Aaron assured him. "Lord Weston will be staying for a while. Please see a room is readied and see to a luncheon for us all." Before the butler could turn away, Aaron glanced at Brien who was moving up the stairway as if trying to escape further scrutiny. "And Peters—"

"Yes, sir?" The tone was long-suffering.

"Send Aggie or one of the other servants up to help Lady Brien."

Peters' eyebrows arched slightly and he sniffed with resignation as he glanced Brien's way. "Very good, sir."

Aaron sprang up the steps after Brien and retrieved his boots and shirt before escorting his father-in-law and potential adversary into the salon. He paused long enough to steal one quick, hard kiss and to place a lusty pat on his brdie's ill-concealed buttocks.

Weston had to admit the Durham fellow looked almost respectable when fully clothed—far better than he had expected. His manner and speech were civil enough, a fair counterfeit of culture, to be sure. But something in the older man went cold at the thought of any man stealing off with his daughter—before even considering what had obviously happened between them. When he remembered the kiss he had unwillingly witnessed he felt blood rushing to his face anew.

Aaron returned with a tray of steaming coffee from the kitchen and poured cups of the pungent brew for himself and Weston. Weston added this ungentlemanly act to his list of objections to the man; such things were best left to servants. But in all fairness, Weston cast the man alongside his wilful progeny and had to admit it was a fair match. *If* they were married, *if* they stayed married, and *if* they had children (he deemed all these possibilities remote) then he would have beautiful grandchildren.

Straining for civility he little felt, Weston launched forth his investigation. "Tell me, Durham, how come you to be in this nobleman's house? Are you some relation to the count?" Weston gauged his words carefully, sipping the hot liquid and scrutinizing the man's casual movements.

"Yes, I am kin; the count is my father." Aaron answered the gaze and the question straight on.

Weston nearly choked on a mouthful of coffee, his eyes wide with disbelief. Either the man was daft or a colossal liar. But the story was too easily checked to be an obvious lie—or was it?

"You find that hard to believe," Aaron stated, still gazing at Weston directly. "I cannot say I blame you. You have had little of the truth of late. If it will help, feel free to check the family Bible in the library and to interrogate the servants. Some of them have been here since before my birth."

"I . . . well, I . . ." Weston stammered. The man was disarmingly direct and Lawrence Weston found himself wishing the story true and liking the man in spite of everything that had occurred. "I will," he said, hoping for some reason that the younger man would not be offended.

Aaron smiled and relaxed a bit. Weston was shrewd, not easily duped or sold a bill of goods. His willingness to stay and hear them out lent credence to his reputation for fairness, but Aaron sensed that the battle was far from over.

"How is it we have never seen you in London . . . if you are the count's son? Did you never travel?"

"I have not lived with my father for some time. I have my own trading company and am often at sea. I have preferred to avoid the delights of London's society."

"Um-m-m," Weston took in the explanation dispassionately. "And where did you meet my daughter, if not in London?" He searched his memory and found no recollection of Aaron Durham's name ever mentioned. Yet now, the memory of Dyso's motionless form on the floor of the hall came back to him. The hulk had attempted to free the man, had he not? The hulk was fiercely loyal to his daughter; Weston knew he would never have allowed this rake near her, unless . . . The answer was not long in coming.

Aaron rose from his comfortable chair and stood near the fireplace's glow, a smile playing at the corners of his mouth. "I captained the vessel that carried Brien to the colonies this last spring. My ship, the *Lady's Secret* is berthed even now in Bristol's harbor."

"How is it you, the son of a nobleman, captain a vessel?" Weston was now truly puzzled.

"It is not usual, I admit freely. I designed my ship and she turns a tidy profit for me. I press no claims to my father's title or wealth. All I have is what I have made in this world."

Now Weston was both intrigued and deflated. He

had hoped, if the man were truly a noble, the situation might yet be saved. But perhaps he was born on the wrong side of the blanket and not entitled to an inheritance. At the very least, Durham admitted to being out of favor with his wealthy father. But what of the man's own worth?

"And just what have you made," Weston strained to contain his urge to sarcasm.

"I own three ships now, a goodly string of shops and warehouses of goods in the colonies, large parcels of land near Boston, and a fair sum of gold held safe in the Bank of England. The latter was mine from my mother as my inheritance from her. Only a small part of it has ever been touched. It will stay intact for my children, should they ever need it."

Children!

Weston gulped, his mind reeling. He could not even choke back the question. "Is Brien . . . well, is she . . . ?" He could not bring himself to say the words, but he had come too far to retreat now.

"With child?" Aaron supressed a smirk at the fatherly delicacy. This was one point he had yet to make clear for himself. "That you must seek from your daughter."

With each word, Weston's face flamed and daggers came to his eyes. This rutting rake had already dishonored his daughter and now had the effrontery to smirk and flaunt it before the nose of her father!

"You rutting blackguard'—" Weston growled, coming up quickly from his chair.

"Father!" Brien stood in the doorway with genuine shock written on her face, ashen at the sight of her two men angry and tense. "How could you?" she breathed, planting herself resolutely between them and turning to Weston. She shoved a rolled parchment at him insistently. "If this will ease your mind and stop your disparagement, so be it. You must think me quite degraded to mistrust my word so. And I deserve none of your contempt."

She turned on Aaron next as her father, red-faced, untied the scroll and read the contents.

"You're not helping matters by provoking him. He, like me, needs time to adjust to changes—and heaven knows there have been many of those of late. Can you not show him some consideration?" Her eyes were an arousing mixture of indignation and pleading that Aaron found irresistible and he relaxed. Brien squeezed his arm against her side as she turned to Weston.

"It all appears i norder," Weston said warily. "But you will admit I have had ample cause to doubt you . . . not the least of which is the fact that until this day I have never heard the name of Aaron Durham, yet, of a sudden I find him entrenched in my family. I came to rescue a kidnapped daughter and found her cozily ensconced in a man's bed, claiming to be his wife, when only days before I heard her with my own ears decry the very institution of marriage as unfit—even abhorrent!"

Brien took his reluctant hand and held it tightly in her own. "Please sit, Father. I know this is hard for you, but it is no less difficult for me, seeing you doubt me so." She drew him down on the sofa beside her and caught his gaze in hers as Aaron drew up another chair to be near them.

Lawrence Weston related how he had received Brien's frantic summons the same evening that a message had arrived from the marquis announcing her engagement to Louis Trechaud. The marquis' letter gave a false report of Brien's delight in the match and begged Weston's forgiveness for the unorthodox manner in which it took place; he blamed the impetuosity of the young. Weston, more than a little confused, had set out from Bristol the previous morning and was better than halfway to Dunstan when intercepted on the road by the marquis, who was searching for the "kidnapped" Brien.

The marquis had woven a story, saying that while the vicar was attending them at Dunstan to plan for the wedding, Brien had been abducted by a madman who'd demanded a ransom. He had, by his own account, rousted soldiers to accompany them—over Weston's objections. He'd repeatedly had warned the redcoats that this outlaw was armed and highly dangerous—admonishing them to shoot on sight.

They were led to this area by the vicar's recollection of the Durhams of Wiltshire. As Weston talked, the clever manipulations of the marquis became ever more apparent. It was obvious the wretch planned to have Aaron killed on sight and to see that Brien's protests would be seen as the tragic result of her overburdened mind. But for Lord Weston's presence and Dyso's rash intervention his hideous plan might have succeeded.

"He had it planned so well," Brien shivered, pale and stunned at the extent of the marquis' cunning.

"With me dead," Aaron put in, "he could have claimed that Brien was not herself—that her mind twisted the events. Even you would have believed him, Lord Weston."

Brien looked at her father's solemn nod. "When I fled London to Dunstan, the marquis guessed that I planned to resist the marriage further. He followed me to Dunstan to force a marriage in your absence." She had avoided the marquis' threat until now. "He claimed I started the fire that killed Raoul. He produced a false witness to swear to it. . . . I was alone . . . I didn't know whether you would be—"

Weston had fidgeted uncomfortably beside her and now grabbed her suddenly into his arms, cutting off the flow of words. At the point where her chin quivered and great liquid drops filled her eyes, he had totally embraced the truth of her story. She was his child, his lovely Brien; he knew her honesty and now her truth. There was a long quiet moment as he held her against him, trying to quell the emotions that clouded his voice. Aaron sat uncomfortably by, knowing that this must be their time of reconciliation, but somehow envious of it.

"When I got to Bristol," Weston continued, "I found the ships late, but not unreasonably so. One docked a mere two days after my arrival and my head clerk disavowed all knowledge of an urgent summons." He released Brien from his tight embrace and stared down into her sweet face. "Probably more of the marquis' work. I had never trusted him completely, but I was frantic with worry for you."

Brien's eyes glistened, very wide and very blue now. "If you hadn't come, Father, he would have succeeded. He could not overrule my pleas with you here. You did 'rescue' me."

Weston's eyes narrowed briefly. "It was only by chance we met along the road. The soldiers were stopping all travelers along the way to inquire of you. He said they were on the way to Bristol to find me— searching as they went. Now I see it for the ruse it was. He counted on being your rescuer"—he turned to Aaron—"and your executioner."

"He narrowly missed." Aaron winked at Brien, now feeling as though a great weight had been lifted from him . . . Weston believed them.

"He'll have no second chance," Weston vowed. "He'll find the climate of all of England poor for his health and his fortunes when I'm through. Not a door in London will be open to him."

* * *

500

During luncheon, Lawrence Weston watched his daughter and her rescuer-abductor-husband. There was clearly more to this story than met the eye—or than they had yet revealed. Why was he always the last to know things where his daughter was concerned? He remembered the womanly glow about her when she returned from the colonies. He had marked well that the rigors of the voyage had little dissipated her vitality . . . in fact, the opposite. She had seemed renewed, invigorated. His eyes narrowed as he regarded Aaron. The captain of a vessel, eh? On an ocean voyage there was plenty of time. . . .

What was he thinking? Further, what did it matter? His daughter was married legally to this man; he doubted it no longer. He watched her as her soft blue-gray eyes flitted shyly over Aaron's face. And he saw the lovely crimson that flooded her cheekbones when the man returned her gaze. The Captain was a big, strong man, rugged and, from the scar on his face, no stranger to conflict. But his unusual golden eyes glowed adoringly when they turned on Brien, casting a gentler hue over his angular features. They knew each other well, Weston judged, and it surprised him that the thought no longer irritated him.

In the end, Weston agreed to stay on another day at Aaron's request and Brien's entreaty. All that Aaron had told him was confirmed that very afternoon as Weston pored over books and documents in the library. Weston found himself liking the man's boldness and honesty in spite of himself. He grudgingly admitted that he could not even have conjured a man whose stature, quickness of mind, and temperament could mate so well with those of his own capricious offspring. Before tea that afternoon, Weston was resigned to the match, if not one of its advocates.

Only one thing disturbed him. Each time he delved

into the man's future or inquired about his prospects, Brien carefully, even slyly, steered them away from it. Weston watched her, troubled by her possible motives, even while admiring her skill.

"And what of this trading company of yours, Durham—what is it called?" Weston tried once more to broach the subject over tea.

Aaron threw a guarded glance at Brien before answering. "The Harrison-Durham Company, thus far. Most of the property is a recent acquisition and I've had little time to plan for its future. But I'm sure it will need a strong, understanding hand on the helm."

Brien looked at him in wonder. She had no idea he had assets other than his ship. What trading—Then the name "Harrison" lodged in her mind. Idiot! He'd done it to her again!

"You!" she sputtered. "You're Harrison! You brought Weston Trading! Of all the nerve . . ."

Aaron faced her with a bemused coolness that fascinated Weston. He hoped the man coul deal with the full fury of his daughter's wounded pride. He would have hated to lose this son-in-law just as he was getting used to the idea.

Aaron leaned forward in his seat, quite near her reddening face as if to launch his own attack. "I told you I would hate to see so promising a venture fall into the wrong hands. It was an excellent investment with a real future in the colonies."

"Of course!" Brien prated. "And made all the more attractive by the specter of my failure!"

Aaron leaded back nonchalantly, staring at his cup. "Don't be so prickly, Brien. I won't be baited on this. I won't deny I had some personal interest in the holdings because of you, but I would never have put part of my mother's legacy into any venture on sentiment alone."

"Your mother's legacy?" Brien's anger was abating

as she realized the solidity of his argument and she was intrigued by this new element.

"My mother's name was Harrison before she married. It was some of the money she bequeathed me that purchased Weston Trading. I felt it only proper that her name should be used." He smiled with warmest intent into Brien's sparkling eyes. "She had a good head for business, herself, and had invested wisely. Unusual for a woman."

Weston looked on, again amazed by this man and his adroitness in handling himself in sticky situations.

"I feel sure Brien Weston Durham will have a real hand in running the business, if she wants one." Aaron had succeeded in thwarting the lash of her wounded pride and now seized the opportunity to air some plans for their future. How she would react, he could not predict. "That is, after she finishes the house." He sat back and crossed his arms across his chest smugly.

"What house?" Brien was aghast. The man had more secrets than a gypsy!

"The one that sits half begun on my land just outside of Boston. You remember the meadow and lane near the stream? It sits there, awaiting your word on its completion. I feel certain you would do a better job at it than I. I have not the patience you display." He watched her struggle inwardly with her pleasure at his revelation and her ingrained need to rebel.

Best to have it all out now, he thought, warming to this next piece of news. "I've already engaged a housekeeper; one quite capable, but with the tongue of a fishwife when crossed. Knowing how you love a challenge, I thought it best you master Ella . . . or perhaps you know a trick or two in dealing with stubborn servants who nip into sherry."

Brien's eyes flew wide as the point of his words struck home. "Ella?" Anger threatened to flash anew in her face, but her mouth twitched uncontrollably as the war raged on inside her. Soon the victor was made known by the slow smile of chagrin spreading on her lips.

"Then Boston it is, Aaron Durham, and let's hope you'll not regret the bargain you've made for yourself."

"Not a minute of it."

Thirty-one

Aaron claimed her hand as they walked in the garden enjoying the coolness of early evening. Lord Weston had discreetly chosen to remain inside, dozing in a chair by the fire after the exertions of the day. The air smelled of damp leaves and must and the warm light of the sunset bathed them in its rosy glow. Their cloaks felt good against the descending chill.

Brien looked about her trying to picture Aaron as a copper-haired moppet, running and jostling about on these very paths. Her face took on a revealing softness as she concocted the scene before her mind's eye. Would her babe be like that? She stiffened at the thought and her hand went of its own accord to her middle, resting there protectively. She was unaware that Aaron watched her intently and read the movement more clearly than she would have wished.

"Does it move yet, the babe?" he asked softly, leaning near her ear. He pulled her gently to a halt beside him.

Her eyes were saucer-sized. Did he also read minds

like a gypsy? Her embarrassed scarlet color betrayed her words. "I don't know what you're talking about." She turned to walk away, now all confusion and longing inside. She had meant to hold this one last thing awhile; she could not bear it if their love, having endured so much, was found wanting in the matter of the babe.

He pulled her back to him and lifted her resisting chin up so that her gaze met his. "It's true, isn't it. You bear a child."

Her face was crimson with shame and she jerked her head away from his touch. "How could you know?" she asked, finding new cause for embarrassment when she realized that only the night before he had touched and explored the secret parts of her freely. How else? This man always seemed to know her better than she knew herself. She dropped her head, turning away from his grasp, wishing fervently the cracks in the paving stones would open to swallow her.

Aaron's hearty laughter at her embarrassment only added to her chagrin. How dare he make sport of her!

"It is a bit late, love, to play the coy, modest maid. Tell me truly, now, we are to be parents, are we not?"

She mumbled it so softly, he barely heard.

"Ah, you can do better, Brien," he chided, grinning broadly, knowing she could not see.

"Yes," she uttered weakly, reddened to the roots of her hair and still unable to look at him. She felt his hands withdraw from her shoulders and she stepped away from him eagerly. She would give him the chance to withdraw now—before she had time to think, to remember how badly she wanted and needed him. She'd not have him pitying her or staying with her from a sense of duty.

"Aaron, I know this changes everything for you." She gripped the edges of her cloak hard and swallowed back the fear that clutched at her throat. "I won't have you bound to me because you feel an obligation." Oh, how could she put it? How could she assure him it was his child and ask him to stay and to love it as much as she would?

"Yes, it changes things, slightly." He grinned as she turned her stricken face toward him and then flushed with color anew at the humor in his face. "I shall have to be more careful with you in bed."

Her eyes flew wide. "That's all you have to say? You . . . you . . . rake!"

"What would you have me do?" He rushed at her and swept her up into his arms whirling her well above the ground. He laughed again, drawing her into his mood as into his arms, and soon she was laughing breathlessly. too. When her feet again touched the ground, his lips found hers and pored leisurely, invitingly across them.

Lifting his face from hers he smiled at her and Brien noted with a little gasp that there was a moistness in the corners of his eyes. "What would you have me say, silly wench? Did you think me callous enough to deny you?" He saw the darkness that flitted momentarily across her eyes in response and the insight came to him.

"Ah, love, you should know me vain enough to assume the babe is mine. I know you well, lady. I doubt there has been another who has gained your hard-won favors and romped in your bed." He caught her hand as it came up to strike him. "Right?" He leered, pulling her tightly against him and blistering her mouth with the heat of a hungry kiss.

"Right?" His voice was hoarse and his head reeled with the passion he meant to infuse in her. Caught, he was, in his own trap, and not unhappy there.

"Right." Brien melted against him, marveling anew

at his special sense that allowed him to know her mind before she did.

"Lady, I want you now and always. And I want your babe, my son or daughter. And I want us to make a good life together in that place where you first became mine and took me to your bed. It is only right that our babe be born in America, seeing he was begun there." Noting her silence he tucked his chin to look into her face as it rested against his chest. "Do you find it hard to accept, Brien, this life I spread before you?" There was a puzzlement in his voice that made her smile.

"No, Aaron." She reached up to stroke his smooth cheek tenderly. "I know now it is all I have ever wanted." She smiled. "But sometimes I find my pride runs well ahead of my own heart's desires. I want so to be a real wife to you, to love you and share with you always. It would hurt terribly to have you at some later time begin to doubt—" But his lean fingers against her lips stopped the flow of words.

"Never, Lady . . . my own Lady. I have searched for you and lost and found you—always counting my happiness and fortunes by your smiles and meager touches. With you I shall be content . . . and I will love the babe all the more for its unlikely start."

They walked on in sweet silence for a short while, his strong arm holding her close to him protectively.

"But how did you know?" she finally asked, burning anew with curiosity. He only laughed and hugged her close to him. "I knew."

Brien left her father and her husband in the salon, sharing a brandy, while she retired. Aaron cast more than one anxious look toward the door as he listened patiently to Lord Weston's latest news of the East India Company and the commodity trade. Weston pretended

508

not to notice Aaron's growing agitation, fully aware that he strained the buck's endurance to the limit.

A commotion in the hallway caught them both by surprise and they rose as one man. Aaron gained the door first and was into the great hall before the familiarity of the action could dawn upon him. He suddenly felt as though he had responded just so a hundred—a thousand—times before.

He stopped short in the hallway as the visual embodiment of the recollection loomed up before him. A face of reddened granite glowered at him, its mouth contorting to cast orders to the servants who scurried about to help him with his cloak and gloves.

For a long, electric moment there was silence in the hallway as father and son faced each other. The confrontation so chilled the room that every muscle was frozen, no one moved—not even in obedience to the master's orders.

Aaron felt his heart drop to his stomach and his muscles coil involuntarily as in preparation for an attack. The dread that wetted his palms and dried his mouth was a relic of former days and he staunched the cause as soon as he recognized it.

"So, you're home." The count eyed his prodigal son appraisingly.

"How did you know? Aaron asked coldly, tilting his chin upward to parry the man's intense gaze.

"Peters."

Aaron placed his hands on his hips in a strong stance and cast an equally appraising eye over the tall, graying figure. "I might have known. Did he also tell you why I'm here?" Aaron's voice was lower, tighter than usual.

"Yes," the count's face was flawlessly dispassionate, "some nonsense about a marriage."

Aaron's voice and mood mirrored perfectly those of

the man he confronted, even to the slight twitch of a muscle in his sqare jaw, telling of impatience—or annoyance. Aaron ignored the high-handed provocation evenly.

"I *am* married. She is here with me."

The redness in the count's face deepened and he turned to the servants and snapped, "Quit your gaping—you have work to do!" And as they scurried out separately to their appointed tasks, the count brushed by Aaron, stridently ignoring Lord Weston in his haste.

Aaron turned in time to see his father enter the salon and his eyes narrowed. Weston considered making a discreet exit, but the drama was too high, too tempting. In the end, he followed Aaron back into the salon and sat down in an out-of-the-way chair, hoping to be as inconspicuous as possible. This did not seem an auspicious start toward an introduction . . . but he would see what manner of family his daughter had married into.

The count poured a brandy and stood gazing into the glowing embers of the fire. "How long have you been married?" he demanded.

"Three days."

"Why did you come here?" the count sounded less hospitable by the moment. Weston winced as he thought of his own outrage upon learning of his daughter's marriage. He now felt foolishly akin to this gruff old aristocrat.

"We needed a place to stay," came Aaron's cold reply.

"Then why not a public house?" The count tossed the words as he would have a javelin. "Or has your waywardness wasted all your resources?"

Weston saw with alarm the way Aaron's fists closed tightly. The small lines at the corners of his mouth were the only other evidence of his inner state.

"We came for other reasons," Aaron answered tightly. Then a reckless urge to honesty goaded him. "To avoid my arrest and possible hanging."

Weston's eyes widened at the ill-timed announcement and the audacious way it was phrased. The cool boldness of the experienced captain became pure, thoughtless rebellion when facing the hostile dignity of his progenitor. Weston's mind raced to gather the sparse facts and nuances and to trace them to their melancholy conclusion. The man, however worthy, would never fulfill the ambitions of his lordly father; however courageous he was, whatever he became or built, it would not matter. He would be an ungrateful, rebellious wastrel in his father's house . . . unless . . .

Weston was jolted back to the present by the count's heated charge.

"Caught cuckolding some fat merchant—or bedding his wayward daughter, no doubt!"

Aaron struggle visibly to rein his unreasoning anger. "No, only for abducting my lawful wife!"

"I was not aware that marriage was a hanging offense," the count sneered. "If you were married legally, then it could not have been honorably, to send you skulking back to the shelter of my house."

"It is not for you to judge my honor, or my wife's." Aaron's voice was too low, too controlled for the heat of his words and Weston sprang to his feet.

"I'll judge whom I will in my own house—you and your strumpet!" the count bellowed.

Only Weston's physical intervention prevented Aaron from striking the older man. But the elder Durham stood his ground regally. Only then did Thomas Durham take notice of the well-dressed observer who had intervened in his behalf.

"No, man, are you daft?" Weston strained against

the youth and strength of his daughter's husband, summoning his every reserve just to match his force. "This will get you nowhere. Think, man, would you bring such disgrace upon your head, upon your wife?"

At Weston's reference to Brien, Aaron's body relaxed somewhat and he straightened. The fury in his face was now cold and Weston suppressed a shudder. He now sensed that the younger Durham was again in control, but with passion full-blown and all the more dangerous for it. What a turn! He now feared for his daughter's abductor when only hours before he had sought the man's head!

Weston stepped slowly aside to keep both men in his sight as he turned to the father.

"Who are you?" the count demanded.

"I, sir, am the 'strumpet's' father . . . who this day led an attack on your son for abducting my daughter." Weston's dress and cultured speech and bearing were all that prevented a high-handed retort. The absurdity of his statement drew an involuntary grunt from the Count that passed for a laugh.

Weston straightened to his full height and delivered a princely, disdainful glare as he continued. "I shall excuse your distasteful reference for it is clear you have no knowledge to speak from. And it is clear you know even less about your son than you do about my daughter. A deplorable fault in a father, sir—however justified."

"The affrontery!" the count exclaimed indignantly. "Just who do you think you are to lecture me in my own house?" Redness returned sharply to his prominent cheekbones to let Weston know his words had found a mark.

"I am your son's father-in-law, sir. Otherwise I am known as Lawrence Weston, earl of Southwold."

At the name, the count's eyes widened; he had heard of the wealthy Lord Weston, but had never met the reclusive nobleman. It would take more than mere assurances to convince him of the authenticity of the claimant. But for the first time that evening, the wheels of his logical mind began to turn and to ferret out the truth if there were any to be found.

The count's brow shot up. "In a pig's eye you are." Before Weston could respond, the count had turned on Aaron again. "Clever you are to bring so accomplished a liar as an accomplice. But it will do you no good. Whatever you seek, you will go away empty-handed."

"You stubborn old fool," Aaron retorted angrily. "What makes you think I want anything of yours? Had I known you would have returned, I would never have stayed."

An ugly curl crept into the elder Durham's lip. "Did you think to rob me blind in my absence? You and your trollop?"

Instinctively, Weston grabbed at the man's arm and growled as he landed the first blow, "You foul-minded bastard!"

Aaron stifled the urge to join the melee but could not bring himself to stop it. They were healthy and evenly matched in age and size. In a bare few exchanges they both panted and swung mightily, but without much effect. At least once each man was brought to his knees—an even bout to Aaron's incredulous scrutiny. At sometime during the fight, his own anger was spent as well.

When Brien's horrified voice split the air, they were more than willing to halt the pugilistic display.

Weston got up heavily from his knee and the count leaned, panting for air on a chair for support. Their clearing gazes turned at once to the young woman in the doorway. And each of them stared—for different reasons.

"Merciful God! What do you think you are doing?

What is going on?'' Her eyes, wide with disbelief, were quickly tinged with wrath. She was a queenly vision in the same shell pink dressing gown that highlighted her perfect skin and winsome curves. Her hair had been brushed and was pinned loosely atop her head, allowing a stray curl to trickle down the alabaster column of her neck. Her cheeks were flushed rosily and her eyes flashed sparks of indignation.

"Well?" she demanded, floating into the room and steadying herself on a nearby chair.

Aaron cleared his throat as the others looked to their clothing and battered flesh. "It seems our fathers had a marked difference of opinion." There was a trace of amusement in the bold curve of Aaron's mouth.

"Father?" She turned on Weston incredulously. "Whatever possessed you?" But without waiting for a response, she moved on to Thomas Durham, who now nursed a sore jaw with one hand.

"And you, sir, to brawl with a guest in your own home!" Then she wheeled on Aaron. "And you let them! You're as daft as they!" She felt a rush of anger at his amusement with this folly.

"What possible provocation could they have had?" she demanded, eying him suspiciously. "What is going on?"

"My father doubts our marriage, your father's word on his identity, and thinks I am here to steal him blind." Aaron's brutally simple summary told Brien all she needed to know.

She approached the count with a display of high-born grace that amazed her father and dazzled her husband. How dare this overproud, stiff-necked old prude doubt his own son's word! Her shock quickly turned to indignation, then righteous wrath. Her effect on the count was harder to read, but his wary, sidelong glance at Weston hinted that he reconsidered his earlier stance. She clearly was not what he expected, whatever that was.

He took Brien's proffered hand awkwardly.

"Since no one seems to have the manners to introduce us . . . I am Brien Weston Trechaud, now Durham. Your son and I were married three days ago. The circumstances, while unusual, cast no doubt on the honor or legality of our union. Tomorrow morning you may inspect the marriage documents yourself if you wish." Her lovely features seemed chiseled in the finest marble.

"I . . . I shall." The count's gaping jaw slammed shut.

Brien withdrew her hand. "I do not know what you have been told, but I shall tell you the truth as I know it. Aaron rescued me from an abduction and very nearly a forced marriage. And before I was aware of what transpired, I found myself married to him instead. I admit, I thought it a cure as drastic as the ill, at first. But now I find I like being Madame Durham, and I intend to be your son's wife for many years to come." Her calm, pleasant voice had the ring of a steel blade against stone. Her coolness in the face of an obviously hostile father-in-law surprised even her a bit. But if the count rejected them totally, at least she would have the satisfaction of setting the pompous, old curmudgeon straight!

"Surely you cannot expect me to welcome you with open arms," the count said defensively. "For all I know this is a ruse—and a diabolically clever one at that. I warn you, you'll not get a farthing!"

Brien's superior gaze was withering as she drew herself a bit straighter. "Were you not such a juiceless old relic, such a pompous old jackass, you would know well that Aaron would take none of your money—and desires your title even less. Having seen how nobly you

515

wear the honor, I make it a condition of my marriage to him that he never even consider it! It matters not what you think of my family or of me. But you must be the world's greatest fool to disparage the honor and courage of a man as exceptional as Aaron Durham, solely on account of his being your son.''

The count's mouth dropped open at the audacity and clarity of the young woman's words. She had driven every reply from his mind with astonishment.

She stepped back slowly, her mind racing and her heart filled with a jumble of indignation, pride, and a twinge of sadness. This was the scorn Aaron had lived with until he could bear it no longer and had fled to the open and hungry arms of the sea. She would love that man all the more dearly to make up for the hurt he had suffered here.

''You needn't worry about being bothered with us,'' she finished her soliloquy. ''We plan to make our home in Boston in the colonies. There at least a man is judged by his own skill and cleverness and courage—and not by the tomes of a lifeless tradition.''

She stepped back raking him with her gaze and her eyes narrowed as she lifted her chin. ''This I will take from you . . . I shall spend what is left of this night in *your* bed. Tomorrow I shall take nourishment at *your* table and I will leave shortly thereafter with *your* son, to make my life with him.''

In the kirklike silence that followed, she crossed the floor to Aaron and took his hands as he extended them to her. She turned to fire the finishing salvo. ''In return, sir, I will give you beautiful grandchildren that will honor both their father and the name of Durham. Only you must come to Boston to claim them.'' She turned to look up into Aaron's adoring face. His eyes poured forth his love into hers.

Aaron gently put one arm about his wife's waist as

they reached the door, and she leaned her head on his shoulder. Their love echoed about the room.

Weston's eyes misted as he stared after them and then reached for the decanter of brandy that stood on the butler tray near him. His fatherly pride bubbled over in an uncharacteristic rush.

"Isn't she something?"

"Um-m-m."

Epilogue

What canvas remained free in the great sails flapped lazily in the breeze, its job well done for now. Four eyes on the deck below scoured the approaching dock for signs of life. The gentle lapping of the water about the piers and the sides of the good ship were mingled with the cries of sea birds soaring and calling, and with the scraping of wood on wood as the vessel nudged the dock. There were dull thuds of calloused, bare feet upon the dock and the low musical chant of hands about the ropes, pulling.

Lawrence Weston breathed deeply of the smells of the harbor and one hand impatiently smacked the other behind his back. He gazed up at the sky and mused on the signs he read there, the clearing of the gray, monotonous clouds and the liberation of the sun once more. His spirits began to lift. A movement on the wharf caught his eye and he turned slightly to better glimpse its cause. A handsome black coach, drawn by two matched roans, turned onto the dock and halted near the ship's mooring. Weston smiled; there would be no need to send a message after all.

Weston paced impatiently until the gangway was in place and immediately he was on and across it, making for the coach with certain stride. But before he reached it, the door swung open and a tall figure bent through the opening and landed on the ground.

Aaron Durham smiled generously at his father-in-law and extended his hand. The older man not only grasped it, but drew the taller man down in a crushing hug with the other arm. Then he nodded to the hulk, Dyso, who stood by.

"By God, man it's good to see you again," Weston's voice was husky and he cleared his throat to hide the emotion welling up inside him.

Smiling broadly at this enthusiastic greeting, Aaron gazed at the older man intently. "And you, sir, you're looking well. Brien will be so pleased to have you with us." Seeing the lord peering into the coach, Aaron reassured him. "She was to have come along, but at the last moment, Garrett began to cry and would not be comforted by any other. Rather than delay us, she sent me on for you alone."

"Ah," Weston was not seriously disappointed. Then as a thought crossed his mind, he voiced it with relish. " 'Twill be a sight indeed to see Brien soothing and mothering a wee one. I never thought to see that in my life . . . or to hear my headstrong daughter constrained to anything she did not want to do."

Aaron smiled warmly at the thoughts, so akin to his own in the past. But his wife surprised him still at every turn. She had reveled in her new motherhood and thrown herself into it with all the passion she possessed. But just when he thought her too absorbed in her son to give business a mere thought, she had come to him with some ideas about expanding their trading into the new Ohio Territory, and he was left wondering once more.

"There is quite enough left you will recognize," he laughed. "She's planned quite a time for you here, I hope you've come well rested."

Weston smiled. "I am eager to get my hands on that grandson of mine. For that privilege I'll endure her worst." He glanced over his shoulder, his face sobering as a thought occurred to him. "Uh . . . Aaron there is something I would speak of now. I have brought a friend with me and would know whether you will allow lodging for us both, or if I must seek it elsewhere."

Aaron frowned slightly at the older man's manner and the tension in his face. His big shoulders shrugged off any concern. "Any friend of yours is welcome in our home, sir, you must know that."

Clasping his son-in-law's arm, Weston sighed with relief and pleasure. "That is as I knew it would be. If you'll see to the trunks, I'll see to my friend." Before Aaron could inquire further, Weston was moving away and back up the gangway.

A friend? A lady friend? Was the old boy bringing his bride now to obtain his daughter's blessing before marrying again? Otherwise why all the secrecy? He shook his head in bewilderment. Weston had acted as though he fully expected his son-in-law to reject the plea and refuse to honor his friend as a guest. Tugging on a large brass-bound trunk and lifting it with Dyso's help, Aaron failed to see Weston's guest and friend descend the gangway and near the coach where they labored with the baggage.

Hearing Weston's polite cough, Aaron wheeled about, leather satchel in hand to flash a welcoming smile at Weston's lady. And he nearly dropped the bag as his eyes met the cold gray of ones he knew well and in which he had found little warmth. Aaron straightened from his labor slowly.

"Aaron," Weston's friend addressed him, proudly,

but with a softer edge than the younger man could remember.

"Father." The pronouncement took great effort and left Aaron utterly speechless. For a long moment, father and son confronted memories of the old, deep hurts within them in silence, each searching the other for clues to the present state of their relations.

Weston drew a long breath, only now realizing that he had held it for a while. The silent start was encouraging; at least there would not be open rancor now. "This is my friend, Aaron. You have generously offered us both the comforts and hospitality of your home, have you not?"

Aaron's gaze tore away from the intense exchange to bore into Weston. The quiet smile on his father-in-law's face struck down any indignation he felt at the presumption, the meddling. He found his heart calming in his chest and a feeling of the rightness of it settled on him. Now was a time for closing old wounds and setting things right. Better that this be settled too.

"I have offered such." He looked at his father, wondering at the anxiousness that flitted across the elder Durham's features. But soon he was sure he had only imagined it. "You are welcome as Weston's guest in our home, Count."

In the coach as they moved along the streets of Boston with the drapes drawn back to afford a view of the city to the guests, Weston relaxed back into the seat and chatted easily about the latest news and the events that had occupied him over the past year.

"I have induced Thomas to buy a house in London near Harcourt and have introduced him to several widows of my acquaintance. He seems to have the Durham touch with women. I swear he is all they see when he is about. I find myself ignored, mostly."

Aaron studied his father, who shifted uncomfortably

under his son's scrutiny. This was a new view of the man, one which unsettled the son even as he welcomed it. Aaron knew the price of pride his father had paid to undertake so long and costly a journey, risking rejection at the destination.

". . . and he is the only man in London who can give me a real game of chess. But he fears I shall make a soft-living idler of him and insists upon returning to Wiltshire frequently to oversee its doings. I've told him the servants manage far better without his interference." Weston chuckled as Thomas Durham chafed at his humor and snorted his disagreement.

"Someone has to see to it things are done." The count left unspoken the part that said neither of my sons will do so. He sighed heavily and looked out the window.

Weston resumed his stream of words again. "He chafes because his younger son has just announced he yearns for the cleric's garb and will stay in Oxford to train further."

"Edward? A vicar?" Aaron sat up straighter, eying his father.

"It seems my mantle has been twice rejected." The august nobleman looked uncomfortable with the topic, but seized the opportunity for one more observation. "It has been a bitter winter. But I see now there are things in my life I would change, were I given the chance to retrace those steps."

It was the closest to an aplogy Aaron had ever heard on the lips of his lordly sire. A sudden catch in his throat prevented him from replying but his look was warm as he turned it on his father.

Weston noted all that transpired and smiled with satisfaction. Things were moving better than he'd expected at first. It had been a difficult task, getting Thomas Durham to end his moping and self-indulgent pessimism and to move to London. More work had been required to constrain his new friend in the matter of his second son's choice of vocation. And this last, the voyage, was nothing short of miraculous. What the man needed was the chubby fist of a little grandchild to grab his rusty heartstrings and shake them free of the debris of years of loneliness and frustration. Brien's child.

In the spacious parlor, the sun streamed through the leaded panes, warming and cheering the comfortable blues and greens and golds of the furnishings. Garrett Durham sat on the floor beside his mother, who held up brightly colored beads on a string and named the colors to him in a low, melodious voice. His chubby cheeks were flushed pink with the warmth of the afternoon sun and his blond hair burned with a fiery cast in the light.

A noise in the hall alerted Brien to the arrival of her husband and father. Noting quickly there was nothing the babe could be harmed by, she got to her feet and started for the hall. Ella took the men's hats and they turned as one man when Brien entered.

With a little cry, Brien ran to her father's outstretched arms, not seeing anyone else in the hall just then. They embraced for a long moment before Weston, his eyes moist, thrust her back to arm's length to study her. If anything her new life lent her greater beauty, a warm and openly contented charm. "Let me look at you."

Looking past Weston now to her husband, Brien's eyes widened as they came to rest of the third member of the party and she stiffened noticeably. She sought Aaron's gaze with a questioning look. Puzzled at his calmness and seeming acceptance of his father's presence, Brien looked back to her own father, who beamed with pride as he surveyed the magnificent house.

"Brien, I must see this grandson of mine—I can wait no longer," he roared.

"Oh, yes!" She was jolted back to the present and caught Weston's hand to draw him into the parlor. Aaron followed close behind, beckoning to his father, amusement apparent in his mood.

When Aaron gained the door, Weston already held Garrett up in his arms, enthralled by the alert eyes and cuddly sweetness of the babe. He touched the little hands that grabbed at his nose fearlessly and his eyes were more than wet.

Aaron went to his wife and drew her lovingly against his big, hard body. Resting his chin atop her head, he watched in silence as love between grandfather and grandson was born. The sweet silence was richer than London's vaults.

Past her husband's arm, Brien glimpsed Thomas Durham standing just inside the doorway, his face an awesome mixture of sadness, memory, and longing. Whatever brought him so far, Brien could not imagine. But she read clearly and compassionately the state of his melting heart just then.

Wordlessly, she pushed away from Aaron and took the babe from her own father's arms. Turning slowly she went to the proud old aristocrat who had come half-way around the world at her invitation to claim his grandchild. With a true softening in his hardened face, he awkwardly cradled the babe in his lean arms. When he raised his eyes to Brien's they were wet and shining with pride and gratitude. He moved farther into the room, carrying the babe reverently and sat down on the sofa.

Brien once more sought the warmth of Aaron's arms as they both watched the mighty flow of destiny binding together the generations at last.

ZEBRA HAS IT ALL!